Table

Dedication v

Acknowledgments vii

Foreword... ix

PART ONE – BILLY 1

Chapter One - Claire 3

Chapter Two - The Tramp 25

Chapter Three – Irene's Secret 35

Chapter Four – Billy's Secret 51

Chapter Five – Billy's Quest 59

PART TWO – MARY **69**

Chapter Six – John and Veronica Jones................................71

Chapter Seven – Mary Jones 75

Chapter Eight – Mount St. Joseph Convent.........................85

Chapter Nine – Peter changes Mary's mind 93

Chapter Ten – Mary goes to Jersey 101

Chapter Eleven – The Twins..117

Chapter Twelve – A place of their own 125

Chapter Thirteen – Mary gets a telegram.............................133

Chapter Fourteen – Looking for Thomas 137

Chapter Fifteen – The Box 147

Chapter Sixteen – Angela 149

PART THREE – TOMMY..**163**

Chapter Seventeen – Orphanages...165

Chapter Eighteen – Thomas goes to Canada 179

Chapter Nineteen – The Bouchards..185

Chapter Twenty – Monsieur Rene Marceau...................................191

Chapter Twenty One – Ellie and Mae 195

Chapter Twenty Two – Eddy Marshall..197

Chapter Twenty Three – Charlie Gibson 203

Chapter Twenty Four – Josie 211

Chapter Twenty Five – Tommy goes to Jersey.................................223

Chapter Twenty Six – The German Occupation 233

Chapter Twenty Seven – Amelie 243

PART FOUR – THE JONES FAMILY **251**

Chapter Twenty Eight – Billy's Search 253

Chapter Twenty Nine– Billy goes to Jersey 255

Chapter Thirty – Brothers United 263

Chapter Thirty One – Ted...269

Chapter Thirty Two – Claire 279

Chapter Thirty Three – Tortue Verte 287

Chapter Thirty Four – Billy meets Guillaume................................291

Chapter Thirty Five – Claire's secret 295

Chapter Thirty Six – Retracing Routes 299

Chapter Thirty Seven – The Feast...305

Epilogue...**313**

Appendix...315

About The Author...319

About the Book...321

The Soldier and the Orphan

Separated by Church and War

ALASTAIR HENRY

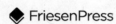

One Printers Way
Altona, MB R0G 0B0
Canada

www.friesenpress.com

Copyright © 2022 by Alastair Henry
First Edition — 2022

www.alastairhenry.com

All rights reserved.

This book is a work of fiction. Names, places, characters and events are either the product of the author's imagination, or if real, used fictitiously.

No part of this publication may be reproduced in any form, or by any means, electronic or mechanical, including photocopying, recording, or any information browsing, storage, or retrieval system, without permission in writing from FriesenPress.

ISBN
978-1-7781567-0-0 (Hardcover)
978-1-7781567-1-7 (Paperback)
978-1-7781567-2-4 (eBook)

1. FICTION, HISTORICAL, FAMILY SAGA

Distributed to the trade by The Ingram Book Company

Dedication

I dedicate this book to everyone who has crossed my path on my journey through life. In some big or small way, you have impacted my thinking, values, and direction and have helped shape who I am. I am indebted to you. We are a product of our environment, our experiences, and our encounters, and these make us unique.

I also dedicate this book to the survivors and descendants of the British Home Children Program. I hope my book helps to create a greater awareness among Canadians of the multi-generational harm this program did to you and pushes the Canadian government to apologize to you publicly for their role in the scheme, as they have with the survivors and descendants of the Indian Residential School program.

Acknowledgments

Primarily, I want to thank Candas Whitlock for her encouragement and unwavering support for me to continue writing my novel, and for her help with ideas in developing the storylines.

Thank you to all my beta readers, most notably Pearl Kim Lee and Frank Banfield, and the Bolton U3A Reading Group for their useful critiques and suggestions. I also want to thank Aldous Smith for his meticulous copy editing, suggestions, and proofing, and my son, Dean Henry, for his help in designing the book cover. Their contributions have raised the literary quality of my novel.

Foreword

Conflict seems to have been built into life on earth since it began. From the microbial and viral level to the ghastly, mechanized slaughter of warfare struggle seems to characterize our very existence. We can all feel conspired against by forces beyond our control at various times. Such a one is the subject of Alastair Henry's book, *The Soldier and the Orphan*.

In twentieth-century England, many working-class people were victims of values and circumstances not of their own making. They were people to whom things were done, not for. Billy and Tommy Jones were such people. They were born out of wedlock at a time when such a thing was regarded as a disgrace. Neither boy knows they have a brother. They embark on quests to find their family and, in so doing suffer consequences of circumstances beyond their control which they must confront and resolve.

These are the bare bones of the story, but the merits of the book lie in what Henry James would call the 'treatment' of the plot. The author has written this book from within, knowing intimately the nature of the society in which he writes. Billy and Tommy move from being victims to becoming their own persons. As they grow in knowledge and confidence, they take control of their destiny and arrive at peace. The author examines his growing awareness and places it in the context of a world in which kindness is all too often a rare commodity. The merit of the book lies in its truth, and its account of lives well-lived which, as the Jewish proverb says, is the best revenge. It can be highly recommended as a rich and heartfelt account of the complexity of life as experienced by one dispossessed family.

Dr. Anthony Heyes.
Retired lecturer, book reviewer, and Fellow of the Royal Society of Arts.

PART ONE – BILLY

Chapter One - Claire

Paris, France.

August 10, 1944

15 days before the liberation of Paris.

Five soldiers in the Lancashire Fusiliers Brigade were on patrol in a Cromwell tank looking for German snipers in a village north of Paris when they hit an unexploded bomb. All hell broke loose. The three soldiers sitting on the turret blasted into the air as the tank flipped onto its side and bits of hot metal violently catapulted into the air, raining down like hail and brimstone. Bobby Taylor, the hull gunner, was killed instantly and Jack West, the radio operator, lay on the ground twenty feet away, still alive, but covered in blood and missing most of his left arm. Billy Jones, the tank driver, miraculously survived. Delirious, in shock, and in pain from the hot shrapnel embedded in his left arm and shoulder, and with eyes stinging and watering from the thick, acrid smoke which now enveloped the area, Billy staggered to his feet and stumbled blindly around looking for his mates.

Ten seconds later, the ammunition in the Cromwell tank combusted, exploding in a ball of fire, instantly killing the commander and the gunner trapped inside, and knocking Billy off his feet.

When the Red Cross arrived forty-five minutes later, they found Billy in a catatonic state, kneeling beside his best mate, Bobby Taylor, and staring at him with cold, fisheyes. The right side of Bobby's face was missing, and the left side was scorched and crispy.

The Red Cross stretchered Billy and Jack West to a waiting ambulance and rushed them to the Hôpital Hôtel-Dieu in Paris where a doctor hooked Billy up to an IV drip, removed the shrapnel, and gave him a blood transfusion and a shot of morphine. Jack passed away in the ambulance on the way to the hospital. Another ambulance took Bobby straight to the mortuary.

For the next twenty-four hours, Billy drifted in and out of consciousness. His body shivered and shook violently, and cold sweat beaded on his brow. He woke up once, flailed his arms about wildly and shouted, and then, just as abruptly, closed his eyes and went back to sleep. Claire, his nurse, stopped by his bed every couple of hours to take his blood pressure and pulse to ensure he had not expired.

For the next two days, Claire came by with his breakfast, dinner, and tea, wiped the sweat from his brow, and bathed and bandaged his wounds, but Billy never woke up enough to know what was happening. Claire took an extra blanket from the storage room, though they were in scarce supply, and snuggled it up around his neck to help him stop shivering, and when her shift ended, she came by his bed and sat with him for five minutes before going home. She held and warmed his hands in hers and anxiously watched his face for any sign of recovery.

On the third morning, Billy woke up, gazed around at the room, and, not recognizing anything, went straight back to sleep.

When Claire came by at noon with his dinner, she startled him. He partially opened his eyes, stared blankly at the woman in the cornflower blue uniform standing in front of him, her angelic face framed by a white starched cap, and wondered who she was.

Claire squeezed his hand, smiled, and wiped his brow.

Am I dead? Are you an angel come to take me to heaven? Reading her smile as an invitation to go with her, he closed his eyes and imagined he was floating through white puffy clouds up to heaven. When she lifted his left arm up to bathe it he sensed she was helping him climb over the pearly white gates. A huge smile spread across his face – he had arrived in heaven.

Besides concern for his mental health, Claire was also worried about his physical health because he hadn't eaten or drunk anything since being admitted to the hospital three days earlier. She decided to force him to eat something in the morning

~

When she brought his breakfast, she pulled back the bedsheet, gently shook his shoulders, and whispered in his ear, in a broken English accent, "Time to get up Mister Jones."

Billy stirred and squinted.

"I will not let you sleep your life away, Mister Jones. You must eat something."

Billy blinked, sat up a little straighter, and stared at her with a half-smile. She looked familiar. *Didn't you take me to heaven?*

Claire was patient. She waited for him to become more alert before placing the food tray across his bed and lifting the lid to reveal a bowl of cabbage soup, a bread roll, two slices of cheese, and a glass of milk. A little grin appeared on Billy's cheeks. His mouth watered and his stomach rumbled. He closed his eyes and gingerly slurped the soup. He then took a big bite of the sandwich and chewed it slowly, savoring every morsel. His grin spread across his face from ear to ear, like the rays of the early morning sun spreading across the fields to greet the day. He was famished. Though the quantity of food was meager and the quality simple, it was a gourmet meal to Billy. After, he lay back down on the pillow, pulled the bedsheets over his head, and fell asleep.

He slept soundly for the rest of the morning and didn't stir even when Claire came by mid-morning to wipe his brow, bathe his wounds, and ensure his bed covers were tucked up around his neck.

When she came by at noon with his dinner, Billy sensed her presence and opened his eyes, eased himself up onto his pillow, and smiled.

"Well, Mister Jones, how are you feeling now?"

Billy stared blankly at her. He didn't know who he was let alone who she was, or indeed where he was.

"Do you feel better than this morning, William?"

The question sunk in, and Billy replied, gruffly, in a thick Lancashire accent, "Don't call me William. Nobody calls me that."

His abrupt answer caught her by surprise. "Well, what shall I call you then Mister Jones?"

"You can call me Billy. That's what everyone calls me."

"Okay, Billy. Take your time. You've been injured. It'll take time for you to heal."

"Injured?"

"Yes. You got hit with shrapnel. That's why you're here, in a hospital, in Paris."

"In Paris? In France? What the bloody hell am I doing in Paris?"

"You're a British soldier, Billy. You got injured. The Red Cross brought you in."

"Me. A soldier? I don't think so," said Billy shaking his head.

"Well, that's what you are."

"I should know if I was, shouldn't I?" replied Billy, irked by Claire's questioning.

She reached under the bed, brought up the box of Billy's Army clothes, and rummaged around to find his Lancashire Fusiliers cap. She handed it to him.

He tried to read what it said on the cloth tag sewn inside, but he couldn't. He handed it back, and asked, "What does it say? My eyes are too blurry to read."

"It says, William Jones. It's your cap, Billy."

Billy was speechless. He tried to remember who he was. He looked at Claire and confessed, "I can't remember a bloody thing! My bloody memory's gone."

"It'll come back in time, I'm sure. Maybe if you eat something, you'll feel better, Billy. You must be hungry," she said placing the food tray across his bed and lifting the cover.

Billy grinned when he saw the chunk of bread, the cheeses, the sliced tomatoes, and the large, floured bun. Sensing this amount of food was not going to be enough, Claire returned to the kitchen to see if she could get more food and returned with an extra bread roll. As soon as Billy had finished eating, he turned over and fell asleep.

He was still asleep at teatime when Claire came by with his evening meal. She considered letting him sleep but concerned about his need to build up his physical strength, she decided to wake him up. She put the food tray on the floor, moved closer to his ear, and said, "Come on Billy. Wake up. It's teatime."

He opened his eyes, peered at her over the bedsheets, and looked around the room. "Where am I?"

"Don't you remember? You're in a hospital in Paris and I'm Claire, your nurse. I've been looking after you for the past four days."

"Oh yes. Now I remember," Billy replied, sitting up and gathering his senses.

"How's your appetite tonight?" Claire asked, lifting the lid to reveal a steaming bowl of potato and cabbage soup, two bread rolls, and a glass of milk.

"I'm bloody starving." As the mouth-watering aroma of the soup assailed his nostrils Billy said, "But this isn't enough. I can eat ten times this. Are they trying to starve me?"

Claire smiled not knowing how to take his remark. "It's great you have your appetite back, Billy. You need to eat lots of food to get better."

"But you can't expect me to get better on this skimpy bit, can you?"

"It'll keep you alive. It's wartime. Everything is rationed. Even here at the hospital, everything is apportioned. I was lucky yesterday, but I won't always be able to get you extra helpings."

As he tucked into his meal, Claire said, "You know Billy, at first, I didn't know if you'd make it because many of my patients with injuries like yours don't. But you did, and I'm glad."

Billy stopped eating and smiled. Holding his soup spoon in mid-air he said with a cheeky chuckle, "You're glad I made it! I'm much, more gladder than you I made it!"

Claire laughed. She liked his dry sense of humor but was unsure about the abrupt change in his personality. Was it for real or was it a weird manifestation of him being shell-shocked?

"I'll see if I can get you more soup. Okay?"

"More soup! Yes, please. Lots and lots of it. Bring me the whole bloody pot of what's left if you can and give me compliments to the chef."

Claire laughed again and said, "I'll see what I can do."

When she returned with another bowl of soup and a slice of bread, Billy was running his hand over his bandaged shoulder.

"Thanks for looking after me, Claire."

As the soup fuelled his body, Billy became more lucid and aware of his surroundings.

"So how come you speak English?"

"Because I teach it. I'm not a nurse. I'm an English Teacher. I'm only helping because of the war. They're short of nurses. My mother is a nurse here and my father is a surgeon. He might have been the one who stitched you up."

Billy smiled, ran his hands over his bandages, and said in a phony business-type voice, while extending his hand for a formal handshake, "Well, I'm very pleased to meet you, nurse Claire."

"And I'm very pleased to meet you too Mr. Jones" Claire replied shaking his hand. "We'll have you up and out of here in next to no time."

Relieved that Billy seemed to be on the mend, Claire held his hand and gently squeezed it. He impulsively squeezed it back, grabbed the other one, and relished the physical connection he was having. The warmth of her hands was therapeutic, and the good feeling spread throughout his body causing him to look at her differently. *What beautiful blue eyes she has! What smooth, tanned skin and what gorgeous hair!* Though it was pinned back under her cap, he could see enough to admire it. *And when she blinks, her long blond eyelashes curl up and down over her eyes, reminding me of the frilled curtains at the Royal Theatre in Blackmoor where I went with my mum to watch pantomimes at Christmas.* He grinned, pleased that his memory was returning, and when Claire stood up to take away his tray, her slender silhouette in the shimmering noon sunshine that filled the ward at that hour took his breath away. He was besotted. He couldn't believe what was happening. He was so happy to be in Claire's care.

~

Billy had a restless night and woke up before dawn, stressed and lathered in sweat. He dreamt he was stumbling over bloodied bodies with missing body parts and gagging on the odious smell of burnt flesh and gunpowder with bombs exploding right left and center. He lay there for the next hour, drifting in and out of consciousness, and wondering what was real. Had it happened the way he had just dreamt or was it all just one big, horrible hallucination? He was unsure, but looking around at the room, he knew one thing for sure. He was in a bed, warm and safe, and that was comforting.

He was sitting up and grinning when Claire came by with his breakfast.

"Well. You look happy today, Billy. What's happened?"

"I am. My memory's coming back. I'm remembering lots of bits and pieces. I remember going to the theatre with my mum to watch Christmas pantomimes and to Burton Park with my mates to watch Blackmoor Wanderers play. Another time I remember was when we were playing cards in my front room and smoking cigarettes. My mum got mad coz she said they weren't good for us. But she smoked."

Claire laughed.

Billy lay back down on the pillow and continued reminiscing and smiling. "I remember playing cards with Bobby and Joe in the barrack's canteen just before Bobby and me were shipped off to France, and I remember landing on a beach with Bobby and being fired on and we had to scramble like mad up to higher ground to get to safety."

"That's wonderful Billy. I told you your memory would come back, didn't I?"

"You did, and I feel great it's coming back, but not all of it is. I don't know where the rest of it is. Can you ask around the ward to see if anyone's seen it?" he said grinning and raising his ginger eyebrows.

Billy's strange sense of humor once again surprised Claire, but this time it convinced her that this was just the way he was. This fun aspect about him was beginning to endear him to her.

"Are you looking after Bobby?" asked Billy. "He's my best mate. He was with me I think when I got injured."

The question caught Claire off guard, and she bought some time by saying, "I'll check, but I don't think any of the soldiers here are called Bobby. Maybe he was sent to a different hospital. I'll check and get back to you." She knew Bobby was DOA when they brought him into the hospital and took him straight to the mortuary. Experience had taught her that giving Billy this grim news at this time could seriously set back the pace of his recovery, so she changed the subject by asking him about his life. He couldn't recall much about being in the service, but more memories of his childhood started to come back. He described their house in Blackmoor, Lancashire, and spoke of how close he'd been to his mum.

"It was always just me and her. Not only was she my mum, but she was also my best friend." Sadness descended his face and his eyes teared up. Looking up, he whispered so no one else could hear, "She died two months ago. I didn't get a chance to go to her funeral. The bloody Army told me too late." Anguish filled every feature of his face.

Claire put an arm around him and gently hugged him. Giving him her handkerchief, she said, "I'm so, so very sorry to hear that, Billy. I can't imagine what a shock it must have been."

"And she was only forty-four – only forty-four!"

"That's terrible. What did she die of if you don't mind my asking?

"They said it was a heart attack, but I don't believe that. When the war's over, I'm going to find out what really happened," he said wiping his eyes and breathing deeply.

Changing the topic to try to lift his spirits, Claire said, "They say the war's going to end soon. The Americans will be here any day now to liberate Paris."

"Is that what they say? Well. I can't bloody well wait to see them march through those front doors and liberate us!" replied Billy, giving Claire a military-type salute.

Claire saw broken bodies in the hospital every day, so there was no reason why seeing another injured soldier should have caused her a different reaction, but it did. There was something special about this young man, Billy Jones, lying there, so damaged, and helpless. Maybe it was his red stubble hair and whiskers, or his ruddy cheeks with a generous sprinkling of freckles that caught her attention. Whatever it was, she felt drawn to him and had a strong desire to help him heal.

Though Billy still had substantial memory loss, was in pain, and was confused for most of the day, he was smart enough to know that as soon as the doctors pronounced him physically fit, he'd be discharged from the hospital and sent back to the Army base. He also knew the hospital desperately needed his bed because he could see that the hallways were littered with bodies on gurneys waiting for beds,

Immediately after breakfast on the sixth day, Billy got up and walked around the ward in his hospital gown and Army boots. He was glad to be up and about, even though he was shaky on his feet and his left shoulder and arm still pained him. To give purpose to his walking, he stalked Claire as she went about her nursing duties.

She came by at noon with his dinner: a fat chicken leg (bone-in/skin-on), two cheese sandwiches, two thick slabs of buttered pound cake, and a pot of tea.

"What the hell? Got a new chef? Where d'ya get all this food from?"

"Shush. You mustn't tell anyone. Just eat it quietly," Claire replied putting her fingers to her lips.

"I don't get it," said Billy, pleased to see such a mouth-watering meal on his tray. "You said everything was rationed?"

"It is, but I have connections, and you need more food to help you get stronger. You're too skinny," she said as she playfully poked his arm with her right index finger. "I'll tell you where it came from some other time. Okay? Just eat up and enjoy."

"I don't care where it comes from, so long as it keeps coming," replied Billy grinning from ear to ear and tearing off a chunk of the chicken leg with his teeth. His smiling eyes told of his pleasure in eating.

Claire disappeared and returned with an assortment of street clothes she guessed would fit him: a pair of shoes, pants and a belt, a shirt, and a jacket. The hospital had a storage room filled with donated clothes so recovering patients, such as Billy, could go outside to walk in the garden as the doctor ordered. She also brought a small brown canvas satchel.

"Is this yours?" she asked.

"No. Never seen it. Why d'ya ask?"

"They said it's yours."

"Who said?"

"The receptionist at the front desk. She told me to give it to you."

Billy opened the satchel and removed the contents: a stack of thirty or so blue aerogram letters tied with brown Army twine. He stared at them, removed the top letter, and inspected it. The handwriting looked familiar. Was he hallucinating? He looked closer and tried to read it. Tears clouded his eyes and trickled down his cheeks.

"Crikey. These are my mum's letters." He blew his nose and wiped his eyes. "But I know nothing about the satchel. Where did that come from?"

"I don't know," replied Claire.

"The letters are from my mum. Matt must have done this to cheer me up. He's in the next bunk to me back at the base. It's something he'd do coz he's like that."

Billy inspected the letters, hugged them close to his chest, put them back in the satchel, and slid the bag under his bed.

~

After breakfast the following morning, Billy put on his street clothes, grabbed the satchel, and went into the garden for some exercise and fresh air. He walked slowly, sitting down when he felt he was going to faint. Three times he had to stop and sit on a bench to rest. He took the top letter out of the satchel and tried to read it, but his eyes were too blurry. Instead, he closed his eyes and thought about his mum. He pictured her sitting at her kitchen table writing the letter. He watched as she put it in an envelope, kissed it, and licked the gum section. He saw her rubbing it shut with the edge of her floury hand and slipping it into the pocket of her blue apron, the one he gave for Christmas when he was seventeen. He saw her go into the living room and put it on the mantelpiece above the fireplace for mailing the next time she went to the shops. Thinking about his mum always made him sad, but now, not being able to read her letters deepened his sadness tenfold. He went back inside periodically to search for Claire because the sight of her always lightened his mood and lifted his spirits. As he walked through the hospital grounds, he thought about his situation and planned.

When Claire brought him dinner, he said, "When I was on patrol, I didn't think I'd make it out of the Army alive. It was hell. This one time, there were bodies and blood everywhere – all around me and on me. I'm pleased I got injured coz now I'm safe. I don't ever want to go back into the Army. But that's where they'll send me whether I'm better or not, won't they?"

Claire didn't answer. She understood his concern. She'd seen this situation many times. When you're not completely healed you get careless, and accidents happen. Some of her patients got injured a second and third time and some were so mentally broken, that they completely lost their minds and took their own life. She was gravely concerned for Billy. She knew he was healing physically, but mentally, he was nowhere near ready to resume his soldierly responsibilities.

She covered his hands with hers, looked into his eyes, and softly said, "I know how you feel Billy. All soldiers feel like you when they have to go back, but there's nothing I can do about it. It's just the way it is. It's wartime. I'm so, so very sorry."

"It's okay Claire. The war will be over soon. The Americans will be here any day now, won't they?"

She nodded, looked him full in the face, released his hands, and stood up. "Have a good sleep Billy and dream of better times. I'm going home. See you in the morning."

She turned around and, partially covering her face with her headscarf to hide her worried face from her work colleagues, hurried out of the ward.

Billy threw back his bedsheets and got up. He was fully dressed in his street clothes. He put on his shoes and coat, retrieved the satchel from under the bed, and followed Claire home.

As he walked, he muttered to himself, *there's no bloody way I'm goin' back into the Army. No bloody way. I don't care what happens, but I'm not goin' back.*

He trailed Claire to her neat, red-bricked apartment on a terraced road about ten minutes away from the hospital. As she was putting the key in the lock, Billy appeared by her side. Shocked, she glared at him. Billy shrugged his shoulders and said, "I'm not goin' back into the Army, Claire. I don't care what happens. I'm not goin' back."

"What are you saying? You must go back. You're a soldier. You can't stay with me."

"I'm not goin' back. I'll bloody well live on the street if I must, but I'm not goin' back."

Claire was speechless. She stood on the doorstep, silently staring at him while her mind raced, thinking about what options she had. Billy stared back. A minute passed. With no options coming to mind, Claire turned the key, pushed the door open, and let him in.

"You can stay the night, but you must go back with me in the morning. I'll get a pillow and a sheet – you can sleep on the couch."

"I can't go back. I'm not right. I'll tell you when I'm ready. Okay?"

She knew he wasn't ready.

Billy sat on the couch in the living room while Claire went to the kitchen to prepare some food. As she sliced the bread and cheese, she fretted over the scarcity of food in her apartment and her dilemma with Billy. She knew she could always supplement her groceries by visiting her parents, but she didn't know what to do about Billy. As she extracted olives from a bottle and placed them on the plate next to the cheese, many questions flooded her mind. *What will happen – tomorrow, next week, or next month? Where's he going to live? He can't stay with me, but neither can he wander the streets. He'd be shot or arrested by the Germans and sent to a detention camp in Germany.* No answers came to mind.

They ate at her little kitchen table without saying a word. Billy washed the dishes as best he could with his one good arm and Claire dried. Neither spoke. Billy relished the silence. To him, it was like eating food he hadn't eaten for a long time. He found it heavenly. For four years, all he'd heard was noise: the noise of boots pounding the pavement for hours on end; the metallic crunch of tanks and machinery grinding along stony streets; the booming of guns and bombs, and Sergeant Majors barking orders at the top of their lungs.

They retired to the couch and sat side by side. Claire removed her nurse's cap, unpinned her hair, and let it spill over her shoulders, chest, and back. Her magnificent blond tresses took his breath away, mesmerizing him, and her sparkling, blue eyes excited him. He grinned, shook his head, and said, "Wow!"

Embarrassed by his physical reaction to her, Claire tried diverting his attention away from her by asking, "You said you lived with your mother growing up, but you didn't say anything about your dad, or if you have any brothers or sisters?"

Billy responded immediately as he had done all his life when asked this very question. "I never knew my dad and I don't have any siblings. My mum never married. It was always just me and her."

Claire couldn't imagine not knowing her dad or not having a brother. "What about relatives? Do you have any aunts, uncles, or cousins you're close to?"

"No. Nobody. Well, that's not quite true. I do have an Aunt Angela, but I haven't seen her since I was a teenager. As I said, it was always just me and my mum."

"How strange? Weren't you lonely?"

"No. I never knew anything else. I did wonder at times though when I saw children playing with their mums and dads and brothers and sisters, what it would be like to be from a big family. But that's all. It was never a big deal for me."

What a sad childhood he's had thought Claire when she went to the kitchen to get a bottle of wine and two wine glasses.

Billy thought it was about time he asked her some questions and found out more about this beautiful young lady sitting by his side. "How 'bout you? D'ya have much family?"

"Oh qui. I have a brother and my dad has three brothers and two sisters and my mother is one of seven. We have a cottage on a lake and most weekends we have large family gatherings there with lots of music, games, and food. I can't wait for the war to end so we can do that again."

"Sounds wonderful," said Billy smiling. "And did you like school?"

"Oh oui. I loved it. That's why I'm a teacher. As soon as the war ends, I'll go back to teaching."

"What are your mum and dad like?"

"They're good people Billy. You'd like them. They'd like you too because you're humble, honest, and funny. You're the type of person they like. I know we had a privileged upbringing because my dad was a doctor, but my parents went to great lengths not to spoil me and my brother. What about you? Did you like school?

"Me? No. I hated it. I got bullied for not having a dad and for having red hair. They said I was the son of the devil. I hated my red hair and I wished I had a dad coz then they wouldn't tease me, and I wished I had a big brother to stick up for me."

He took a moment to reflect. He was pleased he was beginning to remember more details about his youth. "My best mate is Bobby. He's the same age as me and he lives on the same street as me and like me, he doesn't have a dad, but he does have two older brothers and an older sister who always stick up for him. He didn't go to the same school as me coz I'm a Catholic – my mum was Catholic, and he's a Protestant, and he got conscripted at the same time as me. I'm worried about him."

Claire's stomach knotted at the mention of Bobby. She'd forgotten that he didn't yet know that Bobby had died. It was sad enough that his mother had passed away just a few months ago, but how could she now tell him that his other best friend had died? Who would that leave in his life? No one?"

"What about teachers Billy? Who was your favorite teacher? We all had favorites, didn't we?"

"No. I didn't. I can't remember any of 'em being special."

"What happened when you told them about the bullying?"

Billy smiled wryly. "Told them? I never told them! They were all bloody rubbish. They'd just tell me to toughen up: that it was all part of growing up. That's just the way it was at my school. You just had to accept it and move on and hope you didn't get too badly beaten up before you became an adult."

Claire was horrified. She'd never heard such appalling and damaging accounts about a school. She couldn't relate to the cold and brutal school environment Billy had just described.

She faced him, clasped his hands in hers, and said in a voice, full of warmth and compassion, "You are very special Billy. Your hair and freckles are beautiful. There aren't many men, or women for that matter, with gorgeous red hair like you, and I love the way your green eyes sparkle when you smile and how you make me laugh."

Billy blushed, embarrassed by Claire's kind words.

"I think you're special too, Claire. You have such a kind heart and a caring smile, and I love your beautiful hair and I love talking to you. I've never felt as comfortable in my whole life with a woman as I do with you. You are my special angel."

"Your special angel, Billy? Oh. I don't know about that?" Claire replied with a grin, but, at the same time, she liked his description of her. It fit well with the Florence Nightingale image she was trying to live up to.

"You had a horrible childhood, Billy, what with one thing and another, but here you are today. You made it through, and I know you're stronger for it, though you might not think that yet. Those tough years are all behind you and once your wounds heal. you'll be all set to live a good life."

"I hope so," Billy replied, sitting up straighter on the couch. "I hope the war ends soon so we can all get on with our lives."

"Let's save that conversation for another day. It's ten-thirty – my bedtime. I have to go to work tomorrow." She got up from the couch, took the empty wine bottle and glasses to the kitchen, and went to her bedroom.

Billy stretched out on the couch with the sheet and pillow Claire gave him and for the next hour lay there thinking. He thought about his mum, picturing her in the kitchen baking: her hair, hands, and apron spotted white with flour. He smiled at the recollection, and then his thoughts drifted to Bobby. He wondered why he couldn't remember more about what had happened. And then he thought about Claire: how beautiful she was and how easy she was to talk to, and how happy she made him feel. The thought of her lying in bed in the next room with just a wall between them thrilled him and he drifted off to sleep with a big smile on his face.

Billy was up first in the morning and familiarizing himself with the contents of the kitchen cupboards. He brewed a pot of tea, put two slices of bread in the toaster, and found a jar of homemade raspberry jam before Claire appeared, fully dressed in her nurse's uniform and with her hair in a bun ready for her cap.

"I won't tell them where you are," Claire said as she spread jam on her toast. "I'll let you know what's happening when I come home for lunch. Make yourself at home as much as you can. I'll go to my parent's house after work to get some groceries."

Claire went to work, and Billy lay back on the couch, drifting in and out of sleep for the rest of the morning.

⁓

Anna, the night nurse, reported Billy missing when she started her shift. No one had seen him since tea-time the previous evening. Billy wasn't the first patient to go missing. It happened quite often with shell-shock victims. Many suffered from insomnia and wandered the halls and grounds at night, restless and agitated, but they usually showed up in the morning, having fallen asleep behind a counter or in a closet.

No one seemed concerned that Billy still hadn't shown up by noon. Everyone just assumed he would, sooner or later, or the police would bring him in if he'd wandered off the hospital grounds. Besides, it was wartime. The hospital staff was so overwhelmed with admissions, discharges, and procedures that no one had time to look for a missing person. If Billy didn't show up soon, they'd assign his bed to another patient: one of the ones on stretchers in the hall waiting for an empty bed.

Claire went about her business as routinely as she could, but she couldn't stop thinking about Billy. *When will he be ready to go back and face the consequences —tomorrow, in a few days? In a week? in a month?*

When she came home at lunch and saw the kitchen table, she was pleasantly surprised. Billy had laid out place settings for two: two blue placemats with two yellow linen napkins, two glasses of milk, two knives and forks, and two plates with a slice of cheese omelet on each.

"What an inviting table to come home to," gushed Claire.

"I'm not just a pretty face, you know," teased Billy.

She gave him a little hug and asked, "How are you feeling? What did you do this morning?"

"I slept. I'm getting caught up, I think. Did they miss me?"

"Oh oui. But at the moment, no one is overly concerned. They think you'll show up soon. Are you ready to go back with me after we eat?"

"No. I'm still having trouble remembering things and I can't read – my eyes are too blurry, and I'm too shaky on my feet."

Claire knew he wasn't faking it, moreover, she felt he didn't know just how damaged he was. She'd seen a lot of shell-shock victims and was most familiar with their afflictions: the loss of memory, shakes, poor vision – she'd seen it all, and she knew the prognosis for a speedy recovery was not good. She knew he wouldn't be ready to fight again for a very long time, if ever.

After four years of war, people were weary of it and felt fatalistic about life. Many young people adopted a live-for-the-moment philosophy not knowing if they would still be alive tomorrow. And when tragedy struck close to home for Claire, the effect it had on her was devastating. Just two months earlier, two fellow nurses and friends, Lucille and Rebecca, died tragically when the part of the hospital they were in was bombed. The authorities said it was an accident! *That could have been me. How lucky am I to be alive?* she thought at the time and now she thought about Billy. *How lucky was he to still be alive? If he and Bobby had changed places, Bobby would be here instead of him.* She shuddered at the thought, and at that moment, she realized how much she was beginning to care for Billy.

All afternoon, Claire thought about Billy and looked forward to coming home and being in his company again. He intrigued her and his honest and sensitive nature was beginning to resonate deeply with her.

She went to her parents after work to get some groceries. She told her dad about Billy, his injuries, and how he was staying at her apartment for now because he was too sick to go back into the Army. Pierre didn't condone the arrangement, but neither did he discourage it. He was sympathetic to his daughter's dilemma yet he was concerned for her safety.

Her dad, like his dad before him, had made wine all his life from grapes harvested from the vineyard of their ancestral home. Once he became aware the Germans intended to confiscate his home and use it for their purposes, he rented a three-bedroom apartment near the hospital and clandestinely smuggled out one hundred and twenty bottles from his wine cellar. With regards to running out of food, there was no danger of that happening because Pierre was well connected to influential people and the black market. Everything was available for a price, and he had the money. Claire replenished her shelves with goods from her parent's stock and was able to get the chicken leg and extra food for Billy when he was hospitalized.

She brought home four chicken legs, three onions, six potatoes, six long green beans, a loaf of bread, six eggs, and another bottle of her dad's wine.

~

"Hello, Billy. I'm home," Claire called out excitedly, as she closed the front door. She hung up her coat, joined Billy in the kitchen with the groceries, and kissed him lightly on the cheek.

"I was wonderin' what we were going to eat," said Billy lifting the groceries out of the bag. "It's going to be a feast. I'll prepare the spuds and beans. D'ya wanna cook the chicken?"

Claire put the wine bottle that she'd been hiding behind her back on the counter.

"Where d'ya get that from?" said an astonished Billy. "Don't tell me your dad can get wine too?"

"Ah, that's a secret. What did you do this afternoon? I was worried about you."

"I slept. I don't know what's wrong with me. I never could sleep before during the day. Now I can't keep my bloody eyes open."

"You're still recovering from your injuries. You must be patient and let nature take its course," said Claire without thinking, and then, instantly, regretted saying it. She didn't want to give him an excuse for not returning to base.

Billy mashed the potatoes and stirred the pot of beans while Claire sauteed the onions and pan-fried the chicken legs.

She poured two glasses of wine, brought them to the table, and proposed a toast. "To us Billy. May the war end soon, may you heal and go home, and may I go back to teaching."

Billy clinked his glass with hers. "I usually drink beer but wine's okay once you get used to it. Our landlord always gave my mum a bottle at Christmas."

They tucked into their food and ate in silence. Billy took the dishes to the sink, washed them and Claire dried. This time, there was lots of conversation. Feeling stronger and more comfortable in Claire's presence, Billy was eager to ask more questions about her life and about being a teacher.

They retired to the couch and for the next two hours snuggled and enjoyed each other's company, swapping memories and stories about their past lives. Billy now remembered many things, but he still couldn't remember what had happened to Bobby.

"You know Billy, what I like about you is your honesty and your caring nature. I've never met a man so considerate and interested in getting to really know who I am than you. I like being in your company. You make me happy."

"You make me happy too," replied Billy, putting his arm around her and pulling her closer. "I want to stay here in your arms forever." He knew of course he couldn't, but he said it because it was how he felt. It was the truth after all, and she said she appreciated his honesty. Claire grinned, pleased that he felt this way about her.

A little later in the evening, Claire said, "You know Billy. You are the opposite of my last boyfriend. He was so full of himself, not humble like you."

"Well. I'm glad you stopped seeing him. I wouldn't be here if you hadn't. Would I?" Claire lovingly squeezed his hands.

By ten o'clock, they'd finished the bottle of wine, were comfortably snuggled in each other's arms, and feeling blissfully happy.

Billy woke up in Claire's bed with a huge smile. It was a night full of firsts for him. Claire was the first woman he had ever gone to bed with. They were in no hurry to get up and Claire decided to stay home from work for the day. It was a difficult decision for her to make because she hadn't missed a day of work in over two years. They lazed, made love, and fantasized about what they might do once the war was over, even musing about living life together.

In an instant, their world turned upside down. It was dinner time. They were in the kitchen preparing food when there was a knock on the door. Claire opened it and at once got into a heated argument with a man. Billy didn't understand a word being said, but he could tell by the tone of the man's voice that he was angry. The man shoved past Claire, barged into the living room, and raced into the kitchen where he saw Billy in his socks, shorts, and shirt. The man went berserk, violently pushing Billy back against the counter and yelling at him. Claire rushed in and moved in between them as the peacemaker. But the man was having none of it. He slapped her so hard across the face that she collapsed onto the floor like a rag doll. Billy drove his good fist into the man's face smashing his nose, and they struggled, fell to the floor, and brawled. The man broke Billy's nose and jaw. Bright red blood pooled on the white tiled kitchen floor next to where Billy's head was, and something snapped in Billy's brain. He now remembered the last time he saw Bobby - he was lying on the ground in a pool of blood with half of his face missing. The man let out a gurgle and blood sprayed out of his mouth, hitting Billy in the face. Billy recoiled in disgust, and when he turned around, he saw a bread knife sticking out of the man's back. He thought he saw the man move. Impulsively, he grabbed the knife, yanked it out, and plunged it back in, again, and again, and again. The man didn't move.

"I killed him. I bloody well killed him" screamed Billy, feverishly scrambling to get up from the floor.

"No, I killed him. I killed him," cried Claire shaking with tears streaming down her face.

"No. I killed him. I killed him. They'll kill me. I've gotta get out of here," yelled Billy grabbing his satchel and wearing only his shorts, shirt, and socks, raced out of the apartment and retraced his steps back to the hospital.

The receptionist shrieked when she saw the half-naked, blood-spattered man with crazy eyes and a broken nose oozing blood. A doctor injected him with morphine, put him in a straight-jacket, and laid him on a gurney in the hallway. When Nurse Jane came by an hour later, she identified the injured man as Private Billy Jones, a patient at the hospital who'd gone missing a few days earlier. Assured by Nurse Jane that Billy was not violent by nature, the doctor ordered for the straight jacket to be removed, and for Billy to be dressed in his Army clothes which were being kept at the front counter, awaiting his return. Nurse Jane dressed him, covered him with a blanket, and pinned his satchel to his trench coat.

Billy, still under the influence of morphine, slept soundly on the gurney in the hall for the rest of the day and night because they had already assigned his bed to someone else.

He awoke in the morning to chaos. It was August 25th. The Army Corps – the French 2nd Armoured Division and the American 4th Infantry Division – had entered the hospital and everyone was preparing to leave. By nightfall, all the British troops were on their way back to England.

They shipped Billy by truck, boat, and train to the Blackmoor General Hospital in Lancashire, where his broken nose and jaw were dealt with. The hospital was overwhelmed with caring for returning war casualties, but there was little help for those suffering from mental health issues, such as Billy.

Five days later the hospital discharged him, and with nowhere else to go, he went to live at the Salvation Army hostel. His only possessions were his Army uniform and the satchel with his mum's letters.

Chapter Two - The Tramp

Blackmoor, Lancashire
1947

Joe Barton helped his dad and brother run the family's sheep farm which bordered an area of Blackmoor called Westlea. Joe wasn't conscripted into the Army as were Billy and Bobby because farmworkers were exempt from service, however, in 1942, Joe voluntarily enlisted and went to France with his unit. He wanted to do his part for his country in fighting the Germans, but more importantly, he wanted to get away from the farm and see the world.

Joe and Billy knew each other from school. They met again in the spring of 1944, in Caen, France when their Blackmoor accents gave them away. Once they recognized each other, they met periodically after that for drinks and cards or just conversations to get caught up on news from home. Bobby Taylor joined them when he could.

Unlike Billy, Joe had escaped the horrors of war without injury, moreover, his war experience had matured him and had grown his sense of independence and adventure. He was evacuated on 'D' Day and returned to his dad's sheep farm feeling strong: mentally, and physically, and enthused with the idea of going into business for himself.

The economy in northwest England at the time was a shamble. There were severe material shortages, particularly for metals and fabric. Joe's idea was to collect these items from the public, sort them by type, and sell them to further processors. With volume, there was good money to be made and most towns now had scrap dealers and rag and bone men to collect the goods. An old Yorkshire saying, "Where there's muck, there's money" became Joe's mantra.

Joe's dad sub-divided the farm and gave Joe two acres for his business. He encircled his yard with a high wooden fence, put up sheds, and hired a posse of rag and bone men to roam the backstreets of Blackmoor picking up old clothes and scrap metal. Many of Joe's employees were casualties of war, like Billy: people who were having difficulty coping in a post-war world.

After two years in business, Joe was doing all right. He lived with his wife and one-year-old son in a large home in Fern Hills, the wealthy part of Blackmoor, and drove a Bentley. He clothed his five-foot-nine, two-hundred-pound frame in suits and wore white shirts, red ties, and black leather dress shoes. One might easily have mistaken him for a solicitor.

It was a wet, blustery day. Leaves, papers, and grit blew everywhere and the rain, propelled by the wind, was soaking and bitingly cold when Joe drove up to the Barclays Bank on Great Moor Street, parked his Bentley, and dashed into the entranceway. As he shook out his umbrella, he noticed a tramp in the corner. Though the man was huddled and bundled in clothing, Joe sensed there was something familiar about the man's facial profile. There was no mistaking the red curly hair sticking out from under a tattered Lancashire Fusiliers Army cap, the ginger eyebrows, and freckled, ruddy cheeks.

"Is that you Billy?"

The tramp stirred.

"It's me. Joe. Joe Barton."

The tramp looked up and tried to focus on where the words were coming from.

"You are Billy Jones, aren't you?"

A bewildered look crossed the tramp's face.

"It's me, Billy. Remember me. I'm Joe Barton. Your old Army mate

– we used to drink and play cards in the canteen."

The tramp's bewilderment morphed into a wry smile, confirming to Joe that this homeless man was indeed Billy Jones.

"How are you mate?" Joe asked.

Billy didn't answer, but when his smile changed to a grin, Joe knew Billy was pleased to see him.

"Let's get something to eat."

Joe put up his umbrella and held it high so Billy could get under. They crossed the street to the Littlewoods cafeteria and took a seat in a corner away from the crowd.

Joe was nattily dressed in a light-grey raincoat over a serge blue business suit and wore a grey trilby hat. Billy was wrapped in his stained Army trench coat with his old Army cap pulled down over his ears. They looked like chalk and cheese. People gawked at them, but Joe chose to ignore his discomfort – his desire to help his old mate was more important.

"What you having Billy? – my treat."

Billy continued smiling a silly grin, but he didn't say a word. Joe wondered if he could. He sensed Billy was suffering from shell shock and wondered just how bad off he was, mentally.

"Wait here. I'll get us something."

When Joe returned with two heaping plates of chips and gravy and two cups of tea, Billy doffed his cap, unbuttoned his coat, unpinned his satchel and put it between his feet, and drew himself up to the table.

"There you go, mate. Have a good nosh."

Billy tucked into the food with gusto because he hadn't eaten a proper meal in a very long time. Joe ate in silence, letting Billy enjoy his meal uninterrupted. The parable about the Good Samaritan stopping on the road to help a destitute man popped into Joe's mind eliciting a smile.

Joe finished eating, leaned back in his chair, and looking Billy in the eyes, said, "So what have you been up to, mate?"

Billy pushed his empty plate away, looked down at his feet, and muttered. "Not much."

Joe was greatly relieved to know Billy could speak. "So, what have you been doing?"

"Bit of this. Bit of that. You know."

"Are you working?"

"I was."

"Where are you living?"

Billy looked up and met Joe's gaze. "I had a place, but I got evicted."

"So. Where are you living now? Where did you sleep last night?"

Billy grinned, and Joe got the message.

"So, what you're telling me is you haven't got a place to sleep?"

Billy nodded.

Joe realized Billy was in a bad place with no job and no home. Gravely concerned about his friend's destitute situation, he thought quickly of how he could help.

"I've got a place you can have and a job. Interested?"

In truth, Billy was quite ill from living in squalid quarters on the street for the last two years and was at his wit's end. He was paranoid about being arrested by the French police for murder and haunted by memories of seeing Bobby's half-face in a pool of blood on Claire's kitchen floor and a man with a knife in his back.

"What's the job?"

Joe told Billy about his scrap business. "You can stay in my farm-house and collect scrap for me."

Billy was on cloud nine – he felt he'd won the football 'pools'. Impulsively, he got up, went over to Joe, and hugged him, before Joe had a chance to avoid the embrace. The gesture embarrassed him for men in Blackmoor seldom hugged their wives and children in public, let alone other men. Joe looked sheepishly around to see if anyone had witnessed the hug, and to his chagrin, a few had and were smirking.

Joe sweetened his employment offer by giving Billy a premium route in Westlea, the best area in Blackmoor for collections, and a mere five minutes away from where he would live and a large rubber-tired wooden cart to carry the collected goods.

Joe bought a few basic furnishings for the farmhouse, some groceries, and new clothes for Billy.

Like most cotton mill towns in Lancashire in the 1940s, Blackmoor had three separate residential and industrial areas. Fern Hills, where Joe lived, was the wealthiest part of town. Homes there were detached with gardens front and back, and driveways. Old moneyed families lived there as well as professional people, such as solicitors and doctors. The more recent homes were for the nouveau rich: entrepreneurs who'd started businesses during and after the war and were enjoying much success, like Joe.

Westlea was where Billy, Bobby, and Joe grew up. It served as the bedroom community for Mosley Common. Locals called the homes there the three-up and three-downs because they had a living room, a front room, a kitchen at street level, and two bedrooms and a bathroom upstairs.

Mosley Common was where the mills and factories were located and where the poorest people lived in terraced houses, which they called the two-up and two-downs for they had just a kitchen and a living room at street level and just two bedrooms upstairs. The tippler toilet was outside in the backyard in a separate bricked structure.

The town had five major employers: two cotton mills, a foundry, a tannery, and a pet food manufacturer. Besides being the noisiest part of town due to the machinery at the mills and foundry, Mosley Common was also the dirtiest and smelliest, and the worst part of Blackmoor for air pollution. The tannery brought in hairy, smelly hides from all over the world, and processed them using acids and other toxic chemicals into high-grade leathers for shoes, fashion wear, handbags, hats, briefcases, and school bags.

Class distinction was important in Blackmoor. It mattered where you lived, which school you attended, and what your parents did for a living. As a rag and bone man, Billy was on the lowest rung of the social ladder, along with the gypsies. The general public considered rag and bone men to be daft and dangerous, and any contact with them was to be avoided at all costs. Some people even feared them. When they heard them coming down the street shouting rag and bone, they would lock their doors and remain vigilant, making sure that the back gate didn't open and a rag and bone sneak in and steal the washing off the clothesline. Some people did feel sorry for them and wondered what possibly could have happened for them to sink so low on the social ladder, but Billy didn't care what people thought of him. He'd lost his sense of dignity when he returned home from the war and became a homeless person.

The general public put aside anything that was broken, or that they no longer wanted, and gave it to the rag and bone man in exchange for a donkey stone. The stones were about the size of a large bar of soap, and when whetted, were scoured over coal-blackened doors and windowsills of their homes. Once dry, the surfaces came up the same bright white color as the stone. Joe bought the donkey stones in bulk and sold them to his employees for a pittance. Most housewives in Blackmoor scoured their sills at least once a week as if it was a public demonstration of the cleanliness of their homes. When donations were being exchanged for stones, no conversation or eye contact usually took place.

Billy was one of nineteen rag and bone men employed by Joe, and each was allotted a separate section of town. Billy's territory consisted of fifty-two streets which he liked to cover in thirteen working days. His rule of thumb was four streets a day, no matter how many hours it took. If he couldn't do four because it was raining, which happened quite frequently in Blackmoor, he'd do more streets the next day to catch up. He was obsessive now about staying on schedule.

As he rumbled his cart along the cobbled, back streets of Westlea, Billy thought about his good fortune in meeting Joe and smiled. He was now his own boss, could work whenever he wanted, wear whatever he chose, and most importantly, he didn't have to worry about being fired. At the end of the day, he wheeled his cart into the yard where Joe inspected, sorted, weighed his take, and paid him in cash – so much per pound for copper, so much for tin, so much for cotton and wool, and was in his kitchen within minutes of leaving his job, re-counting his shillings and pence, and putting them in the biscuit barrel he used as his bank.

In truth, the work was hard and unpleasant because Blackmoor was damp, dreary, and dirty. The climate was perfect for cotton process-ing and the reason why Blackmoor had evolved into a thriving cotton mill town in the first place. Everyone knew the air they were breath-ing was unhealthy, but people needed jobs to feed their families and that was more important than clean air. Many residents had bronchial problems and died prematurely. Though the buildings were built from stones and bricks of different hues and colors, there was only one color visible in Blackmoor - black. Soot from coal fires and mill chimneys permeated every nook and cranny of the town.

Feeling better now that he had a steady job and a little money in his pocket, Billy invented a new routine to improve his life. Every Friday night, he bathed in a tin tub in front of his coal-burning fireplace, shaved, donned his good clothes, some of which he harvested from his rag and bone collections, and went downtown to the Black Dog pub. He sat in a corner, always the same corner, to sup his beer, stare out at the street, and think.

He thought about his childhood and his mum, and what a hard life she'd had, and how much he regretted not being able to go to her funeral. He thought about Bobby and the good times they had at the Barracks playing cards and drinking beer, but he always stopped short of thinking of how he died. And he purposely didn't think about the murder. For a long time, he couldn't or didn't want to remember anything about it. It was as if his brain had partitioned that part of his memory off-limits.

And then he thought about Claire. He looked forward to going to the pub and to thinking about her just as someone might look forward to going to a restaurant so they could order and enjoy the cheesecake. He always started his reminiscing of her with a fresh pint. Closing his eyes, he recalled in much detail her hair, her eyes, her skin color, and texture, as well as her warm smile and softly spoken voice with a cute French accent. He recalled the look and feel of her apartment – the kitchen, living room, couch, and bed, as well as most of their conversations. Anyone in the pub who looked his way might think he was nuts because he physically reacted to his thoughts by periodically smiling, nodding, and laughing. He saved his most precious recollection until the end of his remembrances. "*You know Billy, what I like about you is your honesty, your humor, and your caring nature. I've never met a man so considerate and interested in getting to know who I really am than you. I like being in your company. You make me happy*" He then imagined putting his arm around her and pulling her closer and hugging her. But there was another scenario ever-present and lurking in the back of Billy's mind that he tried not to think about. *What happened in her flat that day after he left? Was she alive? Was she in prison?*

Guilt and fear troubled his mind and soul every day and he developed a nervous habit of constantly looking over his left shoulder to see if he was being followed.

One day he cut his chin shaving and when he saw bright red blood splash onto the white enamel sink, he had a mental breakdown. He imagined he was sprawled on the floor in Claire's kitchen in a pool of blood, his head just inches away from the man with a knife in his back. His body shuddered uncontrollably as he gasped for air and squeezed his eyes shut hoping for the vision to disappear. He opened his eyes slowly and stared at his strained face in the mirror. He breathed deeply and pressed a wet cloth against his chin. After a while, he removed the cloth and stuck a piece of newspaper on the cut. His breathing returned to normal.

Many times, as he pushed his cart around the streets, he'd think about Claire, and his feelings and concerns for her would percolate in his body, making him feel either warm all over or extremely sad. He wondered if he would ever see her again. *Not bloody likely*, he thought. *I don't know if she's dead or alive; I don't have the money to go to France to look for her and, anyway, I don't know where she lives.*

Chapter Three – Irene's Secret

Blackmoor, Lancashire
1947

On the third street of Billy's route lived a seventy-two-year-old, silver-haired widow by the name of Irene Pilkington. She was stooped and walked slowly with a cane. She had been five-foot-five inches tall in her prime, but over the years, osteoporosis had taken its toll and she was now barely five feet tall.

On Billy's fourth visit to her street, she came out of her house with a broken lamp and noticed the Lancashire Fusilier Brigade inscription on Billy's cap, the same name of the regiment her son, James, and her grandson, Walter, had served in. She guessed Walter would have been about the same age as Billy when he was conscripted. She stared at Billy's cap.

"Were you in the Lancashire Fusilier Brigade, dearie?" she asked, softly.

Billy deliberated a few seconds, looked at the old lady, then at his boots, and reluctantly muttered, "Aye."

Irene pulled her woolen, shamrock green cardigan tighter around her waist and quietly declared, "My boys were in your Brigade," and then she added in a whisper, "But they didn't come home."

Bobby's dead face lying beside him on the street flashed across Billy's mind. He shuddered, raised his head slowly, and looked compassionately into Irene's eyes.

"I'm so very sorry."

Billy's age and seeming vulnerability reminded her of Walter and she wondered how he'd gone from being a soldier in the Lancashire Fusiliers to a rag and bone man now. She was curious. "Let's go in and have a nice cuppa tea love. It'll warm you up. I want to tell you about my boys." Without waiting for a response, Irene turned and made her way to her back door.

Billy grasped her need to talk. "Okay, but I can only stay for five minutes," he said, and with that, he abandoned his cart in the street, and followed Irene through her back gate, down her yard, and into her cozy kitchen. He had hardly spoken to anyone other than Joe since being discharged from the Army and he wouldn't normally have had the confidence to be social, but for some reason, this time seemed different. He felt an affinity with this grandmotherly old lady.

Billy doffed his cap and looked at the bright yellow flowers on the kitchen wallpaper before sitting down on a wooden chair at the green linoleum-covered table. He stretched out his legs, crossed his ankles, and folded his hands, placing them in front of him on the table.

"My name's Irene. Irene Pilkington. What's yours, dearie?"

"Billy."

"So very pleased to meet you, Billy."

"Likewise," said Billy.

She boiled water, poured it into the pot, and brought two cups and saucers and a plate of oatmeal biscuits to the table. She sat opposite Billy so she could clearly see him because, as with many people her age in Blackmoor, her eyesight was poor and she should have had her eyes looked at years ago, but she hadn't bothered.

"Me and my husband, Ernie, both lived on the same street when we were growing up. I'd known him all my life. He was the only man for me. When we got married, we bought a house on Holden Street three doors down from my parents so we could keep an eye on them as they got older."

Billy looked up, startled, and said, "I lived on Holden Street too."

"For goodness' sake! What a small world it is, Billy."

She didn't question him on what number he lived at or when, such was her desire to talk about her Ernie, her boys, and her past.

"We were both twenty-one when we had James. He was born the same day as his dad. Can you believe that? "What are the chances of that happening?" Ernie used to say. James married Theresa at the end of the first war, and they went to live in Liverpool because that's where she was from. Her mum and dad and two sisters lived there. And two years later, that'd be 1920, Walter was born."

She sipped her tea slowly while taking child-sized nibbles out of her biscuit. Using both hands to steady her cup, she carefully placed it back down on the saucer before continuing.

"Ernie put in for a transfer to work at their Liverpool tannery so we could all be family. Five years later, that would be 1925, it came through, and we moved. It was a good time in Liverpool, and I'd still be there if Ernie hadn't died."

Billy felt at ease and was quite enjoying Irene's stories, sad as they were. The companionship felt odd to him after so much isolation and guarded behavior.

Irene spoke of James going off to war and Walter being conscripted into the Army at the age of nineteen, the same as him. "He never had a chance to be a father nor make me a grandmother. They were both killed within a week of each other. Probably better that way – get it all over with in one fell swoop as it were, don't you think?"

"I know what you mean. I think you're right," said Billy.

Irene got up and went to the sink to refill the kettle, but that was only a ploy because she didn't want Billy to see the tears in her eyes. She wiped them with her handkerchief, turned, and with a forced smile, returned to the kitchen table.

Realizing she'd hogged the conversation thus far, she said, "And what about you Billy? What did you do in the war?"

"Oh me? I got injured. A bomb went off and pieces hit me. It messed me up and I had a hard time when I got back."

He didn't tell her about Bobby, but he did tell her about meeting Joe, his pal from school, and how Joe had given him a place to live and a job.

"What a wonderful man he sounds. I'd like to meet him one day."

"He lives in Fern Hills – drives back and forth to the yard every day, but he doesn't hang around Westlea much."

Billy sipped his tea and ate a biscuit, slowly. In a quiet, almost inaudible voice, he said, "When I got injured, they took me to a hospital in Paris and Claire looked after me." He paused and added, "She was my nurse." Tears clouded his vision and his face tensed. Irene noticed the sudden change in his demeanor and was surprised.

Billy abruptly got up, thanked Irene for the tea and biscuits, donned his cap, and left.

"Ta-ra Billy" Irene called out.

"Ta-ra" answered Billy closing the back gate.

As he pushed his cart through the streets, Billy thought about what Irene had divulged and was moved. He felt her grief at having lost three members of her family in such a short time, her loneliness, and her need to confide in someone. He also thought about how he nearly told her about what happened in Claire's flat. He looked forward to visiting her again, but first. he had to stick to his schedule because routine was now important to him. He didn't want to disappoint his other customers who expected him to be in their street at a certain time on a certain day.

He completed his thirteen-day rota, and it was time to start over. When he opened his eyes that Wednesday morning and anticipated his visit with Irene, he had a feeling that it was going to be a special day. He washed his face, shaved (the first time in mid-week for a long time), and put on his best shirt and pants.

"Rag and Bone," he shouted as he turned from Settle Street into the back lane of Ainsdale Rd. "Rag and Bone," he yelled again, and again. This was most unusual for he usually only shouted 'rag and bone' once every fifteen minutes as he moved from one section of the street to another, and when he noticed this, he chuckled, and thought, *Am I losing it?* When Irene's back door opened and she stepped out into the street, a surge of warm feelings coursed through his body

"Good morning, Billy. You look smart today. I've been waiting for you. I'll put the kettle on, and we'll have a brew."

Billy grinned. He followed her down the path and into her kitchen. He doffed his cap, plopped down on a kitchen chair, and stretched out his legs. Irene made the tea and arranged two buns on a plate.

"My boys loved football," she said as she poured the tea. "Every Saturday, rain or shine, they went to Burton Park to cheer on the Wanderers. Ernie went with them too, most of the time. Did you go?"

"I used to, but not no more. I used to go every Saturday with my mate, Bobby, and we'd collect autographs." His face softened and a smile showed in his eyes as he recalled the happier days of his youth. "We'd go early before the bus pulled up with the players, and we'd hand our autograph books to a hand hanging out of the bus window. Ten minutes later, we'd get it back. We couldn't tell whose signatures were whose, but that didn't matter. It was the number of signatures that were important to us." He was enjoying the chance to talk. "Bobby and me swapped stamps. Did James collect them?"

"Oh yes. And Ernie too. And they had big collections. Ernie gave his to James when he turned twelve and James gave his to Walter for his tenth birthday. Ernie had an uncle in Africa, so Walter checked the mail every day looking for a new stamp. He'd steam the stamp off the envelope. Did you do that?"

"Yes. That's what we did. Once stamps were ripped, they were no bloody good. Nobody would swap a ripped one. They'd laugh their heads off if you offered them a ripped one."

"Do you still have your stamps, Billy?"

"No. It all went when I was in the Army and my mum died. All I have are the letters she sent me when I was in the Army."

Irene was tempted to ask him more about his mother but thought it best to let him keep talking.

"I used to build balsa wood planes with Bobby, and I had a big collection of military uniform and bird cards I got from my mum's cigarette packets."

Irene listened and enjoyed his company. The feeling was mutual. To Irene, Billy was like Walter, and to Billy, Irene was like a grandmother. He transitioned into more personal details and admitted his childhood wasn't happy.

"The only happy time I remember were the times I spent with Bobby and knowing that my mum loved me above everything else in the world. My relatives were mean, except for my Aunt May and my Aunt Angela, my mum's half-sister – she was fifteen years older than me."

He sat back, sipped his tea, looked at his boots on the ends of his outstretched legs, and munched on a piece of cake. "Did you know I was bullied at school?" he asked.

"No. Why did they bully you, Billy?" Irene gently inquired.

"Coz children at school called me 'ginger 'ed' coz of my red hair and freckles."

"That's not so bad Billy," replied Irene. "Many people with red hair get called 'ginger 'ed.'"

"They called me 'the bloody ginger 'eaded bastard' coz I didn't have a dad, and then they'd gang up on me and beat me up."

Irene was shocked. Being called a bastard was obviously very hurtful to him.

"That wasn't your fault, Billy."

"I know, I know, but that didn't help. Everyone called me that. They blamed me for being a bastard and made me feel guilty. But most of all, I felt bad for my mum coz I ruined her life." He paused and added. "She never married, and she didn't have any little ones. And now she's gone. And she was only forty-four. And it ruined her relationship with everybody, and it was all my fault."

"My oh my Billy. That's terrible. I can imagine how tortured you must have been as a child. When did your mum die?"

"When I was in France. She died of a heart attack they said. But I think it was coz she had a broken heart. She didn't want to live anymore. Her family was mean to her. Without me there to cheer her up, she didn't have much going for her."

"I'm so sorry to hear that Billy"

She sipped her tea, carefully placed her cup on the saucer, and looked him straight in the face. "I remember you telling me you still have your mother's letters – the ones she wrote when you were in the Army. Right?"

"Yes, but I never read them coz they'd make me sad."

"What about your dad, Billy? What do you know about him?"

"Not much. All I remember my mum saying was that he was called Ted and he was already married and that she'd made a terrible mistake, and it wasn't all his fault that she got pregnant."

And with that, he got up, thanked her for the tea, and announced that he must be getting back to work.

Irene accepted his abrupt departure, sensing that would be back to share more of his pain, but for now, he just needed more time to think about what he wanted to say.

For the next thirteen days as he completed his rounds, Billy thought about what he had told Irene and was surprised to find that he felt relieved and not regretful in any way. Being a bastard was such a touchy subject for him to talk about – it triggered so many unhappy childhood memories he was doing his best to forget. He felt vulnerable and feared what else he might say in the heat of the moment like what happened in Claire's flat.

On another day, as pushed his cart and daydreamed, he realized Joe and Irene were the only people in his life besides Bobby, his mum, and Claire to have shown him kindness and now that his mum had gone, Irene had by default become his surrogate grandmother. He so needed someone special in his life to talk to and to share his joys and concerns with. He felt he could tell Irene anything and she'd keep it a secret.

Irene too thought a lot about what Billy had said, and putting two and two together, she realized an astonishing fact. Billy must be William Jones and his mum must have been Mary Jones, her next-door neighbor thirty-six years ago when she lived on Holden Street.

Irene and Mary had enjoyed a special relationship until she and Ernie moved to Liverpool. Irene had treated Mary as her daughter and Mary had confided in Irene as if she was her mother. They lost touch after Irene moved to Liverpool and Irene only moved back to Blackmoor two years ago after Ernie died.

~

Billy completed his rota and now it was time to start over. "Rag and Bone," he shouted as he turned from Settle Street into the back lane of Ainsdale Road. He went straight up to number ten.

Irene opened the back door, and said, "Good morning, Billy. How are you today? Let's go in and have a brew and a chat. I've made some cheese and onion pasties."

Just as Billy was going to sit down in the kitchen, Irene said, "Let's go in here," pointing to her cozy living room. "It's comfier and I've put out my best China for you." On the little teak table with carved legs in front of the brown leather couch and the fireplace were pieces of a Royal Doulton tea service. Decorated in a dainty rose and powder-blue floral pattern were a teapot, a biscuit barrel, two cups, and two plates holding cheese and onion pasties. Billy gazed at the tea set, raised his eyebrows, and whistled. "Wow. That's special. Never seen anything like that."

"They are special Billy. Ernie's parents gave them to us as a wedding present. I don't have all the pieces now, what with all the moving, but I'll always have these."

Billy settled into the green, crushed-velvet side chair and made himself comfortable, and Irene sat on the brown leather couch next to him. After some small talk, she came right out and said, "There's something I must tell you, Billy. You'll be shocked at what I'm going to say, but it's the truth, and you should know it. Okay? Are you ready? Is your last name Jones?

"Yes, but how d'ya know that?"

"And what number did you live at on Holden Street?"

"Eighteen, but I was born at number ten."

"I knew it! I knew it," declared Irene, clapping her hands and shaking her head. She sat back and paused. Leaning forward and looking intently into Billy's eyes, she said, "Ernie and me lived next door to you at number eight. I remember you and your mum and your mum's little sister. I knew your mum from when she was a baby."

Billy was stunned. "You did. You knew my mum and me and Angela."

Irene picked up her cup and slowly sipped her tea, allowing Billy time to digest the news.

"What was my mum like when she was little?"

Irene closed her eyes and recalled the little girl who lived next door all those years ago. "Your mum was a little sweetheart. She had this gorgeous red hair, like you, but hers was longer and wavier. It fell over her shoulders at the front and went down to her waist at the back, and she had the most beautiful emerald-green eyes that seemed to sparkle when she laughed.

Billy smiled as he transformed Irene's words into a picture of what his mum must have looked like as a little girl.

"She loved her dollies and pushed them in her pram, up and down the back street all the time. I can see her now, fussing and cuddling them and talking to them as if they were real babies."

Billy's imagination was working overtime.

"And as she got into her teens, she blossomed into a beautiful young lady. She was quiet and always very respectful. She always called me Mrs. Pilkington, never Irene. And she was always cheerful." She paused and thought about Mary's home situation. "We knew she didn't have it easy at home, what with her dad being so strict. Many times, we heard sobbing coming through her bedroom wall and we wondered what possibly could have happened, given her sweet nature and obedient manner. It disturbed Ernie and me no end."

Irene sipped her tea slowly, gauging Billy's reaction.

"My mum's parents were horrible. I never liked them, and they never liked me. I always wondered how they could be so bloody churchy yet so cold to my mum, their very own daughter? That's something I'll never understand. Go on. I want to know all you know."

"Your mum's dad didn't like Ernie and me because we didn't go to church. When your mum was seventeen or so, she'd come over to our house to get away from her dad and to tell us about her home situation. She'd knock on the door and not whisper a word until she was in our house and the door was closed. She had no one else to talk to except Ernie and me when she was little. Her dad was pressuring her to become a nun, but that's not what she wanted. She often came over for moral support. One time when she went home, we heard her dad yelling at her about not associating with the heathens next door. They sure were a piece of work, Billy."

"Oh, my God! You can say that again. What bastards!" He felt powerful when he called them that.

"Are you sure you want me to continue Billy?"

"You can't stop now. I want to know all you know about my mum."

"When she was nineteen or twenty, she had a boyfriend. I think his name was Peter, but I can't say for sure because it was so long ago now. We heard her dad shouting at her forbidding her to ever see him again. Everybody in the street must have heard him because he didn't seem to care who was listening. It was as if he wanted everyone to know how he felt."

Billy raised his eyebrows and nodded. "Go on."

"One time when your mum came over, she said her dad was sending her to live with an aunt in Jersey for the summer. She said her dad arranged it to put an end to her relationship with her boyfriend because he was an atheist!"

Billy and Irene laughed, and then Irene said, "But what he didn't know was that her boyfriend was going to America and your mum wouldn't be able to see him anyway. Your mum was pleased she was going to Jersey because she wouldn't have to put up with her dad for the summer."

Billy laughed, appreciating his mum's ploy to get away.

"Your mum sent me postcards from Jersey. How many? I can't remember now, but quite a few. What I do recall though is that your mum seemed very happy in Jersey. A later postcard informed us that she'd met a young man and had fallen in love. Ernie and me laughed at the irony of it. Your mum was supposed to return at the end of summer, but a further postcard said it would be later – something had come up."

Irene got up, excused herself, and went to the bathroom. In truth, she needed a break. This was heavy going for her and what she was about to tell Billy was weightier. Not that she was regretting telling him, on the contrary, now that she was revealing all, she knew from observing his keen interest that she was doing the right thing. Billy needed to know the truth about his birth if he was ever to get a better sense of who he was.

Irene returned to the couch and sat down.

"It's been a long day. You must be exhausted listening to all of this. Should I continue or save it for another day?"

"You can't stop now. I want to hear it all."

"Your mum came home just before Christmas. She didn't send a postcard to tell us this. How we knew was because of the terrible commotion coming from your house. We heard her dad yelling and your mum bawling her eyes out and trying to talk. It was so disturbing that Ernie got up, put on his jacket, and nearly went over there to see what was happening, but he didn't. He thought being a heathen would just make matters worse. The upshot was that your mum was pregnant, very pregnant. With you, Billy."

"Oh, my God. She was pregnant. With me?"

"We heard your mum's dad shouting that she would go straight to hell when she died for what she had done. He said she'd shamed him and the whole family, just like his sisters had done. He called her a whore, and he barked a lot of other horrible things too. We heard every word spoken through the walls, but there's no point in me trying to recall them because I'm sure you get the gist of what he said. He demanded she not go outside of the house until after the birth because he didn't want the neighbors to know she was pregnant. But she did. She came to our house when her parents were at work and told us everything. She was so distraught Billy. We hugged, we cried, and we told her we'd be there if she ever needed anything, anything at all."

"Bastards, bastards, bloody bastards," said Billy raising his voice. "My mum never told me any of this. She said her mum and dad had different opinions about things and that's why they didn't get along. But why didn't she tell me? It would have made all the difference in the world if she had told me" said Billy.

Irene smiled and said, "It's complicated Billy. Believe it or not, there's much more I need to tell you – much, much more. I know you're shocked, who wouldn't be? I didn't know how you'd take it. In the beginning, you were hard to read, but now I know you better."

She picked up her cup and with the other hand brushed the hair off her forehead. She eyed Billy and said, "You have a brother Billy, a twin brother. Your mum had twins – identical twins."

"What!" Billy's face drained to ashen white. "Twins! You've gotta be joking? I've got a brother, an identical twin brother!" He got up and paced the floor, shaking his head and repeating the words, "A twin brother! I've got a twin brother! I don't believe it!"

"Yes Billy, a twin brother. I know because I saw the two of you with my own two eyes. Your mum had you at home. She asked Ernie and me to come to your house the day after you were born when her mum and dad had gone to work, and we saw the two of you."

Shocked amazement filled Billy's face.

"It was to be a dark family secret. No one was ever to know you were twins. Your mum's dad wanted to put both of you into an orphanage, but your mum threatened to kill herself if the priest took both of you. She said she didn't believe in heaven or hell anymore, and anyway, she said it was the shame that would fall on the family if she took her own life that her dad was most concerned about. Not her death."

Billy continued staring, wide-eyed.

"And she would have, Billy, had the priest taken both of you. I feel that for certain because I knew your mum well. In the end, her dad relented and let her keep one baby, and that was you. Your poor mum. It broke her heart to give up one of you. She was never the same afterward. You were her light Billy. You were her joy. Your brother was her heartache."

Billy didn't say a word. He was trying to absorb the full impact of what he had just learned. Thirty years without knowing he had a sibling! A million thoughts raced through his brain overwhelming him. He clasped his head in his hands and tears filled his eyes – tears of sorrow for his mum, for her loss of a baby, and tears of joy for himself because he now had a brother.

Impulsively, Irene said, "Thumbs up."

"What?"

"Turn your thumbs up so I can see them," she said with a mischievous grin,

"What's that?" she asked pointing to a faint dark spot on the fleshy underside of his right thumb.

"A birthmark!"

"No, it isn't. It's a 'lovemark' Billy. Ernie made it for your mum. And your brother has one too."

"A 'lovemark'? What's that? Never heard of it."

"That's because it's very special. It was all your mum's idea. She wanted a way for you and your brother to find each other, should you ever be separated. When she came over to our house before you were born, she knew she was having twins and she asked Ernie to help. Ernie worked at Coopers Tannery, and he brought home a needle he used at work to burn designs into leather. It only took a second."

Billy stared at his tattooed thumb and shook his head in disbelief as the truth sank into his brain. Conflicting emotions swirled around his mind and body, culminating in a wry smile. It was all too incredulous to be true.

"What happened to my brother?"

"The priest came for him in the afternoon and put him in an orphanage."

During a long pregnant pause, Billy digested this latest piece of news and thought about the ramifications of what he had just heard. "So, where's he now?"

"I don't know."

"Why didn't my mum tell me about him?" implored Billy. "She should have. She should have bloody well told me everything. It would've made all the difference in the bloody world if she had."

"How could she, Billy? It was to be a dark family secret. No one was ever to know – not the neighbors, the people at church, or anyone. No one was ever to know you have a brother." She waited a minute and then added, "Your mum didn't have any say in the matter. She didn't have a job and she needed her parents to pay for her room and board, and, of course, there was the expense of bringing you up. She didn't go back to work until you were four or five as I recall. That's when we moved to Liverpool with Ernie's job and over the years, I lost touch with your mum."

Billy was deep in thought, still thinking about his mum and the tattoos and how terrible it must have been for her to have kept these secrets to herself for all those years.

"Believe me, Billy, I'm sure your mum intended to tell you oodles of times, but, for one reason or another, she must always have had a change of heart at the last minute."

As soon as Irene said this, she smiled. It brought up another thirty-year-old memory.

"Your mum wanted Ernie to make the tattoo in the shape of a heart because she said your dad's last name was Heart, but you were too tiny. Ernie suggested a single black dot instead and your mum agreed. I call it a 'lovemark' because I remember that's what your mum called it. She said it would be like a birthmark in that you'd have it forever. I clearly remember the mischievous grin on your mum's face when she said that. I will never forget it."

"You've gotta be kidding. Right?" exclaimed Billy, still staring and smiling at the faint black mark on his thumb. "So, my dad's name is

Heart, and he lives in Jersey, and I have a brother who has a 'lovemark' on his thumb too, just like me. That's unbelievable."

As his brain absorbed the enormity of the revelations, the truth percolated through his body changing his physical being. He gleamed from ear to ear, sat upright, and breathed in and out, slowly, and deeply. Irene had never seen him look quite like this. She went into the bathroom to recover from her ordeal and quietly sobbed with relief. *He absolutely needed to know the truth,* she kept repeating to herself. *I had an obligation, did I not, to tell him?* She was convinced she'd done the right thing and whatever Billy did with the truth was now up to him. She knew he'd suffered a lot in his life from loneliness, depression, being bullied, and whatever happened when he was in the Army and was hoping that now he knew the truth about his birth and brother, his life would be different and better. But, at the same time, she was concerned it might be worse. *Would he be able to manage the deception of all those years?* She blew her nose, wiped her face with a cold cloth, and returned to the living room.

"You know Billy, life is a gift we shouldn't take for granted. I'm sure you know that better than anyone, given the loss of the life you've seen in the war. I want you to think about that, and about what I'm going to say because take it from me, it is most important."

She poured him another cup of tea, refilled her cup, and turned to look at him, face to face. He was smiling and looking at her, eagerly waiting to hear what she had to say.

"There's always someone who needs us, Billy. It's as simple as that. I've been lonely since Ernie died, but then you came along out of the blue and made me feel worthwhile again."

Billy smiled, pleased with the compliment. He knew too that his life had changed for the better since meeting Irene.

"You might not think you need anybody, but you do," she said, "And I'm sure there are people out there who need you."

"I know what you mean. I'll think about it."

Billy stood up, feeling an inch taller than when he went into her house two hours earlier, and grinned. He gave her a long, strong hug and thanked her for everything. She hung on to him tightly, as if he were Walter. She didn't want to let him go.

Billy walked out into the bright sunshine, which seemed to be shining just for him.

Chapter Four – Billy's Secret

Blackmoor, Lancashire
1948

Billy continued his rounds as before, but he was a changed man – he'd been reborn. His new knowledge felt empowering, causing him to look at the world through a different lens. It was as if he'd been in a stupor all his life but was now awake for the first time.

As he pushed his cart through the streets, he held his head high, looked around, and observed. He noticed the air temperature, the heaviness of the clouds, the color of the sky, the wind on his face, and the condition of the houses on his route. He studied his customers' faces and noted their dispositions – were they happy or sad or troubled? His customers must have wondered if a new man was on the job when he greeted them with a friendly hello and a smile. Irene's revelations changed everything for him. Although he'd been a rag and bone man for seven months, in many ways, he felt like it was his first day on the job and he was enjoying it anew.

Now that he had a better sense of who he was, he changed his habits: he shaved every day, switched pubs to the White Swan on Great Moor Street, and talked and laughed with fellow drinkers on a Friday night, even joining their weekly darts team. He went to Irene's house for tea every Wednesday evening with flowers and cakes, and he looked after small repairs in and around her house and came back on weekends to tackle the bigger jobs.

With each passing day, Billy got stronger, mentally, and physically.

As he reflected on his recent past, he realized how the power of kindness and compassion had twice changed his life. Joe had been the first to manifest these virtues by giving him a place to stay and a job, and then along came Irene with the same kind heart and understanding. If she hadn't befriended him, he'd never have known about his brother and father. And all because he chose to wear his old Army cap! The war had given him the gift of a cap and the cap had given him the gift of Irene. *How ironic was that?*

Irene's prophetic words, 'There's always someone who needs us" transformed Billy's thinking and goals. As he went about his business, his mind was now preoccupied with thoughts of his brother, his dad, as well as Claire. He tried to imagine them and wondered what they were doing at that very moment and if they needed him. He so wanted to find them, but he wasn't in a position to search for them. For now, just knowing about these people in his life had to be sufficient.

Joe was amazed and delighted with the changes he saw in Billy. When an opportunity came up for him to start a new car dealership, he asked Billy if he was interested in managing the scrap business. Billy jumped at the opportunity and threw himself into his new job full throttle.

Over the ensuing months, Billy spent every Wednesday evening in Irene's front living room chatting with her about every topic under the sun. One exchange was extraordinary for what was revealed. Irene asked him if he'd ever been in love. His face flushed and his green eyes twinkled brighter than Irene had ever seen. She smiled too, curious as to what was going on in Billy's mind for his face to light up so.

"I fell in love when I was in the Army," he said sheepishly.

Irene noticed the blushing and smiled. "Goodness me Billy. It's nothing to be embarrassed about. I think it's wonderful you know what love is and how it feels to be in love. Everybody should experience being in love at least once in their life. I always wondered because you never mentioned it. Surely, you aren't embarrassed to tell me about it?"

Billy continued smiling. "And I'm still madly in love. Can you believe that? After all these years, I still feel the same way about her."

"While you think about what else you want to tell me, I'll make a new brew and get some biscuits."

Billy leaned back in the chair, stretched out his legs, and crossed his ankles. While waiting for Irene to return with the tea, he folded his hands, twiddled his thumbs, and began talking in a louder voice so she could hear. "I met Claire when I was in hospital in Paris. I was injured and out of it for a few days. When I came to, she was standing in front of me. I thought she was an angel, come to take me up to heaven. That's when I fell in love with her. I can see her now if I close my eyes."

Billy paused. "Seems incredible coz I didn't speak French and the only reason she spoke English was coz she wasn't a nurse: she was an English teacher for God's sake. How lucky for us was that? We were meant to be. That's all I can say."

His eyes twinkled and his grin beamed at Irene, as she returned from the kitchen with the teapot and a plate of biscuits. She sat down and nodded for him to continue. He closed his eyes, breathed in deeply, and his manner took on a more ominous feel. "When I was in the Army I got injured and I didn't want to go back because I'd had enough."

"Go on," prompted Irene.

"Many patients were waiting for beds – the halls were full of gurneys with people on them in worse shape than me. Some were missing their legs and arms and pieces of their face."

He opened his eyes hoping to dispel the horrific pictures in his mind, inhaled and exhaled deeply for two seconds, and continued staring at Irene. He was acutely aware he was getting close to opening Pandora's Box and releasing its secrets.

Irene sensed it too. "Go on. What happened next?"

"I knew the hospital would discharge me soon coz my wounds were healing, and the hospital badly needed my bed. When Claire left work and went home, I followed her. I just showed up at her door. I didn't know what I was goin' to do. I didn't have a plan. I just knew I had to get out of the hospital before they sent me back to the Army."

Irene shook her head, sipped her tea, and nodded for Billy to continue.

"I told her I wasn't goin' back. I knew I was putting her on the spot, and it'd be difficult for her to know what to do with me, but I didn't know what else to do. If she hadn't let me stay at her place, I'd have roamed the streets and tried to stay out of sight until the war was over. I know that sounds crazy but that was my state of mind at the time. I was crazy. She agreed to let me stay in her apartment coz she feared I'd get injured if I went back into the Army or be blown to bits by a German sniper if I was homeless."

Irene knew about the soldier's code of conduct from her husband and that what Billy did wasn't right, yet she grasped how he must have felt at the time and was sympathetic to it. She imagined how horrible it must be to see bloodied bodies with missing limbs.

The kettle whistle blew, and Irene refilled the pot for the third time. She returned to the living room with the tea and sensing Billy had more to tell, said, "Go on Billy. You need to talk it out."

"Claire was so sweet. We talked and talked and talked. Life was wonderful. She even stayed home from work the next day. I remember not caring about anything. I just wanted to stay with her forever." And then he paused, and his facial expression changed as he thought about what he was going to say next. He picked his words carefully. "There was a knock on the door and when Claire answered it, an angry man was there, and he argued with her. And then he barged in and came into the kitchen where I was. He yelled at me, and we started fighting, and fell on the floor."

Irene gasped, clasping her hands over her mouth.

Billy was doing his best to tell the story without becoming too emotional, but he couldn't stop his voice from racing and wavering, nor his face from becoming distorted with anguish. Irene picked up on the signs and said, "Maybe you should take a break, Billy. There's no hurry. You've waited a long time to tell me this, I know you want to tell me, but only tell me when you're ready. Okay?"

Billy took a sip of tea and a deep breath.

"He broke my nose and blood streamed everywhere. He was livid like a bloody mad man. He wanted to kill me."

Billy's face, hands, and legs started to tremble uncontrollably.

Irene's face drained of color, and she had a coughing spell and excused herself to go to the kitchen for a glass of water.

When she returned, she said, "My oh my Billy. You must tell me what happened next and get it off your chest once and for all."

"But it is what it is. I can't change it, can I?" Billy pleaded, with eyes, bloodshot and watery.

"Can't change what Billy? You've got to tell me what happened." She took a deep breath, readying herself for more shocking news.

"Can't change what bloody happened in Claire's kitchen. That's what I can't change," he barked in a louder and angrier voice.

Irene was taken aback.

"You don't have to tell me what happened, but I think it would help if you did. You know you can tell me anything. I've told you all I know, haven't I?"

"I killed him. I bloody stabbed him in the back with a knife," he said looking imploringly at Irene for forgiveness.

"You did what! You killed him?" Irene gasped. "You killed him?"

She tried to cover up her shock, but she couldn't hold it back. Tears welled up in her eyes and her frail hands trembled as she tried to keep them still on the coffee table.

"I ran back to the hospital coz I didn't know what else to do. I was terrified. I was jabbering nonsense and I wouldn't tell them where I'd been or what I'd done. They said I was shell-shocked, and they shipped me back to England the next day."

"My oh my," repeated Irene. "I don't know what to say."

No words were spoken for a long time.

"You didn't go back to see Claire?"

"No. I wanted to go but I couldn't. I've never had enough money and I don't speak French and I've no idea how to find her, but I still love her and that's the worst part. I know I'll never forget her, and I know I'll never meet anyone else like her. Anyways, if I was to go to France, I'd be arrested and jailed for the rest of my life or hanged. I wouldn't be able to spend my days with Claire. I know that for sure."

"So, the last time you saw Claire was in her kitchen, and I take it, you haven't heard from her since?"

"That's right. I know the Police must be looking for me and one day, any day, maybe later today, they're going to find me. I know I'm on borrowed time. I've tried to evade them for as long as I can and just get on with life. What else can I do?"

"Oh, Billy. No wonder you're so tortured. I'm glad you shared your secret with me. Now I understand the burden you've been carrying all these years. You know you've got to resolve this one day, don't you? For your own sake. You can't live in fear for the rest of your life!"

"Oh yes, I can. What choice do I have?"

"And what about Claire? What happened to her and where is she now? Don't you want to know?"

"Of course, I do. I will always love her, and I think about her every day and night, but what can I do? I'm sure she's fine. She's probably settled down with a doting husband and a bunch of little ones by now," he exclaimed, but not sincerely enough to convince Irene that was how he truly felt.

"You don't know that. Remember me telling you there is always someone who needs us, Billy. Maybe Claire needs you. Where there's a will, there's always a way. You just have to find it."

Billy buried his face in his hands. He couldn't see any way to resolve his situation.

After a minute, he stood up, took a deep breath, and composed himself. He realized his relationship with Irene would most probably change now that he'd told her his secret. He felt sad, yet relieved, for he had needed to share his story with her for such a long time.

Their relationship did change, but it was for the better. The sharing of secrets brought them closer.

Chapter Five – Billy's Quest

Blackmoor, Lancashire
December 1950

Irene had suffered from bronchitis for most of her life and it was getting worse with her advancing years. Now seventy-five, weak, and having trouble breathing, she relied on Billy for almost everything. For the past year, Billy had shopped for her, put out her rubbish bins, and did whatever chores came up. For the last three months, he had gone to her house every night after work to make her tea and to ensure she was safe and comfortable.

"What's the matter with Irene?" Joe kept asking.

"She's getting on," was all Billy said.

In December 1950, Irene's bronchitis turned into pneumonia, and she passed away peacefully in Blackmoor General Hospital, two days before Christmas, with Billy at her bedside.

Irene had sensed her time was running out, and, on one occasion about six months earlier, had given Billy an envelope to be opened after her passing. It had instructions on what to do and contained two hundred pounds to cover the cost of her funeral.

Billy called the Nothers Funeral Home and arranged for a small service for neighbors and friends to be held on December 27, followed by her burial at the Westlea public cemetery, and placed a notice in the obituary column of the Blackmoor Evening News.

A few people showed up at the funeral, identifying themselves as distant cousins, but Billy didn't recognize any of their faces or names.

Irene had never mentioned them.

Billy was heartbroken. For the past two years, besides Joe, Irene had been his one and only companion. He stayed in his home, alone, over Christmas and grieved her passing. He imagined she was up in heaven looking down on him. He felt her presence and it consoled him.

Her words, 'There's always someone who needs us,' continued popping into Billy's mind, consistently and uninvited, most days and nights, challenging him for an answer. Was it Claire, his brother, or his dad who needed him the most?

One night as he lay in bed, before trying to go to sleep, he imagined he was in his hospital bed in Paris. The bedsheets were snuggled up around his neck and Claire was by his side, holding his hands and smiling down at him. And then he pictured her coming home from the hospital and taking off her nurse's cap and letting her hair cascade, like a glistening waterfall, over her shoulders and chest. He then imagined moving to the couch and snuggling up to her and hugging her, and then to her bed, where they blissfully spent the night together making love. He used this practice from then on whenever he felt lonely or overwhelmed and it never failed to comfort him.

Irene had often asked if he was going to look for Claire, or his brother, or his dad, and his stock answer was always, "Yes. But not yet."

"And why not?"

"Coz I'm not ready" was always Billy's stock reply.

The truth was that he couldn't go looking for any of them because he simply didn't have the money. When he was a rag and bone man, he barely got by after paying Joe a small amount for rent and paying for his groceries and household bills. Many times, he didn't even have enough money to buy a pint at the pub on a Friday night, so he'd skip his evening out and stay home. He had too much pride to ever ask Joe for an advance.

Now that he was on a wage and had a little more money, he paid Joe a higher rent for the farmhouse and that made him feel better, however, there was little money left over at the end of the week that could be saved.

One of the last conversations Billy had with Irene before she died was about his Aunt Angela. Sensing her own demise and concerned about Billy's mental health and loneliness after she was gone, she said, "And what about you're Aunt Angela, your mum's sister? I'm sure she'd love to see you. Maybe she has children, and they might want to get to know you. I think you need to get to know your family. Do you ever think about them?"

"No, not really, but I will," he replied.

"Promise me you will Billy. You need them and I'm sure they'd love to see you."

"I promise." And with that vow, came a change in the direction of Billy's life.

On January 1st, 1951, motivated by Irene's passing and by his promise to her, Billy made a New Year's resolution that by the end of the year, he would search out his Aunt Angela and find a way to locate his brother and his dad. Irene's words, where there's a will there's a way kept running through his mind. His search became his quest – his reason for living.

On Wednesday, January 4th a late model, black Rover motor car pulled up outside the scrap yard office. A man stepped out of the car and carefully picked his way, in black patent leather shoes, through the yard's mud to knock on the office door. Dressed in a dark grey pinstriped suit with a white shirt and a royal blue tie and carrying an expensive-looking leather briefcase, the man looked out of place in the scrap yard. The slightly balding man, smelling of spiced cologne, said he was looking for a Mr. William Jones.

"I'm him," said Billy, dressed in a cream undershirt and wearing black pants with suspenders, when he answered the door.

The man was taken aback.

"Good morning Mr. Jones. My name is Charlie Dickinson. I'm the solicitor for the late Mrs. Irene Pilkington." He held out his right hand for a handshake. Billy shook it and invited the man into his home.

"Come on in. Don't mind the mess."

Mr. Dickinson put his briefcase down and extracted a business card from an inside pocket of his suit jacket. "There's no need for me to come in. There are some things I need to speak with you about. Can you attend at my office at ten o'clock on the morning of Wednesday, January 11?"

"Yes. I can be there," Billy replied, taking the business card.

Mr. Dickinson then turned around and using the footprints in the mud he had made two minutes earlier, carefully picked his way back to the car.

Billy was surprised at the request, but the more he thought about it, the more it made sense. To his knowledge, he was Irene's one and only friend. She had never spoken of anyone else, nor had he seen anyone ever visit her when he was there.

The next day, Billy had a haircut and bought a new brown and green tweed cap. He was frugal – always had been – that's just how his mum had raised him. Buying anything discretionary was always an enjoyable treat for him, even if it was just a simple tweed cap. He put it on and admired himself in the bathroom mirror.

Jones, Dickinson, and Mathers LLP were a long-established law firm with a suite of well-appointed offices on Great Moor Street in downtown Blackmoor. Billy arrived fifteen minutes early and anxiously strolled up and down the street until it was five minutes to ten. He went in, approached the desk, and spoke to Peggy, the receptionist. The pretty young lady, a tad-too-tarted up to be working in such a prestigious establishment, told him to take a seat while she informed Mr. Dickinson that he had arrived.

One minute later, Billy strode confidently behind Peggy down the dark, wood-paneled hallway to the third door on the right. He gazed at the copper nameplate reading C. Dickinson. LLP and wondered what Mr. Dickinson was going to tell him.

"Come in. Come in. Let me take your coat and hat," said Mr. Dickinson, holding out his hand to accept Billy's duffle coat and tweed cap.

Looking suave in an expensive charcoal grey business suit and wearing a bright white shirt with a decorative ruby red tie, Mr. Dickinson looked established and successful. He sat in his black leather swivel chair and rolled it forward and under his oversized oaken desk. With both hands clasped and resting on a purple felt mat on his desk, he twiddled his thumbs as he readied himself for his next client.

Billy slumped into a large green fabric chair, straightened out his legs, and crossed his ankles.

"I'll get right to the point," Mr. Dickinson said in a polished professional voice, looking straight at Billy. "Mrs. Irene Pilkington left you as the sole beneficiary in her will." He held up an envelope and waved it slowly, enticingly, in the air, motioning for Billy to take it.

Billy smiled and reached for it. He turned the expensive-looking, linen-finish packet over in his hands and studied it. The words, Jones, Dickinson, and Mathers LLP were embossed in small silver letters in the top right corner, and To Mr. William Jones was imprinted across the middle of the envelope in larger letters: black and in a fancy font. He ran a finger slowly over the embossing and imprinting. He was impressed. The envelope felt important and expensive. He carefully extracted the contents; a letter from Irene and read it slowly and silently to himself.

"May 2, 1950
10 Ainsdale Rd,
Westlea.
Blackmoor.

My dearest Billy,

I am of sound mind, have free will, and have informed my solicitor, Mr. Dickinson at 152 Great Moor Street in Blackmoor, of my intention to change my will. You have been

like a grandson to me, and I want my estate to go to you.
There are no conditions attached to this bequest. Do with the
proceeds as you wish. I hope that in some small way it will
enable you to live a happy life. You certainly deserve it after all
you've been through. I can't think of anyone more deserving
of a lucky break than you.

With all my love,
Irene Pilkington."

Billy's eyes narrowed and clouded over with tears. He liked what
Irene had written about him being like a grandson to her. The feeling
was mutual. She'd been like a grandmother to him.

Not only had Irene bequeathed him her house and contents,
but she had also left him her bank account with two thousand, five
hundred and seventy-six pounds. It was incredulous – he'd no idea she
was so rich.

Billy signed the documents and carefully listened to Mr. Dickinson's
instructions about what he must do to effect the changes. As he left
the office, filled with a deep sense of gratitude, he vowed to honor
Irene by emulating her kindness and compassion. He would use his
good fortune to find people who needed him and to help them. He
pictured her, sitting in heaven among a bevy of angels and smiling
down on him.

Only Mr. Dickinson and himself knew the contents of the will and
that's how Billy wanted it. He didn't even tell Joe, but Joe sensed he
was now financially better off because Billy insisted on paying him the
going rate for the rental of the farmhouse.

Billy didn't want the inheritance to fundamentally change anything
in his life, not in the immediate future at any rate. He decided to continue living in the farmhouse and to rent out Irene's furnished house.
He put a rental ad in the newspaper for a tenant.

He looked at everything in Irene's house to identify what could stay
for the benefit of the tenant, what he wanted to keep for himself, and

what he felt was no longer needed. He didn't care much for 'stuff.' And even if he had, there wasn't much storage space at the farmhouse for 'stuff.' What he did want, as a memento to remember Irene by, was her Royal Doulton tea service. He made space for it in the antique hutch and buffet in the farmhouse kitchen and took the framed photograph of Irene and Ernie on their wedding day and another one of them standing in front of the Royal Liver Building in Liverpool and used them as decorative bookends to frame the tea service. He also found a dust-covered biscuit tin in the attic which held many documents, including Irene's marriage certificate, and birth certificates for the entire Pilkington family – Ernie, James, Walter, and Irene, as well as various contracts and deeds that had long since expired.

On the bottom of the tin, underneath the documents, was a stash of six faded colored postcards. As soon as Billy saw them, he knew what they were. A strange feeling erupted in his gut making him feel edgy. He picked up the collection and slowly, reverently, looked at each one. They were the postcards his mum had sent Irene from Jersey. He gazed at the faint writing on the front and back, at the postage stamp, and the scenes on the cards. His heart raced and his eyes teared with love for Irene and his mum.

This is my mum's handwriting. It's her words. She licked the stamp and put it on the card, he thought, clutching the cards to his breast. *She picked out the scenes. I bet she's been to all of these places and seen these sights with her own eyes,* he thought, and in that instant, he promised himself that one day he'd go to Jersey and see those sights with his own eyes. I'll go there as soon as I find my brother. Maybe we'll go together and look for my dad.

He scanned the scenes, imagining his mum in the postcards, and smiled at what he saw. He imagined her laughing and skipping across the beaches at Saint Brelades and Saint Ouens: her long red hair flying in the wind with Ted following behind in close pursuit. In another postcard, he imagined the two of them holding hands and looking out across the English Channel to England from the ramparts of an old castle. He savored every stroke of the pale penciled writing and read every message on the cards at least three times. He couldn't make out every word, but he could read enough to get a sense of the message. His mum had written about visiting the places on the cards with Ted and, from what he could read, he got a sense she was in a very happy state of mind when she wrote the cards. On the back of the La Rocco Martello Tower postcard, she had written: 'Dear Irene. Something has come up and I've been delayed. I'll write later. Love. Mary."

'*That was me! That was me and my brother who came up!*' The realization made him feel warm and excited.

He put the postcards aside and closed the box. As a sentimental gesture to Irene's memory, he put the box on the top shelf of the storage cupboard in his bedroom and lined the postcards up on the mantelpiece above the fireplace so he could see them whenever he wanted.

Within a week of the rental ad for Irene's house appearing in the newspaper, a potential tenant knocked on Billy's door. Harry Warrington desperately needed a place for his family: his wife and a son aged five and a daughter aged two, to stay while their house in Mosley Common, which had been damaged in a fire, was being repaired. As with many families in Blackmoor, the Warringtons didn't have full house insurance coverage.

"It was a chimney fire that caused it," explained Harry when Billy asked him what had happened. "Two months I figure. They say kitchen and living room will be done in six weeks and rest of house in ten weeks," Harry said when asked how long he needed to rent. "Insurance will pay for some of the repairs, but not rent," he added.

Billy could see the desperation written on the faces of Mr. and Mrs. Warrington and the look of uncertainty in the eyes of the children and was moved. He at once thought of how Joe had befriended him when he was down and out, and how Joe had helped him to weather the storm. He offered Harry the same deal as Joe had offered him: pay what you can when you can.

"God bless ye young man. That takes a ton of trouble off my

shoulders. We'll look after your house as good as if it were our own, won't we children? You can count on it." The children nodded, smiled huge grins of gratitude, came over, and hugged Billy. Billy was greatly moved – he'd never felt that much physical warmth from strangers in his life before. Knowing he was helping a family through a difficult time made him feel good inside. He gazed upwards to the heavens and sensed Irene smiling down on him.

As Billy went about his business, he pondered how he might help others in need. At the end of Settle Street lived the Barlow family with three children: two girls and a boy, all under the age of ten. He sensed they were struggling when he saw them on his rounds. The girl's dresses and the boy's pants and shirts were ill-fitting, and their shoes were falling apart.

He guessed the approximate sizes of the children's clothes and began to sort out and set aside shirts, pants, dresses, and shoes from his collections that were clean, in reasonably good condition, and might fit. When he confided in Joe about what he was doing, Joe was intrigued and fully supportive.

"Can I help?" he asked.

"Yes. Can I look through all the clothes that are turned in by the other rag and bone men and I'll pay you for what I take on a per pound basis? That way you're not out of pocket."

Joe agreed.

Billy could have knocked on the Barlow's door and presented the gift, but that would have been too uncomfortable for him. He didn't want the attention. He much preferred to remain anonymous. He also knew that the residents of Blackmoor were a proud bunch and loath to accept any form of charity on a personal basis. That's just the way they were.

One evening, while frying an egg and some rashers of bacon for tea, Billy thought about how he could deliver his gift anonymously when an idea popped into his mind causing him to laugh out loud and slap his sides. I can be Father Christmas. I know how happy he makes children feel. I'll call myself Barnabas, Father Christmas' helper.

"That's hilarious," said Joe when Billy told him about his plan. "D'ya need any help?"

"Yes. You can get me some cards printed. Maybe your friend, Terry, can help. He has an office job, doesn't he? I just need about a dozen business cards with these words: Enjoy... With love... From Barnabas... Father Christmas' helper."

"You're right Billy. I think Terry can do that. I'll look him up and ask him."

A week later, Billy had the cards. Terry had made up a dozen, about the size of a postcard, and printed them on green paper, just as Billy had asked.

Billy put the assortment of clothes – pants, shirts, dresses, and shoes in a pile, wrapped them in brown paper, tied it with string, and attached the Barnabas note. He went down Settle Street to the Barlows and when he was sure no one was looking, hung the package on the handle of the back gate. He knew it would be discovered by the end of the day because everyone used their back gates many times a day to go to and from their homes. They only used their front doors for special occasions, such as when they summoned a taxi to take them to the train or bus station.

Billy continued to do this whenever he became aware of a family in need. Of course, in time, everyone gossiped about Barnabas and took guesses as to who the Good Samaritan was, but no one ever guessed it was Billy, the rag and bone man.

PART TWO –
MARY

Chapter Six –
John and Veronica Jones

Blackmoor, Lancashire
Pre 1900

John Jones was the youngest of three siblings who grew up on Reservoir Street in Mosley Common. He lived in a two-up and two-down terraced house and slept on the sofa in the living room. His two sisters shared the second bedroom upstairs.

Reservoir Street was the roughest and toughest street in Mosley Common: The police were there every Friday and Saturday night to break up bare-knuckled street fights and to arrest drunken husbands for beating up their wives. This was a normal occurrence and to be expected if you lived on Reservoir Street.

John's father was a heavy drinker whose violent ways instilled fear in all who crossed his path. John feared him, as did his mother and sisters. Though his dad earned a good wage at the mill, he spent most of it at the pub. Watching his mum scrimp and save every day to feed and clothe her family, made John angry and resentful of his father.

Constantly being ridiculed by his classmates for living on Reservoir Street and for wearing threadbare pants and ill-fitting shirts, John lived in a perpetual state of embarrassment and self-consciousness. And to add to his tormented soul, he was teased horribly by his classmates when both of his sisters got pregnant at the age of 15.

Seeing how alcohol had ruined his family, John vowed never to touch a drop, and the shame he felt of growing up in poverty and feeling powerless to change the situation, ignited in him a desire to get out of that domestic environment as soon as he could.

John's robust physical appearance and streetwise ways caught the eye of many a girl at school. One such young lady was Veronica O'Malley, a fellow student in his class. All it took to get John's attention was a smile and a friendly hello one morning, as they lined up in assembly. John admired her petite five-foot-three frame, her blazing red hair, emerald-green eyes, and freckled nose, and looked forward to getting to know her better.

Veronica had been a sickly child who hoped to outgrow her health issues and become hale and hearty by the time she was an adult, so she could be a wife and mother one day.

John and Veronica began courting when they were fifteen, much to the dismay of her parents who had serious misgivings about John. They knew where he lived, were aware of his reputation, and were concerned about how he'd treat their daughter, but once they heard him talk about swearing off the booze and of his hopes for his children to become priests or nuns, they came around and were fully supportive of their daughter's relationship.

They married when they were eighteen in St Cuthbert's Church. It was the simplest of weddings with just a little celebration afterward back at her parent's house. John wanted to elope or keep the church wedding a secret from his family, lest his dad showed up drunk and spoil their special day, but as was the custom at the time marriage banns had to be read out at church on three successive Sundays. Everyone in the neighborhood soon became aware of the upcoming wedding and though John didn't formally invite any of his family to the wedding, his mum, dad, and Aunt May showed up at the church, and to his enormous relief, his dad was sober and behaved himself.

~

John and Veronica worked full-time at the Ashleigh Cotton Mill, and after the wedding, lived with her parents to save money to buy a house. Their day-to-day living expenses were minimal, and in two years they had saved enough to put a down payment on a house, located just three doors down from her parent's house when it came up for sale.

Aunt May, John's mother's sister, was the only relative on John's side to stay in touch with them after they were married. She shared John's sentiments and supported his dreams, and she got on well with Veronica. She was thrilled when Veronica told her she was pregnant, and that her expected delivery date was January 1st. Not only would the baby be a New Year's baby, but it would also be a centennial one too.

Chapter Seven – Mary Jones

Blackmoor, Lancashire
1900

The New Century rolled in and the whole town of Blackmoor spilled out into the streets at midnight with their Union Jack flags, hooters, and horns, to celebrate the end of what had been a hard decade for most residents. Everyone was in a great mood and optimistic that better times were ahead.

It was a particularly joyous occasion for John and Veronica because their baby, a little girl they named Mary, was born at home at dinner time on New Year's Day.

Weighing in at six pounds two ounces, Mary was as healthy a baby as you could wish for, but Veronica had a difficult time with the birthing. There were complications in the way Mary was positioned in the birth canal. The midwife hurriedly sent for the doctor to help in the delivery, but by the time he arrived, it was all over. Mary had already arrived.

The doctor attended to Veronica and ordered her to stay in bed for the next seven days. Aunt May took time off work from her job at the Post Office to look after baby Mary and Veronica, while John went back to work at the mill. However, unforeseen infections set in, and three days later Veronica died of child-bed fever.

The whole family was devastated. John blamed the midwife and the doctor for incompetence and even blamed his baby daughter for his wife's passing. The O'Malley's blamed John for not having a cleaner house and Aunt May blamed God.

John was at his wit's end: he didn't know where to turn or what to do.

Aunt May, a thirty-four-years old widow whose husband, William, had died tragically in a boiler explosion at work the previous year came to the rescue by offering to function as a surrogate mother to Mary. She and William had always wanted children, but she was never able to conceive. The opportunity to be the mother of a newborn baby was the perfect antidote for the loneliness and grief she was feeling for the relatively recent loss of her husband. She handed in her notice at the Post Office, rented out her house, and moved her personal belongings into John's second bedroom. Baby Mary slept in a crib by the side of her bed.

To deal with his grief, John immersed himself in church activities and volunteered to take on whatever tasks arose. He went to church every night after tea and again on the weekends to keep himself busy – cleaning, repairing, and generally just filling in time and the only time he spent with Aunt May and baby Mary was when he went with them to church on Sunday mornings. Aunt May had full custody of Mary. To observers who didn't know any better, they would think that Aunt May was John's wife and biological mother to Mary.

For the next three years, everybody seemed to thrive in the Jones household: John was busy with his lay duties at church, Mary was growing like the proverbial weed, and Aunt May was teaching Mary numbers and letters readying her for nursery school.

Given John's seeming lack of interest in his daughter's development, Aunt May thought about asking him if she could adopt Mary and take her to live with her in her home. She hoped John would meet someone and remarry and that's when she'd ask him about adoption. He did meet someone and remarry, but it didn't work out the way Aunt May had envisaged.

Eileen Bailey was twenty-six, three years older than John, and one of three sisters of an Irish family living in Westlea. She was about the same height as John, but a little plumper. Her warm chestnut-brown eyes seemed to be always smiling and her thick, curly jet-black hair always hung unruly around her ears and shoulders. For the past seven years, she'd been caring for her ailing grandfather, and when he passed away two months earlier, he bequeathed his house to her in appreciation for her caregiving.

Now she was free to move on with her life and pursue her dream of finding a husband and having children. She was single, childless, and knew she was a great catch – she had a full-time job and owned her own home, but she was also keenly aware that she was no longer eighteen years of age.

As with John and Veronica, Eileen had gone to work at the Ashleigh Cotton Mill when she left school at the age of fifteen. She knew who John and Veronica were, and had heard that Veronica had died in childbirth and that John was bringing up his daughter with the help of an aunt. Now that she was in the market, actively looking for a husband, she set her sights on eligible John.

She saw him every Sunday at church and had observed Mary's growth over the years – from pram baby to a happy little four-year-old. She admired his seeming no-nonsense approach to life: his sobriety and religious beliefs, and felt he'd make an ideal husband. She was also captivated by little Mary's beauty. The thought of being a stepmother to such a precious, happy child delighted her, intensifying her desire to become John's wife.

She joined the Women's auxiliary at church to give her a plausible excuse to be there on Thursday nights when John polished the pews. She wanted a way to search him out and to be able to speak with him privately in a non-threatening way – to get to know him better without being too obvious.

Arriving at the church half an hour early for the 7 o'clock Women's Auxiliary meeting, she found John working on the pews, as she knew she would.

"Hello, John. How are you?"

Startled to hear his name and curious as to who wanted to know how he was, he stopped what he was doing and looked up.

"I'm okay. How about you?"

"I'm good. I don't know if you remember me. I'm Eileen Bailey and I work at the Mill, same as you."

John smiled a half-smile – the most smile he ever let himself display.

"Yes. I know who you are. What can I do for you?"

"Oh, nothing. I'm on the Women's Auxiliary and we meet here every Thursday. I just saw you as I came in and thought I'd say hello. I see you and your little girl at church every week – my, how she's growing. She must be going to nursery school soon, I imagine."

"Yes. She starts nursery school in the autumn."

"You perhaps don't know, but I knew your wife quite well. She went to the same school as my older sister, and they were good friends. I was devastated when I heard what happened."

John was taken aback by this revelation. He stared at her.

Eileen smiled and added, "And I've watched your little girl grow up, year by the year. You are so lucky to have such a beautiful child."

"Thanks. I take it you don't have any children?"

"No. I'm not married. I was too busy for boyfriends. I looked after my grandfather for seven years when he was ill until he passed away earlier this year. But I'd like to get married one day and have children."

John gave another half-smile and joked, "Well. You better start looking, hadn't you?'

Eileen returned his smile and said, "I am. How about you? Would you marry again?"

"Perhaps. But only if I met the right woman."

"So, who's the right woman?"

"Oh. I don't know. Someone who shares my beliefs and values I guess."

Sensing the door to John's world had opened a little, Eileen decided to jump in with both feet. "That sounds just like me," she teased.

Her frankness caught him off guard. "You think so, do you? And what about you? What are you looking for in a husband?"

"A strong man who doesn't drink and has strong Christian values. Do you know anyone like that?"

John was enjoying this back-and-forth banter, yet, at the back of his mind, he wondered about her. *Were tonight's meeting and conversation just a coincidence, or what?*

Eileen's forthrightness emboldened him to take the next step. "Would you like to come to my house for tea and meet Mary sometime?"

"That would be wonderful, John. I'd like that very much."

And so began the courtship of John and Eileen.

Aunt May was pleased at first to learn that John was dating – it gave him some other interest in life besides his lay church duties – and she thought the pair made a good match. She was hoping they would get married, and that John would agree to her adopting Mary, however, it didn't take long for her to become concerned for Mary and for herself. It was obvious Eileen was going to great lengths to endear herself to Mary as she always brought gifts of toys when she came over to John's house three times a week and sat on the floor playing and laughing with Mary and her dolls. One time, she overheard John and Eileen talking about getting married and moving into Eileen's bigger home in Westlea, but there was no mention of what would happen to her.

John and Eileen courted for two months before John proposed marriage. Though happy for them, Aunt May was also heartbroken, having to give up being Mary's mother. She explained to Mary that now she had a real mummy, there was no reason for her to continue living with them. Mary listened and was upset, but she was too young to fully appreciate what was happening.

Aunt May gave her renters one-month notice and moved back into her home, and the Post Office gave her a job similar to the one she previously had.

John sold his home and moved into Eileen's, and Eileen took over the maternal duties as stepmother to four-year-old Mary.

At first, Mary asked every day about Aunt May's whereabouts, but over time, she grew accustomed to the new arrangement and stopped asking. Aunt May visited every Saturday at dinnertime and in Mary's best interest, was fully supportive of everything.

Eileen now had a husband and a baby girl to care for and that pleased her, Mary had a new mother and was continuing to thrive in an environment of affection and attention, and John had a wife who shared his religious beliefs and his bed. He was most pleased with the way his life was unfolding. Moving away from his detestable family in Mosley Common to a respectable three-up and three-down in Westlea had always been his dream. Now it was his reality.

~

Two years later, John and Eileen had a baby girl they named Angela. Mary, now six years old, was thrilled to have a real little sister to dote on instead of playing make-believe with dolls. Eileen was thrilled she was now a real mother with two little ones to look after, but John was disappointed – he wanted sons.

The sisters could not have been more unlike in physique and temperament. Mary had her mother's thick red wavy hair, her emerald-green eyes, freckles, and her petite stature while Angela had her mother's darker features: her silky black straight hair, and olive skin, and was more robust and outgoing than Mary.

~

Mary was nine and attending St. Peter and Paul Catholic elementary school when her dad invited Father Shields, the parish priest of St. Peter and Paul Church, to the house for tea. After the meal and in Mary's presence he said to Father Shields, "I want Mary to become a nun. Her mum did too before she passed. We need to do this to honor her memory and I'm looking for your help in preparing Mary for the convent."

The Catholic priest's eyes lit up and he gleefully rubbed his hands.

He couldn't stop himself – it was so spontaneous. Self-conscious about how his actions might look and not wanting to appear too eager, he tried to disguise his mirth by giving his body a shake as if he was cold and rubbing his hands together in a more exaggerated manner as if to warm them up.

Mary was pleased with the attention and smiled, but she was too young to grasp the scope of what her dad was talking about, or how it would affect her life going forward, however, the idea of swishing around in a black robe and wearing a white headdress seemed to be such a lot of fun.

The following day, Father Shields went to the school and spoke with Sister Mildred, the headmistress. He told her of John's wish for Mary to become a nun and of his request for the help of the church in grooming her for the convent. The tall, bespectacled Sister Mildred was delighted with the news and said she'd be only too pleased to assist and immediately began to think of ways to help.

The next day, Sister Mildred called Mary into her study. Like all children at St. Peter and Paul's School, Mary was nervous, intimidated, and scared – she had never been in Sister Mildred's study before. She stared down at her brown flat shoes without blinking and clasped her hands tightly and demurely in front of her.

"You are special Mary. Not only do you have the only red hair and freckles in the school, but you are going to be a nun. What do you think of that?"

Mary didn't answer.

"None of the other girls are as special as you." Sister Mildred leaned back in her big, black swivel chair and gloated.

Mary continued to stare at her shoes and squeeze her little hands tightly together. She wasn't going to say anything. With the Sisters, children listened but never spoke.

"That's why I'm going to give you special tasks to do Mary. I'm not going to ask anyone else to do them. I'm going to ask just you. What do you think of that?"

Reluctantly, Mary lifted her gaze from her shoes to look up at the smiling, severe face in the white hood and trembled with fear. She did not answer.

"Now, go. And remember Mary: you are special: God has chosen you."

Mary quietly exited Sister Mildred's study and went to the playground, confused, and scared.

While the other girls frolicked in the playground on their dinner break, Mary had to go into each classroom to wipe the blackboards with a duster, empty the wastebaskets, fill the teacher's ink pots, and every Friday at noon, wax and polish Sister Mildred's hardwood floor. She tied rags to her feet and shuffled along the surface of the floor – back and forth with little steps – once with wax and once to polish, just as Sister Mildred instructed. Sister leaned back in her chair and smiled. When Mary's energy level dropped, Sister commented and reminded her that she was doing God's work. Mary made an extra effort and picked up the pace.

Throughout her childhood, John had conditioned Mary to do whatever was asked of her without questioning, so, when Sister Mildred asked her to do extra chores, Mary simply obeyed and followed the rules. Parishioners and neighbors considered Mary to be the perfect child and parents cited her as a role model when counseling their children on good behavior.

John also wanted Angela to become a nun, but there was no way Eileen was going to let that happen. She wanted grandchildren and with Mary cloistered in the convent, it was up to Angela to have them.

⁓

Over the ensuing years, John became more fanatical about his religion and more determined to follow through on the teachings of the church in thought, word, and deed. He believed all bad behavior, including complaints, was the work of the devil. The church and school knew that Mary's parents wouldn't do anything if Mary complained to them about the chores she was assigned because they believed the church could do no wrong. Consequently, Sister Mildred gave Mary new jobs whenever something extra came up.

Mary changed schools when she was eleven and went to Mount Carmel Grammar School. She thrived in the different environment – no more dusting, waxing, and polishing, and no more Sister Mildred breathing down her neck, hounding her to do more chores. She enjoyed doing homework and applied herself well to everything the teacher asked, always finishing the school year in the top three of her class. This achievement gave her the confidence in herself that she had previously lacked. Meanwhile, Angela was struggling – she wasn't as smart as Mary, and she didn't like doing homework.

While Mary's school life was greatly improving, her home life was deteriorating. Eileen resented Mary's academic success and tried to make up for Angela's shortfall at school by favoring her over Mary. She gave Mary more chores to do around the house and the dirtier ones too, rationalizing that as she was older and destined to become a nun, it was okay to purposely make her life difficult – it was all part of Mary's training to be of service, which John said was a nun's purpose in life.

When Mary turned fifteen, Eileen baked a chocolate cake for her and put fifteen little white candles on it. After Mary blew them out, her dad said, "Just think, Mary. This will be your last birthday at home. I'll start making plans for you to go to the convent after your graduation next year."

"I'm not sure I want to go, dad. I'm not sure I want to be a nun."

"Not sure! Not sure! Did I ask you? It's what you've trained for all your life, isn't it?" said John in a heated voice.

"I know. I know. I just said I wasn't sure dad. That's all."

"You can't let everybody down. Father Shields and Sister Mildred ask about you every time I see them. They've invested a lot in you."

"I know. I just said I wasn't sure. That's all."

"It's what your mother wanted. You know that. You can't let her down too. She'd turn over in her grave if you didn't become a nun. Wouldn't she?"

"Yes. I suppose so," replied Mary, her spirit crushed under the weight of the implied obligations to her mother, to Father Shields, to Sister Mildred, and everybody.

At that moment, Mary accepted that it was her destiny to become a nun and vowed she would never allow herself to question it again.

The O'Malley part of the family only visited a couple of times a year now because they lived in Mosley Common and that was too far away for them to walk, and it made the taxi cost unaffordable. So, you can imagine how delighted they were, when on their next visit, John announced that Mary was going into a convent after graduation. They congratulated him for following through on his promise and left the Jones house in a buoyant mood. But that wasn't how Aunt May felt when she left – she was disheartened. She wanted to speak with Mary on a one-to-one to find out how she really felt about devoting her life to the Church, but there was never any opportunity to do that. Now, fifty years of age and suffering from painful arthritis in her joints, Aunt May had mobility issues. She could only visit when she had a medical appointment in the area, and even then, she seldom saw Mary because she was usually in school.

Chapter Eight – Mount St. Joseph Convent

Blackmoor, Lancashire
1916

A year later, after graduating from Mount Carmel Grammar School, Mary entered the Mount St. Joseph Convent to begin her training as a novice nun. She went there with an open mind and heart, but as she walked through the compound gates and looked around at the environs that would be her home for the foreseeable future, she had second thoughts. *What am I doing?* This was the first time since expressing concerns to her dad a year earlier that she admitted to herself she had doubts.

For ninety days, Mary applied herself, dutifully following all instructions and praying as fervently and devotedly as she could, however, with each passing day, she became more aware that she just didn't seem to have the same conviction and passion for the convent as the other girls. She sensed they were blooming while she was wilting. The desire to be a nun just wasn't in her heart.

Mother Celeste, the Mother Superior at the convent, noticed Mary's seeming lack of conviction but chose not to say anything. After three months of cloistered existence, Mary decided she'd had enough – she just didn't want to be a nun. She wanted to live a normal life: to fall in love, get married, and have children. More than anything, she wanted to experience the love she sensed was possible in a family but that she had never known.

After dinner, Mary went to see Mother Celeste in her study. "I've been struggling ever since I got here, Mother Celeste. I don't have what it takes to be a nun. I've prayed and I've tried. I pray and I try every day."

Mother Celeste put her prayer book down, folded her hands on her lap, and lowered her head. With raised eyebrows, she looked at Mary over her black wire glasses and frowned. "I know my child. I know you've been struggling. Most novices do at first. You must trust in God and keep praying to him to give you the faith you need to become a nun."

Mary wasn't going to be sloughed off with this comment. She was tired of fervently praying every day. She'd already made up her mind to leave. Looking straight into Mother Celeste's tired, watery eyes, she quietly and defiantly declared, "I've been patient and I've done my best. It's not working. I know it never will and I'm going to leave."

"Have you told your father and Father Shields?"

Mary shuddered a little with fright at this question. Taking a deep breath, she quietly replied, "No. It's none of their business."

Her abrupt answer shocked Mother Celeste who was hoping that the question might win Mary over to remain in the program. She tried again and nodded her head implying that Mary should agree with her. "They'll be most upset with you, won't they?"

"Yes, they will," replied Mary, standing straighter and taller and refusing to be intimidated. "I've not come to my decision lightly. I'm well aware of how upset people are going to be with me, but I can't stay," she boldly proclaimed.

Though only sixteen, Mary was showing a level of maturity and self-confidence far beyond her years. "It's my life. I must do what I feel in my heart is right, not what other people want me to do." She turned around, marched out of Mother Celeste's office holding her head high, and went straight to her room to pack.

When she didn't show for morning prayers the following day,

Mother Celeste accepted the fact that Mary was not going to change her mind and so informed the other novices and staff of Mary's impending departure and arranged with the office for the necessary paperwork to be prepared.

Mary returned home, unannounced, to the anger and disappointment of her dad and stepmother.

"What d'ya mean you're not going to be a nun?" her dad thundered with Eileen by his side in full support.

"It's not for me, dad. For three months I've tried and tried, really, really hard, every day. It's not for everyone. It's not for me."

"D'ya know how disappointed I am in you. And I know how disappointed your mother is too – she'll be turning over in her grave. You can't do this to us."

"I'm so very sorry, dad. I don't mean to hurt you."

"Well young lady, you have. And you've disgraced us. What shall I tell Father Shields and Sister Mildred and all the congregants at church when they ask why you left the convent? What did I do wrong? Can you tell me that?"

"You didn't do anything wrong, dad. Not every girl has what it takes to become a nun."

Mary left the room and went upstairs to her bedroom. Eileen followed and knocked on her door. "May I speak with you?"

"Yes," said Mary begrudgingly.

"Your dad will be okay. He just needs more time to get over the shock. Do you think you might give it another try, in say about six months?"

Mary dropped the hairbrush she was holding, raised her eyes, and looked sternly at her step mum full-on. "No. I will never go back. Never, ever. Why can't everybody just leave me alone and let me be?"

Eileen returned to the living room.

Next came the silent treatment, designed to make Mary feel depressed and inconsequential. Mealtimes were the worst.

Two days later, Mary took her school results and went to the unemployment office on Great Moor Street to look for work. Eager to contribute financially towards the cost of her room and board, Mary was determined to get a job, any job, even if it meant being a loom worker at the Mill with her parents. A few vacancies on the Job Board interested her, but the one that most garnered her attention was a job in the typing pool of a company called Wilkins Clothiers, a large mail-order firm specializing in women's clothing. Mary immediately went to the company office to arrange for a job interview. She was thrilled when they said they would see her right away because they were expanding and urgently needed more typists. She passed the typing test and was offered an entry-level position as a junior Typist.

Mary returned home with a Wilkins Clothier catalog tucked under her arm and a face full of smiles. Angela congratulated her and borrowed the catalog — she wanted to see the latest styles of women's clothing and what colors were in fashion. Eileen was pleased that Mary had found an office job and didn't have to work in the Mill, and the only thing her dad said was how much she was to pay for her room and board.

Mary started work the following morning and though shy and quiet, she made friends quickly and settled into the job well. The work and her new environment gave her a fresh perspective on life. Once a week, she went to the cinema with Jean, one of the other six girls in the typing pool, and every two weeks on payday, she went for lunch with them to the Little Panda, a Chinese restaurant, located on the next street.

At home, things weren't going so well. Her dad wouldn't accept the fact that his daughter was never going to be a nun. Until she got the job, he'd been able to orchestrate every aspect of her life, and with a firm hand, as he tried to do the same with his wife and with Angela. It was always his way or no way. He was determined that what happened to his two sisters getting pregnant at fifteen was not going to happen to his two daughters if he had any say in the matter.

One morning after breakfast, John gave Mary an ultimatum. "So long as you're in my house, young lady, you aren't allowed to go out with boys until you're twenty-one. I know what they're like and they'll lead you astray. Understand?"

Mary nodded and went upstairs to her room. She wasn't interested in boys anyway – they frightened her. Other than her one night out at the cinema with Jean and lunch with the girls on payday, Mary was very much a loner. She spent most of her leisure hours in her room reading. She had a few school friends, but she was never close to any of them, and they were not allowed to cross the threshold of the Jones household and meet the rest of her family. But then again, Mary didn't want them to, fearful that her dad would embarrass her. Her only friends were Jean from work, her Aunt May, whom she seldom saw now because she was mostly incapacitated and housebound, and her next-door neighbors, Irene, and her husband, Ernie.

Though Irene and Ernie had lived next door to her all her life, it wasn't until Mary was eighteen that she got to know them well. Irene had always been friendly toward her and had reached out to her on numerous occasions with a greeting and a warm smile, only to be politely rebuffed by her, which Irene assumed was because Mary was embarrassed by her dad's behavior. All of the neighbors must have heard the arguments coming from the Jones house, year after year, just as she and Ernie had, and that must have been mortifying for a young woman. They knew about Mary's failed attempt to become a nun, her dad's disappointment with her, and how fanatical her dad was about his religion.

Irene was concerned for Mary's mental and physical health. When she noticed Mary looking sadder than usual and putting on weight, she decided to try a different approach. She was in her front garden weeding around the yellow primroses when Mary came home from work. "Mary, can I see you for a minute? I need some good eyes to help me with my sewing."

Mary was a little startled, but reluctantly said, "Okay."

She followed Irene into her house and over the next hour and a pot of tea and a plate of biscuits, they began a warm and loving relationship that would last for many years and prove pivotal in Mary's life.

In the following months, Mary came to trust Irene more and more and began to share her thoughts and dilemmas with her. Once, when Mary went home and told her dad the reason why she was late for tea was that she'd had a nice visit with their neighbor, Irene, he was livid. "I don't want you visiting those heathens next door. They don't go to church, and they'll fill your head with all sorts of rubbish. Do you hear me?"

Mary became angry, but she remained silent.

"Do you hear me young lady?" her dad repeated. "I don't want you to ever visit those heathens again."

"Yes dad," she replied, but she had no intention of following his orders, and she didn't. She'd learned the best way to manage her dad's controlling ways was to simply agree with him and do whatever it was behind his back.

~

When Mary turned nineteen, the situation in the home got worse She stopped going to church – told her dad it was hypocritical of her if she didn't believe in the teachings, and he reacted by increasing the pressure on her to return to the convent. "It'll work out this time you'll see. You are more mature now. You were too young before."

"I wasn't dad. I'm just not cut out to be a nun. I never was. It's just not for me. It never will be."

"Let me remind you, young lady, that your mother will never be at peace – she'll be turning over in her grave until you're a nun."

Although Mary didn't believe this bit about her mum turning over in her grave, she still found the comment hurtful and upsetting. By now, she'd gotten used to her dad's constant pressure to make her feel guilty for her mother's death, yet he persisted in saying it whenever he wanted to punish her emotionally.

Mary was gaining weight and becoming withdrawn and sullener

with each passing week. Meanwhile, Angela was thriving. She wasn't in the house much – school and a lively social life with her friends at their homes kept her busy.

Two weeks before her 20th birthday, Mary went next door to give Irene a Christmas card and to have a talk. She admitted she'd been depressed for a long time, and she realized she had to change. "I'm going to make a fresh start in the New Year, and I want your advice."

Irene leaned forward to better hear what Mary had to say.

"I'm shy and I don't like being put on the spot. A man at work asked me out and I said no. I wanted to say yes, but I was too scared to."

Irene smiled. "And why do think you were too scared?"

Mary thought about it for a few seconds and answered, "I worry things might get out of hand, the way my dad says, and I worry I might not be able to say no."

Irene smiled at Mary's naivety and was deeply saddened by the power her dad obviously had over her. "You know in your heart what's right and what's wrong, Mary. The world is a beautiful place. It's not the way your dad describes it." Taking her hands and clutching them, Irene said, "Trust in yourself Mary and ask questions if you're unsure. You're missing out on so much. A girl your age should be happy and carefree. If you feel you want to say yes, say it and see what happens. I think you'll be pleasantly surprised. Don't be afraid of life, Mary. Always remember life is what you make it. It's your life, not your dad's. He can't live it for you."

Mary was buoyed by Irene's words and felt lighter and happier when she returned home. This confirmation about life was exactly what Mary needed to hear at this point in her life.

Chapter Nine –
Peter changes Mary's mind

Blackmoor, Lancashire
1919

Soon after the New Year, Peter, an order-taker at Wilkins Clothiers, asked Mary out. He'd always fancied her, and he'd asked her out the previous year, only to be turned down. He decided to try again, but this time, he'd be more assertive.

He knocked on the glass window of the typing pool to get her attention. When Mary looked up, he motioned for her to come into the corridor. "Hey Mary, I know I asked you out last year and you said no, but I'm asking you out again. I think you're cute and interesting and I'd like to get to know you. Are you seeing anyone?"

"No."

"Great. I like your hair, your eyes, and your freckles. How's that for starters," he teased.

Mary blushed a deeper red than her hair, her emerald-green eyes sparkled and the freckles on her nose and cheeks seemed to glow under the office lights.

"What are you doing after work tonight?"

"Nothing."

"D'ya wanna go for a walk and a talk?"

"A walk and a talk? Sure. That sounds like a whole lot of fun," she said sarcastically making Peter laugh. *I said yes,* she thought and was pleased with herself.

"Let's go to Meadow Park. They say the weather's going to be fine for the rest of the day. Will you be warm enough? – it's still just February after all."

"Yes. I'll be fine. My coat's warm and I have a woolen scarf and beret."

I said yes again she thought and was doubly pleased with herself and with Peter for not giving up on her.

"Great. I'll meet you at the front door at five." Peter was also pleased with himself because he had asked and Mary had said yes.

Peter was tall, skinny, and two years older than Mary, according to the calendar, but many more years ahead of her in terms of life experience.

Mary wore her dark-red woolen topcoat over her pink blouse and brown skirt. She'd put on a few extra pounds over Christmas and was feeling fat and self-conscious and when she checked herself in the women's bathroom mirror, she regretted not having bought a larger coat. She pushed her shoulder-length hair up and under her battleship grey beret and pulled it tight down over her forehead.

When she came out of the typing pool at five, Peter was waiting for her. "Don't you look smart?" she said, complimenting him on his dress – he was wearing a light grey raincoat over a dark blue sports jacket and a white shirt with a royal blue tie with white diagonal stripes. "You look more like the General Manager than the order-taker," Mary teased.

"Or maybe an undertaker?" quipped Peter making Mary laugh out loud. "Thanks for the compliment. I like to dress smartly."

They walked to Meadow Park, which was at the bottom of Calvert Lane, about ten minutes away from work, and headed towards the arboretum.

"How come you walk so fast? Where's the fire?" Mary joked.

"How come you walk so slow?" was Peter's rebuttal. "I'm sorry. I know I walk fast. People always tell me that. I'll slow down. Okay?"

They walked and talked about work and the weather and then, right out of the blue, Mary asked, "Do you believe in God?"

What an odd question for a young woman to ask and only fifteen minutes into our first date!

"I'm not religious and I don't believe in God. Why d'ya ask?"

"Oh. I'm just curious about what other people believe."

"What religion are you?"

"I'm Catholic. I nearly became a nun you know."

Peter was taken aback. "A nun? Why didn't you?"

"I went into a convent when I was sixteen. It wasn't my idea to become a nun. My mum died when I was born. She and dad had talked about wanting their children to become nuns and priests before she died. I was in the convent for three months, but it wasn't for me. I didn't believe like the other girls."

"That's quite a story, Mary. Do you believe in God?" Peter asked bluntly.

"I don't know. I prayed and prayed to Him all my life to make me a nun, but he didn't. They said faith was a gift from God, but He never gifted me. I don't know what I believe anymore. I'm confused. My dad wants me to try again and go back into the convent to see if it'll work out this time."

"You must be honest with yourself Mary. If you don't believe, you don't believe. It's as simple as that. You can't believe it just because your dad wants you to. You've got to tell him to stop pressuring you. How old are you? Twenty or something? You're an adult and you're entitled to believe what you want."

"That's easy for you to say. You don't know my dad. I wish he was more like you."

"My parents are Anglican, and I had to go to church with them every Sunday when I was little. When I turned sixteen, they said I was old enough to make up my mind, so I stopped going. They wanted me to believe all sorts of things that didn't make any sense to me and in all sorts of rules and regulations I think are a load of codswallop."

Mary laughed at Peter's codswallop. She was intrigued. She wanted to be like him. He seemed so light, so positive, and carefree. Just talking to him raised her spirits.

"Can you picture me standing in front of a classroom?"

Mary gave him a questioning look.

"You mean as a teacher?"

"Yes. It's just something I'm thinking about. I know I'd have to go to Teacher's college, but I want more out of life than just being an order-taker. I want something more exciting and enjoyable."

"I can see you as a teacher. I think you'd make a great one. Can you see me as a nun, swishing down the halls in a black habit?"

They laughed.

"Seriously Mary, I'm thinking about going to America to teach. They say it's easier to get into Teacher's college there because they're in dire need of teachers."

"America? That would be so exciting."

"I'm just checking things out now, but I hope to make up my mind before summer comes."

Mary was hoping that her friendship with Peter might develop into something more romantic over the summer, but now that he'd shared with her his news, her hopes of that happening were squelched.

"What do you want to do with your life, Mary?"

It didn't take long for Mary to answer. "I want a husband, children, and a house. If I had these things, I'd be the happiest woman in all of Blackmoor."

Peter smiled at Mary's humble dream and said, "I really enjoyed our walk and talk today. I knew you'd be an interesting person to talk to and that's why I asked you out, but I had no idea you were so profound and had so many questions."

Mary laughed, removed her beret, and shook her hair. They smiled at each other with warmth and friendliness.

"I enjoyed your company too Peter. Can I call you Pete?"

"Sure. That's what my close friends call me. So, I guess that makes you one of my close friends. It's a real honor you know," he said jokingly.

Mary's face lit up with a bright smile. She was thrilled Pete had invited her into his inner circle. They parted company and agreed to go for a walk in the park every Tuesday after work, weather permitting.

As they walked and talked over the ensuing months, they covered a broad range of topics. Many times, the discussion turned back to religion. One time, Pete said, "When I stopped going to church, I thought about my religion, and I pictured it as a heavy package I'd been lugging around all my life. We all have different packages because we all believe in different things. I got this idea that I could put my package in a rucksack and take it off. And then I imagined putting it on the top shelf in my hall closet and closing the door. I wanted to see if I could live without it, and if I couldn't, I knew where it was. I could always go back and get it."

Mary laughed and asked, "And did you ever go back to get it?"

"No. It's still on the top shelf in my hall closet, as far as I know. I never miss it and I know I never will. I feel lighter without it."

"That's insane! Whatever gave you that idea?"

"I don't know. It just came to me one day. Sometimes when I'm thinking about something, crazy ideas just pop into my head. I don't know where they come from. They just do. Like when I was thinking about being a teacher, I got this crazy idea about going to America to teach. And now I'm going – in June."

Mary's jaw dropped and her eyes opened wide. "You are? In June? Wow! So soon?"

"Yes. And I'm so excited, Mary. No one at work knows yet so don't say anything. Okay?"

"I won't. I promise. You can trust me."

She thought Pete was the most amazing person she'd ever met. His self-confidence, his clear vision of life, and his decision to go to America by himself at such a young age impressed her greatly and she wished she could be more like him.

Later the same evening as Mary lay in her bed she thought about

Pete and his metaphor that religion was a heavy package you always carry with you, and it resonated with her. *That's exactly how I feel. What the heck. I'll give Pete's idea a try. If it works for him, it might work for me too. What have I got to lose?*

She puffed up her pillow, put her hands behind her head, and closed her eyes. Concentrating and visualizing a scenario, she imagined she had a heavy, black package on her back secured by straps tied around her waist. She slowly undid the straps, one at a time, and gently let the package fall to the floor, landing next to a large brown suitcase. She pictured herself opening the suitcase, picking up the package and putting it in, and then snapping the locks shut. She visualized opening the door to her clothes closet and with the help of a footstool, climbing up the three steps to the top shelf and placing the suitcase there. As soon as she let go of the suitcase, she imagined a wave of relief moving through her body from her head down to her toes making her shudder. When she mentally climbed back down off the footstool, stepped outside of the closet, and closed the door, a floating sensation consumed her. The feeling was so overwhelming it made her open her eyes and stare at the ceiling. She stayed with it, savoring it mindfully, for a few minutes. Never had she ever experienced such a weird sensation as this. She felt profoundly lighter and freer. After lying on her bed for a few more minutes, thinking about how differently she felt, she closed her eyes again, prepared to let in whatever thoughts might want to appear. She was amazed at how light and guilt-free she felt. Her guilt for being the cause of her mother's death, for not becoming a nun, and for being a disappointment to her dad were now in the closet, on the other side of the door. They were no longer part of her.

Mary's new outlook on life made her more sociable and livelier and everyone noticed. Irene, Jean, and her other workmates thought Mary had fallen in love. Irene and Ernie were delighted with the changes they saw in her, but it was not so with her dad. He was gravely concerned, convinced that his daughter was now having sex – his worst nightmare – and they weren't even married. Mary wasn't honest with him, and this gave her enormous power over him, which she enjoyed to the fullest. She let him believe that she and Pete were more than just good friends, but she didn't tell him Pete was going to America soon to become a teacher, but she did particularly relish telling him that Pete was an atheist. He was livid as she knew he would be.

The mere thought of his daughter spending time with an atheist and possibly having sex with him was not acceptable. What if she got pregnant? Oh, the shame that would bring on the family. The last straw came when Mary began to wear a silver ring with a red agate stone embedded in the middle.

"Who gave you that?" her dad demanded the moment he saw it on her finger.

"Pete."

"Why did he give you a ring?"

"Because he likes me."

"Did he ask you to marry him?"

"No, dad. It's just a friendship ring."

He was convinced Mary was not telling the truth. He felt he had to find a physical way to separate the lovers and quickly put an end to their relationship because words weren't working. He knew Mary wouldn't stop seeing him on her own accord. No. It had to be a physical separation.

Chapter Ten –
Mary goes to Jersey

St. Brelades, Jersey
1920

Eileen had an Aunty Jane who lived in Jersey: a small island in the English Channel, a short distance from the Normandy coast of France. Jane had met her Jersey-man husband, Cyril Boucault, four years earlier during the First World War. When the war ended, they married and went to live on Cyril's farm in St. Brelades parish. The farm had been in the Boucault family for many generations, and, after many different uses, it was now a flower farm.

Eileen wrote to Jane to see if Mary could stay with her for the summer, saying that Mary needed to live somewhere else for a little while because she wasn't getting along with her dad and the tension in the home wasn't good for Angela, her other daughter.

Jane responded at once saying Mary was most welcome to visit and could stay for as long as she liked.

It was June 1920, the start of Mary's summer and her life away from Wilkins Clothiers, and her dad. She embraced Pete's attitude to life and regarded the whole arrangement as a new beginning: an exotic adventure as it were.

She only took a small suitcase and packed it with a few of her favorite summer clothes. Except for her stay in the convent, Mary had never been away from home before, even for one night, so the train journeys by herself from Blackmoor to Manchester, from Manchester to London, and from London to Southampton were most exciting. By the time she found her way to the dock in Southampton for the boat to Jersey, she was confident and eagerly looking forward to her time on the island. *I feel as light and free as Pete* she thought as she strode up the gangplank to board the St. Julian mail boat to Jersey.

As the boat prepared to dock in St. Helier, Mary spotted her name on a cardboard sign being held aloft by a couple on the quay. She jumped up and down, waved her hands high in the air, and her spirits soared. Jane and Cyril made eye contact and waved back.

They welcomed Mary with warm hugs and smiles and Cyril took her suitcase and helped her up onto the wagon. Mary sat in the middle of the bench and looked around in a daze at the new world she found herself in.

Cyril shook the reins and Nelly responded – she'd made the trip hundreds of times over the years and knew the way blindfolded. They ambled along the coastal road, past picturesque bays and inlets, churches, taverns, and houses before arriving at Les Fleurs de Jardin, Cyril and Jane's flower farm in St. Brelades.

As they leisurely trotted along, Mary noticed that the street names were mostly in French and that many homes had French names on their gate posts instead of numbers. She found this aspect novel and charming and it reinforced her sense that Jersey was a very different world from the one she was used to.

The long, rambling stone farmhouse, with its huge sunlit kitchen and cast-iron pot-bellied stove, was built in 1860. It had five airy bedrooms and a vast open living area. The single-story structure with its black slate roof faced east on the large square cobbled courtyard. Jane gave Mary the last bedroom down the hall so she would have the most privacy possible.

On the courtyard's north side sat a large three-story barn holding farm implements and inventory – boxes, paper, and seeds for their flower business. On the west side, a series of cages housed hens, chickens, geese, and rabbits. A vegetable patch took up the whole southern edge of the property.

A wide sandy path from the courtyard curved around the house to the farm acreage behind which bordered the English Channel. The fields were a blaze of color at this time of year. The purple gladioli were in bloom and waving their flags at the white puffy clouds riding high in the azure blue sky. A refreshing sea breeze blew over the farm, gently caressing the purple floral pennants, and filling the house with cool, clean, fragrant air.

Jane and Cyril couldn't have any children, though they wished they could. Mary staying with them for the summer was a gift from heaven as far as Jane was concerned, and she doted on Mary as if she was her daughter.

Mary liked everything about Jersey. It was opposite to everything she had experienced in Blackmoor: the fresh salty air carried on the gentle wind blowing in from the sea was pure and invigorating; the warmth of the sun on her white arms, face, and legs delighted her; the deep blue of the sky and the openness of the beach and sea enthralled her, and the warmth and love of Jane and Cyril soothed her spirit.

Mary was also pleased with her trimmed-down figure – she'd lost fifteen pounds since her first date with Pete, and with her new hair-style. In Blackmoor, she combed her hair straight down over her ears to disguise what she felt was her fat face and to cover up a black mole high up on her cheek near her left ear, which she had always considered hideous. Aunt Jane said she should be proud of her beauty spot, and now she was. Mary let her hair grow long and combed it straight back off her forehead and behind her ears, securing the twirled mane at the back with a bright red ribbon. She liked the feel of her ponytail swishing and swinging from side to side as she sauntered along. She also liked the lightness and freedom that came from wearing new ankle-length dresses made of light cotton, and white ankle socks with her brown oxford shoes that Aunt Jane had bought for her. Mary felt grown-up and free of the pressure from her dad. Without realizing it, she was becoming rebellious and beginning to challenge everything she'd been taught.

She wrote a rambling four-page letter to Pete telling him what she'd done, where she'd been, and what she'd learned about the Channel Islands. She told him about how excited and light and carefree she was feeling and thanked him for helping her to open her eyes, and for the ring, which she said she hadn't taken off since the day he put it on her finger. She added that every time she looked at it, she saw his smiling face encouraging her to take chances and she felt emboldened.

Pete wrote back saying he was happy for her and informed her that he was leaving for America in ten days. He'd arranged his passport and booked a berth on a steamship out of Liverpool. This was to be the last correspondence Mary would ever receive from him.

Mary was ready for romance. She was primed and ready to say *yes* and to let the chips fall where they may, just as Irene suggested, and to *live life to the fullest* as Pete had counseled. There was no heaven or hell in her mind now to intimidate her – she'd found another version of heaven – Jersey. She embraced her new carefree attitude to life with all her being.

Her bright, smiling new face in the community attracted the attention of many young men, many of whom were migrant French farmworkers, who had come to Jersey to pick potatoes and other crops.

Every Tuesday and Friday, Mary went to the neighboring Shaw's dairy farm to buy milk and cheese. She cycled on the sandy path, past the fields of gladioli waving to the sun on one side, and to the prickly bushes with small yellow flowers on the other side that bordered the beach and the sea. She took her time, enjoying the sights and sounds of the scenery on her way while musing on how wonderful life was. The bike she borrowed from the Boucault's shed was old and uncomfortable, but she didn't mind. It forced her to sit upright on the seat with a straight back – she could have balanced books on her head if she had wanted to - and it caused her to open up her arms wide to grasp the curved handlebars. She thought about her open posture and smiled.

Ted Hart was in the yard fixing a post on the farm gates when Mary cycled into the driveway of Les Vaches de Terre, the dairy farm owned by Bobby and Jennifer Shaw. Ted worked for them as a herdsman and general laborer.

When Ted's and Mary's paths crossed, the attraction was instant and mutual.

"Hey. What's your name?" Ted called out.

Mary grinned, wheeled her bike around, and rode up to him.

"Who wants to know?" she teased.

"Me. I'm Ted," he said, laughing. "What's your name?"

"Mary," she replied, aware of the subtle physical attraction she was feeling for him.

"Pleased to meet you, Mary. You must be new. Haven't seen you around."

"Yes. I'm new. I'm brand new you might say," said Mary cheekily. "I'm staying with my aunt for the summer, at her flower farm just up the road."

Ted was smitten. He'd always had this thing for redheads. He stared at Mary's ponytail with the bright red ribbon swaying and glinting in the sun as she steadied herself on the bike. Excitement rushed through his veins. Mary noticed and teasingly swished her hair more.

Ted grinned and said, "Yes. I know the place well and I know who your Aunt Jane is. She knows me too, but she won't know my name. We've said hello many times. I'm the herdsman here."

Ted had a shock of chocolate brown hair that fell over his forehead, causing him to toss his head back in a repetitive, unconscious manner. Mary found his quirky habit extremely appealing.

They stared at each other, exchanging grins. Mary liked the sparkle in his light-blue eyes, but it was his tanned lean body she found most attractive. His skin was light brown, like milk chocolate, and appeared to be just as creamy smooth. Her skin was as white as a bleached handkerchief.

"Why aren't you wearing shoes?" she asked, noticing his feet. "You'll damage your feet if you don't wear shoes."

His feet were as brown as his bare arms. He looked at them and laughed. "I don't like shoes. I only wear them on Sundays if I go to church, or if I go somewhere special."

That's bizarre, thought Mary. She sensed Ted liked her and he did, and a lot. Her long, red wavy hair, swishing in the sunlight excited him, the freckles on her nose and cheeks made him smile, and her pure white skin on her exposed limbs, chest, and face thrilled him. He also found the lilt of her Lancashire accent music to his ears.

"See you around then," Mary said, turning her bike around and riding into the dairy to get the milk and cheese.

They spoke again when Mary came out.

"Do you come for milk and cheese a lot?" Ted asked as he tightened a bolt on the post.

"Every Tuesday and Friday," Mary replied as she pushed off on her bike and went down the sandy path home.

On Friday, three days later, Mary's heart was pumping fast with anticipation and her legs felt jittery when she climbed on her bike to go for the milk and cheese. To her dismay, Ted was nowhere to be seen when she arrived at the dairy. *I have to wait another four days before I see him,* she thought unless, of course, *I make an effort to see him sooner.*

On Saturday, after cutting, boxing, and wrapping the gladioli orders, and completing her other farm chores, Mary called out to Aunt Jane that she was going for a bike ride.

"Have fun," Jane shouted back, pleased that Mary was settling in well and had met a friend at the Shaw's farm.

Mary took her time, cycling slowly in big arcs to the right and left of the sandy path. She was nervous about meeting Ted and was subconsciously delaying her arrival at the dairy.

Ted was still working on the gates when Mary turned into the driveway.

"Hi, Mary. How are you today? Did you get your milk yesterday? I had to go into town."

"I'm good thanks. Yes, I did. What a beautiful day it is, don't you think?"

"Yes. Run out of milk already?" he teased.

Mary blushed. She desperately wanted to say *"No. I came to see you. Silly"* but she didn't. Instead, she said, "And what if I did? It's none of your business."

Ted smiled.

"I'm just checking out the area. I've got some free time, so I thought I'd explore the lie of the land a little."

"Me too. I'm off this afternoon. Do you want some company? Seeing as you're new here, I'd love to show you around."

"Yes. That'd be great," Mary replied, thrilled that events were unfolding the way she hoped they would.

Ted took a bike from the Shaw's shed and cycled with Mary through the surrounding country lanes for the next two hours. By the time they returned to the dairy, they were the best of friends. So began Mary's whirlwind romance with Ted Hart, the herdsman.

The next weekend, Ted came to the flower farm and formally introduced himself to Jane and Cyril, and then set off with Mary to walk along the cliffs, which were just five minutes away.

Mary wore her brown oxfords, and the uneven surface of the path sometimes twisted her ankle, causing her to yelp. One time, when they sat on the path and rested in the warm sunshine, Mary bent over to take a closer look at Ted's bare feet. They looked as hard and as thick as old pieces of leather, but other than that, they appeared to be remarkably healthy.

"Go on. Touch them if you like," Ted joked, smiling, and raising a leg towards her.

"No way. They're not feet. I don't know what they are, but they're not like any feet I've ever seen. Take them away. How long have you been going barefoot?"

"Forever. As long as I can remember."

They laughed and continued with their cliff walk, all the while breathing in the fresh briny air, and looking out to sea and across to France.

"If we were over there, I'd buy you a coffee and a croissant," kidded Ted.

"Why not a glass of wine and a baguette, you cheapskate?" teased Mary, pushing him to one side and running off ahead. Ted caught up. "Or better still, why not a ring like this one?" said Mary sticking out her middle finger. The red agate stone glinted in the sun.

"It's beautiful. Who gave it to you?"

"Wouldn't you like to know," Mary joshed?

"I bet it was from a boyfriend. Right?"

"Are you jealous? What if it was?"

"I'm just curious that's all."

"If that's all then I'm not going to tell you. It's a secret."

"Come on Mary. There shouldn't be any secrets between us."

"Why not? We all have secrets. I bet you have secrets."

Ted laughed uncomfortably.

Mary sensed she'd hit a nerve. "Come on Ted. Tell me your secret and I'll tell you mine."

"You're right Mary. It's okay to have secrets. I shouldn't have pressured you to tell me. I apologize. I don't know what I was thinking." Ted looked sheepish.

~

They helped each other to do the chores on their respective farms, and they did them joyfully with an abundance of energy. Within two weeks, they were spending long hours wrapped in each other's arms on hay bundles in the loft of Les Vaches de Terre.

They met whenever they could: They walked hand in hand along the beach looking for crabs when the tide was out, strolled arm-in-arm along leafy country lanes, inhaling the floral aromas, and admiring the sights of the hedgerows and farms, and sometimes, they caught the bus and went into town.

One time when they were in St. Helier, Mary stopped in front of a jewelry store, captivated by a silver brooch sparkling in the window.

Ted noticed her admiring it. "You like that brooch, Mary?"

"Yes, It's beautiful. It would be too expensive for me."

"Well let's go in and see."

"We can't go in there. You're not wearing shoes. I bet they don't serve people in bare feet."

"I bet they do. This is Jersey Mary. If they won't serve me, they'll lose out on a sale. Right?"

Mary was so excited. She'd never been in a jewelry store before. She'd looked in their windows, but she'd never gone in and tried on jewelry. It made her feel special.

The clerk retrieved the brooch from the window, Mary pinned it on her red summer jacket and looked in the mirror on the counter to admire it.

"It's beautiful. How much is it?" asked Mary.

Ted took the clerk's arm and turned her away from Mary. "Don't be concerned about the cost Mary. I'll buy it for you if you really like it."

"You will?"

Mary impulsively hugged and kissed Ted passionately on the lips. To Mary, the brooch signified a new development in their relationship: a maturing of sorts making her feel more secure about him and his long-term intentions.

Mary sent postcards to Irene with views of the island she and Ted had gone to and wrote a little something on the back of each card about their visits. She didn't send any cards to her dad or step mum, but Jane wrote to them, just a short letter monthly, more out of a sense of obligation than anything else, telling them that Mary was keeping well and enjoying her stay in Jersey. She didn't tell them Mary had a boyfriend.

Mary's dad intended her sojourn in Jersey to be just two months, but Jane suggested that as everything was going so well, Mary should stay on until later in the year. Mary was now paying Jane for her food and keep by doing chores on the farm, and by earning extra money from a neighbor for babysitting her two young children.

Mary was reveling in her independence and new life; however, as they say, everything has a season that sadly, someday, must come to pass.

In September, Mary went to see Doctor Ryan, Aunt Jane's family doctor because she'd been throwing up every morning for the last six days. He checked her over and, with a congratulatory smile, said. "You're pregnant my dear."

"Pregnant?" Mary gasped, but she'd suspected for some time that she might be pregnant.

Ever since Mary was a little girl, she had wanted to be a mother, and marrying Ted was something she often thought about and now it was going to happen.

She was bubbling over with the good news when she met Ted at lunchtime the following day. After they hugged, she said, "I have some fantastic news to tell you."

"What is it? What is it?" Ted asked excitedly.

Mary grabbed both of his hands and looked him straight in the face. "I'm pregnant. We're going to have a baby!"

"You're what?"

"I'm pregnant. We're going to have a baby."

The smile on Ted's face instantly disappeared, replaced by a look of horror.

"What's the matter?" asked a startled Mary, letting go of his hands and pulling away from him.

"You caught me by surprise, that's all," said Ted, sporting a phony smile.

"You had me worried there for a moment. I was thinking you weren't pleased. I'm so happy we're going to have a baby. It's my most precious dream come true Ted. Maybe my aunt will let us stay with her while we save up for a place of our own?" She stared at him with smiling eyes, brimming full of love, and her heart beat faster and stronger with joy and excitement.

Ted's heart was racing too, but out of fear. Holding both of her hands firmly in his and looking her straight in the eyes, he spoke slowly and seriously. "I don't know how things are going to work out Mary. I have to go to Guernsey at the end of this month to work for my brother. The Shaws only hired me for the summer."

Mary was shocked to her core. She pulled her hands free, stepped back, and glared at him. "Go to Guernsey? Go to Guernsey? I don't understand. Why go to Guernsey?"

"I have to go. I have financial obligations and I have a job there waiting for me. I need that job."

"You don't have to go. I'm sure you can get a job here. My uncle will help you find something. He knows everyone."

"I have to go Mary. It's complicated."

"Why didn't you tell me this before now?"

"I should have."

"I'll go to Guernsey with you. Okay, I'll go anywhere with you. Okay?" said Mary convinced that her offer would seal the deal.

"Everything is happening so fast," said Ted. "I was mesmerized by your beauty and your joyful nature, and I've fallen in love with you. But I had no right to your charms and your youthful innocence."

Mary was speechless. She looked at him suspiciously, wondering where he was going with all this fancy talk. He held her hands even tighter. "I can't marry you, Mary. I'm already married."

"Married! You're already married? Mary shrieked and thumped him on his chest and arms with both fists. "Married! You're already married?" She continued yelling and thumping him.

Ted held his arms up and let her beat him.

After a few minutes, Mary, emotionally and physically drained, let her arms down and stepped back. Anger emanated from every part of her body.

"I'm so, so very sorry Mary. And I have a little boy too. They live in Guernsey."

"Oh, Ted. Why didn't you tell me?" she pleaded, tears streaming down her cheeks.

"I was afraid you wouldn't want to see me anymore if you knew I was married."

"Damn right I wouldn't," Mary said without pausing for a breath. She pushed him away and looked him straight in the eyes again. "If you truly love me, you'll get a divorce, and we'll get married."

Ted shook his head slowly. "I can't marry you, Mary. It's complicated. I can't get a divorce."

"Then run away with me to England and we won't tell anyone," Mary said, clutching and squeezing his hands.

He pulled his hands away and stepped back.

"I should never have let this happen. I've deceived you and I've been unfaithful to my wife. I'm not the person you thought I was. You don't deserve me. You know I love you and I always will, but I must first take care of my family in Guernsey. I should have told you about them."

"Damn right you should have told me." Mary spat the words at him.

"Believe me, I never intended for us to get serious. You said you were going back to England at the end of the summer, and I have to go back to Guernsey at the end of September to work for my brother – I don't have another job. I only came to Jersey to get away for the summer while I thought things through about my marriage. I can't just run away from my obligations and responsibilities."

"Damn right you can't. You have obligations and responsibilities right here – to me and our baby. Well. You've got more things to think through now, don't you" Mary said sarcastically. "I want you to think through them tonight, and tomorrow morning I want to hear you say that you will get a divorce, that you'll get things sorted, and that we'll get married in October. You meet me here at noon tomorrow."

She got on her bike and pedaled away fast without looking back. and went straight to her room and lay down on her bed, having called out to her aunt that she'd already eaten and wouldn't be having dinner.

She closed her eyes and thought. *How could I have gotten so serious with someone I knew so little about? Why did no one tell me he was from Guernsey and had a family? Surely someone knew. And why had the neighbors and everyone I passed on the streets encouraged me with smiles and whistles? I feel I've been duped. Was I wrong to assume Ted wanted to marry me? Why did he buy me the brooch if he wasn't serious?*

At noon the next day, Ted was waiting in the yard when Mary arrived. As she was getting off her bike, she looked at him and noted the stress and sadness in his eyes and manner. She prepared herself for the worst.

In a cold, monotone voice, Ted repeated what he had been saying to himself all morning, in preparation for speaking to Mary. "I'm so, so very sorry Mary. I've thought about everything, and I've got to go back to my wife and son. I can't just leave them in the lurch like that. I know I've messed up – we've messed up. You're better off without me. I don't know what else to say."

Mary was not surprised at what he had to say. She glared at him and said, angrily, "You could say you'll get a divorce and marry me. That's what you could say."

"I can't say that Mary. I can't. I must go back to my family. I owe it to them. They need me."

"They need you! They need you!" screamed Mary. She moved closer to within an inch of his face and poking him in the chest with her finger, barked through clenched teeth, "What about me? What about us? It's your baby too. Don't we need you?"

Ted backed off, put his arms up in the air, and said, "I'm so, so very sorry Mary. I told the Shaws this morning something personal has come up and I've quit my job. I'm catching the seven o'clock boat tonight. I'm not going to change my mind."

He turned around, walked quickly away, and disappeared into the Shaws' farmhouse.

Mary dropped to her knees, sobbing with remorse for getting pregnant and with fear and uncertainty about her future. For the next five minutes, she stared blankly at the door to the farmhouse where Ted had entered, hoping he'd reappear. She stood there, dazed, not knowing what to think or do. Ted was her whole life. He was the only person she'd ever loved and would ever love – she was sure about that. Rage rose in her, shaking her body and reddening her face. "You bastard, you bastard," she yelled at the top of her lungs, hoping he would hear her in the house.

She turned her bike around and cycled home, tears flooding and blurring her vision as she continued shouting all the way home, "You bastard, you bastard."

Later that night, as she lay on her bed thinking, she realized Ted had lied to her on more than one occasion. She remembered asking him if he'd ever met anyone he thought of marrying and he said no, never. And then there was the time they were talking about secrets. No wonder he let her keep her secret about who gave her the red agate ring. She was upset with herself for having been so naive to trust him when she knew so little about him. She felt he'd taken advantage of her. He was a despicable scoundrel and she hated him. The warm hot love that had been a fire in her heart for the last four months was now doused, replaced by icy-cold, bitter anger. She was even more distressed and ashamed when she realized that her dad's worst fears about her getting pregnant had come to pass. She didn't know what to do. She couldn't stay in Jersey permanently – tourists and migrant workers could come and go, but they couldn't stay unless they were married to an Islander. She knew she had to go back to England sometime to face the truth, and she dreaded it.

So did her Aunty Jane who felt responsible for not keeping a closer eye on who Mary was seeing and what she was doing.

Mary delayed her return for as long as possible and kept the secret hidden from her parents. She sent a postcard to Irene telling her that something had come up and she'd been delayed.

As if her situation wasn't dire enough, it became much worse on her next visit to the doctor.

"You're having twins, my dear." was what Doctor Ryan said.

Mary blacked out and collapsed on the surgery office floor. The doctor and his assistant carried her to a bed to recover. The assistant made her a cup of tea and sat with her until she came to. As she lay there thinking, reality set in. Many questions without answers swamped her brain, leaving her feeling weak and distressed. *How can I go home and face my dad after all he warned me about getting pregnant? And what about Father Shields and the neighbors? How can I face them? And how can I take care of two babies when I don't even have a job? And where are we going to live? What if my dad throws us out of the house — where will we go? Things were bad enough in the house before — what will they be like now? And who would want to court or marry a woman with two babies?*

The only option for an unmarried mother with no job or home in Blackmoor was the workhouse. Mary shuddered at the thought of it — she'd heard horror stories about the deplorable conditions and the harsh treatment destitute women with children had to endure. She was determined there was no way she was going to end up there. All she could see for her future was abject unhappiness. And the more she dwelt on her pitiful situation, the more convinced she became that her only solution was to simply end it all, right there in Jersey.

All I have to do is close my eyes and jump off a cliff into the raging waters or smash into the boulders on the beach? It would be quick, and it'd put an end to everyone's pain.

For the next couple of weeks, Mary struggled with which of the two options to choose, all the while becoming more aware that the babies were growing bigger — her body was expanding, and her clothes were fitting tighter.

By November, she was four months pregnant and getting used to the idea that she would soon be a mother. If she didn't do something soon, the outcome was inevitable.

She thought more about the babies growing in her womb, and

as she did, something strange happened. All the teachings she had learned in church about the preciousness of life that were stored in her subconscious leaked out and trickled into her consciousness. It was as if a blanket had been lifted off her troubled mind, giving her a sense of clarity, calm, and hope.

She spoke to her babies: *You are entitled to live, aren't you? Who am I to deny you this right? It's not about me anymore. It's about you. I don't care if I die, but you must live.*

Mary decided to go home in December for the birth, give the babies up for adoption, and face the consequences.

Chapter Eleven – The Twins

Blackmoor, Lancashire
1921

Mary's dad was livid when he opened the front door and saw his daughter standing there, bulging with five months of baby growth.

"Close the door," he snapped. "Have any of the neighbors seen you?"

Mary closed the door.

The veins in his neck reddened and bulged. He squinted, shook his head, and wagged a finger. "You little whore! You little, little whore! What have you done? You'll go straight to hell for this."

Mary looked past her swollen womb to the floor and dutifully listened.

"I know you've done this on purpose, haven't you? - just to spite me?"

For the next ten minutes, he continued to berate her in the front hallway while Mary continued looking at the floor and not saying a word. She'd prepared well for the verbal abuse she knew would come as soon as she entered the house and which she was sure would continue for the rest of her pregnancy.

Mary decided not to tell him that she was expecting twins until it was absolutely necessary because she feared that would double the trouble and prove to be too much for her to bear at this time.

Aunt May, who just happened to be in the house at the time, helped ease the tension by showing compassion for Mary's plight. She hugged Mary tightly, while John seethed and fumed with rage. The shock had to run its course. He needed time to say all the nastiest and hurtful things he could think of before he calmed down, and then he forbade her from going outside until after the birth because he didn't want the neighbors to know she was pregnant. He arranged for a midwife to come to the house for the birth and asked Father Shields to take the baby to an orphanage.

When her parents had gone to work, Mary went next door to see Irene and Ernie and told them the whole story about Ted and her predicament. She was in a strange mood and took great delight in informing them that she was having twins, but that she hadn't told anyone else yet, not even Aunt May. Irene was shocked. She got up, excused herself, and went into the kitchen to refill the teapot. When she returned with the brew, Mary spoke about her situation, her dad's disappointment with her, her step mum's lack of empathy and support, and her fear about how things would be in the future. On the other hand, her secret made her feel powerful and the thought of being a mother elated her. Irene sensed her muddled feelings and listened intently, not saying a word.

And then Mary dropped the bomb. "I'm going to keep one of the babies. I don't know how yet, but that's what I'm going to do."

Irene and Ernie exchanged glances and looks of concern.

"Being a mother is the only thing I've ever wanted. If I can't keep one of my babies, I'm going to kill myself. I don't care. I don't want to live if I can't keep one of my babies."

Irene and Ernie knew Mary well and were sure she was deadly serious about taking her own life. They realized she'd made up her mind and there was no point in trying to talk her out of it. So, Irene and Ernie listened and nodded their understanding of her intentions. Turning to Ernie, who was teary-eyed, Mary spoke in a serious tone and gave him a determined, impassioned look.

"I want my babies to be able to find each other. Can you put a mark on them with your needle?" Pointing to the decorative leather slipcover hanging over the armchair in the living room, she said, "As you did with that? Would it work? Can you make it in the shape of a heart?"

"Yes, I can. It'll be like a tattoo, but there will be no room for a heart. How about a single black dot – that's the best I can do? Why do you want a heart?"

"Because Heart is the name of the babies' father."

"I'll give it a try," Ernie said, now smiling and quite looking forward to the opportunity to be a key player in this subterfuge.

A week before the expected delivery date, John sent Angela to stay with a relative a few streets over.

At seven o'clock on Wednesday evening, April 21, 1921, with the help of a midwife, Mary gave birth to William and Thomas at home. When the midwife came downstairs and announced that Mary had given birth to twin boys, her dad went ballistic.

"Twins!" he shrieked. The veins in his neck doubled in size, and his blood pressure soared. He felt the same pain of shame and sin he felt as a teenager when he was teased about his sister's pregnancies. It was as if no time had passed. He was so overwhelmed that for a moment he wondered if the new mother upstairs was his daughter or his sister. He buried his head in his hands and continued to complain about the shame Mary had brought upon the family, and how they were all doomed to go to hell for it.

Aunt May was there, and she was shocked too, but she was joyful with relief that Mary and the babies were healthy, and she hurried upstairs to see if she could be of help.

The next morning, after Irene and Ernie had seen Mary's parents going to work, they slipped next door to carry out Mary's plan. Ernie tattooed the boys with a single black dot on the fleshy underside of their right thumbs and then went home to anxiously await the arrival of Father Shields.

John came home for dinner at 1:00 pm. and went straight upstairs to prepare the babies for Father Shields.

Mary, hugging her babies close – one in each arm - calmly and quietly, announced she was going to keep one of the babies.

"What! No, you're not. Whatever makes you think you can do that?" barked her father, approaching Mary's bed with intent.

Mary clutched her babies even tighter and said, "If I can't keep one of my babies, I'm going to kill myself. How will you explain that to the neighbors?"

Her dad was taken aback. He stared at his daughter and shook his head. "Kill yourself! Kill yourself? You wouldn't dare. You haven't got the guts," he bellowed, raising his voice a few decibels, and angrily wagging his index finger at her.

Mary stared back at him. "Haven't got the guts? You just wait and see. I'll show you. You'll be sorry you said that. I've figured it all out and I know how to do it. I don't want to live anymore, dad, if I don't have a baby to love and care for, and you'll have my death on your conscience for the rest of your life. I don't know what your God thinks about that, but I'm sure he won't let you into heaven!"

John was lost for words. His daughter had never talked back to him so bluntly.

"If you're so smart, young lady, where do you think you and your baby are going to live and who's going to pay for your food and expenses?"

They were still arguing when Father Shields knocked on the door, let himself in, and called out. He climbed the stairs to Mary's bedroom and entered. After removing his coat, he turned around and saw Mary holding a baby in both arms. Shock and questioning replaced his smile.

"You have two babies?"

"Yes, Father, and she thinks she's going to keep one of them. Tell her she can't," John said.

"I can and I'm going to," declared Mary defiantly, looking the hapless priest square in the face.

Father Shields looked at the young mother, put his hand on her shoulder, and spoke in a quiet and as compassionate a voice as he could muster. "I know how upset you must be Mary, but it's for the best if you give me the babies."

"For the best? Who's best?" Mary retorted in a raised and angry voice and stared at the priest with steely eyes.

Father Shields didn't know what to say. He looked at John for guidance.

"It's not for my best Father and it's not for my babies' best. Babies need their mothers. It's for your best, the both of you. You're only worried about what the neighbors and what the Church will think. Well. I don't care anymore. You can both go to hell for all I care." She spat out the words with venom, making her dad and the priest take a step back. And then said, "What are you going to tell the neighbors after I commit suicide? It's not a secret Father. I've told people what I'm going to do if I can't keep one of my babies."

Father Shields was nervous and scared. He gasped, made the sign of the cross, and looked up to heaven for divine guidance. "You shouldn't talk like that Mary. It's a sin. You'll go to hell if you persist in saying things like that."

"Well. I'll see you both down there then won't I," Mary said while clutching the babies closer to her breast.

John and Father Shields didn't know how to respond, until the good Father said, "What if I take one baby now, and in three days, come back for the other one? This will give you time to think straight Mary and to talk it over more with your dad."

"No. I want them both out of the house and now," her dad demanded, and in a threatening gesture moved closer to the bed.

Mary clasped the babies tighter to her chest and glared at him. "I know I can't keep both babies, dad. I just want to keep one of them."

"Come on John. Let me take one now and I'll come back next week for the other one. You can see Mary isn't going to give up both babies today."

Mary knew she would never give up both babies, but she could argue that another day. Father Shields used Mary's acceptance of the compromise to pressure John into going along with his suggestion, and reluctantly, he agreed.

Father Shields was greatly relieved because this turn of events resolved a most distressing dilemma for him – he didn't have a place to take two babies once he left the Jones house. The Catholic orphanage was full and there was just one spot left at the Anglican McIvor Memorial Home for Babies. Time was of the essence. He'd pleaded with the Catholic orphanage to take the baby, but they said they were full to the brim and couldn't possibly make room. Reluctantly, he approached the Anglican McIvor Memorial Home for Babies, and they agreed to take one. Even if they were full to the brim, Father Shields was sure they'd make room because it wasn't every day a Catholic offered an Anglican a soul with no strings attached.

Taking a single-page document from his briefcase, Father Shields handed it to Mary saying, "You have to sign this, Mary."

"What is it?"

"It's a consent form from the Home. It just says you consent to give your baby to them to look after."

"What if I don't sign it?"

"Then the Home won't take your baby. It's as simple as that. You have to sign it Mary."

"Is that all it says? I'm too upset to read all that small print."

"It also says that you agree not to contact them about your child."

"That means I'll never see him again. I can't agree with that! They're twins –identical twins. They'll need each other," said Mary.

"I know how distressing this must be for you, but there is no other option," said Father Shields. "I know the Home and they'll take good care of your baby; I assure you. Just sign the form, Mary."

Mary reluctantly signed the form, and then her dad and Father Shields went downstairs to give her some private time to spend with the babies

She bundled Thomas up in a blanket with his arms above the fabric and placed him in front of her face up on the bed. Clutching William under one arm and holding his right hand with the tattooed thumb, she looked down at Thomas and smiled. With the finger on her other hand, she held Thomas's tattooed thumb and said, "*One day you'll be reunited. You'll find each other, just like I've planned. You'll see. Just don't lose your thumbs. Okay?*" This humorous afterthought caught her off guard and she wondered where it had come from. She was pleased she'd had the thought because it gave her the satisfaction of knowing she'd told her boys about their thumbs.

When Eileen returned home from the mill and saw Mary with a baby in her arms, she was alarmed. However, it would be just a few days before Father Shields came by to take him away, would it not?

When Angela returned home, she was thrilled to bits to have a baby nephew in the house but became most distressed when she heard her dad talk of putting him into an orphanage. For the next week, she pleaded daily with him to let Mary keep him as if William was a puppy.

Aunt May stepped in and said Mary and the baby could live with her. It would be tight financially, but she was sure she could manage. John nixed the idea at once, saying he wouldn't accept the charity of any kind. In truth, he was more concerned about how it would look to neighbors when gossip and rumors told of his kicking his daughter out of the house, leaving her penniless, and with a new baby, and he, a supposedly devout Christian.

Mary was torn. She so desperately wanted to get away from her dad, but she knew her Aunt May couldn't afford to feed and clothe both of them. She intended to get a job eventually and rent her own place, but, in the meantime, she had to live somewhere, and someone had to pay the bills.

Everyone helped: Irene, the O'Malley's, the neighbors, and some parishioners from church all visited the house bearing gifts of nappies, baby clothes, and sundry items. Irene and Ernie supplied a wicker basket for William to sleep in.

It only took a week for John and Eileen to accept the fact that baby William wasn't going anywhere, but upstairs in Mary's bedroom. Angela's support for William had been critical.

Father Shields was shocked when John told him that William was going to stay, but at the same time, he was greatly relieved that he didn't have to give up another Catholic soul to the Anglicans, and besides, when he checked with the Home just before he went to the Jones house, they told him they didn't have room for a second baby.

~

For the next four years, Mary stayed in her parent's home and cared for William. Angela's love and affection for baby Billy helped soften the temperament of her dad, but still, the atmosphere in the Jones home was always stressful. The tension was ever-present in the air of every nook and cranny of every room in the house and in the back of the minds of everyone in the Jones household.

John never forgave his daughter for her indiscretion and for not becoming a nun and neither did he accept Billy: the illegitimate product of his daughter's indiscretion.

Chapter Twelve –
A place of their own

Blackmoor, Lancashire
1925

It had always been Mary's intention to get a job and live on her own when William was old enough to go to school, and now he was four and attending St. Peter and Paul Catholic primary school, she felt it was the right time to make the change.

With her good school marks in hand and the highly complementary reference letter from her boss at Wilkins Clothiers, Mary went to the Blackmoor unemployment office to see what jobs were available.

The National Government Weights and Measures department was looking for an administrative person with some office experience and strong typing skills. Mary read the job description, felt she had the requisite qualifications, and went over to their offices on Great Moor Street to apply for the job. She was granted an interview for the following morning, and by noon the next day, she had the job. She was offered the position at a salary higher than she had expected.

Three doors down from her parent's house lived a Mr. Harry Bickerstaff. He was an elderly widow who rented out two of his three bedrooms to boarders as a source of income to help pay his mortgage and bills. His tenants for the past three years, the Parkinsons, had recently bought a house, and Mr. Bickerstaff was now looking for new tenants. Having lived at that address for the past twenty years, he knew

Mary and William well and was delighted when Mary asked if she could rent the rooms.

~

The arrangement worked out well. Harry appreciated Mary's company and domestic help, and the joy that came from having a happy little four-year-old running around in the home. Harry particularly enjoyed his visits with Mary and hearing William laugh and giggle when his mum tickled him before turning off the light and closing his bedroom door. It was also convenient for Angela because she could visit often and babysit whenever Mary had to go somewhere.

~

That same year, Irene and Ernie moved to Liverpool to be closer to their son and his wife's family. For many years, the Tannery had promised Ernie a factory floor manager's job and one finally came through at their Liverpool factory. Irene stayed in touch with Mary for a little while through letters, but eventually, their communications stopped completely.

~

When Billy was ten, his grandparents moved to another part of Westlea, much to Mary's relief. Though her parents had lived just three doors down from her for the past six years, they'd neither visited nor spoken to her in all that time. They'd nod politely when they met on the street or in a shop, but that was the sum total of their interaction. Angela visited occasionally, but now she was married, she was busy being a wife and homemaker to her lawyer husband in their new home in Fern Hills.

~

In 1932, Mr. Bickerstaff died and bequeathed his house to his son, Terence, who agreed to let Mary have the whole house for the same price. Having taken up knitting and sewing as hobbies in the recent past, Mary used the extra bedroom as her craft room. To keep herself busy and become more independent, should Billy get married and move out, she got a second job on the weekends as a shop assistant at Albert Harrison's iron-monger store. That same year, Billy and his best friend, Bobby, now eleven, graduated and began attending Compton Secondary Modern School.

Mary had always intended to tell Billy about his dad after he graduated, but she could never tell him about Thomas because of the contract she had signed with the orphanage. One night after tea, Mary said, in a soft warm voice, "Come over here Billy and sit next to me. I've got something important to tell you."

Taking his hands in hers she looked lovingly into his eyes. "This is awkward but I'm going to tell you about your dad."

"My dad? You are!" A huge grin spread across Billy's face. He pulled away and sat up straighter in the chair. "You're goin' to tell me about my dad? I didn't think you knew much about him."

"I know I haven't told you much, but now that you're older you deserve to know more."

Billy stared expectantly at his mum.

"Your dad's name is Ted and I loved him with all my heart. When I was with him, I was happier than I'd ever been in my whole life. And I know he truly loved me too. We were as madly in love as any young couple could be. He gave me this brooch. Do you remember when you asked me where did I get it from, and I said it was my secret? Well, now you know. I saw it in a jewelry shop and Ted bought it for me right then and there."

"What about your ring mum? Did he give you that too?"

"No. Pete gave me that before he went to America. Pete was my first boyfriend. We worked at the same place, and he changed my life. He set me free in a way. I'll tell you about him some other day, but today I want to tell you more about your dad."

Mary smiled when she read the question on Billy's face: *So, where is he and why doesn't he live with us?*

"The problem is, Billy, that Ted was already married."

"Already married!" Billy spat out the words as if they were poison. A look of anger and shock appeared on his face. "Already married! What a louse!"

Mary squeezed his hands tighter and fingered the tattoo on his thumb.

"I know. I know. I agree with you. But if your dad hadn't got me pregnant you wouldn't be here right now, with me, would you? Think about that? Maybe we should be thankful to him, not angry?"

Billy reached over and hugged his mum. "I guess not, but still. What he did hurt you. I know it did."

Mary let go of his hands and patted his cheek. "Giving birth to you Billy was the best thing that ever happened to me."

Billy got up and bent over to face his mum, He engulfed her in his arms and hugged her tightly. She hugged him back and ran her fingers through his curly hair with long tender strokes. He patted her hair and kissed her.

"He can't live with us, Billy, because he has another son, as well as a wife to look after. I know he wasn't happy, but he said he had obligations he had to live up to."

Billy was gobsmacked.

"Another son? Does that mean I have a brother?"

"Yes. You have a stepbrother – he'd be a couple of years older than you."

"I wish I could meet him. Can we go see him?"

"That wouldn't be a good idea, Billy. Too much water's gone under the bridge I'm afraid. We've all moved on. You might want to look them up one day when you're older. We must leave it like that for now, but I want to tell you more about your dad. He was so good-looking Billy. He swept me off my feet the first moment I saw him. By the end of our first date, I was head over heels in love with him. His hair was dark brown, and his skin was as tanned and as creamy as a bar of Cadbury's milk chocolate."

Billy laughed.

"His eyes were sky blue, and they lit up when he talked, and he always seemed to be smiling. He had this clump of hair that fell across his face, and he'd flip his head back to get it out of his eyes. Oh, how he made me laugh. And he liked to go barefoot – everywhere. I never saw him in a pair of shoes. I don't think he had any," she said with a laugh. "How strange was that?"

"Barefoot?" Billy exclaimed and laughed out loud.

"Barefoot? That's crazy. Is that where I get my strangeness from?"

"You're not strange. Billy. Whatever gave you that idea?"

"Children at school say I am."

"Nonsense," said his mum.

"Where d'ya meet him, mum?"

"When I was on holiday in Jersey. I don't want you to think badly of him because it wasn't all his fault, I got pregnant. It was as much my fault as his. We were so in love Billy. You were born in love."

Billy grinned. He liked that thought.

"But he didn't tell me he was married and had a child until I told him I was pregnant."

Billy breathed in heavily and snorted.

"It is what it is Billy. I just thought it was about time you knew about your dad. Okay?"

"I'm glad you told me, mum, coz now I can picture him in my mind when children at school ask questions about him. But I won't tell them he goes barefoot. That would prove that I must be weird too."

His mum laughed.

"I'm still mad at him coz he's the reason I'm a bastard."

"Don't use that word. Billy. You know it's not a nice word."

"Well, it's what the children at school call me. They call me the 'little red 'eaded bastard."

His mum wrapped him in her arms, hugged him tightly, and her eyes teared.

"Oh, Billy. I am so very sorry. I had no idea they called you that.

Why didn't you tell me? You should have. Children can be so cruel."

"It's okay mum. I'm used to it now. It used to bother me, but it doesn't anymore."

"But you're not the only child at school who doesn't have a dad. Leslie Thornton and Paul Hubbard don't have dads, do they?"

"They do. Their dads don't live with them, but they see them. They go and stay with them, and they sometimes watch football games together."

"Do you want me to go to football games with you? I will."

"Nah, mum. It's okay. Bobby wouldn't feel comfortable if you came. You do so much for me already."

~

Throughout her life, Mary struggled emotionally, thinking about her sons. She wanted to tell Billy the whole truth about his birth, about his brother, and their tattooed thumbs, and the part Father Shields played in their lives, but every time she thought it through, she arrived at the same conclusion: I can't. It's a dark family secret and I've given my word not to say anything to anyone.

Many times, Mary burst into tears thinking about Thomas: *Where was he? What was he doing? Was he happy?* Sometimes it happened when she was in the kitchen making tea, or when she was at the greengrocer buying a cabbage. She never knew when the thoughts would rise in her. Though she acknowledged that she'd signed a form severing all ties with Thomas, she always entertained in her heart the possibility that one day, when the timing was right, she'd search for him and find him. She knew he couldn't come looking for her because the orphanage would never tell him anything about his birth. That was the deal, Father Shields said, but not a day went by that she didn't look for him when she was on the street. She was sure she'd recognize him because he'd have the same thick, curly red hair, and freckles as Billy.

~

After graduating at sixteen, Billy got an office job in accounts at the local foundry. When he was seventeen, Bobby tried to set him up with Carol, a girlfriend of Marjorie who Bobby was courting, but Billy wasn't interested. His consideration for his mum was paramount. He knew he was his mother's life and all she had was him. He was content to stay home, play cards, and do jigsaw puzzles with her in the evenings.

Chapter Thirteen – Mary gets a telegram

Blackmoor, Lancashire
1940

In 1940, nineteen-year-old Billy Jones was conscripted into the Army and sent to France to fight. All mothers feel the loss of their sons when they leave home, but it was worse for Mary for Billy was all she had, and ever had, in her life.

She wrote him long letters most nights and he wrote back when he could. The post was sporadic. Sometimes, she didn't get a letter for a couple of weeks, and at other times, three or four appeared in the mailbox all at the same time. She delighted in reading them and always re-read them many times over.

Billy wrote about some aspects of the war, but he purposely withheld telling her about the carnage he saw on the battlefield. War was hell was the most he ever said.

Mary knitted him socks and sweaters, and every few months, sent him a care package of clothes, along with bars of Cadbury Chocolate Flakes and the Walkers Shortbread biscuits he liked.

~

In late 1943, Mary had a disturbing dream. She dreamt that she opened her front door to a man dressed in a brown military uniform standing beside a bicycle. He looked directly at her and said, "I'm very sorry, madam," and handed her a telegram. It read that Billy Jones was 'missing in action'. She awoke from her nightmare with a start, sat up, and cried, Eventually, she calmed down and went downstairs to the kitchen to make a cup of tea. The dream was so real. She remembered every second of it and replayed it many times over in her mind, from start to finish. Sitting at the kitchen table, shaking, and staring into space, with her hands clasped tightly around her teacup, she wondered about the dream. *Where did it come from? Was it her fear that Billy would be killed that prompted the dream or was it a premonition of what was to happen?*

The dream shattered her belief that Billy would not be harmed. For the last three years, she'd never entertained the thought that he might not come home, but now she feared he wouldn't.

The dream reappeared to Mary many times in the ensuing months, usually when there was a delay in the letters from Billy. It was always the same dream – leaving every detail etched in Mary's mind. She knew how the dream would unfold yet she felt powerless to stop or change it. Every time she accepted the telegram from the man in the brown military uniform standing beside a bicycle, a shudder of fear coursed through her body, abruptly waking her up in a cold sweat. With each dream, she became more distressed and paranoid that any day her dream would come true. Then what would she do? She couldn't imagine life without her Billy.

Though she kept to herself most of the time at work, she couldn't keep the decline in her mental health a secret from her co-workers. They became increasingly concerned with her advancing anxiety and depression. Some invited her to their homes in the evenings or suggested they all go out together on a girls' night out, but Mary always found an excuse to decline their offers.

~

On April 16, 1944, a British War Office gentleman came to Mary's door with a telegram telling her that a William Janes had been 'missing in action' since March 16. Mary collapsed onto the step in a heap. The messenger helped her into the kitchen and onto a chair.

All-consuming grief filled every part of her body, draining her of the will to live. She stared at the telegram - 'Missing in action'. Rumor had it that this was how the government informed loved ones that their child had died in the war, and she believed it. There was absolutely no doubt in her mind that Billy was dead, and she wanted to die too, to be with Billy. How could she live without him? She was agitated and couldn't think straight. She'd already lost one of her sons. Or had she? She thought about Thomas. Where was he now? Was he still alive? Had he died in the war too? She had to know. She had to go and find him. It wasn't just a wild idea: it was the conviction of a concerned mother desperate to find her lost child.

Chapter Fourteen –
Looking for Thomas

Blackmoor, Lancashire
1944

Instead of going to work the next day, Mary went to St. Peter and Paul Church to see Father Shields, but he wasn't there. He'd been transferred to another parish eight or nine years earlier, but the clerk at the church didn't know which one. Mary explained the purpose of her visit and asked for help in tracking down where Thomas might be now.

"I'd try the Catholic Orphanage in Compton. That's where they took the baby orphans," the clerk said. Compton was a small town, about eleven miles from Blackmoor, and on a bus route.

Mary went straight to the orphanage and poured out her heart to the clerk, who was sympathetic to her distressed state, but said that she could not be of help because the records were confidential. Mary persisted and the clerk acquiesced somewhat by agreeing to see if she could confirm that a Thomas Jones was admitted to the orphanage on April 22, 1921, or a few days before and after that date. She checked but did not find any record for Thomas.

"But there has to be some mistake. I know Father Shields himself brought him here. Please check again – there has to be some record in your files."

The clerk re-checked the records but did not find anything. "I'd try the McIvor Memorial Home. Sometimes when the orphanage was full, they'd take in babies from us, and when they were full, we'd take in babies from them. I see that on April 22, 1921, it was a full house here."

Buoyed by this possibility, Mary hurried over to the Anglican McIvor Memorial Home, which was just five minutes away, and spoke with the front desk clerk: a plump, older lady with thin, greying hair and silver-rimmed glasses.

"Can you help me find my son? I think he was brought here on April 22, 1921?"

The clerk wrinkled her brow, looked over her glasses at the distraught mother, and said, "I'm very sorry madam, but I can't help you. I wish I could. There's nothing I can do for you. The information you're looking for is strictly confidential."

Mary glared at her, tears streaming down her cheeks and dripping onto her green headscarf. She implored the clerk again. "Please, oh please. You have to help me. I've just lost one son in the war. I have to find my other son."

The clerk was moved. She hesitated. Taking a deep breath, she removed her glasses, leaned forward over the desk, and in a quiet voice said, "Rules be damned. I'll see what I can do. I'm a mother and a grandmother too. I know what you must be going through. If I were you, I'd want to find my son too? Take a seat and I'll see what I can do."

With that remark, the clerk went to the backroom and searched the files. Mary sat on a hard chair in the corner and waited patiently for her to return. She closed her eyes and imagined the clerk in the next room thumbing through folders in the filing cabinets looking for a William Jones. *Why didn't I do this years ago?* she asked herself. *I should have done this when Billy was alive. My boys should have known each other. Why oh why didn't I do this before now?* she lamented.

The clerk appeared, clutching a thick, brown manila folder to her chest. She stood in front of Mary and waved it as if she had just unearthed an ancient Egyptian treasure. "I found it," she proudly exclaimed, "I've found your son."

Mary's heart soared.

The clerk sat down on the chair next to Mary and handed her the folder. Mary flipped through the paperwork which was filed chronologically, scanned the file, and settled on the last document in the file. She knew what she was looking for. It was a letter stating that Thomas Jones had been transferred to St. Chads Home for Boys in Swanson, Kent on May 16. 1927. Mary carefully wrote down the information, thanked the clerk, and tried to give her five shillings for her trouble – money she'd set aside as a tip, or a bribe, if necessary. The goodhearted lady closed Mary's hands. "There, there, my dear. This is the least I can do for a grieving mother. I hope you find your son. Good luck and Godspeed."

Mary went home in a positive mood, convinced she was just a couple of train rides away from meeting Thomas. She packed a bag with enough clothes and toiletries for a week and, after tea, went to the home of Sylvia, a work colleague.

"Hi, Mary," said a surprised Sylvia as she opened the door to the distraught face of Mary. "Come in."

They went into the sitting room and sat side by side on the couch.

"I don't know where to begin," said Mary, teary-eyed and nervously fumbling with the clasp on her purse. She took a few seconds to compose herself and then blurted out in a whisper, "Billy's dead. My son's dead." The flood gates opened and, uncontrollably, tears poured down her cheeks and onto her handkerchief.

"Oh, Mary. I'm so, so, very sorry," said Sylvia putting an arm around her and consoling her. "When did you find out?"

Mary blew her nose, dabbed at her eyes with the handkerchief, and looked up. "I got a telegram two days ago saying Billy was 'missing in action'. I'm at my wit's end. I don't know what to do. Do I just sit back and wait for them to tell me they've found him dead? Is that what I'm supposed to do?"

Sylvia hugged Mary a little tighter and stroked her hair. "I don't know Mary, but he's only 'missing in action'. There's a good chance he'll be found and alive, isn't there?"

"They don't fool me. I wasn't born yesterday. I know what they do. They say the soldiers are 'missing in action' because they don't want to say they died, until later. They say that to ease the shock."

"Oh, Mary. What are you going to do?"

Sylvia's question shifted Mary's mindset and helped to calm her.

"I have some personal business to take care of and will be away from work for a little while," Mary said in a stronger voice and sat up a little straighter in the chair.

"Is there anything I can do for you?" asked Sylvia.

"Can you tell Stewart I'll be taking some time off work to look after an urgent personal matter, and I'll explain everything when I get back? I can't say when that will be, for sure, but I expect to be back within two weeks."

"Are you sure you don't want to discuss anything with me? It might help if you were to talk it out, whatever it is?"

"I can't. I would love to, but I can't. I just can't Sylvia. Maybe when I get back, I'll share my secret with you. Okay?"

"What? Wait. What secret? Come on! What is it? You can't leave me hanging like this. Tell me you're secret?"

"I can't Sylvia, and I've gotta get going. Let's just say I'm hoping my secret wants to come back with me," teased Mary as she moved to the door.

~

Mary awoke early the next morning with a sparkle in her eyes – she dreamt she'd found Thomas sitting on a bench in a train station. He looked so much like Billy, except that his hair was longer, and he was not in uniform. She dreamt that she walked along the platform towards him, their eyes met, and he got up, opened up his arms, and hugged her. He knew who she was. She smiled, looked him in the eyes, wished him a happy 23rd birthday, and gave him the same present she had given Billy for his eighteenth birthday: a small blue box holding a set of silver cuff links and a tie pin, all engraved with a heart.

As she brushed her teeth and looked at herself in the mirror, her smile grew bigger, and her frown lines softened. Moving closer to the mirror until she was just inches away and her eyes met with their mirrored image, she thought, *Today is the day I've been waiting all my life for. Today is the day I get to see and hold Thomas again.* She wondered how his voice might sound. She knew it wouldn't be anything like Billy's with his thick Lancashire accent. He'd probably have a Kent accent, but she didn't know what that sounded like. By the time she'd finished brushing, she was in high spirits and feeling giddy.

She took a taxi to the train station at 7:30 a.m., went to the ticket office, and booked three one-way tickets: one for the 8:05 train to Manchester, one for the 9:45 to London, and one for the 4:25 to Swanson.

While waiting on the platform for the train to Manchester, she looked at the other passengers, at the empty train track in front of her, and the sky above, and she felt more alive than she had for many years. The smell of grease and oil from the tracks and the noise of engines and carriages rolling by on the other track excited her. She smiled at the gentleman to her left in the light blue business suit with a newspaper tucked under his arm and nodded to the lady in the green headscarf and brown corduroy coat who smiled back as she passed in front of her.

Before leaving home, she had put Billy's last letter to her in her purse. She wanted a part of Billy to be there with her when she met up with Thomas.

She boarded the train, walked down the corridor, and selected an empty compartment. She put her bag in the overhead rack and sat in a seat next to the window. Two male passengers entered the carriage, politely nodded, smiled, plunked themselves down on the bench seat opposite, and at once opened their newspapers and buried their noses in them, giving Mary the impression that this was what they did every morning.

Mary sat back in her seat and mindlessly gazed out of the sooty window at the scenery as the train chugged down the tracks. She found the rhythmic sounds of the wheels on the tracks soothing. They brought back memories of the last time she was on a train. It was over twenty years ago now when she was returning from Jersey and feeling distraught about having to tell her dad that she was pregnant. The memory was as fresh in her mind as if it had happened just yesterday. She mentally compared how she felt then with how she was feeling now and chuckled at how profoundly different the two experiences were. She was going to Blackmoor then, going to what she knew would be a horrific situation, and was feeling more anxious, more terrified, and more despondent with each mile traveled. Now she was going in the opposite direction and feeling more excited with every mile traveled with the possibility of finding Thomas.

On each leg of her journey, she reminisced and thought about various aspects of her life. For the most part, they were happy memories of Billy, but she tried not to think of his passing and tried consciously to think more about Thomas. *Was he married? Did he have a family? Was she a grandmother? How surprised would they be to meet her?*

By 7:00 p.m. she was comfortably settled in a room at the Wellington Arms Hotel in Swanson, Kent, and by 8:00 am. the following morning, she was on a cobbled street in Swanson, Kent staring in awe at a sign, inscribed in stone on an archway that read St. Chads Home for Boys.

St. Chads was an institution run by the Anglican Church for the Waifs and Strays Society that cared for orphaned boys. The large and imposing stone building, encased in high stone walls, was, to her mind, austere and harsh. The entrance was closed and locked.

Tears welled up in her eyes as she thought of her little boy entering this prison-like building when he was only seven years old. It was more than she could take. She sobbed bitterly and her heart throbbed. She remained in the same place, gaping and sobbing at the building in stunned silence for at least a half-hour.

Eventually, she walked on and returned to the hotel. Before going up to her room, she approached the front desk and casually asked the clerk, "Can you tell me when St. Chads closed?"

"About three years ago, I think."

When Mary elaborated on the reasons why she wanted to know, the clerk became more sympathetic and helpful. She called and spoke with someone on the phone.

"I've asked Mr. Jarvis to come down and speak with you. He taught at St. Chads. He's staying with us while his house is being repaired."

The stars were aligning for Mary, and everything was coming together faster and easier than she had imagined.

Mr. Jarvis came down and sat with her at a table in the lobby.

"Good afternoon. I understand you're looking for information about St. Chads. Maybe I can be of assistance. I taught there for many years." Mary couldn't have found a more knowledgeable and empathetic man to answer her questions.

Mr. Jarvis had reflected on his role at the school since its closure three years earlier and now had strong regrets about his work, the school, and indeed, the whole program that St. Chads and the British government had concocted. "Ostensibly, St. Chads was a foster home for orphans, but I now realize that in reality, it was a holding facility for children until they were emigrated to Canada."

"Emigrated to Canada?" Mary was stunned. She sat up on the edge of her seat, her face as white as a ghost, and fumbled with the clasp on her purse.

"Yes. Child-care organizations, such as St. Chads, considered children to be commodities for export. Since it cost five times more to keep a child in care for a year than it did to emigrate them, the government paid the Orphanages and Homes to ship the children to the colonies, and at the earliest age possible."

Mary glowered at Mr. Jarvis with a fixed stare, shocked at what she was hearing.

"At the time, I didn't realize how insidious the program was. I was a teacher and that's what I did. Perhaps I should have said something, but they said it was all in the best interests of the children – give them a fresh start in a new country."

"A fresh start in a new country?" Mary's hands shook and her lips quivered. "Did my son go to Canada?" Mary asked in a quiet voice. "He went to St. Chads on June 3, 1927. His name was Thomas Jones. Does his name ring a bell with you? Maybe you taught him."

Mr. Jarvis reached back in time for the information stored in his memory. "No. I don't recall the name. How old was your boy when he came to St. Chads?"

"He was seven."

"Let's see then. You say he was seven when he came in 1927. So, he'd be thirteen in 1933?"

"Yes. That's correct," said Mary.

"Well, no then. I wouldn't have taught him. I taught from 1934 until the school closed in 1938. He would have gone to Canada in 1933. All the boys were sent to Canada when they reached their thirteenth birthday."

"Canada! Gone to Canada!" Mary exclaimed. "He's gone to Canada! No, no, no," she cried out before fainting and falling off her chair.

The desk clerk heard the thump and rushed over to help. Mr. Jarvis and the clerk helped Mary to get up off the floor and back onto the chair. The desk clerk brought her a glass of water.

"Gone to Canada! Gone to Canada!" Mary continued mumbling and shaking her head.

Mr. Jarvis asked if he could help, but Mary wasn't listening.

"Gone to Canada. Gone to Canada," was all she kept muttering. She got up from the chair and groggily headed towards the stairs. Mr. Jarvis and the desk clerk watched as she grabbed the banister and slowly climbed the stairs. She wobbled on the top step, lost her balance, and tumbled down the stairs, smashing her head on the hard, tiled floor at the bottom. She didn't move.

Mr. Jarvis rushed over and checked her vital signs. She had a pulse. The desk clerk called an ambulance. An hour and fifteen minutes later, an ambulance arrived. Mary was placed on a stretcher and taken to the

Swanson General Hospital where she lay in a coma for two days before succumbing to the concussion.

It was wartime and police resources were all fully engaged in the war effort. No policeman was available to properly investigate Mary's death. A heart attack was the ascribed official cause of death shown on the hospital and police records and death certificate.

Chapter Fifteen – The Box

Blackmoor, Lancashire
1940

The Police were able to identify Mary and where she lived from the documents in her suitcase and purse. Among the papers were her train tickets and stubs showing she had traveled from Blackmoor, Lancashire two days earlier.

A local policeman went to Mary's home at sixteen Holden Street in Westlea, tracked down the landlord, a Mr. Terence Bickerstaff, and informed him that his tenant, a Mrs. Mary Jones, had died of a heart attack.

"Is that all you can tell me?" asked a stunned and visibly upset Terence.

"All I know is what's on these papers," replied the policeman. "It just says she died of a heart attack in Swanson, Kent. Do you know Mrs. Jones' next of kin?"

"She has a son in the Army, and a step-sister I think."

"Can you contact them to let them know what's happened, and I'll see what I can do from my end? I need to know what to do with the body."

Without hesitation, Terence said, "Tell them to ship it to the Nothers Funeral Home in Blackmoor and I'll see what I can do about contacting her son and step-sister."

"I have a box of Mrs. Jones' personal effects. Can you sign for it?"

"Sure."

Terence went to sixteen Holden Street with the box and on his way in, picked up two aerogram letters and an electric bill from the mailbox. He went from room to room gathering up personal items he thought Billy might want to keep and he put them on the table with the box. Among the items was a box of aerogram letters that Billy had written to his mum and some photographs. Terence put everything into a bigger box, and over the next few days, packed up most of the furnishings in the house, readying it for rental. Some of the furniture he stored in a spare bedroom in his house and gave everything else to St. Peter and Paul Society.

He then wrote Billy a short two-paragraph letter informing him that his mother had died from a heart attack on April 22 and that he would be giving a box of her things to his Aunt Angela, for safe-keeping until he came home. He mailed the letter to the address shown on the aerogram.

Terence came across Mary's address book when he was packing up her things, and diligently perused the listings, page by page, looking for an Angela. The only Angela he found was an Angela Mathers at an address in Fern Hills. Surmising this to be her, he wrote her a letter informing her of Mary's passing, and that he had a box for her son, Billy, for when he returned home from the war. Could she pick it up and keep it for him?

Ten days later, Angela came by his house and picked up the box.

Chapter Sixteen – Angela

Blackmoor, Lancashire
1953

When Billy returned home from the war in 1945, his only possessions were his Army clothes, and a small brown paper bundle tied with brown Army twine holding his mum's letters. Billy treasured this package and no matter what his state of mind at the time or his situation, he always ensured the bundle was safe and dry. Even when he lived on the street, he kept the bundle close to him tied around his chest with string under his coat. The letters comforted and grounded him – they were his emotional and spiritual security blanket – and when he became a rag and bone man, he put them in the bottom drawer of his dresser in his bedroom in Joe's farmhouse

One day when he was thinking about his mum, he decided to read some of her letters. As he began to read, he felt the same exciting feeling he used to get when he was in the Army and a courier handed him a new letter. He paused intermittently to recall where he was and who he was with at the time he read that particular letter, and as he read, he realized just how much his mum had loved him and how much he had loved her. His heart was full and it ached thinking about her.

Underneath the bundled letters was a regular letter, unlike the other aerogram letters, from Mr. Bickerstaff, his mum's landlord, informing him of his mum's passing. Billy stared at it turning it over and reliving the shock he felt when he first received it. He hesitated before reading it, unsure if he wanted to or not, but he did, and it was most fortunate for had he not done so, he would not have searched for Angela and the rest of his life would have taken a different path.

In the second paragraph of the letter, Mr. Bickerstaff wrote that he was giving a box of his mum's things to his Aunt Angela to look after for him – information that he didn't remember reading. He'd either been so shocked after reading the first paragraph that he'd stopped reading, or he'd forgotten what he'd read. Either way, he didn't remember. This was news to him. the letter got him thinking about other members of his family – his brother Thomas, his dad, and Claire, and he was reminded of Irene's words: *There's always someone who needs us, Billy,* and his pledge to her that he would look for his family. Suddenly, he yearned to get to know them – all of them – and the sooner the better.

The following evening, he went to see Mr. Bickerstaff at the address on his letter. Mr. Bickerstaff opened the door, his face blank.

"How are you, Terence?" Billy said, grinning like a Cheshire cat.

Mr. Bickerstaff did a double-take.

"It's me, Billy. Billy Jones. D'ya remember me?"

The penny dropped and a wide smile spread across Terence's face.

"Of course, I do. Who else do I know with curly red hair and a freckled face? You're a one-off mate."

Billy laughed, and said, "Not so Terence. I'm a two-off. I bet my brother has red hair and a freckled face, same as me, coz he's my twin brother. I've got a twin brother you know?"

"You do? Since when? When did you get him? For Christmas or did you get him for your birthday or win him in a raffle at the British Legion?"

Billy laughed and said, "I've had him all my life, but I just didn't know."

Terence didn't know what to make of Billy's claim. He didn't know if Billy was just having him on for a bit of fun or if he was being serious.

"Well come on in and tell me all about it."

They talked at length, mostly about what had happened in Billy's life since he was demobbed, and about what Irene told him about his supposed brother. In due course, Billy asked, "I'm looking for Angela, my mum's half-sister. D'ya remember her? She came by a lot when we lived on Holden St."

"Yes, I do. I met her about two or three years ago. She came by the house to pick up a box for you. Did she not give it to you?"

"No, but that was my fault. I should've looked her up sooner, but I haven't. D'ya know where she lives?"

"In Fern Hills. She goes by her married name now. Let me see if I can remember it. I know she lives in a big house in Fern Hills. Her husband is a solicitor, I think. Mathers. Yes. That's it. That's her name. Angela Mathers."

It didn't take long for Billy to find her address because Mr. Albert Mathers was a prominent solicitor in town and Joe knew of him. He was the Mathers in the Jones, Dickinson, and Mathers LLP law firm, where Billy had gone to meet Irene's solicitor, Mr. Dickinson.

What a small world thought Billy as he sat in the office at Great Moor Street again, waiting for Peggy, the too tarted up receptionist, but this time it was to see Mr. Mathers.

Albert Mathers came striding into the reception area with his hand extended in a warm welcome. "How are you? How can I help you, Mr. Jones?"

"I'm Billy Jones, your wife's nephew. She has a box for me."

"Well, I never. You must be the phantom nephew she spoke of who was in the war."

"Yes. That's me," said Billy, laughing.

"So, Angela was right. She does have a nephew. She always wondered if she'd ever see you again."

"Yes. It's been a while."

"Well come into my office and we'll talk."

"Angela's going to be tickled pink when I tell her who showed up at the office this morning. Your timing couldn't have been better. We were just cleaning out the attic on the weekend and came across the box you mentioned. Another week and it'd be at the rubbish dump."

Billy smiled with relief.

"Do you have a car, Billy?"

"No."

"Well, why don't I drop the box off at your house in the morning on my way to work?"

"Great. That'd be a big help."

Billy scribbled his address on the notepad Albert gave him.

"What are you doing Friday night? Come to our house for tea. I'll pick you up at say five-thirty after I finish work. Angela's going to be over the moon to see you again, and the children too though I don't know if they even know they have an Uncle Billy."

Albert dropped off the box at Billy's house the following morning. It weighed about fifteen pounds, was about thirty inches long by thirty inches wide, and about two feet deep.

He made a pot of tea, put two slices of bread in the toaster, and thought about what he might find in the box as he waited for his toast to pop up.

As he sat at the kitchen table, dipping his toast in his tea, and staring at the box on the table, he noticed his heart thumping and he smiled for it reminded him of when he was a young boy staring at his Christmas present on the kitchen table. His mum always gave him one big box, smaller than this one, but covered in Christmas wrap and holding all his presents. He always got two pairs of socks and a woolen sweater – all hand-knitted by his mum, a new pair of pants and a shirt from the shops as well as the main toy. And as a tradition, he also got an orange, an assortment of nuts in shells, and a Cadbury chocolate bar.

Much of the excitement he felt at Christmas was in him when he slit the tape around the lid, lifted the lid, and peered inside. He removed all of the items and lined them up, side by side on the table. There were two boxes, three photographs, and an assortment of items from his mum's house which Terence had selected and included.

The smaller of the two boxes held a bundle of aerogram letters tied with an elastic band. He picked them up, looked at the writing, and was surprised to see they were the letters he had written to his mum. He paused, sat back in the chair, and sipped his tea. *Well, I never*, was all he could say.

Putting the box aside, he went ahead and opened the bigger box which held his mum's small leather suitcase, her black leather purse, some envelopes and letters, and an assortment of his mother's clothes.

With much curiosity, he opened the suitcase and extracted his mum's purple cotton scarf, her hairbrush, brooch, and ring. When he handled the scarf, he got a whiff of what he thought was his mum's lavender-scented perfume. He held it up to his nose, inhaled, and was disappointed, because the smell was just the musty odor of an old leather suitcase.

He went into the bathroom, placed the scarf around his neck, checking that both sides were of equal length, just as his mother used to do, and looked in the mirror. He imagined his mother's face swaddled by the purple cotton bundle. A tear appeared in the corner of his eye.

Filled with nostalgia and feeling calm and serene, he returned to the kitchen, put the scarf on the table, and picked up his mum's silver brooch. He imagined it pinned to the left side of his mum's dress just below the collar. and turning his attention to the ring with the red agate stone, he imagined it on his mum's finger where it always was. He tried it on for fit, but it was too small for any of his fingers.

Putting everything back in the suitcase the way he found it, he next inspected the purse. It was the only purse he could ever remember his mum having. Even as a child, he recalled the purse being heavily wrinkled and sad looking, and here it was, some twenty years later, looking much the same. As he looked at the yellowed metal clasp, memories of his mum fiddling with it to open it came back to him.

Tucked in a side pocket of the purse were a few small green and white papers. He pulled them out and wondered what his mum was doing with train tickets for travel from Blackmoor to Swanson, Kent. There were three stubs and three unused tickets. *What on earth was she doing in Swanson, Kent? Why did she have unused return tickets?* He read all of the details on both sides of the tickets – the dates, times, and places and the departing and arrival stations – and was gobsmacked. They were for travel on April 18, two days before she died. *She must have died in Swanson and that's why the return tickets are unused.*

He leaned back away from the table letting the news sink in and thought about two questions: *What on earth was she doing in Swanson and how did she die?*

Eager to see what else he might learn, he next picked up her small grey notebook and was made speechless by what he read on the first page. McIvor Home for Babies with a Compton, Lancashire address was written on the first line, and halfway down, St. Chads Home for Boys with a Swanson Kent address, and on the last line written in capital letters the words THE WELLINGTON.

The big picture stared Billy in the face, giving rise to astute observations and perplexing questions: *My mum was looking for my brother. That's why she was in Swanson. Did she find him? Why was she looking for him? How did she find out where he was – who gave her the St. Chads name and address? Why did she die and how? And what was THE WELLINGTON? – sounds like a hotel or a pub but I can't see my mum ever going into a place like that. I need answers and the only way I'm going to get them is if I go to Swanson.*

Moving back to the table and looking in the purse again, he found three envelopes.

The first one, folded in half, held money – two five-pound notes, eight shillings, two sixpences, and two pennies, which he put into his pant pocket. *Thanks, mum.* The second one was crumpled and had no markings on it. He nearly discarded it but when he picked it up, he saw that it contained a document – a light blue typed telegram from the British War Office. He gasped when he read that a Mr. William Janes had been missing in action since March 10. *Who was William*

Janes? and why did my mum have this telegram? He checked the address and was astonished to see that it was their correct home address.

He got up and paced the floor, thinking, and as he did, an uneasy feeling arose in the pit of his stomach that the War Office had made a terrible mistake that might have had something to do with his mum's death. *She must have thought the telegram was about me. How distraught she must have been? She must have got sick with grief thinking I was dead.* Tears erupted, obscuring his vision, but his mind was clear. *I bet that was why she went to Swanson to look for my brother.*

He sat back down at the table, opened the third envelope, and was instantly overwhelmed by what it contained: a faded sepia photograph, with La Cloche Studio. St. Helier, Jersey. C.I. stamped on the backside. It was of a young couple. Billy's jaw dropped and he grinned, *That's my mum and dad! So that's what they looked like? My, they were a bonny couple.* Billy ran his fingers over the images, caressing them and committing the images to memory.

He put everything back in the master box and eagerly looked forward to telling Angela about what he had found out about his mum.

⌇

Three days later, Albert Mathers picked Billy up and drove him to his home on Green Lane in Fern Hills. Billy had never seen this part of Blackmoor before nor a home this size. The house was grand by anybody's standards, but for Billy, it was palatial. As he stood in the driveway gazing up at the massive stone construction of the home with its bay windows and turrets, he thought about when he was living on the street as a homeless person. The extreme differences made him shake his head and chuckle. He was in awe when he stepped into the entranceway and looked at the white-tiled foyer gleaming in the light being emitted by three enormous chandeliers dangling from the vaulted ceiling, and as his eyes followed the curvature of the polished brown staircase up the center of the foyer to a landing with hallways running off to the right and left, he was overcome by the opulence of it all.

Just as Albert had predicted, Angela was delighted to see Billy again. Her last memory of him was of a scrawny teenager, about thirteen or fourteen years old, dressed in a brown school uniform.

"Great to see you again, Angela," Billy said, moving closer and hugging her. She returned the hug and stepped back, looking for resemblances between the Billy of old and the Billy of new. "Let me see you. You haven't changed much over the years – a little heavier around the waist maybe, but then aren't we all?" She winked her right eye the way she used to when she was babysitting him. He remembered and returned the smile.

"And you look the same, only older," said Billy, laughing and nervously straightening his tie and sleeves.

Right behind Angela, nineteen-year-old Michael and sixteen-year-old Patricia eagerly waited to be formally introduced. They only learned a half-hour earlier that they had an uncle called Billy who was coming to tea. Angela had never mentioned him to them before. In truth, she had forgotten about him, not having heard anything about him since Mary died.

Smiling with lively bright eyes, the children shook Billy's hand and Michael took Billy's tweed cap and coat and hung them up.

"Come here. Let's have a hug. It's not every day I get to meet my niece and nephew, or whatever you are to me," said Billy moving closer for the hugs. The children backed off slightly, unsure, and unprepared to be hugged by a total stranger. Billy startled them.

The party moved into the dining room. Angela had this thing about eating meals while they were hot, so she'd purposefully prepared the tea so they could sit down and eat without delay. Billy welcomed the breathing space, before the barrage of questions he knew would soon come his way and eating early was particularly good news for him because he'd had a busy day and had skipped lunch sensing that there'd be lots to eat at the Mathers house.

Angela brought out a large platter, piled high with slices of piping hot roast beef, Michael brought out a serving dish full of creamy mashed potatoes, and Patricia brought out a bowl of green peas as well as the gravy boat, which was sizzling with a thick, rich, brown sauce. Billy's assigned place was at the head of the table at one end, facing Albert at the other end. Angela sat on one side facing Michael and Patricia. Albert opened a bottle of wine and walked around the table filling glasses.

"I'd like to make a toast to Billy. We're glad you're here Billy and we hope to see a lot more of you in the future," Albert said, raising his glass to his lips. They all stood up, took a sip of their wine, and nodded to Billy.

"We're really short of relatives," said Michael, cryptically.

Before anyone had time to read into what Michael might have meant by his remark, Billy held up his glass and said, "Me too. You lot are all I've got." Everyone laughed heartily.

Angela tapped her wine glass. "Tuck in everyone. Have a good nosh. Enjoy."

They ate mostly in silence, politely smiling at each other in between bites. Everyone was hungry. The sights and smells of the various food dishes stimulated everyone's appetites.

After they had eaten, Patricia collected the plates and cutlery, took them to the kitchen, and returned with a large dish of piping hot, freshly made apple pie. Albert poured a brandy for himself and one for Billy and they all moved into the lounge.

The Mathers family was fascinated with what Billy told them about his life. He was careful not to tell them everything, nor did he elaborate on any particular period of his life. Driven by his prepared soliloquy about his past, he did not stop to answer their questions, even though they raised their hands and tried their best to interrupt him.

He'd prepared his speech by selecting some parts while excluding others. It wasn't that he was too embarrassed or ashamed of anything he just wanted to give them the big picture before leading them to his big news. Everyone listened as intently as if Billy was a professional storyteller, hired as an after-dinner speaker to amuse the dinner guests.

When he spoke about growing up with his mum on Ainsdale Road and Angela babysitting him, Angela jumped in, disrupting Billy's speech, saying, "Excuse me Billy but I want you to know how upset I always got with my dad for the horrible way he treated you and my sister, I could never understand why he was so hurtful to the two of you. He was not a happy man, Billy. He's dead now and my mum lives by herself over in Westlea. She's holding her own."

"Can't say I'm sorry to hear he's dead. Best place for him, I'd say."

The room went silent. Billy took a sip of his brandy before continuing with his speech. He spoke of being conscripted into the Army and going off to fight in France. and about being injured and falling in love with a nurse in a Paris hospital. But he didn't mention what had happened to Bobby or that he'd killed a man. Nor did he tell them he'd been a sick, desperate homeless person until he met Joe who gave him a job as a rag and bone man and a place to live. He didn't want to tell them any of the details, but he felt he had to tell them what he was now doing for a living.

"I'm a scrap merchant," Billy announced unashamedly.

Silence filled the room and questioning looks appeared on faces.

"You mean a rag and bone man?" asked Angela.

"Yes," Billy replied, smiling proudly, and sitting back in his chair.

"Are you really a rag and bone man?" asked Patricia. "Do you push a cart and collect things from people?"

"I don't, but my men do. I run the operation."

"Why didn't you come and see us?" said Angela. "We'd have helped you out, wouldn't we, Albert? Last I heard you were in the Army."

"I was. It's a long story, but I have something far more interesting to tell you tonight. I've come to tell you about my brother, Thomas. My twin brother."

The room went as quiet as a graveyard at midnight on a full moon.

"You don't have a brother Billy," Angela replied, looking at her nephew with concern, and talking in a voice laced with understanding and compassion.

"Oh yes, I do, but it was a dark family secret – no one was ever to know."

Angela and Albert exchanged worried glances with one another.

"Why do you think you have a brother Billy? I was there when you were born. There was only you – you don't have a brother!"

"Oh yes I do," insisted Billy in a quieter voice. "Were you in the house when I was born?"

Angela considered her answer with a smile, sensing Billy had a surprise up his sleeve. "Well no. Not exactly. I was at Aunt Bertha's. My dad didn't want me in the way, that's all – he said there wouldn't be any room for me with the midwife and all. I came back two days after you were born and there was no other baby in the house Billy. There was only you."

"That's because Father Shields took my brother and put him in an orphanage before you came home. I never knew I had a brother until Irene told me. D'ya remember Irene? She lived next door to us. Irene and Ernie?"

"Yes. Vaguely."

"Well. I met her about two years ago and she told me what had happened. She and Ernie saw us the day we were born, and Ernie did something to us my mum asked him to do."

Everyone listened to Billy's every word.

"See this?" He held out his right hand, palm up, and pointed to the discoloration on the underside of his right thumb. Irene said that's a 'lovemark'. She said it means my brother and me were born in love. And he has the same mark too."

They leaned in on their chairs for a closer look. "Mum had Ernie tattoo it on us with a needle he got from the tannery where he worked coz she wanted a way for us to prove we were brothers if we ever found each other."

The silence in the room was deafening.

"You mean to tell me that you've had a brother all these years and you didn't know! Your mum never told you! Why?"

"I know why she didn't tell me, Angela, and I understand her reasons," replied Billy.

"Can I touch it?" asked Patricia peering at Billy's tattoo and extending an index finger to touch it.

Billy laughed and theatrically waved his finger at the gawking faces.

"Well, I never!" was all Angela could say.

"So, your brother's name is Thomas and you're telling us you don't know where he is?" asked Albert.

"That's right. But I'm goin' to find him. I recently found out that he was placed in an orphanage in Kent and my mum went there to find him. I don't know if she found him or not, but that's where she died. I don't know why or how but I'm goin' to go there soon and see what I can find out."

Billy then proceeded to tell the whole story of how he'd met Irene on his rounds as a rag and bone man, what she told him about being their next-door neighbor, and about Thomas and their dad.

He paused, and like a magician, reached into his inside pocket, pulled out the postcards Irene had sent to his mum, and handed them to Angela to pass around.

"My, oh my, oh my!" was all Angela could say.

Billy sat back and basked in the aura of amazement and awe that filled the room. When the postcards had made the rounds, he reached into his other inside jacket pocket and pulled out another treasure: the studio photograph of his mum and dad.

"And that's not all there is. Look at this. This is my mum and dad, this is."

"Go on!" said Angela, eagerly reaching for the photograph. "Yes. That's your mum all right. She looks just the same as I remember her. Beautiful red wavy locks and I can just make out the beauty spot on her cheek because I know where to look. She looks so happy. And so does her man. Where on earth did you get this?"

"It was in the box of my mum's things that Albert dropped off," replied Billy, feeling the energizing effects of the second brandy. "In the box were my mum's suitcase and purse and a smaller box filled with my letters to her when I was in the Army. Can you believe that?

Imagine how surprised I was when I realized what they were?"

"Let's give Billy a break," interrupted Angela. "If you can make a pot of tea Patricia, and Michael, if you can put out some biscuits and bring some plates for the apple pie that would be grand. Perhaps you'd like another brandy, Billy?"

"Crikey. I thought you'd never ask. I'm not driving. Yes, please. Isn't it strange how life sometimes works in your favor and sometimes against you? About two weeks ago, I found a bundle of my mum's letters – the ones she wrote to me when I was in the Army, and here I am today, in possession of the letters I wrote to her. I'm glad I've got all the letters even though I probably won't ever read them, but that doesn't matter. Just having 'em is enough for me."

PART THREE – TOMMY

Chapter Seventeen – Orphanages

Compton, Lancashire
1928

The McIvor Memorial Home for Babies was an Anglican-operated orphanage under the Waifs and Strays Society banner. It took in newborns, mostly from unwed mothers, but also from families who couldn't afford to care for another baby and looked after them until they were seven years of age. Father Shields took Thomas there on April 22, 1921, the day after he was born.

On June 2, 1928, Sister Madeline called Thomas and two other seven-year-old boys into her study. "Good morning boys. This will be your last day with us. Tomorrow, you will go to a new school."

She never liked to tell the children this, but she'd learned from experience that it was best if it was done the day before the children changed homes.

The children stared at each other in disbelief.

"Yes. You are all going to new schools in the morning. You will be with boys your own age. Isn't that exciting? Neal Tucker. You will be going to St. Marks Home for Boys in Newcastle. Timothy Stone. You will be going to St. Williams Home for Boys in Bradford, and Thomas Jones. You will be going to St. Chads Home for Boys in Swanson," recited Sister Madeline looking down at the page on her desk.

The announcements fell on deaf ears: the boys weren't listening

– they were so in shock from learning that this was to be their last day at the school, and besides, the names of the schools and towns were meaningless to them. The boys were after all only seven years of age, and this was the most momentous happening in their short seven years of life.

The following day, three lady social workers arrived in taxis to take the boys to the Blackmoor train station at 6.30 in the morning. Sister Madeline pinned name tags written on cardboard on the boy's coats and gave each of them a tin suitcase of clothes.

The suitcases were fourteen inches long by eight inches deep by ten inches wide and contained an assortment of clothing – a cap, a suit, a long nightshirt, a pair of woolen socks, two shirts, and two handker-chiefs. Also included were a ball of wool, a boot brush, and needles and thread for future repairs to the clothing.

It was raining cats and dogs when Beth, Thomas' social worker, came to collect him. With one arm around his little shoulder and hud-dling him under her umbrella to keep him dry, she walked him from the taxi to the Railway station, and down the platform to where the train for Manchester would stop.

"Where am I going?' Thomas asked, looking up at her with his big, bright emerald-green eyes.

Crouching down to look him in the face, and, taking hold of his free hand, Beth said, "You're going to a new school today, Billy. Isn't that exciting?"

He looked down at his shoes and didn't say a word.

"You're going to a school with older boys, dearie. You'll be fine. Look for an empty seat by the window so you can see outside and keep your suitcase by your side and never let it out of your sight. And don't speak to anyone. Can you do that?"

Thomas looked up and mumbled "Yes."

"And when the train stops, you'll be in Manchester. Let the other passengers get off the train first and then wait on the platform. Someone will come to help you."

She smiled and stood up. "Do you have any questions?"

Thomas continued to stare at his shoes and shake his head slowly from side to side the way he had learned to do at the Home when he didn't want to speak.

Beth hugged him, patted his head, and briskly walked away.

Although Thomas was only seven, he was unusually resilient for his age. He'd learned to take everything in his stride from being constantly teased by the children in the home about his red hair and his heavily freckled face. The staff at McIvor had nicknamed him 'Sunny Ginger' because of his happy disposition and red curls. He was glad to be leaving the home as most of the children there were now younger than him, and he wanted to be with older boys.

This was the first time Thomas had been away from the home and to be on a train was the thrill of a lifetime for him. As the engine pulled out of the station and chugged along the tracks, he stared in amazement at the scenery gliding by the grimy window and excitedly listened to the sounds of a world he'd never heard before - the repetitive clickety-click, clickety-clack of the train's steel wheels on the steel tracks and the whoo-whoos of the train's whistle as it sped through tunnels and built-up areas.

He sat quietly against the window, aware of the intermittent glances of concern being thrown his way from a grandfatherly type of man sitting opposite him who he sensed wanted to speak with him. Thomas would normally have made eye contact and smiled and would have spoken had the man asked him a question, but first and foremost in his mind, was to obey, and to do what Beth had told him to do – don't talk to anyone. He ignored the old man's curiosity by staring blankly out of the window.

A young man in a grey striped business suit with a briefcase by his side sat in the opposite corner on the same bench as Thomas. The man was so absorbed in reading his newspaper that he was unaware that there was a little boy in his carriage traveling by himself with a name tag pinned to his coat.

When the train stopped in Manchester, Thomas waited in the corridor for the other passengers to go in front of him, ensuring he was the last to get off. As the crowd from the train walked off, he stayed where he was on the platform, put his suitcase down by his feet, and stared in awe at his surroundings.

Compared with the quiet, two-track-train station of Blackmoor, Manchester station was monstrous. It was cavernous, noisy, and chaotic. Tommy looked up in amazement at the mammoth glass, metal, and stone structure and listened to the cacophony of sounds coming from passengers, arriving, and leaving on the many platforms; from the rumble of carts moving luggage to and from the trains and from the trains shunting in and out of the station. The ear-splitting sound of steam being vented by engines, and the shrill whistles of trains leaving the station made him jump, and the shouts of porters and the PA system announcing which trains were arriving and leaving at what platforms and at what times overwhelmed his senses. The aroma of food and drink wafting down the platform from food vendors assailed his nostrils, increasing his hunger. He deeply breathed in the smell of the oil and grease from the engines and tracks and realized he liked this fascinating new world he had entered.

Susan spotted his name tag and walked briskly along the platform to greet him. "Good morning, Thomas. I'm Susan. How did you like the train ride?"

"It was great," said Thomas, continuing to look around in awe. "D'ya know where I'm going?" he asked with the wide-eyed innocence of a seven-year-old.

"To a new place for older boys is all I know. You'll be fine," she said with a big smile. "You must be hungry. Here's some food to eat on the train. It's a long way to London so eat it all up." She gave him a bag containing two jam sandwiches, two biscuits, and a small glass bottle of milk. His eyes lit up and he smiled.

Susan looked in her bag and brought out two apples. "Poor little thing, Here. Have these because you won't get any more food until after you arrive in London."

She took his hand, picked up his suitcase, and led him through the hordes of people to the platform for the train to London. When she found the train to Euston station, she bent down, straightened his name tag, ensuring it was properly and prominently displayed on his chest, and then helped him climb up the metal steps of the train.

"Let everyone get off the train first and then wait on the platform, but don't talk to anyone. Okay? Someone will come to you. No need to worry about anything. You'll be fine." She turned and disappeared into the oncoming crowd.

Thomas was enjoying the journey immensely and gaining confidence with every leg of the journey. He regarded it all as one big, exciting adventure. He was calm and happy. For most boys his age, this journey would have been traumatic, a nightmare even, but it wasn't for Thomas. He was no ordinary boy, and he knew it. He was pleased he was different.

It was a long journey, but the time was flying by too quickly for Thomas. He sat in an empty seat by the window and immediately ate his sandwiches and biscuits and drank his milk. Though still famished, he decided to save the two apples for later. Riveted by the window, he peered out through the sooty glass, taking in everything. He fell asleep once for a little while and got up twice to use the bathroom.

The train pulled into Euston station in the early evening. Thomas waited until all the other passengers had disembarked before alighting. As he waited for his helper to appear, he gawked at everything happening around him, and was once again, overwhelmed. Not knowing what else to do, he smiled a silly smile while looking up and down with his mouth wide open. Everything was bigger, more vibrant, and more chaotic than in Manchester. Dazed, he stood on the platform mesmerized. Though he still didn't know where he was going, he didn't care. *I'd ride the rails forever if I could*, he thought.

Joan appeared out of thin air, took his hand and suitcase, and told him they had to go on the London underground and travel to the station for the train to Swanson. "That's where you're going, Thomas. Swanson is where your new school is." He looked up at her in disbelief. After being on trains all day, he'd forgotten the reason for the journey.

Before he knew it, he was waiting alongside the train for Swanson. Joan gave him a bag holding two strawberry jam sandwiches, a small packet of digestive biscuits, a bag of crisps, and a bottle of milk, and then she helped him climb up the steps on the train for the one-hour journey to Swanson.

The twelve hours of riding the rails had energized Thomas. He felt like a butterfly emerging from its cocoon. He looked at the other passengers and returned their smiles. It seemed everyone was smiling at him and wanting to make eye contact.

One elderly couple sitting opposite him was particularly friendly. "How are you this evening Thomas?" said the lady, reading his name tag. She opened her purse, took out two wrapped, red and white striped sweets, and offered them to him.

"I'm great, thank you," said Thomas taking the sweets.

"Where are you going, love?"

Though mindful of the instructions he'd been consistently given by his social workers, he couldn't resist responding to this old lady's friendly voice, smile, and generosity.

"I'm Thomas. I'm an orphan and I'm going to a new school," he said.

"Where did you come from, love?" asked her husband.

"Blackmoor and then I went to Manchester and then to London."

"All on trains and all today and all by yourself? How old are you, Thomas?"

"I'm seven," he proudly replied.

The couple looked at each other. "Well. You are an amazing young man to be traveling so far all by yourself and at such a young age. You are going to go far in life, my son. Mark my words, I just know it," said the lady.

Tommy's eyes sparkled with pride.

The lady opened her purse, took out the four remaining sweets, and gave them to him. "Here you are, love. Just in case your mouth gets dry which mine does when I'm on the train for a long time?"

As Thomas was preparing to step down onto the platform, a young nun in a light blue habit and a white starched cowl appeared at the bottom of the steps. Reading his name tag, she said in a voice, soft and warm, "Hello, Thomas. Welcome to Swanson. You must be tired and hungry." She reached up, took his suitcase, and put it down on the platform. Reaching up again, she put her hands under his armpits and swung him down, and then hugged him to her side, saying, "I'm Sister Celia. How was your journey?"

"I'm starving. D'ya have any food?" Thomas asked, with pleading eyes.

"Yes. I thought you might be hungry, so I made you a cheese sandwich. Do you like cheese?"

"I like everything."

She opened her bag, unwrapped the sandwich, and gave it to him.

Tenderly holding his little hand, Sister Celia walked slowly through the crowded, noisy station to the street outside, while Thomas gobbled down the cheese sandwich and looked around in wonderment at the bustling world all around him.

They crossed the street to where a horse and cart were waiting. Sister Celia untied the rope holding the horse to the post, placed Thomas' suitcase in the back of the cart, and helped him clamber aboard the high-stepped buggy. She shook the reins, and they were off. Normally, Thomas would have talked Sister Celia's ear off, but he didn't – he'd simply run out of steam. He just wanted to go to bed. Sister Celia understood and let him be.

Thirty-five minutes later, they pulled up outside a large, imposing two-story stone building. St. Chads was operated by eight nuns of the Sisters of Charity and two lay teachers. The nuns lived on-site in a separate wing of the home and functioned as custodians and parents to the sixty-three boys who lived there.

Mother Hyacinth ran the show at St. Chads. She'd been in charge for the past twenty-two years. Sister Celia was the newest member of the team, having come to the home just four weeks earlier, and was having difficulty adjusting to the austerity and severity of the place and was even having second thoughts about becoming a nun.

A large, cobbled courtyard, surrounded by thick, ten-foot-high black stone walls, served as the children's playground. There were no swings or slides. At one end of the yard was a large vegetable garden which the children tended when the weather allowed. On the ground floor of the home were the communal kitchen, dining room, chapel, and a large auditorium that accommodated everyone. Upstairs were the living quarters and dormitories for the children. It was divided into four sections named Philip Sydney, Francis Drake, George Herbert, and David Livingstone. Thomas was one of three new boys, all seven years of age and all from orphanages in different parts of England to arrive at St. Chads on this day. Charlie hailed from Devon and Eddy was from Birmingham. They were exhausted from their long journeys and just wanted to go to bed, but first, even though it was ten o'clock at night – late for seven-year-olds - they had to assemble in the lobby for their initial orientation by Mother Hyacinth.

Giddy with tiredness and hunger and feeling uneasy in their new surroundings, the boys giggled at each other's funny accents and pushed one another. Eddy stroked Thomas' mop of curly hair and pointed to the freckles on his nose. This didn't offend Tommy in the least bit – he'd been teased about his red hair and freckles for as long as he could remember and was used to it. He chuckled and commented on Eddy's big ears.

Mother Hyacinth, the spry, seventy-two-year-old matron of the home, stomped into the tiled lobby in hard leather-soled shoes and stopped abruptly in front of the boys. Her severe presence was palpable, and she knew it. The boys stood motionless, fearfully looking up at her with eyes wide open. With her hands clasped behind her back, she looked down coldly from her hooded head and with beady eyes visually inspected and assessed each waif at her feet. Charlie and Eddy averted their eyes and stared blankly at the floor. Thomas defiantly stared back. She noted his defiance, beamed a sly smile, and announced in a cold, high-pitched, authoritarian voice, "We have Home Rules at St. Chads that must be followed at all times. If you don't follow the rules, you will be punished."

The threat brought instant tears to Charlie and Eddy's eyes, but Thomas was resolute that he was not going to cry.

She brought her hands around to the front and presented a large pair of red scissors. Raising them above her head and waving them menacingly in the air, she smiled demonically while taking great pleasure from the looks of horror on the faces of the boys.

"Who wants to be first?" she said, casting her eyes from Charlie to Eddy and then to Thomas.

"First for what?" asked Thomas.

"For a haircut," she replied, coldly, reaching down and gripping Thomas' right shoulder. "Keep still and don't move," she demanded. Firmly holding his shaking shoulder, she went ahead to snip off his locks. His gorgeous mop of curly red hair fell to the floor in clumps of little ringlets. He stared at them, astonished at her cruelty, and burst into tears. His hair was the part of him that he treasured the most. Lashing out at her with clenched fists, he demanded, "Why did you do that?"

She held him at bay. A slight smile creased at the corners of her mouth as she turned and proceeded to cut off Charlie's and Eddy's hair. Sister Celia swept up the fallen tresses and put them in a bag.

Mother Hyacinth continued with the orientation. "At St. Chads, we use a Numbering System." She removed Thomas' name tag and said, "You are now Boy 14. You must always use this number. You will be punished if you don't."

Thomas looked at Sister Celia, but she had her head turned away.

Charlie was Boy 13 and Eddy was Boy 15.

Mother Hyacinth then explained the Rule of Silence: "You can only speak quietly for one hour a day after teatime." She glared at the three little cherubic faces looking tearfully up at her, and commanded, "Stop you're sniffling. The Rule of Silence applies to sniffling too." She stood up straight, folded her arms across her chest, satisfied with herself. She looked down at the boys, wagged a finger, and coldly warned, "After tea every day, we have a Punishment Circle for those boys who did not observe the rules. They get caned."

She then took Thomas' suitcase, ceremoniously held it high in the air, and turned it upside down. As the contents dropped to the floor, Thomas' eyes teared – he was trying his best not to cry. She gave him his new clothes, which in reality were old clothes that had been worn and outgrown by other children in the home and proceeded to do the same with Charlie's and Eddy's suitcases.

"Put your new clothes in your suitcase and keep them under your bed. You are all in The Francis Drake dormitory. Now go to bed, all of you. You will find your number above your bed."

Thomas threw up when he went to put his suitcase under his bed – his straw mattress reeked of urine. He went off and returned with a mop and a bucket to clean up his vomit.

⁓

Life in the home was barbaric. In addition to having to wash their clothes and bedsheets every week, the children had to also clean the building and the grounds. This involved scouring, mopping, scrubbing floors, and waxing and polishing them.

The boys went to the Swanson Council School, a twenty-minute walk away, and on Sundays, they journeyed to St. Stephens Anglican Church for the 9 o'clock Mass – a thirty-minute walk. The boys always walked in silence and single file – they knew they'd be punished if they looked around or talked.

Unlike many of the children in the home who always seemed to be sad – haunted by past fond memories of parents and siblings – Thomas had no such memories to trouble him. He'd always been an orphan and for all his life he'd been ordered to do this, that, and the other, and, for the most part, he did what he was told. He accepted whatever happened without challenging it, even the harsh and austere conditions at St. Chads. His caregivers at the McIvor Home for Babies had been generally kind, and the nuns and lay teachers at St. Chads, except for Mother Hyacinth, were mostly sympathetic and attentive to the boys' needs.

When Thomas came to St. Chads, he could already read and write and his love for books continued unabated. As there wasn't much to do in the home and as he wasn't interested in sports, he spent most of his time on his bed reading whatever printed matter he could find. Once, he tried reading the Bible, a copy of which was placed beside every bed, but its language was too archaic for a seven-year-old.

The home had a little library stocked with books well-wishers had donated. Thomas read them all and many times over. His three favorite books were Robinson Crusoe, Treasure Island, and Gulliver's Travels. The stories and pictures in them fuelled his imagination and caused him to dream about the exotic adventures he might have once he was old enough to leave the home. Sister Celia noticed his interest in reading and writing and encouraged him to develop his writing skills by bringing him children's picture books, paper, and pencils. He created many stories in his mind but was reluctant to commit them to paper fearing his work might be viewed by Mother Hyacinth as the product of an idle mind and deserving of a caning.

On more than one occasion, Thomas noticed Sister Celia raise her eyebrows and give strange looks when Mother Hyacinth was speaking. He so wanted to speak with her about it but he never seemed to get the right opportunity. His strong feelings for Sister Celia were beginning to make him feel uncomfortable in her presence, but he didn't understand why he was feeling that way.

Because the clergy ran the home, there were prayers to be recited every morning, noon, and night, and the catechism to be memorized. Every evening after tea, everyone gathered in the auditorium for the Daily Punishment Circle, followed by mass prayers for the souls in purgatory to be released and go to heaven. Heaven, hell, and purgatory were real places in Thomas' mind. He imagined they were out there somewhere in the universe or deep in the bowels of the earth. When eight-year-old Timmy died – they didn't say what of – Thomas pictured him in purgatory: sweating profusely with the infernal heat and shouting and pleading for people to pray for him. These images intensified the sincerity of his prayers. Every evening, he wondered if Timmy was still in purgatory, or whether his prayers had been sufficient to move him up the ladder and into heaven. He imagined the whole process to be like a game of snakes and ladders. Those souls lucky enough to have a lot of people praying for them could go up the ladder and skip ahead of the others.

Thomas had many questions about the dogmatic teachings of the church, but he never asked them – he knew he'd get caned for doubting. Besides, there was little opportunity to discuss or debate anything with others since the Rule of Silence reigned supreme. He believed in God, heaven, and hell, but he wasn't as fanatical about his beliefs as most of the other children in the home, who always seemed to be in the chapel, on their knees, sobbing and praying to God for help, or for the forgiveness of their sins, Tommy prayed for a good life after he left St. Chads. He felt he had nothing to repent.

~

As he entered his per-teenage years, Tommy became stronger physically from the arduous weekly labor of chores, and mentally from reading and dreaming. He knew little at this time about emotions, other than the strange feelings he had for Sister Celia that he didn't understand and couldn't explain.

His book heroes inspired him and nurtured his spirited, vivid imagination and he sensed, from what he saw on his way to church and school, that there was much more to life than what he saw at the home. He couldn't wait to experience it.

Though only twelve, he had the maturity of a much older child. He knew he'd be out of St. Chads in a year and what he did then would be up to him.

His best friends remained Charlie and Eddy, who arrived at St. Chads the same day as him. They looked up to him for inspiration and guidance, though that was challenging, given the Rule of Silence and his preference to be alone. But all that changed as the three amigos entered their final year at St. Chads. They wanted to go to Canada next year when they turned thirteen, just as the boys did the previous year, and began to talk excitedly about it among themselves. They hoped they would all be sent to the same area so they could stay in touch and remain the best of friends, forever.

In 1934, the boys turned thirteen, or so they were told, but none of them had birth certificates to prove it – a key part of the re-education program to eradicate their identities. In January, they were told by Mother Hyacinth that they would be in a party of eighteen boys going to Canada sometime in the summer. Those boys who knew of their family were fearful when they heard the news because it meant that they would be leaving England and might not see their relatives ever again. But for Thomas, Eddy, and Charlie, the news was fantastic. When they got back to their dormitory, they excitedly chanted, "We're going to Canada, we're going to Canada, to the land of the Cowboys and Indians," and danced around in circles, hopping from one foot to the other and making what they thought were Indian sounds by clapping their hands over their mouths. This revelation was a seminal moment in the lives of the boys. It changed their perspective for they now had a specific destination to travel to in their dreams. Thomas now focused all his thoughts on what he believed life would be like in Canada.

Like the other boys in the home, Thomas was unaware that the scheme was not about providing children with a better life in Canada as they were told. It was a politically designed arrangement between the British and Canadian governments to satisfy their needs. The British government wanted to save money because it cost more to clothe and feed the children in an orphanage than it did to emigrate them, and Canada needed more bodies – they needed more farm laborers and domestic servants. Even if Thomas had been aware of this, he wouldn't have cared. To him, going to Canada was the exciting turn of events for which he had imagined, hoped, and prayed for. As far as he was concerned, God had listened and was answering his prayers.

Chapter Eighteen – Thomas goes to Canada

Liverpool, Lancashire.
May 1934

In May, eighteen dark brown wooden boxes, 27.5" long by 14.0" wide and 12.0" high, arrived at St. Chads for use by the boys being emigrated to Canada. Thomas, Eddy, and Charlie helped each other carry their trunks back to their dormitory.

The boys sat on the edge of their beds, running their hands over the smooth patina finish of the wood, and smiling at seeing their names stenciled on the top and sides of the trunks. The trunks were theirs to keep forever. They were the first substantial thing the boys had ever owned in their lives. Ownership was a new and wonderful experience for them.

The trunks were extremely well made with dove-tail jointed corners, two reinforced steel bands wrapped around the sides, two metal handles, a sturdy metal-hinged lid, and a heavy-duty padlock. No other present could have elicited more pride and joy in the faces of the boys than the sight and feel of these boxes with their names indelibly printed on them. Stenciled underneath their names were the words Gibbs Home, Sherbrooke, Quebec.

"That's great. We're all going to the same home. It must be big to be taking all of us," said Thomas. Charlie and Eddy did a little dance and clapped their hands with joy.

Sister Celia arrived with an armful of Thomas' new clothes and returned a little later with clothes for Charlie and Eddy. St. Chads was providing clothes considered appropriate for Canada. Sister Celia made a third trip to the boy's dorm with four books for each of them: The Travellers Guide, the Holy Bible, the New Testament, and Pilgrims Progress.

"What are we supposed to do with these?" Charlie cheekily asked.

"You're supposed to read them, Charlie. That's what you're supposed to do with books," Sister Celia replied with a laugh.

"Yes. Right. Maybe I can sell or trade them for something more useful when I get to Canada," responded Charlie.

~

On June 9, 1934, Thomas, Eddy, and Charlie, along with fifteen other boys and their escort, Master James Albrighton, set sail on the Canadian Pacific Steamship liner, the Duchess of Bedford, out of Liverpool for the eight-day voyage across the Atlantic Ocean to Halifax, Canada.

When the boys marched up the gangplank and stepped onto the deck, a steward handed them a colored postcard of the ship. On the back of the card, handwritten in ink, were the words: C.P.S. Duchess of Bedford. Thomas nonchalantly slipped the card into his onboard bag, unaware that he would ultimately treasure it for the rest of his life.

As the liner pulled away from the dock, the boys excitedly raced to the stern, eager to get one last look at England. They gazed at the Royal Liver Building and waved to no one in particular, each boy wondering if they would ever see England again. Ten minutes later, Thomas raced to the ship's bow and the other boys sprinted after him. They lined up and stared out at the grey wide choppy sea ahead of them and wondered what Canada was going to be like.

Master Albrighton herded the boys down many ladders to their bunk accommodations in the ship's third-class section. Each cabin accommodated six boys. The three-tiered bunk beds on each side had metal frames with chains attached to support the mattresses, and the space between the bunks was narrow and claustrophobic. Despite their pleas to Mr. Albrighton to change their accommodations from different cabins for each of them to one cabin for all he simply said that it was beyond his control.

It was a harrowing journey. The cabins were stiflingly hot, muggy, and smelly because they were next to the engine room. All but five boys (the trio amigos plus two others) were seasick within twenty-four hours of sailing and didn't leave their cabins until seven days later when they were in calmer waters just outside Halifax. The crew brought food down for them on platters, placed them on the floor outside the cabin, knocked on the door, and left. The stench in the sweltering cabins from vomit and the reeking odor in the air of hot oil from the engine room was revolting. So long as they didn't go to their respective cabins, the boys felt fine. They spent their days on the promenade level breathing in the fresh salty air and sleeping on the comfortable couches in the bar area at night.

Since most other passengers were also sick and confined to their cabins, the five boys had practically the whole dining area to themselves. At mealtimes, they were swarmed by waiters eager to please but with few other passengers to serve. Some brought food, some drinks, and some came to the table just to chat and break the monotony of the voyage. Over the next eight days, the boys worked through the menu, ordering dishes they'd never heard of, couldn't pronounce, let alone eat. When they did go to their rooms for a change of clothes, it took a half-day to get rid of the cabin odors lingering in their nostrils and on their clothes.

Master Albrighton stayed in his quarters for most of the journey. Thomas saw him only twice and both times he was drunk and seasick.

On the seventh day, as the Duchess of Bedford entered the calmer waters of the upper channel of the St. Lawrence River, conditions improved. Ten boys, who were feeling well enough, clambered up the metal rungs to get to the deck and meet up with Thomas, Eddy, Charlie, and the other two boys on the promenade deck. They raced each other to the ship's bow to get their first sighting of Canada. The fresh, cool air blasted them in the face, invigorating their bodies and lifting their spirits. Thomas' imagination soared and his heart pounded as he spied the first signs of civilization since leaving Liverpool. There was no mistaking the Christian churches, all built on the highest points of land in the little villages: their huge crosses silhouetted sharply against bright blue skies or thick, white cumulous clouds.

The ship docked and Mr. Albrighton, now sober but looking haggard, herded the boys, single file, down the ship's gangplank to a large dimly lit shed on the quay. This was Pier 21, the debarkation point for new immigrants.

Pier 21 was hot and teeming with people and noise. Thomas was overwhelmed – he longed for the fresh air and the relative quiet and privacy of the previous eight days. He inched his way forward with the crowd to the front and waited in line. Eddy and Charlie lined up behind.

A man in a uniform with a gold patch on his arm that read Department of Agriculture asked him his name. "Boy number 14" he impulsively replied, and then, feeling embarrassed and vulnerable, he said in a quiet voice with a wry smile, "Sorry Sir. It's Thomas Jones." The man smiled knowingly. He'd heard the faux pas many times before.

Thomas straightened up to his full height of five foot nine, took a deep breath, and repeated to himself, *I'm Thomas Jones. I'm not Boy 14 anymore.* In that instant Thomas sensed the heavy chains of his St. Chad's identity fall from his shoulders and clang to the floor, and in its place, a feeling of lightness rushed up from the ground and coursed through his body. *I'm Thomas Jones now! I'm free, and I'm in Canada. No. I'm Tommy now. Tommy Jones. Tommy sounds more Canadian. Thomas is too British and stuffy.* He resolved right there and then that he would henceforth be called Tommy Jones.

A man in a white gown with a white stethoscope dangling around his neck came along the line checking each passenger. He pulled Tommy's eyelids back and looked inside. He told him to open his mouth, say

THE SOLDIER AND THE ORPHAN – SEPARATED BY CHURCH AND WAR

'ah', and he looked down his throat.

"Sixty-two medically fit," he hollered when he got to the end of the line. Assistants untied the roped barricade and let the line of passengers through. Tommy joined the line and waited behind three other passengers for the documentation phase of the proceedings. A 'To Whom it May Concern' letter was the only document the boys were given when they left St. Chads. Tommy's letter stated that his name was Thomas Jones and that he was a British subject. That was it – nothing else. When it was his turn, he handed his letter to the young government man, who stamped it without reading, and shouted "Next."

Twelve boys boarded the train for Montreal and six boys and Mr. Albrighton took the train to Ottawa. In Montreal, twelve boys boarded the train to Sherbrooke, Quebec, where the Gibbs Home was located: the distributing center where the Home Children met the farmers to whom they were assigned.

Tommy gazed out of the train window, wide-eyed, and stared at the fresh green scenery whizzing past. The land was so vast, and empty compared with the English countryside. The huge rivers and bridges took his breath away; the picturesque villages amused him, and the entire travel experience rekindled the fond memories he had of his first train rides in England from Blackmoor to Swanson when he was just seven years old. He felt deliciously free, like a convict released from prison after serving a seven-year sentence. He couldn't believe it was happening. *Was it all a dream? Would he wake up in the morning and find himself back in his smelly bed at St. Chads?*

Canada was in the grip of the Great Depression and unemployment was rampant throughout the country. Accordingly, the Home Children program was being wound down and Tommy, Eddy, and Charlie were some of the last boys to be taken to Canada under this program.

Their farm contracts stipulated that they would be housed, fed, clothed, and sent to school by their host farmers until they were eighteen, and in return, the boys were to help with the chores and general farm labor.

183

Chapter Nineteen – The Bouchards

St. Eloise. Province of Quebec.
June 1934

At the Gibbs Home, Emile Bouchard, the dairy farmer to whom Tommy had been assigned, was waiting for him with his horse and buggy, as were the other farmers waiting to pick up their British boys. Tommy anxiously scanned the grouping of farmers, wondering who he would get, when Mr. Bouchard stepped forward and extended his hand for a handshake.

Tommy noticed Mr. Bouchard's hands were unusually large and calloused and he was missing the tips of two fingers. He thought Mr. Bouchard looked much like he had imagined a Canadian farmer to look like: tallish (about five-foot-eleven), with a stocky build and a weather-beaten face, which was tanned and wrinkled around the eyes from squinting in the sun while making hay. Mr. Bouchard's hair was dark brown, thick, and full. His well-worn, full-length light grey overalls with vertical, dark blue pinstripes that were strapped over his shoulders carried a faint, odor of cows. Tommy couldn't get enough of it. Though unfamiliar with the scent, he found it to be a welcome smell for some strange reason, and he tried to breathe it in deeply by flaring his nostrils. He looked Mr. Bouchard straight in the eyes, shook his hand firmly, and grinned.

"Welcome to Canada and Quebec, "Mr. Bouchard said proudly,

but shyly, in a quiet, thick Quebecois English accent, making Tommy smile. Mr. Bouchard spoke very little English – it was his children who insisted he hire an English boy. They taught him how to say a few words in English to welcome Tommy to Canada.

Tommy was uncertain what would happen next. He didn't know what he should do or say. Sensing his hesitation, Mr. Bouchard gently took his arm, picked up his suitcase, and motioned for him to go with him. They were in no hurry. Mr. Bouchard wanted his new boy to take it all in at his own pace. They went into the big yard adjoining the Gibbs Home where the boy's trunks had been neatly set out in rows. Tommy soon found his trunk and as he and Mr. Bouchard picked it up, he spied Eddy and Charlie just coming into the yard with their respective hosts. They waved and smiled at each other. That was the last time Tommy would see Eddy alive.

Mr. Bouchard placed Tommy's trunk and suitcase on the back of the buggy alongside the groceries he had previously picked up and climbed aboard the buggy. *This is the best day of my life,* Tommy thought as Mr. Bouchard yanked the reins and Ned started to trot. Tommy was keenly aware that this was his first close-up look at Canada and he wanted to savor the experience deeply so that he would remember it forever.

The serenity and novelty of clip-clopping along country roads in rural Quebec in a horse and buggy for an hour and a half were pleasing to Tommy and the sights and sounds of the chicken, pig, and dairy farms and little hamlets they passed on their way thrilled him. By the time they reached the Bouchard's farm, Tommy felt elated and happy, and as he alighted from the cart and glimpsed the cows in the pasture, a whimsical thought flashed through his mind eliciting an ironic smile. *I'm going to be a cowboy after all.*

The Bouchard family lived in St. Eloise, a small francophone farming community about ninety minutes outside of Sherbrooke. They ran a small dairy operation of thirty cows as well as a few goats, chickens, and pigs. Emile and Theresa had two children: a twelve-year-old son, Marc, and a fifteen-year-old daughter, Chantelle. Though French was the family's native tongue and working language, the children were learning English vocabulary at school, and this was the main reason why the Bouchards wanted an English boy to stay with them.

Theresa Bouchard was a large woman with a wide smile and large, jiggly arms, which she wrapped around Tommy and hugged him tightly. He was overwhelmed. He felt her warmth and love and his eyes watered, embarrassing him. Once his eyes cleared, they shone bright with excitement.

Chantelle Bouchard was slim and tall, so unlike her mother in that regard, but she had her mother's hazel eyes and brown wavy hair. She liked all sports, had lots of friends, and was always giggling. Marc Bouchard was of a similar build and height to Tommy and had his mother's brown hair and hazel eyes.

The first piece of business was to find Tommy some new clothes: clothes that would be practical for life on a French dairy farm in summer. The Bouchard family laughed when Tommy opened up his trunk and took out, piece by piece, the flimsy and inappropriate clothing the home had given him. Mrs. Bouchard took one look at the ridiculous clothing and suggested, in broken English, "I think the best place for that lot is in the St. Vincent De Paul bin for the poor at the church! We'll get you fixed up Tommy."

Emile asked Marc to go to his room and bring down some clothes that might fit Tommy because he was about the same size as him. This made Tommy smile and he hoped that one of the items Marc might bring down for him would be a cowboy hat.

Marc disappeared and ten minutes later re-appeared much to everyone's amusement with a scarf wrapped around his neck, a tuque on his head, and his arms overflowing with clothes. He gave Tommy two white T-shirts, a dark blue parka, a wool plaid shirt, a pair of denim jeans, a pair of leather boots, and a pair of thick woolen grey socks.

"There you go Tommy – clothes for all seasons. See what fits. They're all yours if they fit," said Marc. He was as excited as Tommy because he would now get to replace his old belongings with new ones.

The whole family took to Tommy from first sight. His tousled, curly, red hair gave him a lovable, impish look, his twinkling green eyes revealed a happy soul, and his freckles made him look mischievous. On a more practical note, his lean firm body showed he was fit and strong and would be most useful on the farm. Emile was pleased that Tommy looked so fit. The Bouchards' only two requirements of Tommy were that he be useful around the farm and good company for their children.

Unlike the majority of Home Children who were treated harshly and had to live separately from their host family in cow barns or other structures as if they were livestock, Tommy was fortunate to have his own bedroom and was treated by the family as if he was the Bouchard's third child.

Emile Bouchard was aware of the discrimination in Canada against Home Children and had heard of eugenics – a movement from Europe intended to improve the human race by selective breeding. He'd had many an argument in the city about it and intended to prove them all wrong by showing what love and caring could do for a boy like Tommy.

On the night of Tommy's arrival and after he'd gone to bed, Theresa explained to the children that Tommy had come from an orphanage in England, and since he didn't know anything about his parents, they should never question him on the subject. Marc and Chantelle understood and felt sorry for him and agreed to never bring up the subject.

Tommy and Marc enjoyed each other's company right from the start and did all the boy things you could do on a farm. Tommy was the brother Marc had always wanted. In summers, they climbed trees in the forest bordering the farm, and in winter, they snowshoed through them. Tommy learned how to swim and skate on the property's spring-fed pond, and in the fall how to tap sugar maples and boil syrup. When he didn't have anything better to do, he whittled wood into bird shapes.

Emile felt fatherly towards Tommy and from time to time checked in with Marc to ensure everything was going well. Marc said it was.

Tommy ate his breakfast and lunch in the kitchen of the Bouchard farmhouse and joined the family for supper every night in the dining room. The family connection was strong, and Tommy thrived in it.

The Bouchards were staunch Catholics and Tommy went to mass with them every Sunday. Though he'd been brought up Anglican, it didn't matter to him which church he went to. As far as he was concerned, one faith was the same as another – *they all believed in God, did they not?* Tommy went along with the Bouchard's form of worship as a dutiful son would, but he always wondered if indeed there was a loving God. *Where was He when Timmy died in St. Chads? And where was He when Mother Hyacinth was caning the boys for speaking their names and for asking questions?* A loving God didn't make any sense to him.

Tommy's job was to tend to the cows and the cowshed. He had to put the cows out to pasture in the morning, bring them in to be milked in the late afternoon, milk them before supper, and help Emile in the evenings with the transfer of milk to the tankers. He also did whatever jobs came up, such as maintaining and repairing farm equipment and mending fences.

Marc and Chantelle regarded and treated Tommy as their sibling, and Tommy deeply treasured their friendship and company. They helped him to speak French and he helped them with their English. They had chores to do on the farm after school and on the weekends, and Tommy helped them with that whenever he had the time.

Tommy couldn't continue his academic education because there was no English school available, and he wasn't eligible to go to a French school because he wasn't a resident of Quebec. He never liked school much anyway, so he didn't feel he was missing out on anything. On the contrary, he was relieved and delighted he didn't have to sit in a classroom all day and listen to a teacher go on and on about subjects he wasn't interested in. He much preferred to be working in the barn or with the cows, all the while thinking and wondering about his future.

He was a fast and willing learner and quickly became exceptionally helpful and useful around the farm.

Emile opened a bank account for him in Sherbrooke and deposited his contract stipulated pocket money into it every month when he went into town to do his banking, and he also put in extra money, bringing his pay up to what he thought was a fair wage for what Tommy did, but he didn't tell him. He wanted to surprise him with it on his last day when he withdrew the savings. If Tommy left Mr. Bouchard's employment of his own accord before his five-year contract was up, then he'd forfeit all of his savings. That was their arrangement.

Chapter Twenty –
Monsieur Rene Marceau

St. Eloise. Province of Quebec.
November 16, 1935

On Monday, November 16, around four o'clock in the afternoon, a man came into the cowshed carrying a brown briefcase. The man was about fifty years old and overweight. By the time he'd walked down the long driveway to the cowshed, he was puffing, panting, and sweating. He sat down on a low cement wall and laid his briefcase on his lap. After doffing his purple beret and wiping his brow with a red handkerchief, he scanned the cowshed as he let his breathing return to normal, or at least as close to normal as was possible for him. Tommy noticed the man's distressed condition and stopped milking. He got up, went to the table at the back of the shed, and poured the man a mug of water from a pitcher.

"Thank you, son," said the man in Quebecois English, surprising Tommy and making him chuckle. "I'm looking for a boy called Tommy Jones. They told me at the big house that I'd find him milking the cows."

"Well, you've found him. What can I do for you," said a curious Tommy?

"It's what I can do for, son. Let me introduce myself. My name is Monsieur Rene Marceau and I'm the Home Children Supervisor for Quebec. You can call me Rene. Okay? My job is to follow up with you

British boys to see how you're doing and if you need any help. How are things with you Thomas?"

"Good," said Tommy, sitting back down on his stool and resuming his milking.

"How's your health?"

"Great. I seldom get sick."

"That's good," said Rene, nodding his head and smiling as he made notes in his record book.

"And how's your appetite? Are you eating enough?"

"Couldn't be better. I eat what the family eats" said Tommy to an astonished Rene.

"Well, that's a first! Don't tell anyone. Wouldn't want that sort of thing getting around or I'd have a mutiny on my hands," said Rene, laughing. "I have to tell you son that you have one of the best situations of any Home Child here in Quebec that I've ever seen, and I get to see them all – every one of them. Many boys are abused, underfed, overworked, and treated worse by the farmer than the livestock they're tending."

"How awful," said Tommy continuing with his milking. "I had no idea. I don't go to the city much and I never get a chance to talk to other Home Children."

Rene shook his head.

"How's the work going?"

"Great. I love it. I've learned to do so many new things since I arrived. I love farm work and cows. This is Ellie. Say hello to the gentleman, Ellie."

Rene smiled and asked, "And how about school?"

"I don't go to school. There wasn't one for me, but I feel I'm learning more than if I went to school."

"Where are you sleeping?"

"In a bed," replied Tommy wondering what a strange question to ask. *Where else would I sleep?*

"And where's the bed?"

THE SOLDIER AND THE ORPHAN – SEPARATED BY CHURCH AND WAR

"In my bedroom," replied Tommy.

Rene laughed out loud. "I don't believe it. You have a bedroom. Have the Bouchards adopted you?"

"They might as well have. Sometimes I think Emile and Theresa treat me better than they do, Marc and Chantelle," replied Tommy raising his eyebrows and smiling.

"Hey. Do you know Eddy Marshall and Charlie Gibson? They came out with me?"

"Yes, I do. I know all the British boys in Quebec."

"Do they live far from here? I'd love to see them again," said Tommy on his way to get Rene another glass of water.

"It's too far for you to go son. It's not like you can ask anybody to take you there, can you?"

"I bet Emile would if I asked him. Maybe I can write to Eddy and Charlie instead. Can you give me their addresses?"

"I have them of course, but I don't know if I want to give them to you. What are you going to say? That you're living like a king! I know their home situation and it's nothing like yours. That's all I can say about that. Can you imagine how they'd feel if they got a letter from you saying how you eat in the farmhouse with the family and that you have your own bedroom in the house?"

"I hear what you're saying Rene and I understand. Eddy, Charlie, and I have been friends since we were seven. We promised each other we'd stay in touch for the rest of our lives. I just want to say hello to them and to let them know I'm alive and thinking about them."

"I didn't know you were all such good friends," said Rene.

"I'm glad you told me what you did because there's no way I'd do anything to upset them. But I do feel they need to hear from me, and I need to know that they're okay."

"Don't get your hopes up too high son. As I said, their living arrangements are very different from yours. Where are they going to get paper and a pencil from to write you a letter? I bet you're going to sit at a table on a chair and use a clean flat surface when you write your letters.

Can you imagine if you had to write them here in the cowshed?"

Tommy's spirits dipped and he lost his concentration. Ellie mooed that he wasn't milking her correctly.

"But this is what I'll do for you son. I hope you understand. I need to read the letters you write and then I'll give them personally to your friends when I see them. Believe me, if you send them in the post, they'd never get them. Home Children don't get mail."

"When will you be here next?"

"In about four months. It takes about four months for me to get around to see everyone. I was very sick last year so that's why you didn't see me, but I can stop by in the morning before I leave for the day if you write your letters tonight. Leave them with Emile. I'm not tackling that driveway to see you two days in a row!"

Tommy laughed and said, "My friends will be so surprised and happy to hear from me."

Rene waited for Tommy to finish milking – Ellie was the last cow to be milked for the day. They walked up to the house and met Emile coming in from the fields. As he was taking off his boots, he invited Rene to stay for supper. While Rene was speaking with Emile, Tommy quickly wrote two letters to his friends. He wrote that he was in good health, working hard, and looked forward to the day when they could all be reunited. He wished them well and hoped they'd be able to write him back, but if they couldn't, that would be okay – he'd understand.

Chapter Twenty One – Ellie and Mae

St. Eloise. Province of Quebec. June 1936

Though the Bouchards had twenty-eight Holstein cows, it was the two Jersey cows Tommy named Ellie and Mae that most fascinated him. He liked their small size, their gentleness, and inquisitive nature. They became his friends in a way and he talked to them while gazing into their big brown eyes as he led them into the milking shed, and again when he was milking them. He pretended they understood every word he said. Nothing was off-limits. He carried on one-sided conversations with them about the weather, and their milk production, and even told them about the Bouchard family's comings and goings.

When Emile informed him that the breed originated in Jersey, one of the Channel Islands located in the English Channel, Tommy was intrigued. Jersey was close to England and in his mind, it was on his way to where he must go one day to find his family. Emile read his mind and said with a broad grin – his English had greatly improved since they first met - "And they tell me the people there speak French, not English. You must go there to see if the cows understand you."

"What! You've been eavesdropping on my conversations with the Jerseys?"

"No," he laughed. "Ellie and Mae told me, but they asked me not to tell you. They said it was their secret."

Tommy grinned. Emile was always kidding him.

Intrigued, Tommy researched Jersey at the Sherbrooke Library and learned that it was the largest of the Channel Islands, located in the Bay of Mont Saint-Michel in the English Channel, twelve miles from Normandy, France, and eighty-seven miles from England. It seldom snowed there and most of the older people spoke a unique French patois. Tommy also learned when he read the agricultural section of the encyclopedia that Jersey's geographical position, coupled with its ban on live cattle imports for more than two hundred years, had made the Jersey cows exceptionally high-quality milk and cream producers which were in high demand by dairy farmers all over the world. Tommy couldn't wait to get back to the cowshed to tell Ellie and Mae about their excellent parentage! He was jealous.

Chapter Twenty Two –
Eddy Marshall

St. Eloise. Province of Quebec.
December 1936

Rene Marceau, the Home Children Supervisor, came to the Bouchard farm three days before Christmas to give Tommy some distressing news. When Tommy came up to the house at noon for lunch, he found Emile and Rene sitting at the kitchen table, laughing, and embroiled in a playful heated discussion in Quebecois about who was the greatest hockey player in Quebec. As soon as he saw Tommy, Rene stopped laughing and a distraught look appeared on his face.

"Hi, Tommy. I have some bad news for you I'm afraid. I've come as fast as I can because you need to know. Eddy Marshall is dead. He died in an accident."

Tommy was stunned and his hands shook. "Eddy's dead? An accident? Dead? When? Where? What kind of accident?"

"I'm so very sorry to have to tell you this, particularly at this time of year, but I felt you needed to know as soon as possible. He died two months ago they said. I last saw him in August, and he was okay, but when I went to see him last Tuesday, they said he'd had an accident and had died."

"What kind of accident?" asked Tommy, his voice trembling.

"I don't know. The farmer wouldn't tell me. He just said he died from wounds he got in an accident."

"That's nonsense Rene and you know it. We need to know more about the circumstances of his death," demanded Tommy.

"I know, I know, and I will. I must write a full report about his death for my bosses, but I hurried over here to tell you as soon as I could. I'll tell Charlie too when I see him next month. Once I've done my report I'll come back and let you know what I found out. Okay?"

Tommy couldn't talk. He nodded his head while his right leg shook, in agitation.

"When I saw him in August, he seemed to be okay with everything at the farm except he said he was having trouble with the farmer's son who was older than him - he'd be about eighteen or nineteen. He said he was being teased about being a Home Child and he asked me to find him another placement. I told him I'd begin looking immediately. I have a hunch the accident has something to do with him, but you can rest assured I'm going to get to the bottom of what happened. I need to know too."

"Poor Eddy. He wasn't a fighter. And he was only fifteen like me" said Tommy, with tears in his eyes. "I can't believe it. I just can't believe he's gone. We said we'd be friends forever."

"I know. I know. I promise I'll find out what happened, but I'm not hopeful I'll find out the whole truth because the farmer wasn't that cooperative. He just said Eddy died in an accident and it didn't matter how he died because he was dead, and no one cares because he was only a Home Child. That's what I'm up against Tommy."

"No one cares? No one cares?" Tommy blurted out through sobs. "I can't believe he said that. I care. Charlie cares. How could he say no one cares and that he was just a Home Child? What does he think we are – chopped liver?"

"I care too, Tommy. And I'll find out what happened from the police. The farmer didn't call them, but I did: the same day last week that I found out. I'll check with them when I get back."

"What happened to his body? Where is it? What did they do with it?"

"The farmer said they buried it on the farm."

"Buried it. Oh my God!" shrieked Tommy.

"What else could they do with it?" asked Rene. "There was no recorded next of kin for them to call. Sad to say Tommy, but that's what happens to most Home Children when they die in service."

Tommy was stunned. "I never knew that. I never thought about it. How horrible?"

"Unfortunately, that's the grim reality I'm afraid," said Rene.

"What will the police do? Will they dig him up to see how he died?"

"You'd think they should, but I doubt they will. The police are not going to spend a lot of time investigating the death of a Home Child who died in a purported accident two months ago. If I can just find out what happened, I'll be satisfied."

Is that what will happen to me if I die? Where would Emile bury me? Should I speak with him about it? thought Tommy.

"Again, let me say how very sorry I am for your loss, Tommy. I saw Charlie in September and I gave him your letter. He works on a chicken farm, and he asked about you. He's doing okay but he's not living in the lap of luxury like you," he said with a little laugh, hoping to inject some levity into the conversation.

Tommy smiled at his remark, relieved that the news about Charlie was good. His creased brow relaxed and the tension in his jaw softened. "So, he's doing okay. That's good. I hope he writes back."

Rene stood up. "I must be on my way. It's a long drive home for me from here." He put on his coat and boots, donned his purple beret, and bid everyone a good afternoon.

Tommy ate his lunch in silence, realizing that although Emile would not have understood every word of his conversation with Rene, he would have understood enough. The compassion Tommy saw in Emile's eyes was comforting. After listening to Rene's account of what Eddy's host family was like, Tommy was even more appreciative of the Bouchards and vowed never to take their friendship for granted.

On Jan 15, Rene returned to the Bouchard farm at noon expecting Tommy to be there on his lunch break. He was.

"Hi, Tommy. How are you? Did you enjoy your time at Christmas?"

"I did. I love spending Christmas on the farm. We had lots to eat and there was music and dancing. How was your Christmas?"

"Quiet but that's how we like it," replied Rene, eager to get down to business.

"Well, I'm sure you know why I'm here. I've come to tell you what I found out about Eddy's death. It's not a lot but it's all I've got and it's probably all I'm going to get."

Tommy sat up straight, moved closer to the edge of the table, and crossed his hands.

"As I suspected, the farmer's son was involved. He admitted to the police that Eddy was arguing with him because Eddy refused to go outside and repair the fences that had fallen in a blizzard. He refused, saying that it was too cold, but the farmer's son pushed him. Eddy pushed back and they got into a fight. In the melee, Eddy fell over and hit his head on the blade of a plow and that's how he died. He said it was an accident and the police believed him and they haven't laid any charges."

"That's it?" said Tommy in total disbelief. "He lost his life because it was too cold to go outside to repair fences! You should have found him a different placement. You knew he was in danger, didn't you?"

"I thought he might be, but I can't help what happened. Maybe if I had visited him sooner and been more aware of the danger he was in, I might have arranged for him to be transferred to another farm, but I didn't. I did try to find him another placement. We have to leave it at that Tommy. There's nothing more I can do."

"That's it? What about where he's buried? Is anybody going to mark his grave and put a cross on it?"

"Who's going to do that?" asked Rene.

"Me. I'm going to do that. I'm going to speak with Emile and see what we can do."

"I hate to say this Tommy, but the farmer won't let you onto his property."

"Well, it's not right. Eddy should be remembered in some way."

"I agree, but putting a cross in a farm field that no one will ever see or even know why it's there doesn't serve any purpose, does it? Better you remember the happy times you had with him so your memory of him, as he was, will stay alive with you forever."

"I guess so. Thanks, Rene. That helps a lot." A smile formed in Tommy's eyes when he recalled running across the deck of the Duchess of Bedford with Eddy, followed by Charlie in fast pursuit.

"Have you seen Charlie lately?"

Rene consulted his diary. "No. I'm not scheduled to see him until March."

Chapter Twenty Three – Charlie Gibson

St. Eloise. Province of Quebec.
February 1937

Charlie Gibson stumbled into the cowshed, supported by an older, taller, and stronger man. It was late morning and Tommy was busy sweeping out the shed. Tommy took a double-take. "My God, is that you Charlie?"

Charlie was limp and emaciated.

"What happened?" asked Tommy, putting an arm around him and with the help of the man, laying him out on a bale of hay, and covering him with two large feed bags and a blanket.

"What happened Charlie?"

Charlie was too weak to speak.

"I found him lying on the floor in the chicken barn this morning and I didn't know what else to do, but to bring him here," said the stranger. "He asked me two weeks ago if I could drive him here and he gave me your address so I could look it up to see how far away it was. Lucky for him he did, because I doubt if he would have lasted the day had I not known to bring him here."

"Thanks. I'm Tommy Jones and you are?"

"I'm Jim Baker. I'm a feed salesman from Ottawa and Charlie is one of my customers."

"Thanks, Jim. You did right to bring him here."

"He's so light and weak. I carried him from the barn to my car and laid him out on the back seat and I didn't hear him stir once in the two and a half hours it took for me to get here. I've been concerned about him for months now, but I figured it was none of my business. I've noticed him deteriorate more lately though. I don't think he's eating enough for all the physical work he does. And I know his boss, Robert Mendez, has whipped him at least once because Charlie told me that's what the bruises on his arm were from."

Many thoughts raced through Tommy's mind. *Should I call an ambulance? Should I take him to the hospital? Should I call the police? Should I call Rene?*

"I don't know what's wrong with him, but I think he needs to see a doctor. There's a lot of TB going around, particularly on chicken farms. Maybe that's what he's got."

Tommy went off and two minutes later returned with a tractor with a bucket. They lifted Charlie up and put him in the bucket on top of the feed bags and blanket. Tommy drove slowly up the light snow-covered driveway to the farmhouse and called out for Emile to come out of the house. Being the biggest and strongest of the three men, Emile picked Charlie up from the bucket, carried him into the house, and laid him down in Tommy's bed. The three men looked down at the emaciated boy and their hearts ached to see a sixteen-year-old boy so emaciated and pale.

"What happened?" asked Emile as Theresa entered the room and covered Charlie with two blankets and a duvet.

"I don't know. I found him like this on the floor in the chicken barn this morning. I'm not surprised to tell you the truth. I've seen it coming, and now I feel I should have done something. I was afraid that if I said something, his boss might switch feed suppliers and I'd get into trouble with my boss. As well, it probably would have made things worse for Charlie."

Theresa went away and returned with a hot towel to put on Charlie's brow and a pot of tea, hopeful that she'd be able to get him to drink.

The men went into the kitchen. Jim said, "I've known Charlie for about two years. He was one of my first customers when I got this feed job and I always look forward to seeing him because he always makes me laugh. I see him once a month. He tells me what type of feed he wants and how much."

"Let's see how he is in a couple of hours and if there's no improvement, we'll call for an ambulance. Are you okay with that Tommy?" suggested Emile. Tommy said he was.

Emile invited Jim to stay for supper, but Jim declined, saying he had a lot of driving to do before he called it a day.

Tommy patted Jim on the back and said, "Thanks for being such a Good Samaritan Jim. I'll tell Charlie what you did because he won't know who saved his life. I'm hoping we can get him back to good health with lots of rest and good food. I bet he'll be twenty pounds heavier by the end of the week with Theresa's cooking. And drop in any time you're in the neighborhood."

"Thanks for the invite but I'm going to pass. The less I know about Charlie the better. His boss will know I was in the barn this morning and he's going to question me. I'll say Charlie was fine when I left him at ten to go see another customer. He probably won't believe me, and he'll check up on me, but I'm going to cover my tracks well when I get back. I have a lot of good friends in the farming community."

Theresa brought Charlie a cup of warm chicken broth and helped him to sit up by placing a large, white, puffy pillow behind his head, and holding the cup up to his lips. He partially opened his eyes, sipped the broth, and nodded his head when Theresa asked him if he'd like more. When she went to the kitchen, Charlie gazed around at his surroundings, wondering where he was and who the lady was. Theresa returned with another cup of warm broth and a cup of her hearty vegetable soup, which Charlie consumed one after the other without pausing. With each cup, Charlie became more alert and stronger.

Meanwhile, in the kitchen, Emile and Tommy were debating what to do. They agreed to wait and see how Charlie was in the morning and to go from there. Emile raised an interesting question: *Should they tell Rene? What would he do? Would he take Charlie back to the Mendez farm or would he find him another placement? What if there was no other placement available? Would that be better than the Mendez farm or are most of the placements like that? And how would all those options pan out for Charlie in the long term?*

Tommy said, "Jim told me that Charlie was planning on running away two months ago when he last saw him. Things must have gotten worse. He can't go back there, that's for sure."

Emile agreed. "Leave it with me and I'll see if I can figure something out."

⌒

Charlie slept soundly for the balance of the day and night in Tommy's warm and comfortable bed with its puffy pillows, thick, woolen blankets, and duvet. Tommy slept on the sofa in the living room.

"How are you feeling Charlie?" said Tommy, drawing the bedroom drapes and letting in the morning light. Charlie stirred, peered at him over the bedsheets, and smiled. He was still severely emaciated and disoriented, but, nourished by Theresa's broth and soups, his color had returned to his cheeks.

"Good morning, Charlie. Good to see you. I bet you're surprised to see me?"

Charlie rubbed his eyes.

"No. You're not dreaming Charlie. You're at my farm: the Bouchard Dairy Farm. Your friend, Jim, the feed salesman, brought you here."

Charlie stared at him and the room.

"Jim found you unconscious in the chicken barn yesterday and drove you here."

Charlie closed his eyes and smiled, enjoying the plush comfort of Tommy's bed.

"Do you know what happened, Charlie? Do you remember anything?"

"All I remember is feeling weak and dizzy when I was sweeping the floor. I must have passed out. I'm so sorry for all the trouble I'm putting you to." He slowly pushed the covers down off his chest and eased himself up onto the pillow. He looked around at Tommy and the room.

"Jim said you were planning to run away. Why?"

"You've no idea Tommy how bad it was. I never complained before about the work, the food, or the abuse, but I'd reached a point where I couldn't take it anymore. Can you believe I've been sleeping on straw bales in an unheated chicken barn for the last three years and all they've been giving me to eat is stale bread and watery chicken soup? A month ago, I told my boss I wasn't going to take it anymore. I told him I needed better food and I told him that if he tried to whip me again, I'd fight him."

"He whipped you?"

"Yes. With his belt."

"And all you got to eat was stale bread and soup?' How did you manage to stick it out for three years?"

"What else could I do? I had no options. I asked to be moved but that didn't happen. That's why I decided to run away and come here. I thought you might be able to help me."

"What happened when you told him you'd run away if you didn't get better food?"

"He got drunk and came into the barn when I was sleeping. He staggered around calling me a good for nothing Home Boy and slashed at my arms and legs with a stick of wood. I couldn't walk or work properly for days afterward."

"I'm so sorry, Charlie. Well, rest assured you're not going back there. Your days are done there like a dog's dinner. You need lots of rest and lots of Theresa's good food to get you strong. You can stay in my room for as long as you want. Emile and I will figure something out."

"But I can't stay here. What am I going to do Tommy? I want to go back to England."

"Don't worry about anything. Emile and I will figure something out. Get up when you feel you've had enough sleep and go back to bed whenever you feel tired. Okay? Theresa will bring you some food. I'm going to get some breakfast and go to work. I'll see you at noon if you're up."

Emile asked his many friends, relatives, and neighbors if they knew of anyone who could use the services of a strong, industrious, sixteen-year-old British boy with three years of farm experience and landed immigrant status. But unemployment was high across Canada and in Quebec at the time and if a position became available for a general laborer or farmhand, Emile knew the likelihood of it going to a Home Child was very slim.

Emile told his cousin, Robert Trudel, who owned a grocery store in Sherbrooke, about Charlie's horrific three-year ordeal at the Mendez chicken farm and that he was desperate to find him a job that was safe and healthy. If he could put something together, Emile offered to contribute financially to make it work

"Bring him in and we'll see. Syd's been my helper for over thirty years, but he's getting on, and I've been meaning to get him some help with the heavier work. I want to help your boy because I know what he must have gone through and how difficult it is for a Home Child, particularly in Quebec. He'd be working in the back mostly with the heavy lifting – unloading boxes from trucks, opening and sorting and disposing of the garbage, and at night, he'd be stocking shelves, pricing products, that sort of thing. Is he any good with numbers? If he is, I have other jobs for him."

"Thanks, Robert. I knew I could count on you to come through. Poor kid's had it rough since he came to Canada."

～

After ten days of good rest and Theresa's solid food, Charlie was feeling stronger in mind, body, and spirit, and eager to be interviewed by Mr. Trudel for the stock boy job.

A week later, Robert hired him on the spot and paid him the going rate. It was enough for Charlie to pay for room and board in a rooming house nearby, and to have some spending money left over.

Emile and Tommy knew that sooner or later Rene would show up at the farm to tell them that Charlie Gibson had run away. They decided that their best strategy was not to say anything about seeing Charlie, though they knew that would be awkward and uncomfortable. An unfortunate lie seemed necessary to protect Charlie.

On Jan 8, 1938, Rene showed up at the Bouchard farm to tell Tommy that Charlie Gibson had run away from his job at the chicken farm.

"I wasn't surprised. I expected something like that would happen. For months now, I've been looking to find him another position, but nothing's opened up. There are no jobs anywhere. Between you and me, Tommy, Charlie is better off out of there. Mr. Mendez is a cruel man. I only hope that wherever Charlie is, he's in a much better situation than he was."

"So, what happens now? Are the police looking for him?"

"No. They don't care. But he's going to have a difficult time just surviving and getting by every day. He'll probably do odd jobs here and there for people who don't ask questions. I just hope he's strong enough and lucky enough to survive. Many runaways don't — they starve to death, or they die of hypothermia or are murdered, or commit suicide out of loneliness and desperation."

"That's terrible. So that's it? You just cross Charlie off your list as if he never existed?"

"I see why you feel that way, but what else can I do?" asked Rene.

"So, if Charlie shows up here what do I do?"

"The best you can. That's all I can say."

"I'm glad you've been honest with me about everything, Rene, and thanks for coming to tell me," said Tommy, getting up from the table to go back to work.

Chapter Twenty Four – Josie

St. Eloise, Province of Quebec.
July 1938

Tommy had always got by without feeling much emotion about anything or anybody, except for the distinct but distant memory of the warm feelings he had for Sister Celia at St. Chads. He'd learned from a very early age to distance himself from situations and not to get emotionally involved in anything more than was necessary. That all changed when he arrived at the Bouchards. He noticed the affection and love openly shown by family members towards each other, and it intrigued him. Never had he seen people kiss and hug and comfort each other as much as the Bouchards did. Their sincere warmth, compassion, and empathy for each other resonated deeply with him, making him feel joyful, alive, and envious.

Though the Bouchards treated him as one of the family, he knew he wasn't and never would be. Emile wasn't his dad, Theresa wasn't his mother, and neither were Marc and Chantelle his siblings. *Who is my mother? Who is my dad? Do I have any siblings? Where are they?* For the first time in his life, he began to feel strongly that he didn't belong anywhere. *Why don't I have a real family? What happened to them?* As he mulled over these questions, an intense desire to find answers arose in his heart.

One day, Tommy asked Emile if he could use some of his savings to buy a typewriter.

"A typewriter! Whatever for? I've never heard of a farm boy wanting a typewriter. Who are you going to type letters to? Ellie and Mae? The next thing you'll be asking for will be glasses for them to read," Emile said, laughing heartily and slapping his sides.

On his next visit to Sherbrooke, Emile took Tommy with him. They went into an office supply store and ordered the Smith-Corona folding typewriter that the clerk recommended, as well as four spools of typewriter ribbons and three packs of paper.

Next, they stopped at Trudel's Grocery store to see Charlie. Charlie and Tommy walked down the street to a cafe to catch up on what had happened since they last saw each other while Emile and Robert chatted at a counter in the store.

On the way home, Tommy and Emile compared notes. "Robert's very pleased with Charlie. He's turned out better than he expected," said Emile.

"And Charlie is pleased as punch with his whole situation. He loves his job, Robert, Syd, and his pay, and he's made some friends at the guesthouse, and he does things with them. I'm so happy for him."

It took three weeks for the typewriter to arrive. "Not bad, given the times," was what the store clerk said when Emile picked it up. The typewriter subsequently became Tommy's most treasured possession.

Tommy spent all of his spare time over the next two weeks typing up his hand-written notes and took great satisfaction in stacking his typing up in neat piles and discarding his rough notes.

Curious as to what the new clickety-clack sound was in the house, Marc knocked on Tommy's door and asked him what he was doing.

"How do you like my typewriter?"

"I've never seen one. Type something. Show me how it works?"

Tommy sat upright in his chair, raised his arms in preparation to type, and looked at the handwritten note he was going to type. He selected the key with the letter H on it and hit it with his index finger. He sat back and marveled at the clean letter H in black ink printed on the page. Marc leaned in to take a closer look and smiled at the magic.

"It takes a little getting used to, but I'm getting faster at it," Tommy proudly said.

"What are you typing," asked Marc continuing to stare at the H on the page.

Not wanting to be specific, Tommy said, "Oh. All sorts of stuff"

"Must be big stuff with all the typing you do," Marc teased, looking at the stack of typed pages sitting to the right of the typewriter. Tommy just grinned.

Four years had passed since Tommy first arrived at the Bouchards and he was thriving. The fresh air, hard physical labor, and love from the Bouchards made him feel strong and alive. He was quick to laugh and joke and he never took himself seriously.

One evening, while milking the cows, Chantelle came to the cowshed with Josie, her best friend from school, and introduced her to Tommy. Josie was also seventeen, the same age as Tommy, and she spoke a little English. It was awkward at first because this was a new experience for him – he was shy and didn't know what to say to a girl. Josie didn't know what to say either. To her, Tommy was a foreigner, yet she was drawn to something mysterious in this French-speaking Englishman with curly red hair, freckles, and twinkling green eyes. She also admired his tanned, athletic build and his Cheshire-cat smile. She wanted to know him better.

Tommy was experiencing a strong reaction to being in her company. His hormones were kicking in and he felt jittery and awkward. Her beautiful long, black, silky hair spilling over her slender shoulders and onto her full and firm breasts left him breathless. He looked closer at her face, at her long black eyelashes, and the sparkle in her sultry, coal-black eyes, and was smitten. Noticing his sudden keen interest in her made Josie embarrassed and uncomfortable, and she abruptly got up, excused herself, and left, only to immediately regret leaving.

For the rest of the evening, they each thought about one another and excitedly looked forward to the next night when they hoped they'd see each other again.

The following evening, Josie showed up at the cowshed looking even more alluring. Her makeup was a little more vibrant and her red blouse was a little tighter. Tommy too looked more dapper and sharper. He'd showered and shaved before he milked the cows, and he wore his best clean shirt.

Chantelle had previously cautioned Josie about asking Tommy any questions about his parentage, instead, she asked the typical questions people ask on first dates when they want to get to know someone better.

"Where are you from?" she inquired in broken English making Tommy chuckle.

"I'm from England, but believe it or not, I prefer to speak French if you don't mind. I haven't spoken English in such a long time, but if you want to practice your English, go ahead."

Josie returned his smile, and they went ahead and conversed in French. He answered her questions freely and honestly with just a few mispronunciations, resulting in funny grins from her.

"I've gotta be honest with you Josie. I don't know anything about my family so I can't tell you what you probably want to know."

Stuck for something to say, he began to tell her what he could remember of St. Chads. Josie's eyes lit up and her keen interest prompted him to continue.

"We slept in dormitories in beds with stinky straw mattresses, just a few feet apart, and we had to use numbers instead of names. I was Boy 14, and we couldn't talk, or else we'd get caned."

He stopped abruptly when he realized how appalled Josie became with these revelations. Her eyes narrowed reflecting the hurt she was feeling, for him and for the other children in St. Chads. He changed the topic by talking about Ellie and Mae and his work at the farm, and then he asked her what she wanted to do in life.

"I'm going to be a veterinarian. That's all I've ever wanted to be — ever since I was a little girl. What do you want to be?"

Tommy had to think about this question. Nothing came immediately to mind. He didn't know where he'd be, let alone what he'd be doing in one year when his contract with the Bouchards was up. He had thought about it often, but nothing definitive ever took root.

"Umh, let's see. Maybe a writer."

"A writer!" Josie's eyes opened wide, and she leaned back on the haystack and kicked her feet in the air. His answer surprised her.

"A writer! Of what?"

"Stories. I like to write stories. I'm going to be a famous writer one day," he quipped raising his eyebrows and grinning.

His response reinforced Josie's opinion of him as a strange and mysterious young man, but at the same time, she felt herself being drawn closer to him.

Tommy loved the way she smiled and the way her lips parted, so slightly, when she was listening, and the way she laid her folded hands on her lap and crossed her thumbs. He loved everything about her. She was the most beautiful and alluring female he'd ever encountered in his whole life, and he wanted to be with her forever.

When she answered his questions about her life, he listened attentively and earnestly, committing every morsel of information to memory. Tommy was in another world with his French Quebecois angel and Josie felt the same way about him. Had Chantelle not returned and called them to supper, they might never have come back down to Earth.

Josie came to the cowshed most nights after supper and homework and waited patiently for Tommy to finish his chores. It didn't take long for their relationship to blossom into something special. It was the first love for both. They delighted in each other's company and bathed in each other's glow and warmth.

Tommy regretted not knowing about his family as Josie so wanted to know more about him. When he confided in her, she listened compassionately. He wondered out loud about who his mum and dad were, and if he had any brothers or sisters, or other relatives. He questioned what the circumstances were resulting in him being an orphan, and sometimes, he even doubted if his name was Tommy Jones. Maybe someone just dreamed it up and assigned it to him. Josie laughed. He confessed he didn't really know who he was, and sometimes, he even doubted if he was seventeen – he felt much older, but he didn't have a birth certificate to prove it

"I just advance my age by one year every January" informed Tommy.

Josie laughed. "You don't have a birth certificate? Everyone has one. I can't believe you don't have one."

"No. Most of us at St. Chads didn't."

"So, you've never had a birthday party?"

"No."

"The Bouchards have never had a birthday party for you?"

"No, but I never mentioned it to them. It's no big deal, Josie. I've never celebrated my birthday because I don't have one."

"That's terrible. Everybody is entitled to celebrate their birthday once a year."

Tommy agreed. "Okay. I'll fix that right now."

"How?"

"I'm going to pick June 9 as my birthday: the day I left England to start a new life in Canada."

Josie was amazed. "Can you do that?"

"Why not? Who's to say I can't."

They laughed and went up to the house to announce the good news. The family thought it was hilarious that Tommy now had a birth date while he didn't have one an hour earlier. They regretted not having ever inquired about his birthday but promised to have a big party for him when he turned eighteen next June. He was thrilled. Secretly, he'd always wanted to have a birthday party like Marc and Chantelle, with cake and candles and presents.

When friends and relatives came to the house, Tommy usually came out of his room to socialize with them. He was now fluently bilingual and able to hold his own in any conversation, and after four years at the farm, neighbors no longer regarded him as a Home Boy. They thought of him as a Bouchard: a quiet young man with a happy disposition who liked the farm life.

Tommy was a pragmatist. He accepted, non-judgmentally, every situation that he found himself in and every event that had happened in his life as part of his life journey. He didn't feel shame or regret for being a Home Child in the same way as most other Home children did. This was mostly because Josie, the Bouchards, and the community accepted him for who he was.

～

Though short on schooling, Tommy was mature beyond his years in other ways. He was a handsome, well-muscled, strong youth with a personal resume full of practical skills and achievements that any young man his age would die for. While most seventeen-year-old boys were struggling with transitioning from school to work, Tommy already had four years of work experience under his belt and the abilities, common sense, and strength that came with that experience. He also enjoyed nature in a way few boys his age would ever experience. He lived mindfully in the moment, noticing the changing colors of the sky and how the temperature dropped as clouds moved past the sun, and the meaning of the different moos of the cows in the fields. Nature energized him, the love in the Bouchard family nurtured him, and Josie inspired him. She was the icing on his cake of joy. He composed and typed love poems for her, all set in nature, which she promised to treasure forever.

Chantelle got a brownie camera for her birthday and asked Marc to take two photographs of her and Tommy. One was with Ellie and Mae: the Jerseys were in between them with their heads down munching on grass. The other photo was a headshot of the three of them. Chantelle also took a headshot of Josie and Tommy, and a neighbor took a group photograph of the whole Bouchard family assembled on the front steps of the farmhouse with Tommy front and center.

Life for Tommy was idyllic, but he knew that nothing lasts forever. As he approached his eighteenth year, he began to think about what he would do when his contract ended in June. The family noticed a change in his demeanor, particularly at mealtimes, and were concerned.

"Yes. I know I've been preoccupied lately and I'm sorry. I just don't know what I'm going to do when my contract is up. That's all. It's nothing you've done or anything you can help me with. I just must sort it out myself. It's a big decision."

"Well, Tommy. If we can help you in any way just ask," Emile offered.

Tommy and Josie had discussed their future many times. Now he was bringing the subject up every time they met. He was eager to get married, settle down and start a family, but Josie, on the other hand, was set on following her childhood dream of becoming an animal doctor. She was unwavering in her decision to go to the veterinary college in Montreal next year after graduation.

Tommy was becoming more amorous and physical every time they met and although Josie enjoyed the increased physical intensity of his enthusiastic embraces, she resisted his advances because she was a Catholic and believed pre-marital sex was a sin. Her fear of going too far began to sour their relationship and, where it had once been light and carefree, it was now heavy and problematic.

"Everything would be perfect if we just got married," beseeched Tommy, but Josie wasn't ready to settle down.

It was quite a dilemma. There was no doubt that they loved each other and wanted to be together, but Josie was smart enough to foresee the problems on the horizon if Tommy was to go with her to Montreal. He was concerned too in his own way. What would he do in Montreal? He only had a Grade Five education and five years of dairy farm experience and the only document he had to prove anything was his 'To Whom It May Concern letter' from St. Chads. There was another aspect of grave concern to him and that was the discrimination in the city against his type. When he went into Sherbrooke on errands for Emile, he noticed many job vacancies in shop windows now included the wording, HOME CHILDREN NEED NOT APPLY in large, bold capital letters on the bottom of the advert.

He also acknowledged to himself privately that he felt uneasy about living in Quebec long-term because he wasn't French. His past and family were in England, where he belonged, and where he should probably go next.

Josie was mature beyond her years and better able to think more rationally than Tommy about their situation. She knew he was obsessed with her and was closed-minded about seriously considering other options.

"You should go find your family Tommy because you'll never know who you really are until you do. You should do it now while you're still young and free. Then you can come back and tell me all about yourself. We'll get married, settle down, and have lots of children. I'll be a vet by then and we can have a great life together," she said, hugging him tightly.

Tommy knew in his gut she was right, but he wanted to think more about it. Later that evening, when he was milking Ellie and Mae, he told them what Josie had said and he shared with them his concern about being a Home Child in Quebec. He came away from the cowshed convinced his bovine friends agreed with him. He should just go to England to try to find his roots, once and for all, and get it over with.

In May 1939, one month before his self-ascribed eighteenth birthday, Tommy announced to the Bouchards after supper one night that he would be going to England soon to search for his family. They weren't greatly surprised because he'd spoken on many occasions about his desire to go there one day.

Despite his outwardly happy disposition, Tommy's heart was heavy and aching. The thought that he would soon be leaving the Bouchards, the only family he'd ever known and loved, and Josie, the love of his life, was sometimes too much for him to bear. He cried most days – he couldn't help it. He felt weepy all the time. When he least expected it, sadness consumed him, and the tears would flow. He struggled to control his emotions and secretly wished he was leaving immediately for England.

He booked a berth on the Empress of Britain sailing from Quebec City to Southampton on May 28, two weeks after his contract ended and twelve days before his self-declared birthday. The timing was unfortunate, but he was so eager to leave he didn't want to wait around for a later sailing.

Now that he had a sailing date confirmed, he went into Sherbrooke with Emile and withdrew his savings.

"Here Tommy. This is all yours," Emile said, handing over a thick stash of banknotes secured by elastic bands.

Tommy's jaw dropped. "It's all mine. I don't believe it. How's that possible?"

"It is and it's none of your concern how it got to be so much," said Emile, smiling broadly and proudly. "Consider it my gift to you for being such a good role model for my children. They've learned so much from you."

Tommy hugged Emile tightly, saying "Thank you, thank you, thank you."

❧

Tommy bought a brown leather suitcase and a completely new wardrobe for his journey, consisting of a pair of brown leather Oxford shoes, two long-sleeve white shirts, a pair of grey flannel pants, a tie, two pairs of grey cotton socks, and a warm windjammer coat. He had considered asking Josie to go with him to help pick out the clothes, but he decided against it. Intuitively, he knew it would be too upsetting for both of them.

He gave his trunk to Marc and asked him to look after his typed notes until he was settled.

"I'll keep them in the trunk where they'll be safe and dry until you ask for them," said Marc with a grin.

"I don't know where I'm going to end up or how long it will be before I'm settled, but I'll write and let you know."

❧

The Bouchards organized a joint early birthday party and farewell celebration for Tommy and invited everyone who knew him, including Robert Trudel and Charlie. They also invited Rene, knowing full well that Charlie's presence at the gathering would raise a lot of questions, which it did.

Charlie seized the bull by the horns by approaching Rene first and asking him how he was?

Rene blinked and stared. "Surely, that's not you Charlie? Tell me it isn't you?"

"It is and I'm doing great," replied Charlie.

"My God, man. I thought you were dead. You're looking well, Charlie. Where have you been?"

Before Charlie had a chance to answer, Emile interrupted and said, "They need you over there Charlie for photographs," and turning to Rene, he said, "Let's get together after Tommy leaves. Charlie and I will tell you all about what happened."

Rene was still shaking his head and repeating to himself: *I don't believe it. I don't believe it. Charlie Gibson is alive and well. I don't believe it.*

It was a grand gathering of about sixty people and a fun time was had by all with food, cake, and presents. Mindful of Tommy's plans to travel light, Emile had asked his guests to gift money instead of stuff. Tommy appreciated this practical and generous gesture to boost his savings.

After supper, a fiddler and an accordion player belted out square dance music for two hours. Everyone, who was fit and able, got up and danced. Josie spent the evening in Tommy's arms on the dance floor, being twirled here, there, and hither, and Charlie had a wonderful time in the arms of Chantelle. They would all remember this night as the most enjoyable night of their lives.

Chantelle had extra copies printed of the photographs she had taken and gave them to Tommy as her parting gift.

Josie and the Bouchard family went to the train station in Sherbrooke to see Tommy off, and Charlie and Rene joined them.

Not knowing for sure where he was going, Tommy only took two pieces of luggage with him because he wanted to travel as lightly as possible. He had his brown leather suitcase filled with clothes and toiletries, his postcard of the C.P.S. Duchess of Bedford, the photos from Chantelle as well as a pack of copy paper and a spool of typewriter ribbon. His second piece of luggage was his typewriter and case.

It was agonizing for Tommy to say goodbye. He could not compose himself. Josie was strong and she let him go without much fuss. They hugged one last time on the station platform, promised to write to one another every week, and then Tommy boarded the train.

As the train slowly chugged out of the station, Tommy waved goodbye through an open carriage window with the white cotton handkerchief Theresa gave him to wipe away his tears.

Chapter Twenty Five – Tommy goes to Jersey

Quebec City, Province of Quebec
1939

In Quebec City, Tommy boarded the Canadian Pacific Steamship, the Empress of Britain, for the week-long sailing to Southampton, England. As he stepped off the gangplank onto the deck, a steward gave him a postcard of the ship. Remembering the other postcard he had in his suitcase, Tommy smiled, put it in his inside pocket, and went ahead strolling around the deck, familiarizing himself with what would be his quarters for the next seven days.

As he explored further afield, nodding with a friendly smile to the other passengers, he thought about how different his circumstances were now compared with five years ago. He particularly appreciated the relative luxury of his cabin.

As he put away his clothes in the dresser drawers, the ship's horn blasted, indicating it was getting ready to sail. Exciting anticipation, triggered by a memory, coursed through Tommy's brain. He raced upstairs and across the deck to the bow where he watched and listened as the ship's engines fully engaged and roared, moving the ship slowly away from the dock. A tugboat appeared and pulled the ship up the St. Lawrence River towards the estuary of the Atlantic Ocean, where it released its ties, and the big ship gained speed, its bow slowly rising and falling and crashing through the oncoming waves. Tommy stared straight ahead, letting the cold breeze slap his face and the cool air take his breath away. Memories of Eddy and Charlie surfaced in his mind, threatening to dampen his spirits, but he intentionally vanquished them by wondering what was on the menu for supper.

He stayed at the bow for a long-time, noting other feelings that were now involuntarily coming and going in his heart and mind. One moment he was sad with memories of Josie and the Bouchards, and the next he was fired up with the prospects of finding his family in England.

As the days passed and the boat sailed eastward, he sensed he was moving forward with his life: leaving behind Canada and the past and heading for England and his future. There was no leaving Josie behind though: she was always with him in his heart and mind. He was determined to take her with him on all his adventures until he returned to Canada and married her. Every night after supper, he went to his cabin and typed her a letter about his day: who he'd met, what he'd seen and what he'd ate. When he felt in the mood, he continued writing and composed more chapters about his life. As he reflected on his days at St. Chads, his voyage to Canada, and his sojourn with the Bouchards, he realized he was now free from obligations for the first time in his life and living his dream.

With each new dawn, Tommy's outlook brightened, and his perspective shifted.

After three days at sea, he began to earnestly think about how he was going to find his family. His priority was to find a job. He had enough savings to cover at least half a year of living expenses, he guessed, but he had no idea how long it would take to find his family. *What if it takes longer and I can't find a job?* After much thought, he concluded that his best bet was to go to Jersey and using Emile's glowing testimonial letter about his abilities and his knowledge of cows, find a position on a dairy farm. And then, when he had saved up enough, go to England to the address in Swanson, Kent as shown on his 'To Whom it May Concern' letter and start his search there.

THE SOLDIER AND THE ORPHAN – SEPARATED BY CHURCH AND WAR

By the time the boat docked at Southampton, Tommy's happy and carefree disposition was well entrenched in his psyche. He felt great, but he did have some questions about what would happen at the Customs shed because he didn't have a passport, a birth certificate, or any other identifying paperwork other than the 'To Whom It May Concern letter' and Emile's testimonial. What would he do if they wouldn't allow him to enter the country?

As it turned out, he got a sympathetic immigration officer – a grandmotherly type who listened attentively to his story about being a Home Child who was sent to Canada at the age of thirteen to work on a farm. When he told her that he intended to go to Jersey and find a job, she thought for a moment, and, empathizing with his dilemma, said, with a wink, "So you won't be staying in England if I let you through?" A grin spread across Tommy's face and his eyes twinkled.

She helped him fill out the forms, stamped them, and with another wink, handed them back, saying, "You'll need to show these if you come back to England."

"Thank you so very much for all of your help," said a greatly indebted Tommy. He was now on a high and feeling invincible, convinced that what Josie said about him was true. *You've got horseshoes up your bum Tommy.*

Swinging his cases merrily by his side, he marched confidently through the dock area and sought out the booking office for the Mail Boat steamers to the Channel Islands. He bought a one-way ticket on the Isle of Sark to St. Helier. Three hours later, he was leaning on the rail watching the Isle of Wight pass by as his boat steamed down the Solent.

When he alighted in St Helier, he was surprised to note that everyone seemed to be shorter than him and he was no giant at five foot nine. He chuckled when his imagination caught fire and remembered the story about Gulliver landing in Liliput.

He rented a room at the Royal Arms hotel and bought the Evening News to look for jobs. Nothing interested him. He asked fellow guests at the hotel and random people he met on the street if they knew of anyone looking to hire, but no one knew of anyone.

Three days later, just as he was beginning to lose hope and doubt himself, he got a lead from a fisherman at the pier mending his nets, who said his brother-in-law might have something of interest. How lucky was that? His faith was instantly restored. But then again, he wasn't surprised because he had horseshoes up his bum, did he not? The old salt with no teeth and only little wisps of hair scribbled his brother-in-law's name and address on the inside of a cigarette packet. "Good luck and tell him Wilfred sent you. Tell him I'll come by for a visit soon?"

The Therin family lived in St. Brelades parish on the southwest corner of the Island, a relatively short bus ride from St. Helier. Tommy was learning fast that nothing was too far away for Jersey was a small island.

The following morning, as he brushed his teeth, combed his hair, and smiled at himself in the mirror, he got a déjà vu feeling that this was going to be a great day. He'd had that same feeling many times in his life and he'd never been disappointed with the outcomes.

With Emile's testimonial in hand and his strange Quebecois accent, eighteen-year-old Tommy set off early the next morning to get the bus to take him to St. Brelades and wanted to get there before Mr. Therin went to work.

The bus driver signaled for him to get off at a church. He then asked a person on the road for directions to Les Petite Vaches de Brelades, the Therin farm.

Tommy knocked on the door and while waiting for someone to answer, looked around at the environs, imagined he worked there and liked what he saw.

When Frank Therin opened the door and saw a heavily freckled, red-haired young man standing in the doorway, he smiled and was curious. And when the young man spoke in a French Quebecois accent and told him that Wilfred had sent him and that he would visit soon, his smile turned into a heavy laugh.

Frank invited him into the parlor where they got down to business. Tommy showed him the testimonial letter and that seemed to be all he needed to make a decision. After a brief exchange of other ancillary information, such as wages, duties, accommodations, and the answer to the question, where on earth did you get that crazy accent? Frank gave Tommy the job.

"Thank you, Mr. Therin, you won't be disappointed."

"Just call us Frank and Elsie, Tommy. No need for formal titles around here."

Frank, Elsie, and their son, Terence, ran a dairy farm that had been in the Therin family for many generations. They had two bulls, twenty-four Jersey milking cows, three goats, two pigs, and a dozen chickens.

Terry was three years older than Tommy and had been accepted by Cambridge University in England to further his studies to become a doctor and would be leaving shortly for England. Frank was at his wit's end not knowing how he would cope when his son was no longer available to help with the chores. He'd been looking to hire someone for over a month, but no one had applied. The island had a severe farm labor shortage since it was harvest season for potatoes and other field crops. Tommy was the answer to Frank's prayers – another one of those serendipitous happenings that seemed to benefit both parties.

There was a bunkhouse on the farm for Tommy to live in – a separate, self-contained brick structure with a small bedroom, a living room with a desk and chair, and a small kitchen. The outhouse was set back thirty feet from the main house. This was more than adequate for Tommy had learned how to live minimally years ago when he was at St. Chads. He was comfortable with not having much of anything and rather enjoyed the feeling of being light and unencumbered.

He took pride in his typed letters to Josie and fretted that one day his supply of ribbons and paper would run out and then he'd have to handwrite his letters. Though the quality of his handwriting had been exceptional when he was thirteen, it was now poor, and it embarrassed him. He'd not had cause to handwrite much in the last five years and the physical laboring of milking cows and doing other farm chores had thickened and calloused his hands. The thought of Josie struggling to read his chicken scratch was most upsetting and he hoped she'd never have to do that.

Frank was unsure if Tommy could get replacement ribbons for his typewriter on the island and suggested that he might have to find someone going to England to buy them for him there.

Tommy sat on his bed, opened his typewriter case, and lifted it out. Lying on the bottom of the case was a sealed manila envelope addressed to him. He picked it up, turned it over, and wondered who was it from? Josie? Marc? The letter was from Emile.

'Dear Tommy,

I just wanted you to know how much we all appreciated having you with us these past five years. You've been like a son to us and a good brother to Marc and Chantelle. Rest assured, we will remember you forever!

I'm sure Josie will keep us abreast of your adventures. Know that you are always welcome here, and if we can ever be of help, just ask. We look forward to the day we see you again.

We understand what you must do and wish you the very best of luck in your search for your family.

With all our love and best wishes,
Emile Bouchard.'

Tommy's heart warmed with an abundance of joy and appreciation for the Bouchards, for his time in Canada, and for Josie.

Terry went to England to continue his studies and Tommy began his employment as the herdsman of the dairy farm. But more than that, he helped fill the void for the Therins. Their only child was gone, but

Tommy, their surrogate son, was here, performing all the tasks formerly done by Terry, with a willing and happy heart.

Tommy went with Frank on his early morning rabbit-hunting escapades with the dogs: Bear, an older, big, black overweight mutt, and Rex, a young, short-haired, black, and white terrier. The dogs took to Tommy at once, as did all animals. Every morning, just before dawn, Frank and Tommy walked along the grassy commons bordering the beach, while the dogs sniffed for rabbits in the gorse. Occasionally, one would dart out from the underbrush. Frank would aim his gun, and when he got lucky, they'd have rabbit stew for dinner, but most of the time the rabbit got away. "I'll get you next time," Frank vowed, putting the gun back over his shoulder.

Tommy settled in quickly and greatly impressed everyone with his expert skills in milking cows and in sterilizing the dairy equipment and the premises. His knowledge of cows, together with his practical skills in the repair and maintenance of farm equipment, buildings, and structures, was second to none. Whether it was electrical, plumbing, or carpentry work that was needed, Tommy seemed capable of doing it all.

Word spread throughout the parishes about this strange, funny-speaking man, who lived at Les Petite Vaches de Brelades. Rumour had it that he could do anything and everything on a farm. Other farmers hired him on his time off and invited him to their homes for meals and social times. Tommy laughed at their French patois manner of speaking because it was as strange to his ears as his Quebecois accent was to theirs.

Tommy thrived on the diversity of jobs that came his way. His favorite task was driving Mr. Vautier's tractor to the beach to rake up vraic, a type of seaweed. Mr. Vautier grew Jersey Royal potatoes and fertilized his crops with vraic, giving them a distinctive flavor that everyone, at home and abroad, enjoyed.

Tommy continued his habit of speaking to the cows while milking them and was soon as at home on the Therin farm as he was at the

Bouchards. He told his bovine friends about their cousins, Ellie, and Mae, in Canada, and about how much he loved and missed Josie.

~

Towards the end of 1939, a grave concern spread throughout England and the Channel Islands. Would Germany invade the islands, and if so, when? This was the big question on everyone's mind and the topic around every dinner table. In the past six months, so many young men had left Jersey to go to England to enlist that the labor shortage on the island was now severe. Tommy worked long days and weekends, helping wherever he could, and he made a lot of money, far more than he ever dreamed possible, and by December, he estimated he had enough savings to cover a whole year of living expenses. He planned to go to England in July after most of the field crops on the island had been harvested to search for his family.

By the New Year and with each passing month, the news from Europe about the possibility of a German invasion of the Channel Islands became direr and the talk around dinner tables intensified about the need for civilians to evacuate from the islands before the Germans came.

Tommy and Josie had exchanged letters weekly since he first arrived in Jersey and in March 1940, he wrote to her about the situation developing in Jersey and that he intended to go to England in July. On June 18th he wrote to her again and asked her not to write until she received a letter from him postmarked in England. This proved to be his last correspondence with her for five years.

On June 20, 1940, two days after he mailed his letter and ten days before German troops arrived, the evacuation of Jersey began in earnest. The British government sent boats giving everyone the option to leave. In Jersey, slightly more than ten percent of the population left. Tommy decided to evacuate, but he waited too long. The boat he awaited never arrived. German gunboats in the English Channel turned it back.

Initially, Tommy wasn't overly concerned – he never was. The British government had declared the Channel Islands to be open islands with no armed forces on them, and no one expected there would be any fighting. The common understanding was that Germany would first build coastal defenses on the islands and then invade the United Kingdom.

Chapter Twenty Six –
The German Occupation

St. Brelades, Jersey.
1940

On June 30, 1940, the Germans began their invasion of the Channel Islands. They immediately set about issuing proclamations imposing new laws on the residents. Mostly, the new laws were inconvenient, and at first glance, it seemed that the Germans were allowing everyone to get on with their lives as if they weren't there. The island government adopted the same approach. Live and let live seemed to be the order of the day, however, it wasn't long before additional laws with more onerous restrictions were enacted, and little by little, the lives of the Therin family were increasingly affected. They could no longer go rabbit hunting or fishing because the Germans confiscated their guns and boats; they couldn't get any news about the outside world because radios were banned; they were denied access to the beach; and they had to abide by a nine o'clock curfew every night.

Hitler decreed in 1941 that the Channel Islands would be made into an impregnable fortress and between 1940 and 1945 more than 16,000 slave workers were brought in to construct coastal fortifications, roads, tunnels, and bunkers in preparation for their planned invasion of the United Kingdom. Eventually, 49,000 Germans were stationed in Jersey.

Tommy and Frank continued their early morning walks with the dogs and saw the huge cement mixers on the beach being operated continuously throughout the day. They were gravely concerned about the health of the slave workers who pushed and pulled oversized wheelbarrows, sloshing over with heavy cement, across the sand in the summer heat. They went back and forth for twelve hours a day until they dropped. They were weak, their bones protruded out of their chests, and their eyes were popping out of their sockets. If this wasn't bad enough, at the end of the day they were frog-marched back to camp. The sight of this brutality sickened them, but they were helpless to do anything about it. If they were to intervene, they'd be arrested and sent to an internment camp in Germany.

One day on their morning walk, they saw a worker collapse in front of a cement mixer. Nothing could have prepared them for what happened next. Two German soldiers picked up the worker and dumped him into the mixer. He was to be part of the seawall. Frank and Tommy gagged and threw up. They no longer went on their morning walks.

⁓

In the fall of 1941, Tommy became alarmed when he heard that the Germans were rounding up any man, woman, or child, who couldn't prove they were born in the Channel Islands and deporting them to Germany. He took refuge in speaking his Quebecois French, hoping the Germans would mistake his French accent for the Jersey patois.

Tommy was well-entrenched in the community by then and considered by all to be such a valuable resource to so many that they decided they had to do something to save him from being arrested and deported. They met at the Therin's farmhouse one Sunday evening in July and devised a plan. Tommy would become Terry, Frank and Elsie's son, and be given a copy of Terry's birth certificate.

Rumors about deportation materialized in September 1942 and anyone who didn't have a Channel Island birth certificate was to be rounded up and shipped to a labor camp in Germany. Though Tommy always carried Terry's birth certificate with him, his neighbors were concerned because Tommy didn't look anything like a Therin – he was taller, had red hair and freckles, and was never seen in the company of a woman. Everyone knew of Tommy's betrothal to Josie and why he didn't show any interest in any of the local girls, but they were concerned that his solitude might attract much attention and scrutiny. The German police might consider him to be homosexual, and that possibility was more life-threatening than being taken for an English soldier.

The same group of people who devised the birth certificate scam met again at the Therin farm on the evening of Sunday, October 4. Tommy attended, but he was asked not to actively take part in the discussion. They assured him they knew best and promised to come up with a workable solution before anyone went home. Many ideas were bandied about before the group arrived at a new life story for Tommy. Desperate times call for desperate measures. This was wartime and they had to pull out all of the stops.

Tommy's new life story went like this: he got his height, red hair, and freckles from his Irish dad, Patrick Jones, who came to Jersey as a migrant worker on the Vautier potato farm twenty-one years ago. After he got Ethel Le Cheminant, a local girl, pregnant, he went back to Ireland promising to return to face up to his obligations, but he never did. Ethel gave birth to Thomas Jones at her cottage, La Petit Chalet, on June 9, 1921. Tommy lived with his purported mum and her aging parents until he married Amelie, the Vautier's youngest daughter, in 1941. His grandparents were said to have passed away in the '30s, and his mother was said to have been evacuated to England before the German invasion. Tommy was a conscientious objector, living on the Vautier farm with his wife, Amelie, and helping his father-in-law with the potato operation, and the Therins with their cows.

When they asked Monsieur Armitage, Jersey's clandestine forger, to create a birth certificate for Tommy and a marriage certificate for Thomas and Amelie, he rubbed his hands with glee. Tommy was speechless – he couldn't believe what he was hearing, and they were all in on it, but he agreed to go along with it, and out of it, finally get a birth certificate for a Thomas Jones

Tommy moved into the extra bedroom at the Vautier's farm and Amelie began to accompany him wherever he went. He knew Amelie quite well – she seemed to have always been around when he went for the Vautier tractor, and they had often exchanged greetings and small talk. Had Josie not been in Tommy's mind and heart and in the photographs in his suitcase, he might well have asked Amelie to go out with him. She was a year older, about a foot shorter and sixty pounds lighter. The texture of her jet-black silky hair was similar to Josie's, but she wore her hair cropped short and straight across above her dark eyebrows, giving the illusion of a black picture frame holding a portrait of an olive-skinned young lady with a heart-shaped face and lips and warm brown eyes. Every time Tommy saw her approach, he thought picture-perfect, and the thought made him smile.

The more time he spent with Amelie, the more emotionally tortured he became. He never forgot about his betrothal to Josie, but his heart was gradually warming to Amelie, and his body kept reminding him that he was a virile, young twenty-two-year-old man. He began wondering why he hadn't been inclined to look at Josie's photographs in over a year and that concerned him.

Amelie believed she was in love with him and had been ever since the first day she saw him four years ago when he appeared in their driveway to get the tractor. Everyone knew how Amelie felt about Tommy and gossiped about what a shame it was that he was betrothed to someone else.

Amelie understood and respected Tommy's situation. She was satisfied for now to have a platonic relationship with him, though, secretly, she wished for more, much much more. While everyone wanted the German occupation to end, Amelie was in two minds about it. So long as the Germans were on the island, she had Tommy all to herself. She was technically married to him, was she not? She couldn't be seen with other men, and neither could Tommy be seen with other women. They had to live with the ruse for now. Amelie sensed that as soon as the occupation ended, and the Germans left the island so would Tommy – he'd go to England or Canada, and he'd be lost to her forever.

Tommy was ambivalent. Because he'd told everyone of his love for Josie and their plans to get married, he felt pressured to stick to the script and not waver. However, he was wavering.

They say absence makes the heart grow fonder, but in Tommy's case, it seemed to be facilitating a change in direction. The more time he spent with Amelie, the stronger his urge to become more intimate with her. He considered changing his mind about Josie to see how his relationship with Amelie might develop if it were left to blossom, but he didn't. He felt he couldn't. He owed it to Josie and to everyone who had supported him to live up to his promises and obligations. He hid his feelings, resisted temptation, and fervently wanted the occupation to end so that he could get on with the rest of his life, whatever that might be.

In the meantime, Tommy and Amelie carried on as best they could. Both enjoyed each other's company, but neither allowed themselves to share their true feelings about one another with anyone, They were two people in love, pretending to be friends.

On June 6, 1944, the Allied Forces launched the D-Day landings and liberated Normandy, France. The Allies bypassed the Channel Islands because they were occupied by the Germans, and heavily fortified. Consequently, the German supply lines for food and supplies from France were completely severed, and there was now very little food available for both the islanders and the Germans.

Frank began slaughtering his cows to help alleviate the growing food shortage on the island. When Tommy noted which of his dear friends was missing, he got depressed, and for the next few days, grieved their passing. Pets began disappearing and people made soup out of whatever wild plants and vegetables they could find –nettle soup was popular. Everyone was desperate to stay alive. Some even boiled newspapers to make cellulose soup. Their situation was dire.

On November 3rd, a slave worker appeared in the Vautier's yard. He was skeletally thin, his work clothes were encrusted with cement and instead of shoes, he had sacking wrapped around his feet. The man didn't speak English. Tommy put him over his shoulder and carried him into the kitchen and propped him up on a stool. Amelie gave him some homemade bread and a glass of hot milk. Her heart sank when she saw his attempt to smile in appreciation for the food – he had no teeth. She washed his face and arms with a warm cloth and soap and soaked the hard, dry bandages on his feet in warm soapy water before she could separate them from his skin.

Tommy went to his bedroom and returned with a pair of boots, pants, and a shirt, and then helped the man take off his pants and shirt and put on the new clothes. Considering how heavily calloused and swollen the man's feet were, it was a miracle the boots fit as well as they did. It helped too that Tommy's shoe size was bigger than the man's.

Harboring and helping a slave worker were still serious offenses, resulting in deportation, but now that Jersey was isolated from the rest of the world, it was an empty threat.

About an hour after the guest had donned his new clothes, he stood up and groggily made his way to the door. Tommy took Amelie's hand, drew her close, and together they followed the slave out of the door and into the yard. They looked at each other and smiled as they waved and watched the man hobble off down the driveway in his new shoes.

After months of negotiations, the Red Cross ship SS Vega was finally allowed to bring medical and surgical supplies to the starving islanders in December 1944. The Vega made five further trips to the islands before the islanders were finally liberated on May 8, 1945.

On May 9, 1945, HMS Beagle arrived in St Helier and the German forces surrendered unconditionally. Tommy and Amelie went down to the harbor to bear witness to this historic event. The weather was cold for May, and the air was unusually blustery. Tommy seized this opportunity as an excuse to put his arm around Amelie's shoulder and pull her close and wrap her in his big tweed overcoat. She looked up at him with a loving gaze, and their eyes met. Love was in his eyes too. She was sure of it. She put her arms under his coat and cuddled up to him. Neither said a word, but there was no mistaking how each was feeling. They stood there for a few minutes, enjoying the experience. The warmth of their bodies so close together, and their loving feelings so strong, but, as yet, not openly shared.

They hurried to the front of the Pomme d' Or Hotel on the Esplanade, where the crowds were the noisiest. People were shouting to the British troops to throw more sweets. Every so often, a shower of sweets rained down on them – they hadn't had sweets for more than four years. They continued walking along the Esplanade to the front of the Grand Hotel, where they stopped and watched what was happening on the beach. It was hectic. German soldiers were being boarded on three gigantic landing craft, which sat on the sand like beached whales. They were to be taken to England as prisoners of war. There was an unspoken solemnity to the occasion. Everyone had prayed for this day for years and now it had finally arrived.

On their way home, Tommy stopped at a general store to order three notebooks, four packs of paper, and four typewriter ribbons.

The first thing Tommy did when he got home was to write Josie an eleven-page letter. It wasn't a love letter, but it was the best he could do, given his confused state of mind and heart. Now that the Germans had left, he was unsure of what to do. *Should I even write to her after all this time, and if I was to what should I say? Goodbye or I'll see you soon?* On the first page, he wished her well and inquired how she was doing and if she was a veterinarian yet. He wrote that he hadn't found his family because he hadn't gone to England due to the occupation, but he would be going soon. The next ten pages were an account of his life in Jersey under the Germans. He didn't mention Amelie.

Seven days later, his paper order arrived. He typed out Josie's letter and sent it to the Bouchard family with an accompanying letter to Chantelle requesting that she forward it to Josie.

Tommy moved back into his lodgings at the Therin's farm, resumed his duties at the dairy, and resolved to distance himself from Amelie until he heard back from Josie.

He inquired about how to get a U. K. passport. Though he was confident his fake birth certificate and marriage license would convince most bureaucrats, he felt it was time to legitimize himself with authentic documents. He wrote to the Head Office of the Waifs and Stray Society asking for his birth certificate and for any other documentation that might be useful in his application for the UK. passport. Three weeks later they replied saying that his birth certificate had been lost, but it confirmed he was a British subject and that his birth date was April 21, 1921. It also stated that he was born at home in Blackmoor, Lancashire, and sent to Canada when he was thirteen as a Home Child. The letter went on to say that this information would be sufficient for the British government to issue him a passport and it provided him with the HM Passport Office address. He immediately wrote a request letter.

Tommy was surprised at how often he thought about Amelie now, and how little about Josie. He found himself aching to see her, but he resisted the temptation, sensing it would only complicate matters further. To help him take his mind off her in the evenings, he resumed writing about his life. He felt he needed to document his journey from the earliest times he could remember. His memory was sound and his eye for detail had always been uncanny. These traits allowed him to capture the key events of his past substantially and eloquently.

When he did not receive a reply from Josie or Chantelle to his letter of five weeks earlier, he wrote Chantelle again asking if she had forwarded his letter to Josie. He also asked her to tell Marc to post his typed papers.

Tommy's life was on hold, and he didn't like it. He was eager to move on, one way or the other.

Three weeks later when he came in for lunch, there was a letter with a Canadian postage stamp waiting for him at his place setting at the table. He excitedly picked it up, turned it over, and was surprised to find that it was from the Bouchards, not Josie. He eagerly ripped open the envelope and read the letter.

'My dear Thomas,

We were pleased to get your letter and to read that you are well. Everyone here sends you their best wishes and Marc hopes you come back in the fall to help him with the maple syrup. He says no one works as fast as you on the lines.

With regards to Josie, I haven't and will not be giving her your letter. She visited us last summer on her vacation with her husband and two children. Josie and her husband, Marcel, are both veterinarians and have an animal clinic just outside St. Eloise. They seemed to be a very happy family.

Best wishes on your search for family. I hope you have a good life. You will always receive a big welcome from us if you come back to Canada and visit.

Your friend,
Chantelle.'

Tommy was stunned. He felt weak and went outside to clear his head. As he walked along the path, he thought about Josie and their plans to get married and to be together, forever. His mind raced with thoughts and his emotions swirled. As reality settled in that this would now never be, his demeanor changed. He was now free of the obligation to marry her. He went back into the house, to his room, and lay on his bed with a pillow propped under his head. He re-read Chantelle's letter, slowly. He wanted every word to sink in and to take hold, just as rainwater feeds and replenishes roots, and as he did this, he felt his confusion about where he was going in life float up to the ceiling, and, like a popped balloon, disappear. He read the letter a third time.

He pulled out the suitcase from under the bed and rummaged through its contents looking for the four photographs Josie had given him and the two postcards of the ships. He wrapped a black typewriter ribbon around them, tied the ends into a bow, and put them in a manila envelope, which he placed in his suitcase, which he slid back under his bed. With all the reverence and care he had shown in his handling of the package, it could well have held Josie's final ashes. Sitting upright on the edge of the bed, feeling calm and satisfied with a job well done, he took a deep breath and thought, *now I can get on with my life.*

Chapter Twenty Seven – Amelie

St. Brelades, Jersey.
1945

As he stepped out into the sunshine, Tommy felt as if he'd lost a few pounds in body weight and his mind was clearer. Josie was no longer in his heart and on his mind. Amelie was. And if truth be told, she'd been there for a very long time. He smiled at how profound it all was. By packing up his past he'd unwrapped his future, all at the same time, and all in less than a minute.

This seminal moment in Tommy's life abruptly changed his demeanor and strengthened his resolve. Full of confidence and conviction, he excitedly put together a wicker picnic basket of goodies and boldly strode over to La Grande Pomme de Terre Royale.

Amelie was in the shed sweeping the floor when Tommy poked his head around the corner and asked in a softly spoken voice, "Hey Amelie. Wanna go to Quaisne with me? I've packed a picnic for us."

Amelie's heart skipped, as it always did when Tommy spoke to her in this tone of voice. She was surprised he'd asked her to go to Quaisne with him because the last time they went there, he let his guard down and became a little too amorous. She loved it, but he apologized profusely for his misbehavior and promised he'd never misbehave again. He hadn't. Would he this time? She hoped he would.

"Love to. Give me five minutes to finish up and get changed. I'll meet you by the gate."

Tommy went back out in the sunshine, bubbling over with excitement to tell Amelie the good news about Josie, but he decided not to tell right away.

As Amelie changed into her shorts, she reflected on Tommy's invitation and picked up on a change in him that she couldn't quite put her finger on. He seemed different. She had a sense that he might intentionally misbehave, and this possibility prompted a rush of adrenaline to course through her body, making her light-headed.

With Amelie's hand in his, Tommy skipped over the sandy beach down to the water's edge and to the rocks that served as the border between St. Brelades Bay and Quaisne beach. It was low tide. Excitedly, they clambered over the wet, slippery stones with Tommy in the lead. Amelie followed, being gently pulled along by Tommy's strong hand. She'd never seen him this relaxed and carefree.

Tommy spread out a blanket for them to sit on and opened the lid on the picnic basket. Like a magician, he pulled out a large red tablecloth, shook it theatrically in the air, and spread it out on the sand, ensuring it was flat. For his next trick, he plunged his hands into the basket and pulled out a bag of sandwiches: four crab with lettuce and four chicken with lettuce with the crusts trimmed off to make them look daintier, more like what the Queen might eat. Next out of the basket was a bottle of red pop and two drinking glasses. He ended his performance by producing two red cotton napkins and then he took a bow.

Amelie stared at him, clapped her hands, and roared with laughter. "You are such a clown. I love it when you make me laugh."

As they lay on their backs, side by side, breathing slowly and watching cloud shapes form and dissipate, Tommy thought about what he was going to say, and how to say it.

"I just got a letter from my friend in Canada."

Why is he telling me this? It must be from Josie. I wonder what it says.

Though Amelie knew that one day Tommy would get such a letter, she found herself caught off guard and didn't want him to see her reaction. She pretended to retie her shoe and nonchalantly said, "Oh, yes? What did it say?"

Tommy smiled, looked up at the sky, and with some obvious embarrassment said, "Seems Josie got married."

"Got married!" Amelie exclaimed, sitting up and turning around to stare wide-eyed at him. "She got married! I can't believe that. I'm so sorry Tommy. She must have got tired of waiting for you. Are you upset?"

"No. More surprised than anything. I'm happy for her. My friend said she married a veterinarian, and they have two children."

Amelie lay back on the blanket and continued staring up at the sky. A smile spread across her face as she realized what this could mean for their relationship. *So, that's why he's so different today.* "So how are you feeling now that you've had time to think about it?" she asked.

With a twinkle in his eyes and a grin on his lips he looked sideways at her and winked. "Great. I feel great. To be honest, I feel free. I can get on with my life now."

"And what does that mean?" she asked, returning the smile. "Get on with your life?"

"You'll see."

They lay together for a few more minutes staring up at the sunny sky, each consumed with their thoughts. Tommy turned on his side, put his arm around her, and pulled her to him. She was like a doll in his hands. He stroked her cheek and her hair and stared into her smoky brown eyes. He caressed her face and neck with his fingers as she lay there with her eyes closed, enjoying his every touch.

"You are beautiful. I've thought that ever since I first saw you," he said slowly in a lower tone of voice.

Amelie's eyes misted over a little. "You think so? I always wondered what you thought of me because you never said anything." She ran a finger over his lips and eyebrows and kissed them.

"Oh, Amelie. If you only knew how much I've loved you all these years. It's been a living hell to be with you but not be able to be honest with you about how I felt. I'll tell you a secret, okay? I stopped thinking about Josie a long time ago, but I didn't want to let her and everybody down. You've been in my heart and on my mind for a very long time and I didn't know what I was going to do if Josie said she was still waiting for me. I'm so glad I don't have to make that decision.

"I love you, Tommy. I always have. Ever since the first day, I saw you when you came to the yard to get the tractor. Do you remember?" She wrapped her arms around him and hugged him tightly.

"Remember? How can I forget? If it wasn't for Josie, I'd have asked you out right there and then in the yard." His lips found hers and he gave her a long, lingering kiss. She kept her eyes closed and shared the kiss.

He whispered in her ear, "I'm so sorry Amelie for taking so long to tell you how I feel. You've been such a good, loyal friend. I don't deserve your love."

"It's all water under the bridge now as you say. We'll just have to make up for it by not wasting any more time, won't we?" With that, she moved her body and lay on top of him.

Tommy moved his hand slowly up to her shoulder, slipped his fingers under her bra, and touched the side of her breast. His hand quivered with excitement, and pleasurable surges ebbed and flowed through his body. The physical contact thrilled Amelie too and convinced her that this was for real. She wanted to give all of herself to him right there on the beach. Tommy had always been the only man she'd ever been interested in.

They continued lying on their backs and gazing at the clouds while listening to the gulls screeching overhead and the waves roaring and breaking onto the shore. Their love was steeping, and it felt good.

When the tide turned, they packed up the picnic basket, and clambered back over the rocks to St. Brelades Bay, to continue their passionate embraces in Tommy's room at Les Petite Vaches de Brelades.

They went back to Quaisne beach the following Sunday. It was a glorious afternoon – the sky was bright blue, and the sea was sparkling with diamond flashes as the waves broke and slapped ashore. Tommy had packed the same provisions as he had the previous week plus he had one extra item. He repeated his magic show and after the table was laid, pulled out the last item from the picnic basket: a little black box.

Facing Amelie and on bended knee, he popped open the box and showed her the ring. "Will you marry me?"

"Yes," she replied without hesitation, "Yes, yes, yes, thousand times yes," she said, wrapping her arms tightly around him.

Finally, Tommy was all hers to keep and forever. "This is the happiest day of my life," she said, hugging and smothering him with kisses.

"Me too," said Tommy, pulling himself away to look into her smiling happy eyes.

They lay on the beach for the next hour, basking in their love and the joy of their commitment, and talking about their dreams and wishes for a future with one another.

Word soon spread through the community that Tommy had proposed to Amelie, and the news pleased everyone. A joyous atmosphere permeated kitchens and dinner tables throughout the parish, putting instant smiles on people's faces and warmth in their hearts whenever they spoke of Tommy and Amelie. Everyone knew they were in love and had been for a long time and all knew about Tommy's dilemma concerning his betrothal to Josie. They had been waiting patiently with Amelie for Tommy to resolve his issue, and now it was resolved.

As the Vautiers were Catholic (her parents went to the Church of the Sacred Heart in the little village of St Aubin's every Sunday), Amelie asked Father Desmares, the parish priest, to marry them. Though Tommy was brought up as an Anglican, he told Father Desmares a little white lie. He said he was a lapsed Catholic, but he couldn't prove it. Aware of some of Tommy's background, Father Desmares just smiled and said OKAY. It simplified matters.

On Sunday, October 14, 1945, Tommy and Amelie married in the Church of the Sacred Heart. It was an auspicious occasion. The Church overflowed with family, friends, and well-wishers, and to make their special day even more memorable, the weather was glorious with a bright blue sky and a refreshing breeze. The air was warm enough to go without a jacket.

The Vautiers invited everyone back to the Therins for a reception in the courtyard. Tables with chairs and red tablecloths to seat family members were set out in the compound. Well-wishers sat on the surrounding low-rise wall and the grass. A buffet-style meal was set up in the large farm kitchen with chicken, Royal Jersey potatoes, and green beans.

Speeches followed the meal. Michel Vautier, the bride's father, told stories about Amelie and of his joy in the union of his daughter with Tommy. He said that he had a sense right from the start that they were in love and would marry one day, but he didn't think he would have to wait this long for that day to come.

Frank Therin brought Tommy up to the front and, putting his arm over his shoulder, spoke at length recalling his journey with him over the past seven years. Lacing his speech with humor, Frank had the crowd laughing heartedly. He spoke of the first time Tommy knocked on his door, and with a strange French accent, asked for a job. He spoke about how everyone was so impressed with the abilities and expertise of the young man, not only in the dairy but also with fixing equipment and building things.

"I couldn't have had a better surrogate son these past seven years. I am so proud of you Tommy." Grabbing a lock of Tommy's red curls, he said, "For four years, Tommy pulled the red wool over the German eyes." The crowd hollered and clapped. Frank was pleased they appreciated his joke. He decided to try another one. "Did you know Tommy was a bigamist? He married a second time without getting a divorce from his first wife!" The crowd cheered, and chanted, "Amelie, Amelie, Amelie." Amelie came up and joined Tommy at the front, put her arm in his, and smiled lovingly at the crowd.

When the laughing subsided, Frank said, "And now dear friends, I want to tell you about Elsie and me. As you know, our son Terry is a doctor with a wife and a practice in Great Melton, Oxfordshire. Well, Elsie and I are retiring and we're going to live in Great Melton so we can be near him and his family when he has one – we heard one is on the way." He finished his announcement by proudly proclaiming, "And Tommy and Amelie are going to run the dairy and they can buy it, for a very good price I might add, if that's what they want." The crowd clapped and banged their fists on tables.

Frank then turned the proceedings over to a fiddler and an accordion player who entertained the happy throng for the next three hours.

Over the next thirty days. Frank and Elsie moved out of the house and Amelie and Tommy moved in. Tommy received a replacement birth certificate and his UK. Passport in the mail. Now that he had the proper documentation to travel, he quickly thought about his roots and family. *Should I go in search of them?* He decided not to. It wasn't as important to him as was Amelie. He had a wife, a homestead, and one day, hopefully, children. They were his real family. For now, he was content with his new wife and life.

PART FOUR –
THE JONES FAMILY

Chapter Twenty Eight – Billy's Search

Blackmoor, Lancashire
1951

Now that Billy had money from the sale of Irene's house and the rental of it, he decided to go to Swanson, Kent to look for his brother

"Good morning, Joe. I have to take some time off work to go look for my brother."

"Yes of course Billy. That'll be fine. I know you've been wanting to do that for some time. I'll get someone to cover for you. Maybe Jimmy Nuttall can do it. I heard he's looking for a job. He got laid off last month when his boss retired and closed up shop."

"I don't know how long I'll be away, but I'll be as quick as I can."

"Take your time. You must do what you must do. Don't worry about us. We'll manage."

"Thanks, Joe. You've always been a good friend and you've always helped me out. I appreciate it."

The following day Billy traveled by trains to Swanson, Kent, and rented a room at the Wellington Arms hotel. While checking in, he asked the gentleman behind the reception desk what he knew about St. Chad's Home for Boys.

"It closed a long time ago – that's all I can tell you, son."

Billy obtained the information he was looking for the following day from a local librarian. She said it was an orphanage for boys until it closed in 1938.

"I'm looking for information on my brother. He went to St. Chads."

"Well then. Your brother is probably in Canada. The Anglicans ran the orphanage in those days, and they shipped all the boys to Canada when they got to be a certain age."

"Shipped to Canada!" said a shocked Billy. "You've gotta be joking. Why would they do that?"

"I don't know. You'd have to ask the Anglicans."

"And how do I do that? What about records?" asked Billy?

"Sorry, but I can't help you. I don't know who you can talk to except for the Anglicans."

Realizing this was the end of his search for his brother in England, Billy surmised that it was probably the end of his mum's search too and might very well have been a contributory factor in her untimely death.

He checked out of the hotel the following morning and returned to Blackmoor, disappointed, and disheartened. He'd set his sights on going to Jersey with his brother to look for their dad. Now he'd have to go by himself.

Chapter Twenty Nine– Billy goes to Jersey

Blackmoor, Lancashire
June. 1951

Billy had never been away from Blackmoor except for when he was a soldier, but that was a long time ago and a duty that didn't count as an adventure in his mind. Now he was going to Jersey of his own free will to look for his dad and was the most excited he'd ever been in his life.

When he thought about meeting his dad, his heart raced, and his palms got sweaty. *Should I be angry with him for the way he treated my mum and for abandoning me, or should I be pleased I found him?* He vacillated between the two points of view and had countless mental conversations with himself. In the end, he decided to let bygones be bygones as his mum used to say.

He began to put his affairs in order to get ready for his big adventure. He went to Syd, his barber, for a shave and asked him to cut his hair short.

"They call that a crew cut in America, Billy. It's all the rage over there now," Syd said stepping back from the chair and holding up a mirror so Billy could see what he had done. Billy ran his hands over his head and grinned. "Nice job Syd, I always wondered what I'd look like if I was as bald as a coot. Now I know. I like it."

He went to the bank to get traveler's cheques, to the train station to buy tickets to Southampton, and to Ward's Clothiers to buy a suitcase and some lighter clothes.

As he packed, he hummed, and his mind wandered, lifting his spirits and putting him in a light-hearted mood. He picked up Irene's six postcards and the photo of his mum and dad and looked at them closely for a minute before slipping them into a manila envelope and placing it on top of his clothes in the suitcase.

When he got up the next morning, the first thing he did was to poke his head outside to see what the weather was like. He was pleased. The sky was clear, the pavement was dry, and the air was brisk. Excitement coursed through his body making him feel happy and carefree. Before getting into the taxi, he looked up and down the street and wondered how long he'd be away. He sensed it might be a long time.

By the end of the day, after three interesting but uneventful train rides, Billy was in the Black Dog Pub in Southampton, supping a pint of bitters and salivating over whether to order the steak and kidney pie with chips or the liver and onions. He opted for the pie. While waiting for his order to arrive, he closed his eyes and reminisced about his day, recalling, and relishing every detail he could remember.

"Your dinner, Sir," the waiter announced in a strong voice, purposely designed to snap Billy out of his reverie. Billy opened his eyes, sat up straight, looked at the huge plate with the steaming pie and fat chips covered in gravy, and grinned. It had been a long day and he was starving. "Thanks, mate, and I'll have another pint when you're around this way. I'm on holiday."

Billy slept solidly for nine hours, three hours more than was normal for him, and awoke feeling refreshed and raring to go. After breakfast, he went to the docks and bought a ticket on the mail boat to Jersey.

The good weather persisted, allowing Billy to stay on the deck of the Isle of Jersey for the entire voyage and to enjoy the full experience of crossing the English Channel. As the ferry sailed down the Solent, past the Isle of Wight, and into the English Channel, he saw lighthouses and boats plying the waters, heard the waves slapping the bow as it cut a path through the sea, and listened to a cacophony of sounds from ship's engines, whistles, and horns.

Hanging over the ship rail and sucking in the sharp ocean air, Billy imagined it was pure white oxygen, and it was filling his lungs. He exhaled, imagining he was expelling grey, sooty air that he'd brought with him from Blackmoor.

When he disembarked in St Helier an hour later, he was bemused to note that most people seemed to be shorter than him, but not only that, they seemed to be friendlier- they nodded and grinned as they passed giving him the impression that they knew him. How odd he thought, but how nice. He felt important.

After renting a room at the Royal Arms Hotel, he strolled around the harbor for the rest of the afternoon familiarizing himself with the lay of the land. He wanted to know where the bus station was as well as other important landmarks. The feeling of relaxation and joy that he felt when he first opened his eyes that morning was still with him.

He sat on a bench overlooking the fishing boats, took out the manila envelope that he'd brought with him, and pulled out the photo of his teenage mum and dad. Gazing at the photo, he imagined they were sitting next to him. He turned sideways to face them and smiled, convinced he could feel their presence. The soothing warmth of the sun on his bare arms felt good and deepened his sense of contentment.

I wonder what my dad looks like now – he'd be fifty-three or fifty-four I'm guessing. Maybe I passed him on the street earlier today! The thought made him chuckle and sent a shiver of excitement rippling through his body.

He took out Irene's postcards and excitedly thumbed through them, looking for the one showing Elizabeth Castle. Raising his eyes and staring straight ahead at it lying out there in the Bay, he compared it with the picture on the postcard and beamed with a heightened sense of pride and satisfaction. *I always knew one day I'd see it with my own eyes.*

He looked at the postcards again and as he scanned the views, he imagined his mum and dad in the scenes, smiling and holding hands, and he felt their love.

As he sat there daydreaming, memories of Irene drifted into his mind. He remembered what she told him about his brother and dad and, as he recalled other key events in his life and people he'd met, a strange feeling came over him. He sensed he was piecing together a jigsaw picture of his life and was on the verge of finding the last few remaining pieces. Though he didn't fully understand what was happening, he enjoyed the bizarre feeling and the realization that he was now more content and confident than he'd been in his life for a very long time. His only regret was that he hadn't set out earlier to look for his dad.

Before he left Blackmoor, Angela wrote down the name and address of her great aunt's flower farm for him, where she said his mum stayed when she was a teenager.

Billy boarded the bus to St. Brelades the following morning and showed Angela's paper to the driver, who nodded knowingly.

It was a beautiful day to be anywhere, but to be on a local bus in Jersey on a quest to find your dad was extra special. As the bus rumbled along the country roads, Billy's excitement grew. The bucolic sights he saw from the window pleased him and the Jersey patois, spoken by the couple in front of him made him smile.

The driver stopped the bus at the entrance to Les Fleurs de Jardin and motioned for him to get off.

It was about noon when Billy strolled down the driveway to the house, knocked on the door, and waited. There was no answer. He walked around to the back and called out in a loud voice. "Anybody here?"

Aunt Jane, now sixty-two, and Uncle Cyril, sixty-eight, were both working in the fields when they heard Billy's shout. They stopped what

THE SOLDIER AND THE ORPHAN – SEPARATED BY CHURCH AND WAR

they were doing and came to the driveway to see who was calling.

Before Billy had a chance to introduce himself, Jane said, with a severe look of concern on her face, "My God Tommy, what's the matter with you? You look terrible." And Cyril, shocked at the sight of Billy's crew cut, said, "What on earth have you done to your hair? You look ridiculous."

Billy was stunned. "Why are you callin' me, Tommy? You don't know me. I'm looking for Jane and Cyril. Are you them?"

Jane and Cyril looked at each other in disbelief.

"Of course, we are. Who did you think we are? What a ridiculous question," said Jane.

The three of them stood there motionless, not knowing what to say.

"What's going on Tommy? Why are you speaking like that?" asked Cyril in a concerned voice.

"Tommy! Why d'ya keep calling me Tommy? I'm Billy. My name's Billy."

Cyril laughed, perplexed by Billy's answer and behavior.

"So. If you're not Tommy, then why are you here?" said Cyril, hoping to catch him out in what he thought was a trick Tommy was playing.

"Coz I'm related to you."

"You are? Who told you that?"

"My Aunt Angela. She lives up in Blackmoor."

"We know an Angela who lives in Blackmoor – Angela Mathers. Is that who you mean?" said Jane.

"Yes. That's her. And her husband's name is Albert. She's my aunt and she gave me your name and address."

"You're not Tommy then?"

'No. I told you. I'm Billy. Billy Jones"

Suddenly, the couple realized who this young man was.

"Oh my God! Are you William Jones! Is your mother Mary Jones?" Jane asked.

"Yes."

"Do you have a twin brother?"

259

"Yes, but how d'ya know that?"

"Your mother told us she was having twins. She was staying with us when she got pregnant."

Billy shook his head in disbelief. "I've never met my brother. He went to Canada years ago, but I know my mum named him Thomas."

Jane and Cyril looked at each other and then at Billy.

Jane laughed and said, "I don't know what's happening Billy, but Tommy Jones is living right here in Jersey. He's just one farm over."

The news hit Billy as if he'd been hit over the head with a two-by-four. The color drained from his face and his knees wobbled. "How can that be? He went to Canada?"

"Well. He's here now and he looks like you, except he talks differently, and he's kept his hair. What happened to yours?" Jane asked.

Billy ran his hands over his shorn head. "So. What's he doing here? Does he live with our dad? That's why I'm here. I've come to find my dad."

"Your dad lives in Guernsey, Billy, or at least that's where he used to live. Tommy's married and lives with his wife and two children on the Therin dairy farm. We'll go see him tomorrow if you like and get everything sorted."

It was like they were in the twilight zone. The facts were too serendipitous and preposterous to be true. Everyone just stared at each other, waiting for a plausible explanation by someone to explain what was happening.

"You can stay with us. We have lots of room. We're so interested in learning about you, and if you like, while I work on dinner, Cyril can show you around the farm and take you to your room."

～

They retired to the lounge after tea and settled in chairs facing the fireplace to share what they knew about the Jones family. Billy went first. He brought out the La Cloche studio photograph of his mum and dad and Irene's postcards and handed them to Jane. Her face lit up. She took the photograph, held it up to her eyes, and smiled.

"Well, I never! That's your mum all right, and that's Ted. What a scoundrel he turned out to be!"

"Mum said he was already married when he got her pregnant."

"That's right. He had a wife and a child in Guernsey, but he didn't tell your mother that. He went back to Guernsey when your mother told him she was pregnant, and we've never seen or heard from him since." Jane continued scanning the photo. "We heard your mum put both of her babies into an orphanage – that's the story we got."

"No. She kept me. Thomas went into an orphanage, but I lived with my mum until she died."

"She died? Oh, how sad. We had no idea she had passed. We lost track over the years. How did she die and when?"

"When I was in the Army. They said it was a heart attack. She was only forty-four."

"Oh. So young. I'm so very sorry Billy. You must miss her terribly?"

"I do. It was just me and her all my life."

Thinking more about Ted, Jane asked, "Are you sure you want to find your dad?"

"Yes. I don't have much family. He's still my dad. That's why I want to find him."

"Well. You've got a brother now. And he's been here right under our noses for the last ten years. I still can't believe what I'm seeing and hearing."

"Neither can I. They told me he went to Canada twenty years ago. I don't know how he got here or why he's here."

"But we're going to find out soon enough, aren't we?" said Jane, nodding and raising her eyebrows.

"We sure are," said Billy, sticking his fork into another piece of Madeira cake.

They talked late into the night. Jane said his mum and Ted truly loved one another and that he made her laugh all the time and that he never wore shoes – he was always barefoot when she saw him – and when she offered to buy him a pair of shoes, he just laughed.

"I knew he didn't wear shoes. Mum told me that."

"You know Billy, just before your mum went home for the birth, she confided in me that she didn't regret a thing. I think you should know that. She said it had been the happiest summer she'd ever had in all her life by far. She said it was blissful. Yes, that was the word she used. Blissful."

Blissful resonated with Billy. That's the word he used to describe his time with Claire. He recalled telling Irene when she asked him what his relationship with Claire was like, that it was blissful. He stared at the photo of his mum and Ted and smiled at them, repeating the word, blissful.

Jane repeated what she had earlier told Billy about his dad, hoping he'd change his mind about looking for him. "As I said, your dad was from Guernsey, but he didn't tell your mum he had a wife and son there. He's never been here inquiring about her, or you that I know of," she said. "No one has."

"So, I have another sibling – a half-brother. My family's getting bigger all the time. Jane smiled at Billy's remark and then Billy shocked her by saying, "I'm glad he got my mum pregnant."

"Why is that Billy?"

"Well. I wouldn't be here, would I? And I wouldn't have a twin brother, would I?"

They all laughed and went to their respective bedrooms for the night.

Billy didn't sleep much. He was much too stimulated to enter a deep sleep even though he was exhausted from a long day of travel. He spent the night thinking and composing what he was going to say to his brother in the morning.

Chapter Thirty – Brothers United

St. Brelades, Jersey.
June. 1951

It began as just another day at the Les Petite Vaches de Brelades dairy farm, but that was soon to change with Billy's arrival. By day's end, it would turn out to be one of the most significant days in the lives of the thirty-two-year-old twins.

It was still early morning – around six-thirty – but everyone at Aunt Jane's house was up, dressed, and ready to go, all eager to witness the reunion of the brothers.

Jane sat in the passenger seat of the little truck, a Bedford CA pickup that she and Cyril used to transport their flowers to the dock in St. Helier, and Billy jumped onto the flat deck at the back. Cyril drove slowly down the road for the five-minute ride to the dairy and parked on the road. Jane and Cyril stayed in the truck while Billy jumped off, strode confidently up to the front door, and knocked loudly.

It was ten minutes to seven when the door opened, and the brothers saw each other for the first time in their lives.

Tommy was stunned. Billy was smiling.

"How are you, Tommy? I'm Billy, your brother. Your twin brother."

Tommy stared transfixed, trying to get a grasp on what was happening.

"I know it's crazy, but I really am your twin brother Tommy."

Billy grinned and his eyes sparkled with excitement. He'd waited a long time for this moment.

Tommy continued to stare up and down at Billy, examining his red hair stubble, his green eyes, his ruddy freckled face, and shook his head. "You've got to be kidding me! Who are you? Where did you come from?"

"I'm Billy. We're twins,"

Still in shock, Tommy began to smile at the outrageousness of the situation.

"I am your brother, and I can prove it," said Billy, grinning madly and nodding his head. Show me your thumbs?"

"What?"

"Show me your thumbs."

Tommy held out his hands.

Billy sensed the gravitas of the moment and reverently reached out, lovingly turning Tommy's hands over. "See that," he said, pointing to a dim dark spot on the underside of his right thumb. "That proves we're brothers."

He showed Tommy the underside of his right thumb. "See. I've got one of them too. It's supposed to be a heart coz our dad's name is Heart. Our mum did this to us when we were born so we could prove we were brothers! She called it a 'lovemark' because she said we were conceived in love."

Tommy continued staring at his brother in disbelief, but no one could deny that Billy looked like him except for the haircuts.

Billy turned around and motioned for Jane and Cyril to come up. They joined him on the doorstep. Billy turned to the grinning couple and introduced them. "These good people, Tommy, are your great aunt and uncle."

"Go on," said Tommy, laughing and shaking his head and looking around, expecting someone to step out of the bushes to offer a reasonable explanation of what was going on.

Not knowing what to say or do, Tommy invited everyone into his house and went off to get Amelie and the children.

Once everyone was seated and settled around the big table, they went around the room and, amid all the laughing, introduced themselves.

"I'm Billy, Tommy's twin brother. I came here to find my dad, but I've found my brother instead! How about that?"

Amelie and the children were stunned. They stared wide-eyed at Billy, then at their dad, and burst out laughing. They thought it was spooky to see another man look so much like their dad, and the funny way Billy spoke made them laugh.

"Well, as you all know, I'm Tommy and this is my wife, Amelie, and this darling little six-year-old with the flaming red hair is Louise and that's Sarah. She's two. We run the St. Brelades dairy farm."

"I'm Cyril and I'm confused!" Everyone laughed.

"I'm Jane. And not only are we your neighbors, but we are also your relatives. We just figured it out last night with Billy. Cyril and I are your great aunt and uncle, Tommy."

Billy said, beaming with pride, "We're all family. Can you believe that? There's seven of us and we're all family." Tommy looked at Amelie and shook his head. "This is unbelievable."

Louise giggled again at her uncle's strange way of speaking. Billy looked at her, winked, and did a magic trick for her. Waving his arms around, he said abracadabra and pulled a sepia photograph out of his inside pocket. "This is your grandma and granddad," and to Tommy, he said, "It's our mum and dad, Tommy."

Tommy took the photo, brought it up close to his eyes, and scrutinized it.

"Look at our mum's red hair and freckles. That's where we get it from," said Billy.

Tommy stroked Louise's red hair and smiled. The excitement in the room was palpable.

Billy looked at Louise who was still giggling, as six-year-olds do when they find something funny to laugh at, and he winked at her again. Flourishing his hands in an abracadabra fashion once more, he reached into his other inside pocket and with a hocus pocus pulled out six postcards. He waved them in the air and gave them to Tommy. Louise kept giggling.

"Look at these Tommy. Our mum lived in Jersey and sent these to her friend, Irene. It's her handwriting."

"Let me see! Let me see!" squealed Louise, jumping up and stretching her little hand as high as it would go. Tommy put a postcard into her wiggling fingers, bent down, kissed her on the cheek, and hugged her.

Amelie filled a pitcher with farm-fresh milk and put out some biscuits. She passed the plates and cups around while Billy told them a little about himself. He spoke briefly of growing up in Blackmoor with his mum, of being conscripted into the Army at nineteen, of going to St. Chads to look for Tommy, and what he knew about his mum and dad from conversations he'd had with his mum, Irene, and Angela, but he didn't tell them much else.

Tommy's eyes clouded over with warm tears of emotion for his new family. Amelie and the children put their arms around him and patted his back comforting him. It was all too much for him to take in.

"I can't believe what's happening here. I've known Jane and Cyril for all these years and now you tell me that we're related and then my brother shows up out of nowhere. I've gone my whole life believing I'd never find my family. and just like that, three of you appear. It's unbelievable."

Billy moved into a spare bedroom at the dairy and helped Tommy with the chores. They talked, laughed, and worked together. By the end of the week, they knew a lot more about each other, but there was still much more to learn. The understanding, love, and compassion shown by all family members towards each other were cathartic and bonding, but more than that, the familial bond that only comes from being identical twins made the twins feel unique and complete. It didn't take long for Billy to decide that he wanted to live in Jersey, to be closer to his brother and his extended family.

Every evening after chores, the twins sat at the kitchen table and shared stories about their past. Each wanted to know every detail the other could share. They were thorough and Tommy insisted Billy tell his stories in chronological order because he sensed Billy's life had been one of progression and by listening to him tell his stories, year by year, he was able to get a better sense of who he was.

The only part of Billy's chronicle that intersected with Tommy's tale was his visit to the St. Chad's Home for Boys. Tommy regaled Billy with his recollections about what went on behind those cold, stone walls, though at the time, none of it was a laughing matter, and to bring Billy up to speed, he gave him his typed papers, showed him the postcards of the ships he'd been on, as well as the Bouchard photographs and letters. Billy was astounded and in awe of all that Tommy had done. He read the documents over and over and got to the point where he felt he knew the Bouchards and Josie intimately.

With help from Tommy, Billy wrote a letter to Joe Barton formally resigning his position at the scrap yard and informing him that he was going to live in Jersey. He wrote that he would visit Blackmoor with Tommy soon to put Irene's house up for sale and to collect his things. He included a check for three months' rent for the farmhouse.

He also wrote a similar letter to Angela asking for Albert's help in selling Irene's house and giving Albert the power of attorney over his property to act on his behalf.

Billy told Tommy what Jane had said about their dad and asked him if he wanted to see if they could find him. "I say we go and see if we can find the scoundrel and see what he has to say for himself," suggested Tommy grinning mischievously.

"I agree. Can you imagine how surprised he'll be when we show up at his front door, looking like the Bobbsey Twins, and we call him dad?"

Tommy clapped his hands loudly, and said, "If he has a heart attack, then that serves him right."

"I can't wait to see what happens," replied Billy, laughing so hard his sides were aching.

Tommy arranged with Bobby Hampson, his neighbor, to help Amelie with the farm chores while he and Billy went to find their father.

Chapter Thirty One – Ted

St. Peter Port. Guernsey.
September 1951

The following morning, the twins boarded the Isle of Jersey for the one-hour sail to St. Peter Port, Guernsey.

Soon after their arrival, they discovered that their father's name was probably Hart, not Heart because there was a large Hart clan in Guernsey, but no Hearts. The locals knew where all the long-established families lived, and Hart's lineage went back a long way. The first person they asked, a heavily whiskered fisherman with a weather-beaten face and a black leather patch over his right eye sitting on a wooden bench on the dock stitching his net, told them where to find one of them – a Richard Hart. He directed them to the Mon Plaisir potato farm in St. Martin's parish.

Richard Hart looked puzzled when he opened the door and confronted two look-alike men with red hair, green eyes, and ruddy freckled faces, asking about a Ted Hart?

Bemused, he said "I'm Richard Hart. Some people call me Ted. How can I help you?"

"We're looking for a Ted Hart. A man in his late fifties or early sixties," Tommy replied.

"That could be my dad. He's called Ted too. What do you want with him?"

"We want to speak with him if that's okay?" Tommy said.

"He's very sick – he's in bed – so I have to say no. Is there something

I can help you with?"

The twins looked at each other, raised their eyebrows in unison, and smiled with a twinkle in their eyes. Billy looked at Richard and said, "We think your dad is our dad."

"What! Are you crazy?" replied Richard, smiling too, but with a different kind of smile – one of disbelief, accompanied by a slow cynical shake of the head.

"I don't think so. Whatever gave you that idea?"

Taking the photo of their parents from his pocket, Billy held it up close to Richard's face and said, "D'ya recognize this man? Does he look like your dad?"

Ted recognized the face at once but wondered for a moment whether he should acknowledge it.

"So, what if it is? Who's the lady?"

"That's our mum. And the man is our dad," said Billy.

The twins paused for a moment to allow the revelation to sink in and then Tommy said, extending his hand for a handshake, "Well brother Richard. We're your Jersey siblings. Nice to meet you."

Richard ignored them. Instead, he invited them into the front lobby, closed the door, and said, "Now what's all this about?"

"Your dad got our mum pregnant. The lady in the photo is our mum," said Billy.

Richard looked at the photo again. "Yes, that's my dad. But that doesn't prove he's your dad, does it?"

The twins showed Richard the dim black marks on their thumbs. "Our mum had this tattooed on us the day we were born. It's supposed to be a heart coz she said that was our dad's name."

Tommy chimed in. "But we were too little for it to look like a heart."

All Richard could do was shake his head in disbelief.

Tommy then asked, "How sick is your dad? We need to speak with him before we leave. We have to get the three o'clock ferry back to Jersey. I've got cows to milk."

"He's very sick – he had a second heart attack last night. I think he's asleep right now. Let me get my sister. She's staying with us and she's his primary caregiver."

He went to the bottom of the stairs and called up, "Mary. Can you come down? There are two men here who'd like to speak with you."

Mary! The twins smiled and looked at one another. *Out of all the possible names they could pick for a girl they'd named their daughter Mary!*

Mary emerged from her dad's bedroom and began to descend the stairs. Richard looked up and said with a cynical grin, "I'd like you to meet your brothers from Jersey!"

Mary stopped in her tracks, stunned, and peered over the banister at the two men waiting at the bottom of the stairs.

"Who are you?"

"We're your brothers," Tommy said.

"Who are these men Richard?" asked Mary, not convinced of their identity.

"They say our dad is their dad!"

Mary continued to descend the stairs and stare at the odd couple at the bottom, wondering what was going on.

As she stepped off the last step, Billy approached her and showed her the photo.

"Is this your dad?"

The look on her face confirmed it was.

"The lady is our mum. Your dad got her pregnant."

"My dad got your mum pregnant?" she exclaimed, angrily spitting out the words. "There's no way he did?"

"Well, he did. And we've come to see him," replied Tommy.

Richard and Mary glared at each other, their eyes narrowed, and their faces softened. "Wow! What other dark secrets does dad have that we don't know about," asked Richard of his sister.

Billy was going to say, *"Well for starters, let's talk about why you're called Mary?* but he didn't. Instead, he suggested, "I think it would be a good idea if we were to speak with your mum first. She has to know sooner or later and sooner would be better."

"Our mother lives in England. She's been gone for more than thirty years. We've only seen her twice since she left and that was many moons ago. I still don't believe our dad got your mum pregnant. Can you prove it?"

"We need to speak with your dad to do that," replied Tommy.

"He's very sick. I don't think he's strong enough to have visitors."

"So be it Mary, but we must see him. We will make it quick. We must know, once and for all if he is our dad."

"Let me see if he'll see you."

She took the photo and went upstairs. She was there for a couple of minutes before coming back down. "He will see you, but he's upset – it's a big shock, and he's crying."

"Crying!" exclaimed Richard bolting up the stairs two at a time to comfort his dad. By the time the twins entered the room, Ted was sitting up in bed, holding the La Cloche Studio photograph with trembling hands, and staring at it in astonishment.

He looked up and was astonished to see two young men looking so much alike. "There's two of you?" he said, shaking his head. "I didn't know your mum was having twins." His sallow face beamed with pride as his sons approached his bed. He extended his arms, inviting them to come to him. The deep group hug lasted for more than a minute. All three sobbed quietly, holding on to each other tightly as if they were the last three people on the Titanic before it sank.

The twins sat on either side of the bed, clasped their dad's hands tightly, and observed and examined, in silence, every nook and cranny of his face. He was not well. He was thin, frail and his skin was pale; his eyes were bloodshot and watery, and his breathing was labored. The twins chose to ignore these aspects and instead put on brave faces.

"We've got your nose and pointy ears, dad," said Tommy, smiling.

Ted smiled weakly, thrilled to hear Tommy call him dad.

"And we've got your creased brow, dad" added Billy, grimacing with an exaggerated furrowed brow.

No one spoke for the next minute. Everyone soaked up the positive energy in the room and shared in the joyous occasion.

Billy broke the silence. "Do you still not wear shoes, dad?"

Ted was puzzled. He looked at Billy inquisitively. Then he remembered and chuckled when he realized where Billy must have got that intimate piece of knowledge about him.

Richard and Mary looked at each other. "What's he talking about dad? – not wearing shoes?"

"I'll tell you later," said Ted in an almost inaudible whisper. "Please leave the room. I need to speak with my sons alone."

As soon as they had left, Ted asked, in a quiet voice, "How's your mother?"

"She died seven years ago," Billy said. "Of a heart attack."

Tears rolled down Ted's cheeks. "I'm so, so very sorry." He took a moment of silence to remember and reflect.

"I'm so pleased you've come. I've wondered all my life what happened to your mother."

He rambled on, punctuated with tears and emotions, while the twins listened intently. They saw he was having trouble talking – there didn't appear to be any strength in his voice, and he seemed to be exhausted. Billy put an arm around him, and said, "We just wanted to meet you, dad. That's all. You don't have to speak. We understand."

Tommy brought Richard and Mary back into the room.

Sensing their dad's precarious state of health, the twins hugged him and moved to the door. "You get some sleep now dad. We'll come by another day when you're feeling stronger. Come and visit us in Jersey. A vacation would do you good!" said Billy. Ted raised his trembling hands in a wave, acknowledging their departure, and attempted to smile.

Mary noted her dad was much weaker than before the twins' visit and was concerned.

They went downstairs, Mary made tea, and the four of them sat around the kitchen table and talked. Billy told them what he knew about their dad and his mum and showed them the postcards she sent to Irene and answered their questions as best as he could. They read the writing on the cards and when they saw the word Ted their lips parted in warm smiles.

Just as the twins were getting ready to leave, they heard a heavy thump come from upstairs. Richard raced up the stairs first and found his dad in a hump on the floor beside the bed, motionless. He couldn't find a pulse.

They called for an ambulance, but it was too late. Ted had had another massive seizure and this time there was no reviving him.

Mary went ballistic. Tears streamed down her face, anger gripped her body and shook it. She attacked Billy with both fists, shouting, "You've killed him. You've killed him. Get out. Get out."

A distraught Richard tried to intervene and hold his sister back.

"We don't ever want to see you again," Mary shouted, shaking uncontrollably. "You got what you came for, now get out and leave us alone and never come back." She pushed the twins through the door and slammed it shut.

Standing on the doorstep, Tommy banged on the door and shouted, "Please, please let us in, Mary. What can we do? There's got to be something we can do." No one opened the door. They waited five minutes and banged on the door again, even harder. "Come on, Richard. Let us in. Let us help." He didn't open the door.

The twins headed back to the dock, shocked to their core, and boarded the ferry.

They were quiet for a long time, lost in their thoughts.

"I think the least we can do is to send some money to cover the funeral expenses and buy a headstone. What d'ya think, Tommy?"

"I agree. I can't see what else we can do. We've got to try to go to the funeral, but I don't know how that's going to work?"

As they stood on the deck holding the railing, Billy had a flashback. With Mary's angry accusation *you killed him* ringing in his ears an image of a man with a knife in his back suddenly appeared in Billy's mind. His body shuddered and a cold sweat broke out on his brow. Tommy noticed Billy hanging onto the railing with white knuckles, sobbing and almost incoherently mumbling, "I killed him. I killed him."

"No. You didn't Billy. You didn't kill him," said Tommy.

"I did. I did," insisted Billy, nodding his head up and down.

"He was a very sick man, Billy. He had a heart attack last night too and we weren't there."

Billy wasn't listening. Possessed by his demons, he continued lamenting, "I killed him, I killed him. He was still alive when I killed him. I had to."

Tommy realized Billy was having a breakdown and not making any sense. He put his arm around his brother's shoulders and hugged him. "It's okay Billy. You're here now with me, Tommy, your brother. You're safe now."

"I stabbed him," muttered Billy. "I had to."

Sensing Billy was making some form of confession, he asked, "Who did you stab Billy?"

"The man who hit Claire."

Tommy was even more confused. He cradled his brother in his arms and said in as soothing a voice as he could muster, "Take a deep breath, Billy. Fill your lungs. I'll do it with you, okay?"

They breathed in deeply together, and stayed at the rail, inhaling the sea air for the next five minutes in silence.

Eventually, Tommy asked, "Are you okay, Billy?"

"Yes. I'm okay now thanks. The horrors of war still haunt me. I don't know if I will ever be free of them. Now and then I get flashbacks. They just come into my mind as this one did, and I can't stop them. They're horrible. The doctors say it's shellshock."

"So. What's all this about you stabbing someone? Did you?"

"Yes, but I must first tell you the whole story. I've wanted to tell you for a long time, but the right opportunity never seemed to come along. When I was in the Army, I got injured and was hospitalized in Paris. Claire, a nurse, looked after me." Billy looked out across the sea and continued inhaling while hanging onto the ship's rail as the boat rose and fell. "I fell in love with Claire, and life was wonderful. I'd never been with a woman before. It was like I was in heaven, and she was my angel, looking after me and healing me. I didn't care about anything, and I didn't want it to end." He went quiet for a few seconds. "Everything was going great. I was living in her flat when a man came to the door and barged in. He saw me in the kitchen and rushed at me yellin' and screamin'. Claire came to my defense, but the man hit her hard and knocked her to the floor. I went crazy and lunged at him. We fell to the floor and brawled. Next thing I know he's got a knife stickin' out of his back, and there was a big pool of blood under him. I thought he was dead, but then he moved, so I pulled the knife out and plunged it back in. Claire was screamin' and cryin' her heart out."

"You killed him!"

"Yes. I killed him."

Tommy was speechless. The boat was pulling alongside the quay and passengers were preparing to disembark. Billy held Tommy back and said, "I didn't know what to do. I was so scared, Tommy. I left Claire and raced back to the hospital. I didn't tell them what I'd done. They said I was shell-shocked, and the next day, they shipped me back to England."

Tommy didn't know how to respond so he didn't say anything.

They disembarked and walked along the front in silence, each deeply preoccupied with their thoughts. Billy guided Tommy to the bench he sat on when he first arrived in Jersey. Though they were in a public place, he felt he had enough privacy to continue telling his brother about his situation and his wish.

"I know what I did was wrong. I was a coward, and it's bothered me ever since. I worry the police will show up any day and charge me with murder. I live in fear, Tommy."

Tommy felt his brother's pain, and turning sideways, took his hands in his and clutched them tightly.

Billy sat up straighter, wiped his eyes, and blew his nose. He straightened his back and looked out to sea. After a few minutes, he turned to Tommy and said, "I always intended to go back to find Claire, but I couldn't. I didn't speak French and I never had enough money. Now I do, and I want to find her coz I still love her. I can't stop thinkin' about her. I've never loved anyone else. It might be the end of the line for me coz I might have to go to jail, but I've got to go. I've got to find out what happened to her and if she needs me? That's what Irene always said to me: "There's always someone who needs you." You speak French. Can you help me find her?"

"I would love to brother. Just let me know what I can do."

Chapter Thirty Two – Claire

St Brelades. Jersey.
October 1951

So long as Billy wasn't thinking about Claire, he was fine. Being in the daily company of his brother and his family gave him the sense of belonging he had so craved all his life. One day while milking the cows, Tommy asked Billy how they might go about finding Claire.

"I've thought a lot about that over the years, and I don't have much to go on. I know her dad was a surgeon, and her mum was a nurse at the hospital I was in, but I can't remember the name of it, and I don't know what her last name was coz it was a French one. I do remember teasing her about it though, coz it sounded like 'cut toe' to me. I will always remember saying to her that if I were a surgeon like her dad, I'd change my name to sound more like 'mend toe' or 'cure toe.'"

"Cut toe, cut toe – maybe her name is Couteau. That's a common name in France and in Jersey too," Tommy said. "Couteau means knife in English. What a great name for a surgeon, eh Billy?"

They laughed and Billy mimicked a surgeon slicing into a slab of meat.

"That's all you have?" asked Tommy.

"Yes." But then he remembered. "No, she had a brother. I met him once, briefly. He came to the door and Claire spoke to him. I was on the couch, and he smiled and waved. Now I remember. Claire said he was a teacher, the same as her, and if my memory is correct, his name was Dominic. I remember it coz it was a French name I could pronounce."

"That's all. That's all you have. I don't think it's enough to go on."

"It's all I've got, but Irene always used to say, "Where there's a will, Billy, there's always a way – you just have to find it." And I believe her."

Where to start? That was the baffling question. They couldn't just go to Paris and walk around for weeks checking out every Couteau name in the Paris phone book. What if their name wasn't Couteau? Tommy had to be pragmatic – he was a busy dairy farmer, and he couldn't embark on a wild goose chase, though he sensed that was what Billy had in mind.

Marcel was a salesman from Paris who sold sterilizing chemicals to Tommy and other dairy farmers in the Channel Islands. On his next sales call, Tommy spoke to him about Billy's predicament and asked him how he'd go about checking out the Couteaus in Paris if that was all he had to go on. Marcel made a note of the names of Claire's family members and promised to see what he could do.

Marcel also sold sterilizing solutions to hospitals and had many long-time friends in the health services sector in Paris. It didn't take long for one of them to speculate that Claire and Dominic must be the children of Pierre and Elise Couteau who worked at the Hôpital Hôtel-Dieu in Paris. Pierre was an esteemed surgeon there and Elise was the Matron of nursing. Marcel did some sleuthing around and confirmed the guess. He looked up Pierre's home address and gave it to Tommy.

Tommy wrote a letter, in French, to Pierre, inquiring about his daughter, Claire. He asked for permission to communicate with her directly, adding that he was writing on behalf of his brother, Billy, who'd met Claire in a hospital in 1944.

Two weeks later he received a reply from Claire. She wrote in English that she remembered a Billy Jones and was pleased to learn that he was healthy. She also said she'd been concerned about him and agreed to accept future communications from him.

Billy hand-wrote a letter to her, and Tommy typed it up. In it, he wrote that he was pleased to learn she was in good health. Pleased was an understatement. He'd wondered and worried for seven years if she had died. Just hearing that she was alive was a tremendous relief. He explained the reasons why he hadn't been able to contact her in the past and why he could do so now. He needed to see her in person he wrote – he had apologies, regrets, hopes, and wishes he wanted to share with her in person, face to face. Would she agree to meet with him?

Two weeks later, her response arrived. It was straight to the point – she would be delighted to see him. Billy hoped that the reason she said 'yes' was because she still loved him. This possibility made the hair on his arms stand on end.

The twins took the ferry to St. Malo, got a train to Paris, and then a taxi to Claire's house. She lived in a stately brownstone building with a large stained glass front window on a quiet residential street near the Saint Germain des Pres quarter in the sixth arrondissement near the Seine. Six steps took them from the street up to the landing.

Billy was nervous, shy, and hesitant. Tommy reached over and pulled the cast-iron knocker on the door in the shape of a lion's head. Though the twins now looked almost physically identical – Billy's hair was the same length as Tommy's and cut in the same fashion by the same barber, their minds were worlds apart. One second, Billy was on Claire's couch sipping wine and laughing, the next he was looking down at her lying on the kitchen floor, screaming, and covered in blood. He tried desperately to vanquish this vision before the door opened. Tommy was deep in thought, considering what he wanted to do in Paris before going home.

The door opened, and Billy's angel hovered there. She was as beautiful and serene as the first moment he saw her at the hospital. Claire did a double-take. Though Billy had told her he was bringing his identical twin brother, she was unprepared for the shock. Seeing two look-alike men on her doorstep was astonishing. She knew which one was Billy though by his grin – there was a warmth and an energetic sparkle to it. It was the look of love.

Billy stepped forward and introduced his brother. "Hello, Claire. This is Tommy."

Claire returned his grin and motioned for them to enter her well-appointed apartment. She led them down a thickly carpeted hallway into a lounge and invited them to sit on the couch. She sat on an upholstered chair facing them.

Billy wondered how to start the conversation when Tommy declared in Quebecois style French, "Billy loves you, Claire. He always has, and he worries about you every day."

Tears formed in the bottom corners of Claire's eyes. She impulsively looked to one side, hoping Billy didn't see them. She blinked and turned to face Tommy. Amused by his strange French accent, she said, "It's okay to speak English, Tommy. I use it every day in my classroom."

"Well. That's great news. Billy won't need me to interpret for him then. In that case, I'll take my leave and come back in a couple of hours." Winking at his brother and Claire, he added, "That'll give you two love birds a chance to catch up," and with that, he let himself out, armed only with some francs and a Paris Tourist guidebook.

❧

Billy looked around and was surprised at how comfortable he felt with the room and with being in Claire's company. "You look great Claire. I'm so pleased and relieved to see you. I've had bloody nightmares for years, wonderin' how you were?"

Claire smiled demurely. "I'm pleased to see you too Billy. I also wondered how you were doing and if I would ever see you again."

"Yes. It was really tough at times. The first few years when I got out of the Army were the worst. I had shellshock and all sorts of problems. But what was worse was not knowing what had happened to you. I had nightmares that you died or were wasting away in a dank prison cell. It was horrible – my mind was all mixed up and I couldn't cope." His voice was now a trembling whisper.

Claire came over and sat by his side, took his hands, and gently squeezed them. Looking him straight in the eyes, she said, 'Well. I didn't die and I didn't go to prison if that's what you came to find out."

Impulsively, Billy took his right hand away, put it around her shoulder, pulled her closer, and gave her a firm, gentle hug. "I'm so happy. I haven't been this happy since I was last sitting on your couch like this." He leaned over and gently planted a light kiss on her cheek. "I was never in a position before to come to see if you were okay or if there was anything I could do."

Claire continued smiling and staring. "I can't believe you are actually here, Billy Jones, in my apartment, sitting on the couch next to me." She hugged him and they savored the mood and their good feelings in silence for a few minutes.

After a while, Billy said, "I'm sure it's no surprise to you that I need to know what happened in your flat after I left."

"Do you really want to know?"

"Yes. I think so. Coz I'll always wonder. I think I need to know so that I can put it behind me and hopefully move on. I keep having horrific flashbacks of that day."

Claire was silent and thinking. Billy noticed the concerned look on her face.

"It's okay Claire. I guess I don't really have to know. It doesn't matter coz you're here and you're okay, and that's all that matters."

Their eyes met and a calm understanding passed between them.

"I'll tell you one day, but not today. I know you need to know, and you will, one day, but not today. Today is a celebration. You are here. I always wondered if I'd ever see you again or if you'd met someone else?"

"I've never had a girlfriend besides you. I've never thought about anybody, but you and I didn't have enough money to come to look for you and I didn't know how to speak French, but now I have the money and Tommy speaks French. That's how come I'm here."

His words resonated deeply with her.

"So. You're not married, and you don't have any children?" she asked.

"No. As I said, I've only ever thought about you."

"And what about you Claire? Are you married?"

She laughed. "No, but I could have, mind you. I've had a few proposals over the years."

Billy's facial features relaxed and he breathed easier, sensing there were possibilities for him and Claire in the future.

"I didn't accept their proposals because I was concerned for my child."

Billy's eyes narrowed. "You have a child!"

His shock changed to a grin and then into a huge smile that lit up his eyes. He was happy for her. "You have a child? A boy or girl?"

"A boy. He's called Guillaume."

"Geeume. What kind of name is that? You should've called him Billy. I can pronounce that," he teased.

His suggestion caught Claire off guard. She raised her eyebrows, bent her head towards him, and smiled.

"Guillaume is French for Billy."

"Get out of here," said an amused Billy, but the penny still didn't immediately drop.

"And he has red hair, just like you. It's not as red as yours, but it's red and it's curly."

Billy stared at her.

She nodded, and with a big smile, said, "Yes Billy, we have a son."

"You've gotta be kiddin' me. We have a son. I'm a dad!"

"Yes, Billy. You have an eight-year-old son who has red hair and freckles just like you."

"I'm a dad?" shouted Billy. "A bloody dad. I don't believe it." He wrapped his arms around her and embraced her with every fiber of his body. Tears rolled down his cheeks. She joined him. She couldn't hold back the emotional tsunami surging through her body. It came in waves, one after the other. For seven years, she'd waited in the hope that Billy would one day return, and here he was, in her arms. She clutched him tight as if to prevent him from getting away.

He held both of her hands, taking turns kissing them.

"Where is he?"

"At his grandparents. I didn't know how you'd react to the news, so I arranged for him to go there for the day."

"When can I see him?"

"Are you sure you want to?"

"Oh, Claire. This is the best day of my life. I've been waiting to see you ever since I got back to England. I'm a dad as well, and you, a mum. We're a family. That's more than I could ever wish for."

She pulled away from him a little, looked him in the eyes, and said sternly. "I don't want any surprises, Billy. Before you meet him, I want to know what your plans are. Absent dads do a lot of harm I'm told."

"I know what you mean. I didn't know my dad. It was horrible not having a dad. My mum told me about him, but I never met him until two months ago and then he died. I'll tell you that sad story another time."

Billy got off the couch, knelt on the carpet in front of Claire, and holding her hands in his, said, "My darling Claire. Will you marry me? Will you be my wife? I've waited all my life for you."

Claire was shocked. She didn't expect Billy to propose this quickly, yet the thought of a marriage proposal did enter her mind when he wrote to say that he was coming to visit.

"So, are you goin' to marry me, or not?" asked Billy. "I need to know before I buy the ring coz I don't want to waste money on a ring if you're not goin' to marry me."

Claire was puzzled and then she realized he was joking. "Glad to see you still have your strange sense of humor, Billy. Yes, yes, yes. Of course, I'll marry you."

Billy gently pulled Claire to her feet, put his arms around her waist, and lifted her off the floor. As he twirled her around the room, she giggled with laughter. He was back in heaven with his angel.

They spent the next hour catching up on the past. He told her about Blackmoor, about his friend Joe, his rag and bone job, and about being united with Tommy. He also told her about the other important people in his life: Irene, his mum and dad, and Angela.

"What about you? I want to know everything about you."

"Well. I teach English as a Second Language at a High school here in Paris and I have four private students who I teach on Monday evenings. I'm teaching Guillaume to speak English in case he ever wants to go to England," and then, playfully punching him in his ribs, added with a laugh, "To look for you."

Meanwhile, Tommy went to the Louvre Museum for the afternoon. He returned home at about four o'clock. Billy went to the front door to meet him, and before he had a chance to close the door, Billy confronted him with the good news. "We're getting married. Claire and I are getting married. And we have a little boy. And he has red hair like us."

Tommy was gobsmacked. He stared at Billy and when he did find his voice all he could say was, "What? What? You've gotta be joking!"

He followed Billy down the hall to the living room, where he straightened up to his full height and hugged his brother. "Congratulations brother. It's about time you settled down and had a family!" Hugging Claire, he said, "Congratulations Claire. I'm so happy for the pair of you and your little boy. I know how much Billy loves you. You're all he ever talks about. He'll have to find something else to say now, won't he?"

Billy and Claire's blissful energy permeated the room, making Tommy feel light-headed. "My God Billy. I leave you alone for a couple of hours and now look what you've gone and done. Wow! A wife and a son, and all in the space of two hours? You are amazing my brother!"

They sat in the lounge and for the next hour planned their futures. There was a lot to discuss.

Feeling jubilant about being reunited with Claire and the revelation that he was a dad, Billy suggested they go to a good restaurant to celebrate. Claire suggested the Tortue Verte, a fine-dining establishment not far from her apartment.

Chapter Thirty Three – Tortue Verte

Paris, France
1953.

The host seated them at Claire's favorite table: the one in the corner facing the street. As soon as they were seated, the server appeared with a starched white towel folded and draped over his right arm, and in his left hand, he held a bunch of oversized menus which he offered the guests with an ostentatious flurry as if fanning a fire. The twins exchanged glances and smirked, sensing this was going to be a night to remember for neither of them had ever dined in a real French restaurant.

The twins were in a light-heated, giddy mood. They found everything in the restaurant a bit over the top and laughable. It pleased Claire to see them so bonded and happy.

Claire ordered a bottle of champagne and quietly began to translate the menu into English for Billy, but he was distracted – he was looking around the room in awe trying to see what everyone was eating.

Claire smiled and said, with mischievous intent, "What if I order for all of us?"

"Thanks," said the twins, smiling with relief.

"Let's see. We'll start with an appetizer. How about I order three different dishes and we'll share. You might never have another opportunity to eat like this," and under her breath, she said to herself with a smile, '*and you might never want to eat French food again*'. "I'll order the Foie Gras. That's goose liver that's been cooked, seasoned, and pan-fried. And I'll get six Escargots – those are snails simmered in butter, garlic, and parsley."

Billy and Tommy grinned.

"Don't they have fish and chips?" Billy teased.

Claire laughed. "No. We're here Billy because you wanted to go to a fancy restaurant to celebrate. Remember?"

"Only kiddin'. I'll eat anythin'. I usually like everythin'. Mind you, when I was in France, I didn't eat livers or snails. They gave me real food!"

Ignoring his remark. Claire continued, "And for our third appetizer, we'll have Cuisses de Grenouilles à la Provençale. I'll get six so we have two each," sensing that neither of them knew what she was talking about.

"We get two each! Two of what?" asked Tommy.

"Frogs legs. Just close your eyes and enjoy them. They're delicious – they melt in your mouth. They do them here in tomatoes with white wine and shallots and season them with garlic and parsley."

"Yummy," feigned Billy.

"And let's see what we shall have for our main course? My! Everything on the menu is so tasty. I've been coming here for five years – ever since I got my apartment and I've never been disappointed."

Billy was in paradise. Just being in Claire's company, able to see her, and hear her, fulfilled his yearning for her. He was feeling the same as he did seven years ago when he was in her apartment.

"I think we'll get three different entrees to try, as we did with the appetizers. Let's see. The Beef Bourguignon is my favorite – it's a succulent rich dish of beef, stewed in red wine and hearty broth. I'll get another stew – the Bouillabaisse, I think. That one's a saffron-flavored mix of four different types of fish and a variety of shellfish. It's different from fish and chips, Billy. It's not battered, but I'm hoping you'll like it."

"If you like it, I'm sure I'll like it too," Billy replied, affectionately.

"And you, Tommy. Do you like chicken?"

"I'm like Billy. I eat everything."

"Well then," Claire said, "Our third dish will be Coq au Vin. That's a rooster cooked in a red wine sauce with bacon, butter, and beef stock. Rooster is a type of chicken but with a much stronger flavor and it's ridiculously scrumptious."

And so began the feast to commemorate this most remarkable day in the lives of Claire, Billy, and Tommy.

When the server had cleared the plates and brought coffee and chocolate éclairs, the party resumed their discussions about the future. Where to live? That was the critical question. Billy didn't want to take Claire to Blackmoor, except for a visit, and Claire knew Paris wouldn't be suitable for Billy, for many reasons. That left Jersey. She'd been there with her parents on two separate occasions in the past. Though she was just fourteen the last time she was there, she remembered it well and regarded it as a dream destination.

"So, we're going to live in Jersey," Billy proclaimed with an air of finality. "How can we do that Tommy?"

"Well. Our dad's from Guernsey so that qualifies us, but I don't have a birth certificate with his name on it to prove he's my dad." Tommy laughed and said with a devilish grin, "And I only have a copy of my birth certificate."

"How about you Billy? What does your birth certificate say?" asked Claire.

"It doesn't say anything. There's no name in the father column. But now he's passed, we'll have to figure something else out."

"You and Claire will need to work. What jobs are you thinking about?" asked Tommy.

"I could help at a hospital or a school or in a shop. They might not understand my Parisian French, but my English is quite good."

Billy smiled as he thought about how he was going to answer. "I was thinking about getting two carts – one for me and one for Claire – and getting into the rag and bone business."

They all laughed.

"Seriously Billy. What will you do?"

"Become a fisherman? I heard it's a real good job to have in Jersey." He noticed Tommy getting frustrated with his teasing. "What if Claire and I ran our own business? We'd be sole proprietors," he said jokingly, but at the same time, he was testing the waters.

"Well. That's one way of getting residency," said Tommy.

'Well," said Billy. "That's settled then. We'll be proprietors. Right, Claire?"

"Right Billy."

"What do you think Geeume's going to say when you tell him we're all going to live in Jersey?"

"He's going to say, "Thank goodness we're not going to live in Blackmoor, mum.""

The twins laughed out loud. They couldn't help it. Other patrons in the restaurant looked disapprovingly in their direction.

"You'll meet Guillaume tomorrow night. He's going to be thrilled to bits. He'll be fine with whatever I arrange," Claire explained to a somewhat anxious Billy.

The twins split the bill and tip and gave the necessary francs to Claire to pay the server. They talked some more, then parted company. Claire went home and the twins went to the Hotel Rouge where they had booked rooms for the night.

Chapter Thirty Four – Billy meets Guillaume

Paris, France
1953

The next morning, Claire went to see her parents. Pierre and Elise were mildly surprised when she told them that Billy and his brother had visited her but were shocked to their core when she told them that Billy had proposed marriage, that she had accepted his proposal, and that they were going to live in Jersey. They had always believed their daughter's reluctance to marry was because she was waiting for Guillaume's dad to appear, and now he had, but they were surprised by the abruptness of his marriage proposal, by her immediate acceptance of it, and by her agreeing to move to Jersey to live with him. They were concerned about her rushing into things. On the other hand, they'd always hoped that one day he would show up, if only for the sake of their daughter's happiness and that of Guillaume's. It was all too much and too fast in their opinion, however, by the end of their talk, they realized this was all she had ever wanted, and they wished her well and assured her of their support.

At noon, Claire went to her brother's school and told him about Billy's visit. He was just as astonished as his parents were, and, like his parents, he was happy for her and especially for Guillaume who would now have his real dad in his life. He agreed to her request not to mention anything to anybody about what happened in her flat in Paris nine years ago. She invited the twins for tea and spent the rest of the afternoon in the kitchen preparing a meal.

⁓

Claire first spoke to Guillaume about Billy two months earlier, when she began exchanging letters with him. She told him that someone who she had always cared deeply about wanted to come for a visit and asked him if he was okay with that. He said he was.

When Guillaume came home from school, she sat him at the kitchen table and told him about Billy's visit. She said Billy had asked her to marry him and she had accepted. Guillaume was surprised, but when he saw the happiness in his mother's eyes, he got up off the chair and gave his mum a big hug. She was greatly relieved. This was exactly how she hoped he would react.

She opened the map of Europe she had placed on the kitchen table and pointing to Jersey, asked, "How would you like to live there?" pointing to a little round dot in the English Channel.

Guillaume liked maps, adventures, and surprises. He moved his head closer to the map, narrowed his eyes, and focused on where his mother was pointing.

"Can we, can we?"

"Yes. That's where Billy lives."

She faced Guillaume, held his little hands firmly, and lovingly looked him straight in the eyes. "Billy is your dad. He's from England, but he lives in Jersey now. He couldn't come to see us before. When you're older we'll talk more about it, but for now, it doesn't matter. He's here now and he'll be with us forever."

"Billy's my dad? My real dad?"

"Yes, and you're going to meet him in about an hour and we're all going to live together in Jersey."

"He's my dad? My real dad? Are you sure?" Guillaume queried.

"Yes, he is, and you're going to be surprised because he has an identical twin brother who's here too. They look alike. Not only that, but they have red hair and freckles like you. That's who you got it from."

Guillaume put his arms around his mother and squeezed her tightly. "I love you, mama."

"Jersey isn't big like Paris. There's lots of water and beaches and places to explore, and you're going to have lots of relatives and cousins to play with." Guillaume clapped his hands and gave his mother another hug.

An hour and a half later, the front door opened, and the twins stepped inside. Positioned between the door jambs and backlit by the sun, the brothers looked more like a pair of ornate knights from a chess set or a pair of bookends than people.

Guillaume was excited, but he held back. Peering around the corner of the lounge, he looked down the hallway to catch his first glimpse of his dad. He wasn't known for being shy, but this was an exceptional event. He stared at the figures in the doorway and wondered which one was his dad.

Billy spotted Guillaume, or at least his head, for that was the only visible part of his body he could see. He stepped forward and strode briskly down the hallway. With open arms and tears dripping down his cheeks, he said "Come here, son. I love you so much." Guillaume hugged his dad, and at that very moment, in the hallway, father and son connected for the first time in their lives and bonded for life.

"And when you come to Jersey, Geeume, you're going to meet lots of relatives. I've been counting and we have eighteen uncles, aunts, and cousins. Bet you didn't know that did you?"

Guillaume was in a daze: so much new information for a little eight-year-old to comprehend.

The rest of the evening unfolded just as Claire had planned.

Chapter Thirty Five –
Claire's secret

St. Brelades. Jersey.
1953

Tommy returned to Jersey the next day and resumed his work at the dairy. Billy stayed on, married Claire in a civil ceremony the following week with just her immediate family present, and three days later, returned to Jersey. As there wasn't time to arrange a formal honeymoon, they decided to postpone it until they were reunited in Jersey. Being together as a family was more important than a honeymoon, Billy said.

Claire planned as she prepared to join Billy. She needed to look after Guillaume's schooling, secure passports, and investigate nursing and teaching opportunities in Jersey.

One month later, in November 1953, Claire and Guillaume moved to Jersey, and with Billy, occupied the two vacant bedrooms at Tommy and Amelie's farm.

Billy continued working as a hired hand on his brother's farm and Claire worked with Jane and Cyril on their flower farm while looking for a nursing position at the hospital. Guillaume attended Vauvert Primary School, the same school as his cousin, Louise. He proudly carried her lunch bag and lovingly held her little hand when he walked her to and from school, and they soon became best friends. Guillaume could speak enough English to get by and it didn't take long for him to increase his English vocabulary.

When Billy and Claire were alone in the yard one time, Billy asked her, right out of the blue, "I need to know what happened in your flat that day. Not knowing bothers me every day. I have to know Claire."

His request caught her off guard. She composed herself and said, "I know you do. I've thought about what I'd say when you asked me that question because I knew you would one day if you were ever to show up. It's too upsetting for me to talk about it, Billy. I've moved on and put it behind me, and I never think about it now. I've written down what happened for you to read, but I don't want to discuss it. Okay?"

"You have?" said Billy.

"And after you've read it, we're going to burn it. And that's the end of it. I never want it mentioned again. Okay"

"I promise," said Billy

Claire disappeared and returned with the letter.

'My Dearest Billy,

The first thing I want you to know is that no one knows you were in my home that day. I haven't told anyone you were there, not even Dominic.

The man was Max – my ex-boyfriend.

When you left, I cried on the floor until Dominic arrived, He always came for tea on Wednesdays. He came in, saw me, and took charge of everything. I told him I got into an argument with Max, and I stabbed him. I slept at Dominic's flat that night and, in the morning. I went back to my flat with him and his friend, who was an ambulance driver. After a bombing, his friend went around to bomb sites picking up casualties and taking them to the hospital or to the mortuary for people to identify and claim. He took a stretcher into my flat, wrapped up Max's body in a sheet, put him on the stretcher, and drove away. I cleaned up the blood.

I expected to be visited by someone at some time, but no one has ever come. It's been nine years now so I'm confident I'm in the clear. The three of us made a pact never to talk about it, and we haven't.

So now you know the rest of the story, my dearest Billy.

Love, Claire.'

As Billy read Claire's account of what happened, he felt a key turn in his brain and unlock the padlock that had shackled his mind for the last nine years. His secret emerged from the dark archives in his brain, hesitated, and fluttered away like a butterfly high up into the sky. He had been set free.

Together, they lit a match and burned the letter.

Chapter Thirty Six – Retracing Routes

Blackmoor, Lancashire
January 1954

Billy got a letter from his Uncle Albert advising him that he had received an offer from the tenant of his house with a closing date of February 28. Billy approved the offer, signed the enclosed forms, and put them aside to take with him to England. He was astounded at the price – he'd no idea Irene's house was worth so much.

Two weeks later, after arranging with neighbors and hired hands to manage the dairy, the twins set off for England. The rest of the family wanted to go and meet their relatives in Blackmoor too, but with the dairy, that was too impractical at the time. Instead, the Mathers would just have to come down to Jersey one day to meet them on their turf.

The brothers took the mail boat to Southampton, boarded a connecting train to London, where they stayed at a hotel for the night, and in the morning, took the northern train to Manchester and then another one to Blackmoor.

Albert picked them up at the train station and drove them to his home, and like Billy, Thomas was impressed by the sheer size and grandiosity of the place.

Angela was startled by the sight of her two identical-looking nephews on her doorstep, and stared in disbelief at them for a moment, speechless. Then her face broke into a huge grin. Though she knew Billy, she hardly recognized him now with his long, curly hair. The brothers just looked at each other, raised their eyebrows, and grinned.

Once the laughing and kidding abated, Angela led them down the hallway to the dining room, where Michael and Patricia were waiting. They were pleased to see their uncle again, though they didn't know for sure who was who until Billy spoke.

Before anyone had time to begin any lengthy conversations, Angela asked that everyone go into the dining room and sit down. She'd arranged for the food to be ready when they arrived, assuming they'd be hungry after traveling all day. She surprised Billy with his favorite dish: Lancashire hot pot. She hoped Tommy would like it too, but she had other dishes for him in case it wasn't to his liking.

She made the dish in the traditional manner, which most Blackmoorians preferred. She used dripping to brown the lamb chunks and kidneys and added fried chopped onions, sliced carrots, a little flour, Worcestershire sauce, and a cup of lamb stock. Then, she placed the sliced potatoes on top of the meat, covered the casserole, and left it to cook slowly in the oven for three hours. Once the potatoes were cooked, she removed the lid and browned them under the grill to make them crunchy. This was the magic touch in the Lancashire hot pot which Billy most appreciated.

"That was amazing. Best meal I've ever had," said Tommy licking his lips.

"Come on brother? Better than the snails and frog legs you had in Paris?" teased Billy.

"Ugh. You didn't really eat snails and frog legs, did you, Uncle?" Michael asked, scrunching up his nose.

"That's disgusting," said Patricia, with a similar facial grimace.

"When in Rome, you do as the Romans do," quipped Tommy with a smile. "They were delicious."

"And when you're in Blackmoor, you do as we Blackmoorians do. We have Lancashire Hot Pot, don't we Billy?" said Angela. Everyone laughed.

They retired to the lounge, where everyone had much to say and talk about. Tommy, being the newcomer had the most to say. "It's too long a story to tell you now, but in a nutshell, I went from an orphanage in Kent to working on a farm in Canada when I was thirteen."

"At thirteen?" Patricia's eyes widened and her jaw dropped. "Weren't you scared?" she asked.

"I don't think so, but that was a long time ago now. Maybe I was. I might have forgotten."

Tommy told them he went to Jersey when he was eighteen and, within a matter of half an hour, had covered off, briefly, his whole life journey from birth to present.

Billy then recounted his journey since leaving the Mathers' house. Everyone sat back, sipped their sherry, and was regaled by the tales he told.

"Show them your thumb," Billy said to Tommy.

The boys put their thumbs side by side to show the discolorations that were their 'lovemarks'. "I told you this was how we'd prove we were brothers, didn't I?" said Billy.

"You did," replied Angela, "but I've got to be honest with you. I didn't think you'd ever find your brother."

Michael and Patricia questioned the twins at length about various aspects of their lives, and the entire Mathers family promised to come to Jersey in the summer to meet the rest of their family.

"Did you find your dad?" asked Angela.

"Yes," said Tommy. "He was very sick, and he died in his bedroom when we were right there in his house. It was horrible."

They all gasped.

Billy jumped in and said, "And now his children blame us for his death. Maybe we did cause his heart attack, but he'd had one the night before, and we weren't there. I don't know if they'll ever forgive us."

The Mathers family offered their condolences, and, on that sad note, retired for the night. The twins slept in the vacant fourth bedroom on beds Angela had prepared for them.

The following day, after transacting the house closing business, Albert drove the twins to Joe Barton's house. They could have walked there since it was only ten minutes away, but it was raining. Aware of their visit, Joe had booked off work for the day. He was thrilled to see Billy again and to meet Tommy. They embraced, laughed, and reminisced about the good old days when Billy was a rag and bone man. Joe brought out the box he was keeping for Billy. The boys stared at it as if it was an ancient holy relic. Billy unlatched the lock, lifted the lid, and removed his mother's suitcase and purse. He opened the suitcase first, slowly removed the contents, and handed them to Tommy who focused his attention carefully on each article Billy handed to him, and as he held them, he thought about his mother whom he'd never met and never would. He felt the softness of her scarf and admired its faded deep purple color. He held her hairbrush, brooch, and ring, and imagined her handling and putting them on. This imaginary activity saddened him, yet he was pleased to finally have made a tactile connection with his mother.

Billy next opened the purse and handed Tommy the train ticket stubs and the notebook and showed him the two bundles of letters: one was his to his mum and the other was hers to him. Tommy stared at them imagining his mother writing them, while at the same time, he was worlds away posing as Terry Therin in Jersey and Billy was a soldier in France.

Joe drove them to the Post office where they arranged for the box to be re-wrapped and shipped to Jersey, and then on to the farmhouse where Billy used to live and to the scrap yard. Tommy wanted to see it all for himself and to get a feel for what it was like. They went to Sammy's Fish and Chips in Mosley Common for lunch, where they gorged on battered cod and chips, flavored by malt vinegar and sea salt. Billy relished the memories triggered by the taste. Sammy's had always been his and his mum's favorite chippie.

Their next stop was the McIvor Memorial Home for Babies in

Compton. The building was still there with its gritty playground encircled by a high rusty iron fence, but it had been abandoned years ago and was in a terrible state of disrepair. The sight of it left Tommy feeling as cold and heartless as the building itself. His only recollection of it was his last day at the Home when a social worker came and took him to the train station, pinned a cardboard sign to his coat, and put him on a train. His mood brightened as he told Billy about the many train rides he took that day and the many strangers he spoke to.

"And you were only seven years old? How did they get away with doing stuff like that, is what I want to know? They should all be locked up for doing that to little children," said Billy staring at the dilapidated structure.

One last stop at the Westlea public cemetery to look at the headstone Angela had arranged for their mum, and it was back to her house for the second night of hospitality, conversation, and accommodation.

The next morning, Albert took them to the train station where they continued their journey to Liverpool. They arrived at noon, walked around the waterfront environs, and then Tommy took Billy to the dock where he boarded the Duchess of Bedford.

"I remember how in awe I was at the size of the ship when I walked up the gangplank and a steward gave me this postcard," said Tommy, pulling out the postcard from his pocket. He stared out to sea and smiled. "I was so excited to be going to Canada, the land of the Cowboys and Indians, with my friends, Eddy and Charlie." Billy patted his brother's shoulder and smiled proudly at him. Tommy turned around and pointed. "See that, Billy? That's the Royal Liver Building. That was the last thing I saw before our ship sailed out of sight." Tommy took a minute to reflect and savor the memories and smile at the naivete and innocence of his youth. Each shared experience was bringing the brothers emotionally closer, and the more they learned about each other, the greater was their desire to learn more.

They were back on the train to London the following morning, and on to Swanson, Kent where they booked a room at the Wellington

Arms. They walked over to what had been St. Chads Home for Boys but was now offices. Though it had been refurbished and looked very different than when Tommy had attended, there was enough old architecture left to trigger in Tommy many memories, both good and bad. He identified various parts of the buildings for Billy and told him stories about his days in that institution: some humorous, some sad.

By noon, they were on their way back to London, and on to Southampton to get the boat back to Jersey in the morning.

Chapter Thirty Seven –
The Feast

St. Helier, Jersey.
1954

Pelegrin Printers was up for sale. Peter Pelegrin, who had taken over the family printing business from his father thirty years earlier, was looking to retire because of ill health. His lungs, they said, were burnt out. It was an occupational disease they said caused by years of inhaling toxic chemicals they used to use in the printing process. Unfortunately, Peter's only son, George, who was expected to take over the family business, was killed in the war in France in 1942.

Pelegrin Printers had a solid customer base with a wide assortment of printing equipment and products. They printed postcards, tourist maps, guides, and promotional literature, as well as a weekly newspaper, and prospects for the business were excellent. With the arrival of new immigrants and businesses to the islands since the war, demand for printed material was growing.

Tommy first became aware that the company was for sale when he approached Mr. Pelegrin about a business proposition. He wanted to know if Mr. Pelegrin was interested in printing a novel he was writing and running it in weekly installments in his newspaper.

Though intrigued by the idea, Mr. Pelegrin declined, saying that he would prefer not to commit to any long-term deal in case it would complicate the sale of his company. *The sale of his company!* Tommy's ears perked up and his mind raced. *Pelegrin Printers was for sale? What if Billy and Claire were to buy it as a means of qualifying for residency status?*

Over the next month, Billy and Claire met with Mr. Pelegrin and researched the printing and publishing business in Jersey. Peter Pelegrin liked the young couple and felt they had the requisite interest and motivation to be successful. Billy reminded him of his son George.

Tommy was interested in the company too, but for a different reason. Though he had a standing opportunity to buy Les Petite Vaches de Brelades from the Therins, he was losing interest in being a dairy farmer and wanted a new career. After nineteen years of looking after cows, he was ready for something different. Amelie supported his sentiments.

To help Billy in his buying decision, Tommy researched the local printing and publishing business on the island, and to his surprise and delight, discovered that there was a strong demand for services other than printing.

It would be challenging, but I need to be challenged. I want to learn how to design book covers, how to compose, edit and proofread scripts for other people, and do whatever else Billy might want me to do. I reckon that over the years I've spent at least ten thousand hours on my writing so that surely must account for something, thought Tommy.

The twins decided to see if they could buy the business together. They had more than enough cash between them to pay for it, but this fortuitous opportunity was not only about money. It was a way for them to satisfy their life-long yearning to be with family and get a sense of belonging.

They met with Mr. Pelegrin and settled the purchase price and terms. He agreed to stay on for the rest of the year and to work with them to get them started.

Tommy wrote to Mr. Therin and told him about the purchase and that he and Amelie would be moving to St. Helier as soon as he could find and train a manager to run the dairy.

On April 1st, Billy and Claire bought a small two-bedroom house on Rue de l'Est in St. Helier, and Guillaume changed schools. Claire got a job at Jersey General Hospital as a nurse in the pediatric ward, starting on April 15th.

By June 1st, Tommy had a replacement dairy manager in place, and he and Amelie were the proud owners of Millais Park, a four-bedroom residence in St. Helier – ten minutes from Billy's and Claire's house.

Albert and Angela in Blackmoor, and Claire's parents, Pierre and Elise, were all eager to come to Jersey to meet the rest of their extended family and to learn more about the lives of their relatives. When Claire discussed this with Amelie, they thought it would be a brilliant idea if everyone came at the same time and treated it as a Jones family reunion. Tommy picked the first week in August as the designated Jones Homecoming week and the Wednesday of that week as the Jones Family Day celebration.

Claire and Amelie looked after the invitations and rented a banquet room at the Hotel de France for the Jones Family Day celebration. They invited the Mathers in Blackmoor, Claire's family in Paris, Amelie's family as well the Bouchards in Quebec, the Therins in England, and Richard and Mary Hart in Guernsey. They selected a menu for a catered tea at five o'clock, and Amelie arranged with Andy Smith, the La Cloche Studio photographer, to take family portraits at three o'clock. It had been Andy's father, Steven, who had taken the photograph of their parents, all those many years ago.

The Mathers, Angela and Albert, and their two children, Michael and Patricia, came down and stayed at the newly opened grandiose, Hotel de France. Albert insisted on picking up the total tab for the Jones celebrations: the banquet room rental as well as the catered meal. Joe also came down with the Mathers and stayed at the Hotel de France.

Claire's parents, Pierre and Elise, and her brother, Dominic, his wife, and son came in from Paris and stayed at Tommy's and Amelie's house for the week because there was more room there than at Billy's and Claire's house.

Aunt Jane and Uncle Cyril, Amelie's mother and father, and Becky, her younger sister, left St. Brelades at twelve-thirty in Cyril's truck and arrived in St. Helier just before one o'clock, as requested in the invitation.

The banquet room had a large table in the center of the room, and enough chairs around it to accommodate all the guests. On one side of the room, two long tables were set up, side by side, to hold the Jones artifacts being provided by Tommy and Billy. Items and mementos from their past lives were displayed on the table for people to view and question.

Tommy brought in his Smith Corona typewriter, his St. Chads 'To Whom It May Concern letter', his two postcards of ships, his Quebec photographs, and his fake marriage and birth certificates.

Billy put out pieces from Irene's Royal Doulton tea service, the contents of the box Angela kept for him: the bundled letters, the postcards to Irene, and the photograph of his mum and dad. He also put out two photos of their dad's tombstone in Guernsey that Mary and Richard had sent. The inscription on the closeup photo read that Ted had four children: Richard, Mary, Thomas, and William.

At the end of the table was the donkey stone Joe provided because Amelie told him to bring along any "artifact" that he thought might be of interest.

Billy and Tommy acted as hosts, introducing people, and clarifying their relationship with one another. For the next two hours, the brothers stood behind their tables and explained to the guests the significance of the artifacts and answered their questions. Guillaume stood proudly by his dad's side, listening, and absorbing what he had to say. Joe stood on Billy's left, ready to add to Billy's stories about being a rag and bone man.

Everyone was fascinated by what they saw and the stories they heard. Joe's donkey stone and Billy's retelling of his days as a rag and bone man got the most laughs, and Tommy's recounting of how he deceived the Germans for four years by impersonating another person was the scariest and most intriguing tale.

Though Dominic and his family's ability to speak English was limited, it didn't matter to Patricia and Michael. By the end of the evening, they were all the best of friends, and would, in years to come, keep in touch with one another.

Andy Smith came in at two-thirty, set up his photographic equipment, and sharply at three o'clock, began creating family portraits. He took many different groupings, including a special one Billy wanted of just the six "red-headed" family members: Tommy, himself, and their three children: Guillaume, Louise, and Sarah.

A delicious catered meal featuring local meats and produce was served at five o'clock. Billy and Tommy sat next to each other at the head of the table.

After the meal, Amelie stood up and read a telegram from the Bouchards congratulating Tommy on finding his family and sending their regrets for not being able to attend. A postscript added that Ellie and Mae sent their love too and asked Tommy if he would pass along their best wishes for great milk and cream production to their Jersey cousins. Tommy had some explaining to do because people wanted to know why he spoke to cows. He was taken aback because he didn't know Amelie had invited the Bouchards, but he was pleased she did because they now knew he'd found his family.

Amelie also read a telegram from the Therins. They congratulated the Jones family on their reunion, sent regrets for not being able to attend this auspicious inaugural event, and wished Tommy and Amelie a good new life in St. Helier.

Billy stood up, cleared his throat, and looked closely at the faces of the people seated around the table. The room went quiet. Even the children sensed a certain solemnity to the occasion and paid attention by staring, silently, at Billy.

Billy was visibly moved.

"I want to thank all of you for comin' today. If just one of you hadn't a made it, it wouldn't have been the same. It'd be incomplete like a pie with a slice missing. So, thank you all again for comin'." Everyone chuckled. "I'm amazed. Who'd a thought it possible? I wouldn't have. There's twenty of us plus Joe and he's family as far as I'm concerned, so that makes twenty-one and we're all family. How's that possible?"

Billy wasn't expecting anyone to answer his question. He let it sit there for a few seconds for people to think about.

"Well. I'll tell you how it's possible. It's coz of the kindness of two very special people and one of em's here today. Stand up, Joe."

Joe pushed his chair back and stood up. He grinned and slowly moved his head from side to side, taking in the smiling faces looking at him. His chest swelled with pride in response to the clapping and congratulatory shouts.

"If Joe hadn't a given me a place to stay and a job we'd not be here today."

The clapping and shouts intensified. Joe's chest swelled another inch and his grin got bigger.

Billy picked up Irene's Royal Doulton teapot from the table and held it high above his head. "See this. This is Irene's teapot."

Everyone stared, wide-eyed in great expectation of what he was going to say. Billy knew he had the crowd fully behind him and he intended to milk the occasion for all it was worth. He wanted his speech to be memorable. "Irene showed me the same kindness and compassion that Joe did. She felt sorry for me coz I was lonely, and I didn't have anyone in my life. We became great friends and this 'ere pot made us tea every time we met. It was over cups of tea that I learned the truth about my birth and my family. That's how I learned I had a brother and a dad."

Everyone hung on to Billy's every word. Most had heard bits and pieces, here and there, but Billy was now telling the whole story. It sounded like the book of Genesis for the Jones family – In the beginning.

"I want to thank Albert and Angela for picking up the tab for the room and the meal today. It was money well spent I'd say, and I want to thank everyone again for comin' and for listenin' to me." He sat down. The crowd applauded with thunderous claps and congratulatory shouts.

Most people used the opportunity to tell their stories and to elaborate on their connection to the Jones family tree. Claire and Amelie spoke briefly about how they had met their spouses but talked more about their children, their situation, and their hopes and plans. It was an entertaining three hours of talks full of laughs, tears, and revelations.

When the evening ended and the Jones family members left the Hotel de France, they felt a great affinity for one another. What they learned was to bond them forever.

Epilogue

When classes resumed after the summer holidays, Guillaume and Louise attended Victoria College Secondary school, and three-year-old Sarah went to Victoria College Preparatory school.

Billy learned the operational side of the printing business from Mr. Pelegrin, and Tommy focused on sales and marketing. By December 31, the twins were ready to run the business by themselves. Mr. Pelegrin retired, and Billy and Tommy renamed their business, Jones Brothers Publishers. As well as keeping every Pelegrin customer, they grew the business by fifty percent over the next two years by expanding into the book publishing business.

Their first book was Tommy's biography, The Soldier and the Orphan – Separated by Church and War.

Appendix

Home Children

British Orphanages and Homes

In the late nineteenth century (1850-1900) there were a lot of homeless and destitute children living on the streets of England and as a result a lot of petty crime and disease. Some children were orphaned when their parents died from diseases or accidents; some were abandoned by their parents because they couldn't afford to feed them; and some were runaways from workhouses and/or abusive situations.

To address the situation, the government, and some philanthropic benefactors, such as Annie Parlane MacPherson and Dr. Barnardo, built orphanages and homes to house the children. And to make them into God-fearing, law-abiding Christians, the British government developed a re-education school program and arranged for it to be implemented and administered by the religious orders running the institutions. It was so successful that the British government saw fit to export it to the colonies where it was used in their residential school programs for Indigenous children.

The Home Children scheme.

In 1868 Annie Parlane MacPherson opened the Home of Industry for orphans and waifs. A few years later, she founded the Home Children scheme whereby she sent children from the Home of Industry to Canada to work on five-year indentured labor contracts. She arranged with Barnardo's Homes in London, Quarriers Homes in Scotland, Smyly Homes in Ireland, as well as the Catholic and Church of England orphanages to send their children.

Though the scheme was said to be in the best interest of the children, it soon became a politically designed arrangement between governments for their benefit. The British government wanted to save money because it cost five times more to keep a child in care for a year than it did to emigrate them, and the colonies needed more farm laborers and domestic servants. For the orphanages and homes, the scheme was a lucrative income generator because both governments (British and Canadian) paid them for every child they sent, and in addition, they collected finder's fees from farmers and other employers, proceeds from insurance policies, etc. The income earned by these sending organizations was in the millions of dollars in today's money.

Over 100,000 children between the ages of four and fourteen were sent to Canada between 1860 and 1948 to be adopted or to work as laborers. Most boys, such as Tommy, Eddy, and Charlie worked on farms while most girls went into domestic service. They were known as Home Children and were generally not welcomed as family members by the host family. Many children, like Eddy and Charlie, were physically, sexually, and emotionally abused, malnourished, and neglected. They faced stigmatization for being a Home Child and were made to feel worthless. Many committed suicide.

The scheme was indentured slavery that created a domestic servant and farm laboring class of British children in the colonies. It was not solely in the best interests of the children as the authorities proclaimed it to be. Sound familiar? The residential school program for Indigenous children was presented to the public in the same way.

The British and Australian governments and Dr. Barnardo's have publicly apologized to the victims and their descendants for their part in the scheme and offered financial restitution, but Canada has not done this. In 2009, the immigration minister said there was no need for Canada to apologize for the abuse and exploitation suffered by the Home Children because Canadians don't expect their government to apologize for every sad event in our history. He said Canada was taking measures to recognize that 'sad period' that would include a parliamentary motion to declare 2010 the year of the Home Child, for Canada Post to issue Home Child stamps, and for the Pier 21 museum to recognize the Home Children.

On Feb 7 2018 the Canadian House of Commons passed a motion: "That, in the opinion of the House, the government should recognize the contributions made by the over 100,000 British Home Children to Canadian society, their service to our armed forces throughout the twentieth century, the hardships and stigmas that many of them endured, and the importance of educating and reflecting upon the story of the Home Children for future generations by declaring September 28 of every year, Home Child Day in Canada."

But recognizing is not the same as apologizing. No Prime Minister has formally apologized to the victims and descendants of the Home Children program for their part in the scheme as they have done for the victims and descendants of the Indian residential school program. Why not? What is the difference between the two? We've allowed this part of Canadian history to be swept under the carpet, yet it is estimated that 10% of the Canadian population can trace their Canadian ancestry back to a Home Child.

In 2009, the immigration minister said it was a non-issue in Canada because people don't care. They don't care because they don't know! How many people reading this article knew about the Home Child program before reading this book?

To get our Prime Minister to apologize we need to raise awareness among Canadians about this social injustice situation We can do this by copying and pasting this document and sharing it with friends and by talking about it publicly.

To learn more about Home Children in Canada click on https://canadianbritishhomechildren.weebly.com/

About The Author

Alastair emigrated to Canada from England by himself when he was 19. He became a typical yuppie – family, a house in the suburbs, and a big job in the corporate sector. Following London Life's Freedom 55 plan he retired at 57 and went to live in the country.

Two years later, disillusioned with the passivity of retirement, he shed his material possessions and went to live for two years with a small First Nations band in a remote fly-in location in the N.W.T. Cultural differences and a challenging environment ignited in him fresh perspectives, inspired a new way of being, and fueled his soul searching. The experience changed the direction of his life which he wrote about in his memoir: *Awakening in the Northwest Territories*.

He left the north two years later and motivated about helping others less fortunate than himself went to Bangladesh on a two-year assignment as an International Development volunteer.

On his return To Canada, Alastair met his new partner, Candas Whitlock, who subsequently sold her house, shed her material possessions, and went with Alastair to Jamaica and Guyana as International Development volunteers on one-year assignments. They co-wrote *Go For It – Volunteering Adventures on Roads Less Travelled* to encourage boomers to consider international volunteering

In between volunteering assignments, they backpacked Central America and Southeast Asia for four months at a time and co-wrote *Budget Backpacking for Boomers.*

In 2016, they went to Alert Bay, BC. on a four-month volunteer placement with the Namgis First Nations as part of a Truth and Reconciliation Committee 'Call to action' initiative. Alastair served as the business coach to ten First Nation would-be entrepreneurs. The experience was so profound they felt compelled to write about it in a memoir entitled *Tides of Change,* which is a free download from Alastair's website: www.alastairhenry.com

For the next three years, Candas and Alastair were entertainers, presenting their audio/visual shows based on their books to audiences in retirement residences, service clubs, and libraries throughout Ontario.

Alastair has three children and seven grandchildren and lives in London, Ontario with Candas.

Alastair's double lung transplant in 2020 enabled him to finish writing *The Soldier and the Orphan* which he began writing in 2016.

About the Book

In twentieth-century England, many working-class people were victims of values and circumstances not of their own making. They were people to whom things were done, not for. Billy and Tommy Jones and Mary, their mother, were such people. The boys were born out of wedlock at a time when such a thing was regarded as a disgrace -the sins of the father being visited on the sons.

Neither boy knows they have a brother. The trajectory of their lives takes them to different parts of the world where they suffer the consequences of circumstances beyond their control which they must confront and resolve.

Billy is injured in WW2, falls in love with his nurse, and is left struggling with PTSD after being discharged from the army. Eventually, through the kindness and compassion of strangers, he regains his health and, in a surprising turn of events, learns the truth about his birth.

Tommy is a victim of the British Home Children program and is sent to Canada when he is thirteen to work on a five-year indenture labor contract on a dairy farm in Quebec. When his contract ends, he travels to Jersey, a Channel Island, just before the Germans invade and occupy the island. To avoid capture and deportation to Germany, Tommy becomes resourceful in surprising ways.

The Soldier and the Orphan is a fast-paced, emotionally packed novel with strong characters and surprising twists. It will elicit unexpected tears of joy and sadness as the story touches on colonialist attitudes, discrimination, love, and tragedy. And for readers wanting an extra taste of mystery and suspense, **The Soldier and the Orphan** brews up a good share of deceits and secrets, and even murder as the novel threads to a powerful, heart-warming conclusion.

The Soldier and the Orphan will appeal to readers of all ages and backgrounds but will be of special interest to those who have traced their Canadian ancestry back to a British Home Child. Readers who enjoyed the *Orphan Train* and *The Guernsey Literary and Potato Peel Pie Society* will enjoy the unique plots and settings of this novel.

Printed in Canada